"ARE YOU EXPECTING COMPANY THROUGH THAT WINDOW?" TOREY ASKED IRRITABLY. "OR DIDN'T YOUR MAMA TEACH YOU ANY MANNERS?"

The man turned to face her. Torey's knees almost buckled. God in heaven! No. His fathomless gray eyes were no longer bloodshot and unfocused. His hard-edged face held no hint of the lazy, sensual smile of the night before. The growth of beard was gone, and she caught the scent of lye soap and bay rum. The dark-haired stranger from the Take Your Chances Saloon had shaved, bathed, changed clothes, changed everything. Everything.

Everything but Torey's own excruciatingly vivid memories of being in this man's arms, feeling him touch her, hearing him whisper sweet, tender lies. *We can go upstairs, lovely lady, forget our troubles, just for one night*. One night . . .

Torey coughed, choked. Did Killian recognize her? Here, now, in her guise as a man? Heart hammering, she dared to look at him again.

His eyes were flint-hard, stone-cold, seeming to stare right through her. But blessedly there was no hint of recognition in them, no acknowledgment that they had ever in their lives met before.

Her role as Vic Langley, bounty hunter, was safe.

For now.

PRAISE FOR JESSICA DOUGLASS
AND HER BEST-SELLING NOVELS

WISH ME A RAINBOW

"*Wish Me a Rainbow* is a glorious, powerful love story deftly crafted by a truly talented author. This tale of childhood friendship that slowly grows into adult love is destined to make you weep with joy. . . . The sheer power of the characters' emotions, the stunning plotline and the sweet romance make this book a very special read."

—*Romantic Times*

"Fast moving and exciting. You will care about the characters. You will cheer for Amelia who shows strength and sensitivity, and sympathize with Matt . . . a winner!"

—*Rendezvous*

"This book is tough-love, tender, touching, tumultuous and triumphant! . . . Jessica Douglass manages to bring pain, joy and reconciliation to a happy ending."

—*Heartland Critiques*

ALL MY HEART CAN HOLD

"From the very first page, Jessica Douglass grabs the reader and never lets go!" —*Romantic Times*

"Powerful, intense. A hero you'll remember forever."

—Kimberly Cates, author of *Crown of Dreams*

Other books by Jessica Douglass,
winner of a *Romantic Times*
Career Achievement Award
for Indian Romance:

ALL MY HEART CAN HOLD

SNOWFIRE

WISH ME A RAINBOW

JESSICA DOUGLASS

A DELL BOOK

Published by
Dell Publishing
a division of
Bantam Doubleday Dell Publishing Group, Inc.
1540 Broadway
New York, New York 10036

If you purchased this book without a cover you should be aware that this book is stolen property. It was reported as "unsold and destroyed" to the publisher and neither the author nor the publisher has received any payment for this "stripped book."

Copyright © 1994 by Linda Hender-Wallerich

All rights reserved. No part of this book may be reproduced or transmitted in any form or by any means, electronic or mechanical, including photocopying, recording, or by any information storage and retrieval system, without the written permission of the Publisher, except where permitted by law.

The trademark Dell® is registered in the U.S. Patent and Trademark Office.

ISBN: 0-440-21188-3

Printed in the United States of America

Published simultaneously in Canada

January 1994

10 9 8 7 6 5 4 3 2 1

RAD

For Lin, who loves Noah as much as I do.
For all the years of caring and sharing
and some of the best laughs I've
ever had. I treasure our friendship.
This one's for you.

The Promise

1

Dawn chased banners of rose and gold across a china blue sky like a child frolicking after her mother's ribbons, innocent, heedless—unaware of the blade of darkness that still clung to the rim of blue. Unaware of the night sky's whispered warning.

Victoria Lansford felt no inkling of foreboding as she woke that beautiful spring morning on her father's central Kansas farm, no hint of the descent into hell the day would bring.

Rising eagerly, Torey snatched up the woolen robe she'd tossed across the foot of her bed the night before. It might be spring, but the morning air still had a bite to it. Quickly she slipped the robe over her pale blue flannel nightgown, hugging it tight to her slender body. But even the dawn chill did nothing to quell the excitement threading through her. This was the day, the day she'd been looking forward to for weeks. Today she and her older sister, Lisbeth, would indulge themselves in a rare trip to town. Winter—filled with snowstorms and isolation—was over at last.

Padding across the wood planked floor to her gingham curtained window, Torey eased open the multipaned glass and gazed out on the patchwork of fields that were the life's blood of the Lansford farm. A vagrant breeze wafted over her, bringing with it the pungent sweetness of freshly turned soil. She inhaled deeply. Eli Burkett, the farm's handyman, had started plowing the near section just yesterday, getting it ready for corn and spring wheat. Winter wheat, planted last fall and accounting for a third of the Lansford crop production, was all but ready for harvesting over in its own section.

The new season's planting was still a month of backbreaking work away, but Eli had acquiesced to Torey's request that they take this one day and drive into Boden for seed and supplies. She grinned a trifle guiltily. That is, Eli had finally succumbed to her constant pleading.

All around her the world was greening again, beginning the cycle of life anew—fresh shoots of buffalo grass, early wildflowers, the budding oaks her father had had brought in as saplings more than ten years earlier to shade the yard surrounding the house and barn. Central Kansas was good land, but it was flat, virtually treeless land, interrupted only rarely by willows and cottonwoods ribboning along meandering streams.

The breeze intensified and Torey shivered slightly, hunching her shoulders, but she didn't move away from the window. She was feeling too good to let a little thing like a slight chill in the air disturb her. What mattered was that there wasn't a cloud in the sky, no hint of a brewing storm. There would be no excuses to postpone the trip to town.

Her blue-green eyes danced as she toyed with the silken tips of her waist-length plait of dark hair. The cloudless sky was a sign. She was certain of it. It was going to be a good year. The bad years were behind them, the years of struggle and doing without.

She and her family had first come to Kansas from Ohio in the spring of 1858 some fifteen years before. She had been only five at the time, Lisbeth eleven. The '60 drought had nearly driven them under before they'd really gotten started.

But her parents had been determined. Even through the bloody Kansas war years the farm had survived. She loved it here. She couldn't imagine living anywhere else.

Even so, there were times when she liked to get away from the sheer isolation of the farm, to be around other people, exchange a little gossip, look through the latest fashion magazines at Mrs. Willoughby's Seamstress Shop. And—she felt her cheeks heat—maybe Boden held one other allure as well. A trip to town would offer the perfect opportunity to do a little flirting with a certain shopkeeper's son.

Torey sighed dreamily. Had it really been five months since the harvest dance last fall? Jim Buckley with his wavy blond hair and sea-blue eyes had looked positively divine in his broadcloth suit and string tie. Every other unattached young woman in town had thought so too. But she had been the one he'd singled out for the last dance.

She smiled to herself, remembering. It had all been so exciting, so romantic. Jim Buckley had never even seemed to notice her before, and then suddenly there he was, sweeping her out onto the dance floor for the final waltz of the evening.

Until that moment she would have judged the entire night a crushing disappointment. She'd only been asked to dance twice. It wasn't that she was unattractive. She had enough self-confidence to realize that. Rather it was that so many men were put off by the one physical attribute she most loathed about herself—her height. Five feet ten in her stocking feet, Torey had long since discovered the majority of men to be intimidated by, if not openly disapproving of, a woman who was as tall or taller than they were. A judgment she regarded as highly unfair. After all, it wasn't as if she'd had any say-so in the matter.

An inch taller than her father, five inches taller than her sister, Torey had had more than one man's interest end before it had even begun, simply by standing up. That was why it had been such a genuine pleasure to dance with Jim Buckley. At six five, he was one of the few men she'd ever met who was taller than she was.

And even after the dance, Jim hadn't relinquished his role as Prince Charming. Before saying his good-nights, he had stolen her away from the crowd, drawn her into his arms, and kissed her!

She had been reliving that kiss for five months. It had been her very first. His lips had been so warm, so soft, softer than she would have imagined a man's lips to be. His breath had been warmer still against her cheek and a strange heat had seemed to simmer to life inside her.

Had Jim Buckley felt a similar heat? Torey wondered. Had he spent the winter thinking of her as often as she had thought of him? Her blush deepened. Today would be her opportunity to find out.

But not if she spent the day dawdling in front of the window, she chided herself inwardly. Quickly she crossed the room to her wardrobe and flung it open, catching up one of her more serviceable cotton day dresses. She had chores to attend to. The faster she finished them, the faster would come the trip to town.

Still, she couldn't help lingering for just a moment as her gaze snagged on a dress not meant to be serviceable, just pretty—a forest-green velvet—hanging amidst the ginghams, calicos, and wools. It had been her mother's favorite. Though it had required altering and an added flounce above the hemline to fit Torey's taller, more slender figure, the garment's simple style had allowed it to remain in fashion for over a decade.

Torey's smile was bittersweet as she remembered the last time her mother had worn it. It had been at a party nearly eight years ago, some five months before Emma Lansford died. The entire family had been in town celebrating the end of the war. Everyone had been so happy that day. Doubly so because Lisbeth's fiancé, Tom Evers, had come home from the war, safe and alive.

That very day to the delight of absolutely everyone, Tom and Lisbeth had rounded up a preacher and gotten married on the spot. Tom's blustery good looks and boisterous sense of humor had proven the perfect balance to Lisbeth's delicate beauty and quiet sensibility. They had both been positively glowing.

But Tom and Lisbeth's joy had come to an abrupt end two years ago, when Tom was killed in a hunting accident.

Torey stilled, an unpleasant shiver skittering along her spine. She had been the one who had found Tom's body. In a ravine three miles from the house. He had been tracking a deer and must have tripped. His rifle had fired and . . .

Torey trembled, repelled, transfixed. Why did she have to remember such an awful event on this beautiful day?

Stay home.

Her skin prickled. *Stay home.* Now where had that thought come from? In her mind's eye Torey could see Lisbeth pleading with Tom not to go hunting that day, that she had a terrible feeling. . . .

Torey drew in a steadying breath. She was being ridiculous. Lisbeth had always been fretful. It was not the first day she had asked Tom to stay home.

No! Enough of memories! It was time to get on with the day.

Resolutely, Torey headed out of her room and down the hallway toward the kitchen. She was instantly aware of the aroma of bacon frying. Lisbeth was obviously up and about.

At the kitchen's entryway, Torey paused. For a long minute she just stood there taking comfort in the warm familiarity of the scene—Lisbeth bustling back and forth between the counter and the stove, indulging her one true labor of love—cooking. Her sister could make a meal out of a saddle blanket and have people begging for seconds. A most fortunate skill, in Torey's estimation, since she herself had been known to turn the finest steak in the county into a charred brick.

Just seeing her sister so happily engaged with her cornbread and flapjacks and bacon made Tory feel all the more foolish about what had transpired in her bedroom. With an impish grin she marched over to the rough-hewn oak table and snitched one of Lisbeth's corn muffins. Her sister had her back to her, busily stirring a panful of scrambled eggs. "Morning, Lissa!"

Lisbeth jumped, nearly dropping her wooden spoon into the eggs. She turned, planting her hands on her hips and scowled with mock ferocity. "Victoria Lansford, could you please make just a little more noise when you come into a room."

Torey made a face. "But just yesterday you accused me of sounding like a herd of buffalo when I tromped into the kitchen. What's a girl to do?"

Lisbeth rolled her eyes. "A compromise? How about one small buffalo?"

Torey giggled. "I'll consider it. So, are you looking forward to our trip into Boden?"

"As a matter of fact, I am."

Torey's brows lifted in surprise. For two weeks Lisbeth had been fussing and complaining about having too much work to do around the farm to allow for any frivolous trips to town. "What changed your mind?"

Lisbeth went back to stirring the eggs. "I think a change of scene would be good for Papa."

Good for you too, Torey thought. Only recently had the shadows of grief over the death of her husband finally begun to lift from Lisbeth's pale green eyes.

Again Torey felt a chill. *Stay home.* "Is Papa up?" she asked abruptly to distract herself.

"I heard him in his room earlier. But maybe you'd best look in on him."

Torey hurried down the corridor to the last room on the right. She knocked softly, but received no response. Nudging the door open, she stepped inside the small, austerely furnished room. Abel Lansford was lying on his back atop the quilted coverlet on his bed. He had indeed been up. He was fully dressed, but he had apparently lain back down and fallen asleep. Torey worried her lower lip. Even in his sleep, her father looked haggard, pale.

Crossing the room to his side, she gave him a gentle shake, careful to keep the concern she felt from showing in her eyes. "Sleep poorly, Papa?"

"Not too bad," he managed.

"You should have called Lisbeth or me."

"I'm fine, Torey. Just fine." He struggled to rise, the simple exertion almost too much for him. Very casually, Torey offered him her arm for support. She knew how much he detested feeling helpless.

Abel Lansford had been the most robust of men, always laughing, full of life. But last fall during the harvest he had suffered a stroke. A mild one, the doctor had said, but nevertheless it had sapped much of the strength from his right arm and leg. He could walk again, but only with a considerable limp, and he tired easily.

"Lisbeth's got breakfast cooking."

He smiled, the spark in his eyes cheering her as it always did. The stroke hadn't taken that from him.

Torey helped her father down the corridor. She could tell he was trying hard not to lean on her. But he only too gratefully slumped into his chair at the kitchen table.

"Papa, what is it?" Lisbeth asked, alarmed.

He shook his head. "Nothing, sweetheart. Nothing at all. Just an old man who didn't get a whole lot of sleep last night."

Lisbeth and Torey exchanged glances.

Torey was the first to suggest what they were both thinking. "Maybe we'd best postpone the trip to town."

"I won't hear of it," Abel said. "You've been looking forward to it for too long." He gave Torey a teasing wink. "I may be getting old, young lady, but that doesn't mean I missed the look on your face when you were dancing with Jim Buckley last fall."

Torey flushed. "He's waited five months, he can wait a little longer."

"Nonsense," Abel said. "Besides, there are even more important things to tend to in town than young love. I checked the pantry yesterday. We're almost out of coffee and sugar."

Lisbeth smiled a little. "That's true enough. We're low on molasses too."

"That settles it," Abel said. "No molasses means no gingerbread cookies. A man's got to have the necessities. We're going to town."

They all had to laugh. Torey felt better. Except for being tired, her father did seem more animated than he'd been in a long time.

"Now what does a man have to do to get fed around here?" Abel grumbled good-naturedly.

Lisbeth quickly went to the stove and began to fill her father's plate. "Why don't you go out and fetch Eli?" Lisbeth asked Torey. "We'll eat before chores today."

"I'm on my way." Torey hurried outside and headed for the barn, where the crusty ex-frontiersman made his home in a small room in the back. The uncertainty of Abel Lansford's health had prompted Torey and her sister to hire on an extra hand for the first time last fall. Eli had ridden up to the house one afternoon and offered to do a few chores in exchange for a meal—a not uncommon occurrence on the Kansas plains. One day's work had led to two, had led to a week, until it was agreed he should stay on permanently. Torey had come to adore the bewhiskered giant with his wild tales of the wild West. But no amount of persuasion would convince him to move into the house. In fact, more often than not, even on the most frigid of nights, Eli would drag his bedroll outside and sleep under the stars.

His primary role on the farm involved doing the tasks requiring the heaviest labor—like plowing and blacksmithing.

But since there would be no plowing today, he was probably mending harness or repairing the slat in the front stall that Rosabelle—the county's most cantankerous cow—had kicked into splinters last week.

It was also remotely possible that Eli was still asleep, taking the rare occurrence of the trip to town as a chance to get some extra shut-eye. He was forever muttering about "not getting any younger," though he worked harder than any two men Torey had ever seen. He drew the line at doing any chores he might consider beneath a mountain man's dignity—like milking the cow or feeding the chickens or gathering eggs.

Torey was thus astonished to find Eli in the barn urging a dance-stepping Rosabelle to stand still in the same singsong voice Torey used on the uncooperative bovine every morning. Out in the yard the chickens were pecking at freshly spread grain, a few kernels still clinging to the fringe of Eli's buckskin leggings.

"Why, Eli," she crooned, unable to resist the moment, "I thought a respectable mountain man wouldn't be caught dead milking a cow."

He scowled darkly, though the mood was not reflected in his brown eyes. "I'm not milking her," he said, "that is, well . . . I knew you'd be kicking up a fuss about getting to town." His bearded, leathery face reddened just a little. "And well, maybe I didn't want chicken feed in the milk strainer and cream poured out for the rooster."

She giggled. "I know you hate it when I tell you how sweet you are. But you are, you know. Thank you."

He cleared his throat. "Just never mind. If'n you're here, maybe you should take over."

"But you're doing such a fine job. I think Rosabelle's in love."

He shook his head. "You are the limit, Miss Torey."

"I try. Breakfast is almost ready, by the way."

Eli tied off Rosabelle's halter to a support post, then retrieved a bucket and a stool. As Torey watched, he settled himself on the three-legged perch and with a royal grimace began to milk the cow. "The things I do for this family. I think I may have been bit by one grizzly too many."

Torey leaned over the side of the stall. "You only do it because you love us."

She was teasing, but Eli looked away suddenly and she feared that she had gone too far. That she had truly embarrassed him. "Pa was looking awful tired this morning," she said, by way of changing the subject.

"Abel's stronger than you think. It's just that old bones don't move as quick as younger ones."

"I worry about him."

Eli looked at her. "I know."

Torey ambled back to the rear stall and offered a sugar cube to the black gelding who bobbed his head in greeting. "I'll turn you out in the pasture later," she promised, stroking the horse's velvety nose. She called him Sir Galahad because she'd always been fascinated by the legends of knights in shining armor. Her father could have been such a knight. He had indulged her with the riding horse when practicality demanded that a spare plow horse would have made more sense. Galahad served no useful purpose on the farm other than to give her pleasure. He wouldn't even pull a buckboard. "What about your family, Eli? You tell me all kinds of adventure tales of your life in the Rockies, but you've never said much about family. Why did you leave the mountains?"

A faraway look came into his deep-set brown eyes. "I had my reasons. Afterward, I rode scout for the army for a while—Fort Bridger, Fort Laramie." His mouth twisted as though the recollection left a bitter taste in his mouth.

"What is it?"

"Nothing. Just thinking of something that happened to a friend of mine at Fort Laramie, an officer . . ." He seemed to shake himself, then stood. "I think Rosabelle's given all she's going to. Besides, I don't want Miss Lisbeth giving up on us and feeding them heaven-sent corn muffins of hers to the hog."

Torey was quiet as she followed Eli to the house. He'd regaled her of only the most outlandish tall tales since the day he'd first set foot on Lansford farm, but never had he revealed more than the vaguest clues about his personal life. She had the feeling that this morning he'd said more than he'd intended. And though she had no desire to pry, she couldn't help but wonder about the secrets locked away in that bear-sized heart.

She forced her curiosity aside as she entered the house and found to her dismay that her father was no longer seated at the table.

"I convinced him to lie down for a while," Lisbeth said. "I know he doesn't want us to worry, but I don't think he should make the trip to town. You two go on ahead. I'll stay here with him."

"Do you think I should fetch the doctor?" Torey asked.

"No. Pa's just tired. Get him his coffee and sugar and maybe some licorice twists. You know his sweet tooth. The accounts are all paid up at Buckley's Mercantile."

Again Torey offered to postpone the trip, but Lisbeth convinced her that getting the supplies would actually do more for their father's spirits than everyone's staying home.

Torey and Eli ate quickly, saying little, and then while Eli hitched up the team, Torey went to her room to change clothes. Her earlier enthusiasm for the trip had waned considerably. It wasn't going to be nearly as much fun without her father and Lisbeth along.

Even so, she had to admit that it felt good to be wearing the velvet dress. She'd let her hair down, too, freed it from its normally confining braid, so that it cascaded to her waist in waves of spun midnight. That should impress Mr. Buckley, she thought, then wondered guiltily if she was being vain.

Was it vain to consider herself attractive? To not for once have to worry about her height with respect to a man?

Fiddle faddle! she thought. It was a day to be a little fanciful, even a little vain. What could be the harm?

She said her good-byes to her father and Lisbeth, then headed out the front door. Determinedly eager, she joined Eli in the buckboard. She wasn't going to give her silly misgivings about this day another thought.

"I want to hear some tall tales, Eli," she announced as he gigged the horses out onto the dusty, wheel-rutted path that would eventually connect them to the road that led to Boden. "I want to hear tall tales about heroes and villains in the wild West."

Eli was only too happy to oblige. He seemed in need of some distracting himself. But even the whopper he spun out for her about the time he spent two months living in a snow cave with a hibernating grizzly had an edge to it.

As they rode on, the stories took an even more serious turn. "I seem to be thinkin' a lot about a friend of mine lately. You want hero stories, Miss Torey, well, I'll tell you about a man who was a hero right here in Kansas during the War of the Rebellion. Except you won't be readin' his name in no history books."

"Who was he?"

"Name's Noah Killian. For a time he took on Quantrill and his butchers almost single-handed."

Torey had heard many stories over the years of William Quantrill and his Confederate irregulars looting and burning their way through Kansas. One particularly heinous morning in '63 Quantrill had led an attack on civilians in the border town of Lawrence. His soldiers slaughtered every man they could find. Before they rode out again, nearly one hundred fifty townspeople were dead. Shortly thereafter, Torey's father had dug out a storm cellar under the parlor, saying it was to protect the family against tornadoes, but Torey had suspected even then that it was meant more as protection against Quantrill's human storms of violence.

"Quantrill was an outlaw who used the Southern flag as an excuse to rob and kill," Eli muttered. "Noah Killian believed in fighting fire with fire. He convinced his superiors to let him have his own secret band of Union irregulars. He kept Quantrill and his bunch on the run for months."

"He must have been very brave," Torey said. "Who knows, he might even have saved my life. Rumors were all over Boden that Quantrill was going to burn it to the ground because some merchant had overcharged one of his soldiers for a pair of boots." Torey found the notion of owing her life to this unknown hero almost romantic. "What happened to him?"

Eli's voice grew fierce with a very real anguish. "Killian was ambushed, shot in the back by one of his own men. A man Noah once considered a friend, but who turned out to be a spy, an infiltrator working for Quantrill."

Torey gasped. "Did Killian live?"

"It'd take more than one bullet to do in Noah. After the war, he was assigned as a captain to Fort Laramie in the Wyoming Territory." Eli twisted the reins around work-callused fingers. "One of the best men I've ever known and those bastards . . . " He stopped, flushed. "Sorry, Miss Torey."

"What became of him?"

"I don't want to say. It's done. It can't be undone."

"Is he dead?"

Eli thought about that a long minute, then said, "Maybe in a manner of speakin' he is. At least the Noah Killian I knew. Ah, hell . . . I'm sorry I brought it up."

"No, I'm the one who's sorry," she said softly. "I shouldn't have pushed you to talk about him."

"It's all right."

"Thank God the war times are over," Torey said, trying to lighten the mood. "Kansas is even pretty much safe from

Indians now. We just have to worry about drought, grasshoppers, blizzards, hail, and tornadoes. Hardly a reason to turn a hair."

They talked no more of Noah Killian as Boden came into view.

Front Street, the wide dirt road that split the town down the middle, was lined with stores on either side. It was a typical frontier settlement, if Torey could believe Eli's comparisons of it to the many others he had visited in his life. But for her Boden was quite the metropolis. Its offerings included three mercantiles, four saloons, a bank, a cafe, a millinery shop, a barber, a bathhouse, the undertaker, jail, livery, and blacksmith. What more could a girl want?

It was nearly noon and everywhere she looked people bustled up and down the boardwalk. She waved at several of them, but her eyes were drawn again and again to Buckley's Mercantile. Her heart thudded. Was Jim working behind the counter today? She would make it her first priority to find out.

As Eli halted the buckboard in front of the livery, Torey didn't wait for him to lift her down. She hopped to the ground, sidestepping the puddled evidence of recent rains. "Meet you back here a couple of hours before sunset?" she called.

"Sounds good."

She flipped her hair over her shoulders and strolled toward Buckley's. Strangely though, after her conversation with Eli, her plan to engage in a little flirting with a man who'd kissed her once five months ago seemed not nearly so important anymore. She was annoyed to find herself fretting instead over a man she'd never even met, and likely never would—a stranger named Noah Killian.

Is he dead?

Maybe in a manner of speakin' he is. At least the Noah Killian I knew.

Now what could that mean?

Torey shook her head. She didn't know, and she told herself she didn't care. Obviously, talking about Killian was upsetting to Eli. She wasn't going to bring up the subject again.

She was in town, just as she'd wanted to be, and she was going to get on with what had brought her here. Stiffening her spine, she marched into Buckley's Mercantile. She was careful to hide her disappointment from the clerk, when Jim was nowhere in sight. Quickly she ordered the supplies she needed for the farm, then casually asked after the Buckleys. She was rewarded with the clerk's telling her Jim was just up the street at Daisy's Cafe having his noonday meal.

Torey wasted no time heading for Daisy's. Her earlier enthusiasm for this long-dreamed-of moment was again stirring to life inside her. Her skin tingled as she remembered Jim's kiss, soft, heady, sweet. Could they possibly steal away for another?

Her fantasies ended the moment she walked into the cafe. Torey stood just inside the doorway and stared across a sea of red checked tablecloths. Jim was there all right. He was seated in the room's far corner, facing in Torey's direction. But he was not looking her way. Those deep-set blue eyes of his were locked in moon-eyed adoration on his dining companion—a stunningly attractive blonde.

Torey took a step back, desperate to be gone before Jim could even take note of her arrival. She didn't make it. Maybe he'd felt her eyes on him. She didn't know. In any case, he looked up. Their eyes collided. He nearly upended his chair in his haste to get to his feet. "Victoria, ah, I mean, Miss Lansford, I—I didn't expect to see you . . . I mean, it's not planting season . . . I . . ."

The blond woman rose beside him, looping her arm possessively in his. The top of her head barely came to his chest. "Please introduce me to your tall friend, Jim darling."

Torey felt her cheeks burning.

"Uh, Miss Lansford, you remember Myra. Myra Parks. She was at the harvest dance last fall."

Torey vaguely remembered the banker's daughter. The Parkses were new to Boden, having arrived just last September.

"Jim and I had a quarrel that night," Myra clucked sadly. "A silly argument over . . . well, I don't even remember, to tell you the truth. When I went looking for him to apologize, I saw him dancing with you. Let's just say, Jim got my attention."

Torey's quick glance at Buckley caught the guilty flush staining his cheeks. "I'll just bet he did." Torey dug her nails into her palms to keep from crying. All these months she had dreamed of him, relived the wonder of that night—the dance, the kiss. And the man had only used her, used her to make his girlfriend jealous! How could she have been such a fool?

"Myra and I are going to be married," Jim said lamely, his eyes betraying how clearly he knew just what she thought of him.

"We'll be sure to invite you, Miss Lansford," Myra said.

"You do that." Somehow Torey managed to excuse herself, stammering something about meeting Eli for lunch. She all but ran from the restaurant.

She found Eli at the Silver Dollar Saloon having a well-deserved beer.

"Something wrong, Miss Torey?"

"Not a blasted thing," she said as she yanked out a chair and sat down beside him. "Except that I hate men. They're vile, loathsome, conniving, disgusting, sneaking, rude, deceitful creatures who don't deserve to live." Her lower lip trembled dangerously.

"I certainly hope you don't include all men in that description, little lady."

Torey looked up to see the face of a stranger. A sandy-haired man with eyes nearly the exact same shade of blue as Jim Buckley's. It did not enhance her first impression of him.

"I beg your pardon?" she asked, steadying herself. "Do I know you, sir?"

The man tipped his hat. "The name's Cole Varney, miss. Just passin' through your little town, waitin' on some friends of mine. Though it might be I'll tell 'em to keep ridin'."

Torey blushed. She was flattered in spite of herself, especially after so raw an encounter with Jim Buckley.

Eli cleared his throat meaningfully. "I'm gettin' a mite hungry, Miss Torey," he said. "Maybe you and I should go somewhere to get a bite to eat. I hear Miss Daisy's has good food."

"No! I mean, no," she added more calmly. "They serve steaks here too, don't they?"

"Your pa would have my hide if he thought I'd let you sit around in a saloon."

"Sarsaparilla for the little lady?" Cole asked. "My treat."

The bartender obliged. Torey sipped the sweet concoction. "Thank you."

Cole smiled, a most dazzling smile. "Never seen such hair," he said. "You must be some kind of an angel."

"That's enough," Eli gritted, shoving to his feet.

"No offense, mister," Varney said smoothly.

"Eli, please . . ." Torey touched his sleeve. "I'm sure Mr. Varney meant no harm."

Eli remained standing, making it clear that he intended them to leave. Now.

Reluctantly, Torey stood, pleased when Varney gallantly reached out to help with her chair. She was starting to thank him, when he straightened. Her spirits plummeted as she noted an all too familiar look in his eyes. She was a full half a head taller than Cole Varney, and it was obvious he didn't like it one bit. Gruffly, he excused himself and headed back to his beer.

Torey sighed. "Oh, Eli, why can't a man like a tall girl?"

"If a man is tall in his heart, your size won't matter a whit."

Torey didn't believe a word of it, but she had no strength to argue. She and Eli headed outside.

"You want to eat?" he asked. "I'll buy. And we don't have to go to Miss Daisy's. The hotel serves food."

"I'm not hungry, Eli. Honestly. I'm afraid my big adventure into town isn't working out exactly the way I'd . . . hoped. If it's all the same to you, I'd just like to head home."

"You're sure?"

She nodded.

With a shrug he walked her back to the buckboard, which they then drove to the mercantile to load up on the supplies she'd ordered.

The next time she plotted some elaborate fantasy, Torey vowed, she would pay more attention to her premonitions. Stay home indeed. She should've stayed in bed.

Eli was about to gig the team into motion when someone called out for him to wait. A gaunt, dark-haired man in a calfskin vest strode up to Eli's side of the buckboard. On the vest was pinned a tin star. Torey nodded a greeting to Sheriff Jack Hutchins, trying to ignore the nauseous-looking wad of tobacco the man had squirreled away in his right cheek.

"I heard you were in town, Eli," Hutchins said. "Can I talk to you a minute?" He spat a wad of brown juice into the dust.

"Sure thing, Sheriff."

"I just got word of a bank robbery up in Hays two days ago. That's less than fifty miles north of here."

"You think they're headin' this way?"

"Don't know. Seems likely they'd run south toward the Badlands, or maybe west into Colorado. Nine of 'em. As brazen as the James gang, only bloodier. They never leave anybody alive to tell what they look like." Hutchins swiped at a dribble of tobacco juice on his chin. "This would never have happened if Bill Hickock was still sheriff up there. Damn fool voters." He touched his hat brim. "Beggin' your pardon for the language, Miss Torey."

She smiled. She'd heard a lot worse when Eli hit his thumb with a hammer last month.

"Something you need from me, Sheriff?" Eli asked.

"I hired on a couple of extra deputies this morning, just in case. No predicting these gangs. Hit hard and run fast. Learned from Quantrill and his devils. Don't suppose you could stay on overnight, Eli? Give me a hand trainin' 'em. They're pretty green."

Eli glanced at Torey. "I'd best not, Sheriff."

"Don't turn him down on my account," Torey protested. "Please. I can handle the buckboard."

"If I stay, then so should you. You can get a room at the hotel."

"I want to get home. Lisbeth might need help with Pa." She could hardly bear the thought of being in town another minute, let alone overnight.

"I seen Nate Hardy up the street at the livery a few minutes ago," the sheriff put in. "He was getting ready to ride out. You know him, Miss Torey. His farm is about ten miles east of your place. He could ride along with you, I'm sure."

Eli scratched at his beard, giving her a look that spoke volumes. "No hijinks. You stick to the main road."

"You know I will."

He hefted his rifle from under the buckboard seat and checked the load before handing it back to her. "I wish I would've given you another lesson or two."

"I can hit what I aim at."

He chuckled. "I reckon you can at that, but I wouldn't be letting you ride home even with Hardy along if'n I really thought you'd run into trouble."

"I know."

With that Eli headed off with Hutchins toward the lawman's office. Torey caught up the reins.

"Miss Lansford, hold up!" came a voice Torey did not

recognize. She turned to see Cole Varney striding toward her. She eyed him warily.

"I don't blame you for being put out with me," he said cajolingly. "In fact, that's why I'm here. I want to apologize. That was mighty rude of me to walk away from you like that in the saloon, and me tryin' to defend the male of the species. It's just that I never run across such a tall lady before." He gave her that dazzling smile again.

Torey felt her legs go rubbery. It was a good thing she was sitting down.

Just then, Jim Buckley and Myra Parks chanced by on the boardwalk. Torey smiled inwardly when they paused.

"Why, Mr. Varney," she trilled, in a voice louder than necessary, "I do declare, you could turn a young woman's head with such talk." She touched his arm. She was rewarded with a scowl from Jim Buckley and another smile from Varney.

"This man giving you any trouble, Tor—uh, Miss Lansford?" Jim asked.

"Not at all," she purred.

Jim's scowl deepened, and Torey was pleased to see Myra tugging on his arm. The petite blonde had to practically drag the man away.

"That fella's got an eye for you," Varney drawled.

"Oh, I don't think so. That was his fiancée with him."

"Man would be a fool not to choose you over her."

Torey ducked her head, embarrassed but pleased. "You do know how to flatter a girl, Mr. Varney."

"Oh, no, I don't use flattery, Miss Torey. I use the truth. You are one pretty lady." He glanced up the street with seeming nonchalance. "I noticed the sheriff talking to your friend . . . Eli, was it?"

"Oh my, yes, that was something," she said, enjoying the thrill of being the one to pass on a bit of gossip. "It seems the sheriff is putting on extra deputies because there's a possibility of the bank being robbed. Can you imagine?"

"You don't say," Cole said blandly.

"That would be pretty exciting, don't you think? Not that I want it to happen, of course."

"Oh, no; of course not."

The plodding arrival of three horsemen made them both look up. A coarse-looking, trail-dusty bunch, Torey noted, as they tied off their mounts to the hitch rail in front of the buckboard.

Cole grinned. "My friends."

He introduced her to them in an offhand way. Torey paid little attention. She found them smelly and uninteresting, though she tried not to show it. She didn't want to offend Cole. She was glad when the men wandered off toward the saloon.

Cole lingered. "Maybe you wouldn't mind if I called on you sometime."

"I thought you were just passing through."

"I was. But a lady like you can change a man's mind."

"You're very kind."

He chuckled, but the sound was more of a secret mirth than a shared one. "That's me," he said. "Kind."

Torey had the sudden urge to head home. She lifted the reins.

"You alone?" Cole asked. His voice was mild, but something flickered in his eyes that made Torey suddenly uneasy.

"Well . . . "

Nate Hardy rode up astride his gray mule. "Sheriff says I'm to escort you home, Miss Torey."

"Thank you, Nate. I'm obliged."

The wiry Hardy headed out.

Torey snapped the reins, setting the team in motion.

"Bet them legs of yours go on forever."

Varney's parting words hung in the air, so soft Torey wasn't even certain she'd heard them. When she turned to look, he was already striding away, probably to join his friends.

She felt her face grow hot. Surely she'd just imagined the outrageous comment.

Stay home. The chill was back, stronger than ever. Torey suddenly couldn't wait to be home.

Behind her, Cole Varney turned and watched the retreating buckboard. He was smiling, a big, broad smile that didn't quite reach his eyes.

Torey was home. She should have felt safe. It was late afternoon when she guided the buckboard into the yard. She halted the team under the oak tree nearest the house and called out a grateful good-bye to Nate Hardy, who declined her invitation to join the family for supper. As she watched Hardy ride on, she had to resist the urge to go after him, insist that he stay. She would have been able to offer no logical explanation for her request. Other than that the unease she'd felt off and on all day was with her again, steady now, unrelenting.

She was frightened. For no reason she could fathom, she was frightened.

Muttering an uncharacteristic oath, Torey hopped down from the buckboard. She'd had just about enough of this. Her so-called distress was nothing that couldn't be cured by a good hot bath. Everything was fine. All she had to do was look around and see for herself.

From the near pasture just past the barn her father waved a greeting. He was making a valiant effort to currycomb Galahad. His movements were awkward, even weary. But at least he was up and around. Torey felt better just looking at him.

Lisbeth strolled out onto the front porch, wiping her hands on her apron. "You're back early, aren't you?"

"Got what we need right here," Torey said, patting the canvas-covered supplies in the back of the buckboard.

"That's not what I meant," Lisbeth said. "And where's Eli?"

Torey explained the sheriff's request that Eli stay on overnight.

"Goodness!" Lisbeth exclaimed. "I certainly hope there isn't any trouble."

"Eli and the sheriff can handle it," Torey said, tossing back the tarp.

"So," Lisbeth prompted, coming over to help Torey lift a small keg of molasses and carry it toward the house, "are you going to keep me in suspense all night, or are you going to tell me how things went with Jim Buckley?"

Torey straightened, maintaining her grip on the heavy keg. She decided to spare her sister none of the details.

By the time they'd finished offloading the supplies, Lisbeth was outraged, perhaps even more so than Torey herself had been. "Jim Buckley is a disgrace," she huffed, pressing the back of her hand to her perspiration-damp forehead. They had settled themselves onto two rocking chairs on the front porch to watch the sun set, but Lisbeth was in no mood to reflect on nature's handiwork. "The man should be horsewhipped. Why the next time I see him, he's going to wish—"

"Oh, no, Lissa, please," Torey cried, "I couldn't bear it if you said anything to him."

"No man is going to take advantage of my little sister. When I—"

They both looked up at the sound of a rider approaching.

Lisbeth stood, shading her eyes. "A stranger," she said, her voice mild, unconcerned.

"Cole Varney," Torey said, trying to match her sister's nonchalance and failing. "I met him in town. He was—"

Varney pulled up and dismounted.

"Good evening, ladies," he said, doffing his hat to reveal a tangled shock of sandy brown hair.

Lisbeth gave him an uncertain smile as Torey introduced the two of them.

"It's nice to see you again, Mr. Varney," Torey said, not at all sure that it was.

"It would please me greatly if you called me Cole," he went on smoothly. "It's such a beautiful night, isn't it? So beautiful that I just couldn't get the picture of a certain beautiful lady out of my mind."

Torey studied the man's offhand stance. Maybe she had misheard his bold comment in town. He seemed charming enough, polite. "Would you care to join us for supper?" she asked, deciding politeness would mollify her own jittery nerves. "My sister is a wonderful cook."

Varney glanced back in the direction he'd come. "Now that sounds mighty friendly. Mighty friendly indeed. I like my ladies friendly."

Torey saw Lisbeth frown.

"Did you ride out for something in particular, Mr. Varney?" Lisbeth asked. "We're not exactly on the beaten path."

"Indeed I did, ma'am." He looked at Torey. "I come to thank you."

"Thank me for what?" Torey asked.

Varney put one booted foot on the porch, leaning an arm negligently against his knee. "You saved me and my friends from making a big mistake in town today."

"I don't know what you mean."

He went on as if she hadn't spoken. "And now we're going to have a little party to celebrate." He stepped onto the porch. "You're invited too, sweet thing." He touched Lisbeth's chin.

Lisbeth slapped his hand away. "My sister spoke out of turn, Mr. Varney. I'm afraid I'll have to ask you to leave."

"Oh, I'm not leavin', Miss Lisbeth." His voice was as silky smooth as a spider's web. "Not just yet. And neither are my friends."

Torey gasped. Three riders, four, the farmyard exploded in a thunder of hoofbeats and curses. They seemed almost to rise up out of the ground. And then there were more, their horses swirling up so much dust that Torey could no longer be certain of their number. Eight? Nine?

"What is this?" Torey demanded. "Cole, make them stop!"

Cole did nothing of the kind.

One of the men dismounted and joined Varney on the porch. He was shorter than Varney, and almost nondescript, except for the scar that slashed across his right cheek. And his eyes. Torey had never seen such black, soulless eyes.

"I'm so glad to see that you didn't exaggerate, Cole," the scar-faced man said, his cultured voice at odds with the cold menace in his tone. "This is indeed going to be a pleasure. I'll bet those legs do go on forever."

Lisbeth stepped in front of Torey. "We have no money. I want all of you off our land. Now."

The man chuckled. It was not a pleasant sound. "My men are tired. We rode a long way today only to be left empty-handed. I can't allow that. They need some sort of . . . recompense for their trouble. If not money," he mused, "then the next best thing. The company of a beautiful, *willing* woman." He chuckled again. "Or maybe one not so willing."

The other seven riders had dismounted, one of them holding the reins of the horses, while the remaining six hovered on the porch's edge, waiting.

Torey had the impression of wolves closing in on a cornered doe. And then one of the wolves attacked.

Cole Varney lunged for her, catching her arms, seeking to pin her against the house. Stunned, horrified, still not quite believing any of this was really happening, she cried out. "Cole, stop this! Cole, you don't have to—"

He tore at her dress front, the cherished velvet giving way. His sweaty palms groped beneath the thin layering of her chemise, closed on her breast. An animal sound of pure terror ripped from her throat.

She heard Lisbeth screaming.

A gunshot split the air. Varney whirled, instinctively going for his pistol, but stayed his hand when another shot rang out.

"Get away from my daughters!" Abel Lansford shouted. "All of you! Or I'll send you to hell where you belong!"

Torey leaned against the house, shaking, sobbing as she watched her father coming toward them from the direction of the barn. She recognized the rifle he was carrying as the extra Winchester from Eli's room. Even in her terror she could see how desperately her father was trying not to limp, not to show these men any sign of weakness.

Abel kept the rifle trained on the men. To his daughters he barked, "Get in the house! Now!"

Lisbeth and Torey scrambled inside and shut the door. Almost in the same motion Lisbeth jammed the crossbar into place, while Torey raced through the house, yanking shutters closed and battening them down.

The scenario had been a game once, played out by Abel and Emma Lansford with their children as a drill in the event Confederate soldiers had ever attacked the farm.

Today it was no game.

Lisbeth was shoving her father's desk to one side, flinging back the parlor carpet and exposing the trapdoor to the storm cellar beneath.

"No, Lissa!" Torey cried. "That won't work. If we go down, there's no one to put the rug back in place. No one to help Papa."

Torey was at the hearth, grabbing up the rifle that hung over the mantel. She snatched at a box of cartridges on the ledge, but her hand was trembling so badly, she dropped it. The box hit the floor, spilling open, bullets clattering in all directions. Torey dropped to her hands and knees, grasping them up with shaking fingers, shoving the bullets one after another into the rifle's chamber.

"Lisbeth!" Torey screamed. "Help me find the rest of the bullets! Help me—"

"No! You know what we're supposed to do! Get in the cellar. Get in the cellar now."

"Lissa! Papa's out there all alone! He can't hold them off forever. I have to help—"

A gun sounded, a shot that seemed to echo and reecho. Lisbeth rushed to one of the rifle slits in the shutters and peered out into the yard. Her face went ash white. She looked at Torey, her lips forming a single, agonized word. "Papa."

Torey allowed no time for the horror to sink in. To do so would be to allow her father's sacrifice to be in vain. She levered a cartridge into the rifle's chamber. It was up to her now. Lisbeth didn't know one end of a gun from the other.

Torey took dead aim on the front door, expecting any second that Varney and his men would try to batter it down.

Lisbeth huddled at Torey's side. "They're going to kill us," she said numbly. "You can't fight them all. Papa wouldn't want me to let you."

Torey was scarcely listening. Her eyes were locked on the front door. Someone was trying to kick it in. She took a deep breath.

With a sudden violence Torey felt herself being hurtled sideways and down. She tried to catch herself, failed. Lisbeth was pushing her, shoving her through the open door of the storm cellar. "Lissa, no! What are you—?"

Torey tripped, stumbled. The rifle slipped from her grasp as she fell heavily down the half dozen wooden steps to the earthen floor below. Her head connected solidly with a support post. She cried out, felt her world spin. "Lissa!"

Desperately Torey fought off the pain, the dizziness, pushing herself to her knees. Above her the cellar door slammed shut, plunging her into absolute darkness.

She was aware of sounds. Lisbeth dragging the rug back over the trapdoor, pushing the desk on top of the rug.

No.

Then came the sound of wood splintering, glass breaking. The front door was being battered to pieces.

Torey stumbled to her feet, groping for the gun. Her world spun crazily. She had to help Lisbeth. Had to . . . She pressed her hand to her forehead. It came away wet, sticky.

She pitched forward and lay still.

From somewhere far away she heard a scream. It took her a minute to remember where she was. And then it all came crashing back to her. Lisbeth!

Torey forced herself to her knees. Her head throbbing, she crawled to the steps, feeling her way up to the top riser. Hunching beneath the trapdoor, she pushed upward with every ounce of her strength. The door didn't budge.

She sagged onto a lower step. How much time had passed? How long had she been unconscious? She trembled. How long had Lisbeth been up there alone? The sounds coming from beyond the trapdoor seemed removed somehow. Torey realized then they were muffled by distance. They were coming from outside the house. The men were in the yard. Shouting, cursing, laughing—having fun. Fun.

Lisbeth screamed again.

Torey banged on the cellar door until her fists were bloody. No one came. She dropped to her knees, sobbing.

Lisbeth's screams went on and on. Endless.

And then, abruptly, they stopped. And there was no sound at all. Only silence. Terrible, awful silence. No screams, no sobs, no . . .

Like a wild woman, Torey again pounded on the door, screaming. Footsteps echoed overhead. The desk was being shifted, toppled.

Torey scrambled back to the bottom of the steps. Gun ready, she waited. They would kill her, but she would take as many of them with her as she could.

Above her head the door yawned open.

A man leered down into the darkness. "A fresh one," he grunted, taking the first step down.

It was his last. Torey fired the rifle.

The man's eyes widened in surprise, pain; then he pitched through the opening and collapsed at her feet. Torey paid him no mind. She was trying desperately to lever another cartridge into the rifle's chamber.

Cole Varney's fist closed around the slender barrel and used it to haul her up the stairs into the parlor. "You're going to regret that, little lady."

Varney caught her arm and dragged her outside. The sun was gone. Lanterns had been brought out from the barn, their glow casting macabre shadows on the yard. Hours had passed. Torey shuddered. Hours.

Torey saw Lisbeth then. Naked, bleeding, sprawled on her back by a budding oak tree. A man hovered over her, his pants around his ankles. He turned toward Torey and touched himself, making her an obscene promise with his eyes.

Torey felt her mind recede for just an instant, as though she weren't there at all. She couldn't even summon the strength to scream.

"Time to join the party," Varney said, maintaining his viselike grip on her arm.

"Let me go to my sister. Please."

"All in good time. You and I have got some unfinished business first." He trailed a hand along her torn dress front, insinuated his fingers beneath her chemise.

Bile rose in Torey's throat. She forced it down. "Don't. Please . . . "

"You don't want me to stop. I know what you want. I knew it from the first minute I saw you."

Another man staggered over, smelling of whiskey and sweat. "Don't hog her all to yourself, Cole," he grumbled. "I never had me a tall one before." The man grabbed Torey's arm, trying to pull her away from Varney. Varney resisted. Torey screamed.

"Stop!" a cold, clear voice commanded.

It was the man with the scar across his cheek. He had held himself aloof from the others, watching from the porch. But now he stepped toward Varney. "This one is mine."

"I saw her first," Cole said.

The black-eyed man glared at Varney.

Abruptly, Varney released her. "Sorry, boss." He coughed. "I didn't mean nothin'."

The man with the scarred face trailed his fingers along Torey's cheek, her throat and down. "Now, Cole," he asked, "what have I tried to tell you about being more subtle? You can't be rough with every woman. Some need a gentler touch."

Without warning he gave Torey's arm a savage twist, pinning it behind her back. She couldn't move. She could scarcely breathe. Involuntary tears sprang to her eyes.

"There now, see?" the silky-voiced man said, bringing his face to within inches of her own. "A gentler touch. You trust me, don't you, dear?" He gave her arm another twist. "See? I'm not going to hurt you."

Torey spit in his face.

The man's features contorted. He cursed and backhanded her across the mouth, sending her sprawling backward in the dirt. Torey tasted blood.

"That was a mistake, bitch," the man said.

From somewhere deep inside her, Torey called on a resolve she hadn't known she possessed. If she lived through this night, she would remember this man, remember them all. She scanned the circle of leering faces. Every eye color, every nose, every mouth. She would remember these men, all eight of them.

No, not eight. Nine. Out of the corner of her eye Torey spied one more, a lone, shadowy figure over by the corral with the horses. One of the riders, hanging back. Not taking part in this savagery. But not stopping it either.

"Help us!" she screamed. "For the love of God, help us!"

He only turned and retched into the dirt.

"I'm disappointed in you, my dear," the scar-faced man said. "You're not being at all cooperative. Your sister cooperated. In fact, she begged for more." He chuckled malevolently. "Begged on her knees."

Torey lunged at him. Like a wild animal she tore at his face, his hair, his clothes. Her hand snagged on his sleeve, ripping the fabric. On his right forearm she saw a crossed-saber tattoo. She would remember that too.

The man laughed. Despite her size, her strength, she was no match for him. He pinned her arms above her head as he forced her to the ground. She felt something hard, rigid against her thigh. "I'm going to show you how it's done, honey," he said. "When I'm through with you, you're going to know what it is to be a woman."

Torey felt her sanity slipping away. "Kill me," she said. "I'd rather be dead than have you touch me."

"All in good time, my sweet."

He had to use one hand to unbutton his fly. Torey screamed, bucked, kicked. One foot caught him a glancing blow to the groin.

The man rolled off her, gasping, cursing. He drew his gun. "You shouldn't have done that," he shouted, thumbing back the hammer on the Colt.

Torey waited for death. Prayed for death. She closed her eyes.

A gun roared.

Torey jumped, startled, but felt no bullet tear through her body. She opened her eyes in time to see one of the outlaws clutching at his chest, a splotch of crimson spreading beneath his palms. He was dead before he hit the ground.

More shots rang out. The bullets were coming from somewhere out in the darkness. Another of the outlaws fell. Then another. The latter regained his feet, gripping his arm, yowling in pain. Everywhere the outlaws were scattering, scrambling for their horses, clawing for their guns. Blindly, they fired into the night.

Torey spied the gun of one of the dead outlaws lying within her reach. She grabbed it, brought it to bear on the man nearest her—Cole Varney, seeking to mount his terrified horse. The animal reared just as Torey fired. She missed. Varney wheeled on her, firing his own six-gun. Reflexively, she fell back, pretending to be hit as the bullet whizzed past her head.

For long seconds she didn't move. Didn't dare. Even as horses thundered past her out of the yard.

Then she felt hands closing around her. She screamed, struggled, kicked.

"It's all right, girl," a familiar voice soothed. "It's all right. It's me. It's Eli." He was still holding his smoking pistol.

Torey caught the sound of other riders heading off after the six fleeing outlaws. Eli answered her unspoken question. "The sheriff and his posse."

Torey shook loose from Eli's comforting embrace. "Lisbeth . . . " The word was a half sob. On her hands and knees she crawled to her sister. Everywhere Torey looked, there was blood. Lisbeth was so still. Her eyes were open, but Torey couldn't even tell if she was breathing.

"I'm sorry, Lissa, so sorry," she whimpered.

She glanced over to where her father lay crumpled near one of his beloved oaks. Eli was bending over him. The bearded ex-scout raised his eyes to hers and shook his head.

But she already knew. If her father had been alive, he would still have been fighting to protect his family.

Eli rose and went into the house. He returned carrying a blanket, which he used to tenderly cover up Lisbeth.

"Why, Eli?" Torey asked. "Why did this happen?"

"The sheriff thinks it was the same bunch that robbed the bank in Hays, that they were plannin' to hit Boden. Varney was the front man, checking out the town." He raked a hand through his shaggy hair. "Maybe he spotted the extra deputies. I don't know."

Torey began to tremble. . . . *come to thank you*. "Oh, God, oh my God. I told him! I told Cole Varney about the deputies, about the bank. I told him. I did this. I did this to my sister, my father."

"No! *They* did this."

"But if I hadn't talked to him, flirted with him . . . " She said the words with self-loathing.

"Stop it! I need your help. Lisbeth needs your help."

"Lisbeth's dead."

"No, she's alive."

The words hit Torey like a fist. "We have to get her into the house. Hurry."

Eli lifted Lisbeth's blanket-covered body and carried her into her bedroom. Gently, he laid her atop the quilted coverlet. "She's in a bad way. I don't know . . . "

"She's not going to die," Torey said. "I won't let her die." Torey rushed about the house, gathering up cloths to use for bandages. Together, she and Eli dressed the scores of cuts and slashes that covered Lisbeth's brutalized body.

But the wounds of the flesh were not the ones that frightened Torey the most. It was the look in her sister's eyes. They were wide open, but they seemed aware of nothing, no one.

"Some kind of shock," Eli said. "I'm sure she'll come out of it."

"How did you and the sheriff know to come here?" Torey asked, needing to focus on something besides the ghost-pale face of her sister.

"Almost didn't." His voice was bitter. "Barkeep at the Silver Dollar come to the sheriff's office about three hours after Varney and his friends rode out. It worried him that they kept mentioning your name. But not so much that he didn't wait until his shift was over."

He had to swallow hard before he could continue. "At least we got three of them."

"Six got away. Varney was one of them."

"Did you recognize any of the others?"

She shook her head. "But I'll never forget them. Any of them."

"Anything special about them. Size? Scars?"

Torey sensed that he wanted to keep her talking. That he was afraid if he didn't, she would somehow slip away from him too, just as Lisbeth had.

"The leader had a scar," Torey told him, "a slash across his right cheek. He gave the orders, not Varney." She cringed as she saw the man again in her mind's eye. "Medium height, maybe a little shorter. Brown hair. Mean eyes. The meanest eyes I've ever seen. Cold, like a snake's. And he had a tattoo."

Eli frowned. "What sort of tattoo?"

"A crossed-saber tattoo on his right forearm."

Eli went still. "The one with the scar had the tattoo on his arm?"

She nodded.

"It can't be." Eli rose to pace to the window, gazing out into the darkness. "It can't be."

"What is it?"

He didn't answer, saying instead, "We'd best get some soup into Lisbeth."

Torey sat up with her sister the rest of the night and all of the next day. The only change was a chilling one. Lisbeth began talking, but not in a manner Torey recognized.

"Mama's baking cookies," Lisbeth said in a voice that belonged to a very young child. "I smell them. They smell so good. Papa, tell me a story. Please."

"Lisbeth," Torey pleaded. "It's me. Torey. Please . . . "

"Can you tell me a story, Papa? Please tell me a story."

Eli brought in a doctor, but the medical man could do no more for Lisbeth than she and Eli had done.

"The mind is a complex thing," the doctor said. "I've seen similar occurrences in soldiers during the war. Those who had seen too much, more than their minds could bear. It's like they build a shell, a barrier around themselves, a protection against remembering."

"Will she . . . will she get better?" Torey asked.

"Some do, some don't." His eyes were sympathetic. "This is difficult, I know, but you might want to consider a sanitarium if she shows no improvement soon."

"No." Torey took her sister's hand in her own and pressed it to her cheek. "No."

Eli spoke briefly to the doctor. The man nodded and left.

"She's going to get better, Eli," Torey said. "I know she is. She's just too hurt to come back right now. Too scared. But she'll be back. She will."

Eli squeezed Torey's shoulder but said nothing.

A week went by, then another. Torey went through the motions of doing her chores, but every spare moment she spent with Lisbeth.

Eli watched, worried and waited. Torey thought about telling him he was free to go, get on with his life, but she couldn't bear the thought of being alone.

The nights were the worst, filled with dreams, nightmares in which Varney and his scar-faced friend returned to finish what they'd started. She would wake screaming, terrified.

Then somewhere in the midst of one of the dreams, her terror changed. When she woke the following morning she was no longer afraid. She embraced a new emotion.

Hate. Cold and dark and all consuming.

She started to think clearly again, to plan.

She was sitting with Lisbeth one late afternoon when hoofbeats sounded in the yard. Reflexively, Torey grabbed up the rifle that was never more than three feet from her grasp anymore. She hurried to the front door, looking out before she opened it. Relief washed through her. The sheriff. It was the first she'd seen of him since he and his posse had taken off after Varney and the others two weeks ago.

Hutchins was alone.

Torey stepped out onto the porch. Carrying his own rifle, Eli came from the direction of the barn to join them.

Grime-covered, red-eyed with exhaustion, Jack Hutchins slapped his Stetson on his thigh to rid it of several layerings of dust. "Trailed 'em as far as the Badlands," he said.

"You let them go?" Torey's voice was shrill.

"No jurisdiction in the Badlands." He shook his head and looked at Eli. "Never saw 'em. Not once in two weeks, though one of 'em put a bullet in one of my men. I swear it was like we were trailing a ghost."

" 'Ghost' might be the right word," Eli said.

"What's that mean?" Hutchins asked.

Eli didn't answer.

"Mighty sorry I don't have better news Miss Torey," Hutchins went on. "If you could come into town sometime, maybe we can get some wanted dodgers out on these men. That is, if you seen 'em clear enough to identify—"

"She didn't see any of 'em clear," Eli put in. "It was too dark."

"But—" Torey began.

"She didn't see anything," Eli repeated.

Torey fell silent.

Hutchins tipped his hat. "Best if you and your sister not stay here. If you got relatives somewhere, go to them. If you do remember something, you know where to find me."

She nodded.

Eli walked off with the sheriff. For several minutes the two of them spoke in low tones that Torey tried to, but could not, overhear. Then Hutchins mounted and rode out.

"What were you two talking about?" Torey demanded. "And why wouldn't you let me tell him that I know what all six of those animals look like?"

"Because I don't want 'em coming back here to finish the job, that's why. I told the doc and I told the sheriff, as far as Boden's concerned, you and your sister are dead. In a couple of weeks, when Lisbeth's able to travel, I'll take you both out of here, someplace safe. Do you have any other people?"

"My mother has a sister. Aunt Ruby. She's a spinster. She lives in Denver. We've never met, but we exchange letters two or three times a year."

"Good. I'll take you there."

Torey didn't argue. Aunt Ruby's would be a fine place for Lisbeth. She'd be safe, taken care of. But Torey wouldn't be going there. She had something else she had to do.

It was dark, the moon was high, bright overhead when Torey went out and stood over her father's grave. Eli had dug it for her, buried him next to their mother. It was what he would have wanted. Her eyes burned, but she didn't cry. "I miss you, Papa. I miss you so much."

Abel Lansford had never been a man for big dreams, just a man determined to fulfill smaller ones. One day, one hellish day had shattered those dreams, changed all of their lives forever.

"You need to come inside," Eli said, coming up behind her. "Get some rest."

Instead Torey turned to him. "What do you know about the man with the tattoo, Eli? I think you've kept it from me long enough."

"It couldn't be who I'm thinking of. That man is dead. Or at least he's supposed to be."

"Who?"

"His name is John Pike. He rode with Quantrill during the war."

Torey frowned. "And you thought he died with Quantrill?"

"No. Pike didn't die during the war. He died with—" Eli bit off the words, and stood there shaking his head. "My

God, this could change everything. Everything. I have to get word to Noah."

But Torey wasn't listening to Eli's words, only his tone. "You're not leaving?" she demanded.

"No. I'm not going anywhere, gal. Don't you worry."

"Good. I need you here."

Eli looked puzzled. "You can't keep the farm going by yourself. Besides, it isn't safe. I told you—"

"The farm is dead," she cut in. "Dead like my father. I'll have it sold. Use the money for Aunt Ruby to take care of Lisbeth. That isn't why I need you." Her voice was steel hard. "I need you to teach me how to use a six-gun."

"Don't talk crazy, girl. This is for the law to handle."

"The law," she sneered. "You heard the law. The law has boundaries and rules. I don't."

"Your sister needs you."

"And I'll stay with her as long as she does." Torey didn't say aloud what had been in her mind for days now. That Lisbeth was never going to get better. "I'll need time to learn to handle a six-gun anyway."

"Miss Torey, you can't—"

"I can and I will." She looked him straight in the eye, an icy shroud closing around her heart. "The Lansfords take care of their own. My father taught me that. Taught me well."

"This wasn't your fault, girl," Eli pressed gently, maybe a little desperately.

Torey wasn't listening. She sagged to her knees. Eyes burning, she scooped up a handful of the wounded earth that marked her father's grave. "They're going to pay, Eli. Every last one of them, they're going to pay." Her fist closed around the cold, damp soil. "That's my promise to you, Papa. To you and to Lisbeth."

"What promise?" Eli demanded. "What can you do to them animals that the law can't?"

Her voice was cold as death. "I'm going to kill them."

The Fire

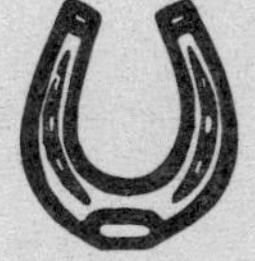

3

Four months later

Bleary-eyed customers in the Red Dog Saloon missed the brass cuspidor near the bar's foot rail far more often than they hit it. Sticky brown splotches fanned out in irregular concentric circles on the boot-scuffed plank wood floor. A slump-shouldered swamper with a bucket and a mop did his best to stay ahead of the faulty-sighted oafs. None of the handful of customers in the Red Dog took much notice, one way or the other.

The essential dreariness of the place was exacerbated by the midnight hour and by the dog-eared posters stuck up over the windows, inside and out. Customers of the Red Dog liked their privacy. Some placards proclaimed events long past—a boxing match, a traveling circus, a dance troupe performing "genuine fandangoes." Others offered varying amounts of money for varying dregs of humanity—horse thieves, murderers, arsonists, even a hundred dollars for an authentic, practicing "consumer of human flesh."

Any or all of the subjects of those posters could have been in the Red Dog this night. No one would have batted an eye or lifted a finger either to claim the reward or facilitate justice.

Including the trail-dusty stranger sitting at the table in the far corner of the room. The man lifted the bottle of whiskey from the spur-scarred table in front of him and took a long pull, barely noting how fiercely the amber liquid burned all the way down to his stomach. His gray eyes were bloodshot, unfocused, and yet to a canny observer they were not entirely unaware. Some inborn survival instinct was still at work in him, which explained why he took care to keep his back to the wall.

Noah Killian tilted his dark Stetson forward, the gesture not intended to shade his eyes against the dim annoyance of the saloon's kerosene-lit chandelier, but rather to screen his features from anyone who might decide to get curious after all about an unknown drifter. He had already stayed too long in this one-horse town, even though, truth to tell, he couldn't remember the town's name or why he'd come here in the first place. Some rare pleasant memory perhaps, though whatever it was had long since escaped him.

From the inside pocket of his black vest, Noah extracted an envelope. He had carried it with him for over two weeks now. From the date on the postmark it had taken much longer than that for the letter to catch up with him. The envelope was still sealed, and his fingers trembled slightly as he held it, though he could have put no name to the emotion that was keeping him from opening the blasted thing. As careless as he had been with the letter these past two weeks, he could almost think he was trying his damndest to lose it.

"Buy me a drink, honey?"

Noah looked up. He noticed her bosom first. He couldn't help it. It was practically in his face. A woman dressed in gaudy blue silk with cleavage as lush as the Great Divide was leaning toward him. He dragged his hat from his head—old habits died hard—and she grabbed it and tossed it on the table. With practiced fingers she began toying with the shoulder-length waves of his dark hair.

"Bet this gray at your temples could tell a tale, eh, cowboy?" she murmured, her smile as false as the warmth in her hazel eyes.

Too much makeup marred what might once have been a pretty face. Too many nights with too many men like him had long ago robbed this particular soiled dove of any dreams that might have nudged past dawn tomorrow.

He shoved the bottle at her. "Help yourself."

Her false smile broadened.

He didn't mind.

She pulled up the chair next to him and snuggled close, pressing her ample breasts against his arm, whispering lewd suggestions in his ear. His body didn't respond. He scowled. He must be drunker than he thought.

"My room's upstairs, cowboy. A dollar can buy you enough time to forget whatever's troublin' you."

"There isn't enough time or enough dollars to forget what I need to forget, sweetheart."

She slid her hand over his crotch. "Are you sure about that?"

Noah curled his hand around the whiskey bottle. "Have another drink. I've got mail to read."

He peeled opened the envelope. At once he recognized Eli Burkett's barely decipherable scrawl. *Come to Cuttersville, Colorado Territory. Urgent.* The words were followed by a series of dates. Dates still a couple of weeks off.

He grimaced. Evidently, Eli had figured on the letter taking a while to find him. The missive went on to assure him that even if he arrived ahead of Eli—*it'll be worth your while to wait,* compadre. *I guarantee it.*

The woman was opening the top button of his shirt, teasing the dusting of hair on his chest. "I'm awful lonely, cowboy. And you sure are handsome."

He reread the letter and cursed inwardly. Eli had been

deliberately obscure. Why? *Trying to rouse my curiosity, old man?* he thought irritably. Or was Eli just being cautious? Too specific and Noah could easily have reached a decision without having to face the old coot. The letter could have wound up in pieces in the cuspidor near the bar.

Noah sighed, a twinge of guilt rippling through him. Or was Eli merely being what he had always been? A good friend. A friend who had stood by him when no one else . . .

With an oath he crumpled the letter in his fist.

The woman clucked sympathetically. "Bad news from home?"

He didn't answer.

"I need you, honey. Please." She nuzzled her face against his neck.

"Need me or need your cut from the bartender for taking me upstairs?" He said the words without judgment.

She affected a hurt look.

"Sorry." He tipped her chin, kissed her cheek.

I'll tell you everything when I see you, Eli wrote.

"Please, honey." The woman cast a worried look toward the bartender. "Lute's going to think I'm losing my touch."

"Well, now, we can't have that, can we?"

It's a chance to get your life back. I swear it.

Stuffing the letter back into his vest pocket, Noah fixed his attention on the woman. "How much could five dollars make me forget, sweet thing?" he asked.

Her smile grew genuine. "Honey, in the morning you won't even remember your name. I promise."

Noah didn't smile. If only. "Lead the way, sweetheart."

. . . a chance to get your life back. What kind of a life would it be anyway after three years in hell?

Long buried emotions niggled at him. Feelings like pride and honor. Maybe, just maybe, he owed it to the old man to find out.

* * *

Victoria Lansford gripped the walnut handle of her Colt revolver and stared down at the two lifeless bodies sprawled grotesquely at her feet, their sightless eyes peering skyward into a blazing Colorado sun. Had it been her bullets or Eli's that had killed the two? She didn't know. She didn't care.

Easing down the hammer on the six-gun, Torey jammed it into the holster she wore strapped to her right thigh. She told herself she was glad the two bastards had decided to shoot it out. Glad that they were dead. She hadn't been practicing with the pistol three hours a day seven days a week for the past five months to turn them over to the law.

Then why was she trembling? Why did she suddenly need to turn her back on their corpses?

Torey drew in a deep, shuddery breath, her eyes burning. Then she cursed. She would not cry. She would not. She hadn't cried since the night of the attack on the farm. She wasn't going to start now.

Damn them anyway. Damn them both. She and Eli had given them every chance to surrender, every chance to throw down their guns. She was not about to feel guilty. They deserved to be dead for what they had done to her father, to Lisbeth.

Torey's gaze swept the rock-strewn slope. Blast! Where was Eli? She expected to see the rough-hewn frontiersman scrabbling toward her. She would need his help to get these two killers slung across the backs of their horses. But Eli was nowhere in sight. She frowned. He was moving more and more slowly these days, his aging bones protesting the relentless pace she had set them on since leaving the farm behind for good three months ago. But the pace couldn't be helped. These two might be dead, but there were still four to go. Including Cole Varney, including John Pike.

Stretching wearily, Torey raised the black Stetson she wore and rubbed a hand across her sweat-damp, close-cropped dark hair. She winced. Even after all these months the shortness of her hair felt foreign to her. But she didn't regret the sacrifice. Like the denims, gray chambray shirt, and black vest she wore, it helped perpetuate the illusion she now presented to the world.

She was no longer Victoria Lansford.

She was Vic Langley, bounty hunter.

From the back pocket of her Levi's jeans, Torey extracted a folded sheet of paper. Smoothing it open, she steeled herself to compare the line drawings on the reward dodger to the faces of the two dead men. The resemblance was almost uncanny. Cleve Jensen and Wade Scott. Cousins, born and raised in Missouri, and reputed to have been rebuffed when they tried to join up with their Missouri kinsmen and fellow killers, Jesse and Frank James. She was certain the sheriff in the nearby town of Cuttersville would have no trouble identifying them from the poster.

Wanted Dead or Alive, the banner blazed across the top of the flyer, while toward the bottom some particularly creative scribe in the print shop had added: "Preferably Dead—It'll Save the Courts the Cost of a Rope."

Her fist tightened, the paper crumpling as she read again their accumulated litany of horrors. Multiple counts of armed robbery, rape, murder, and arson—committed throughout Kansas, and the territories of Colorado and New Mexico. Evidently the two cousins hadn't always felt obliged to ride with Pike and Varney. They had masterminded plenty of unholy work on their own. Some of their victims had survived long enough to describe them to the law.

Torey had first come across the wanted poster on a clandestine trip to Boden three weeks after the attack on the farm. Clandestine, because Eli had remained adamant that no one else learn that she and Lisbeth had survived the assault. Entering the sheriff's office through a rear door, Torey had settled into a dimly lit cell and spent hours poring over scores of old reward dodgers, hoping to attach names to the faces of the four members of John Pike's gang for whom she had none—alias or otherwise.

She'd all but given up when the next to the last dodger had yielded Jensen and Scott. Seeing their faces again made her blood run cold, and yet she'd been exhilarated as well. Two more murderers had names. Yet when she'd pointed them out to the sheriff, he'd only shrugged, telling her that they were likely out of the state and there was nothing he could do.

"You mean there's nothing you want to do," Torey had snapped.

Hutchins bristled. "Now, you listen, Miss Torey. I sympathize with what happened to you and your family, but my hands are tied. I can't go outside the law."

"Then the law stinks," she hissed.

"You could contact a federal marshal," he suggested, his voice tight, "or," he added with a tinge of sarcasm, pointing to the poster, "you could always go out and hire yourself a bounty hunter."

She frowned. "What's a bounty hunter?"

"About the lowest form of life there is," Hutchins said, shifting his chaw of tobacco from one side of his mouth to the other. "A man who'll track another man for money."

"Scott and Jensen aren't men, Sheriff. They're animals. Savages. Or has it slipped your mind what they and their friends did to my father? To Lisbeth?"

The sheriff stood, his face red, his voice now defensive, as it always became whenever he was around her for any length of time these days. "I've done all I can, Miss Torey. Me and my posse chased after them killers for two weeks and all I got to show for it was a deputy with a bullet in his arm. We had no choice. We had to turn back. I have responsibilities here.

"And so do you," he added, spitting a wad of juice into his cuspidor. "In fact, you should be home tendin' to your biggest one right now. Just be grateful you and your sister are still alive. From what I've heard about Cole Varney and his bunch, that doesn't happen very often."

Torey resisted the urge to tell Hutchins that Varney hadn't been giving the orders that night. The leader of the outlaws had been the scar-faced man Eli had called John Pike. But Eli had made her promise not to even so much as describe Pike—to the law or anyone.

And so she had done what Hutchins had told her to do and gone home. But she'd taken the poster with her. At the time she'd intended only to show it to Eli. The plan had come later.

And now she and Eli would be collecting their first bounty. Eight hundred dollars—four hundred dollars per corpse—though the money itself meant nothing to her. She would accept it only because she needed it to continue her search for the others. In her three months on the trail she'd learned early on that information that could be gleaned in no other way often could be bought. It was through such sources that she and Eli had identified one of the two remaining unknown members of Pike's gang—a petty thief named Cal Grady. There was no bounty on Grady, but Torey had learned of an arrest warrant that had been issued for him a year ago in Rimrock, Colorado, on charges of stealing money from a church. It was a start. The final unknown, the young man who'd watched but had not participated in the brutal attack on Lisbeth, remained unidentified.

Even so, Torey had little doubt it would be Pike and Varney who would prove the hardest of their quarry to run to ground. For one thing, she had yet to uncover a single wanted poster on Varney. The attack on the farm was not yet an official crime, because to bring charges against specific individuals was to alert Varney that he had left survivors. As for Pike—Pike was believed to be dead. And nothing she'd turned up thus far had proved otherwise.

Though loath to consider it, Torey knew too there was a chance that Eli could be wrong. That someone else merely had the same tattoo as this man named John Pike. What if word got back to such a man that a bounty hunter was on his trail? He could arrange some sort of ambush before Torey could even—

Behind her a scraping noise sounded. She jumped, startled. In the next breath her Colt was in her right hand. Her gaze locked on the two outlaws, her heart thundering against her ribs. They hadn't moved. She let out an odd choking sound, irrationally relieved. Then she stood there berating herself. Had she actually expected retaliation from dead men?

The noise had come from one of the outlaws' horses scuffing at a clump of buffalo grass. Torey reholstered the gun, assuring herself it was only natural to be on edge.

"Dammit anyway," she muttered aloud. *Where was Eli?* Even he couldn't be that slow. Still agitated, she called out his name.

No answer.

A sudden chill gripped her. Jensen and Scott had gotten off several shots before they'd been cut down. "Eli!" she called again, louder.

Nothing.

At once, she started down the slope. She moved cautiously at first, mindful of loose stones, then more rapidly as each succeeding shout elicited no response. Eli couldn't be dead. He couldn't be, her mind thrummed. He was all she had left.

She spotted him at the bottom of a ten-foot drop-off. An apparent misstep, and he had fallen heavily to the rocky surface below. He was on his back, his eyes closed, his left leg twisted at an unnatural angle beneath him. Torey's stomach lurched. Swiftly, she found a deer trail and clambered down the embankment to his side. She started breathing again only when he stirred at her touch.

"Thank God," she murmured.

"Them varmints?" he demanded, struggling to rise, though his features contorted with pain.

"Dead," she assured him, pressing a hand against his shoulder. "Both of them. Now you just rest easy."

He sagged back. "Leg's busted."

Torey pulled a six-inch hunting knife from the sheath in her boot. "I'd best have a look." Gingerly, she cut away at Eli's buckskin legging. She heaved a relieved sigh to discover that the bone was not protruding through the flesh. But there was definitely an ugly swelling in the skin where the snapped shinbone jutted out of place beneath it.

Her palms were sweating, and she wiped them on her trousers. "This has to be set."

"Maybe there's a doc in Cuttersville."

"Can you ride?"

He shook his head. "You'll need to rig up a travois."

Torey glanced across the slope. "There's a small stand of aspen about half a mile from here. I'm sure I can find a couple of saplings." She started to rise, but Eli caught her arm, gripping it with surprising strength.

"You all right?" he asked.

"Fine. Not a scratch."

"That's not what I meant. We just killed two men."

"I killed one the night of the attack, remember?"

"You sayin' it's got easier?"

"I'm saying," she returned tightly, jerking her arm free, "that they were trying to kill us."

"Those two up the hill are different, and you know it. We tracked 'em like a hound on a blood scent for near two weeks, ever since we got wind of where they were."

Torey stood and paced. "You make it sound like we were too hard on them, that maybe we should have backed off. And what? Let them get away?"

Eli lay back, breathing hard. "That's not what I mean, and you know it. But they could've been heading for Pike and Varney, maybe getting ready for another bank job. If we would've held back just a little—"

"We've been through all this."

"And now we're goin' through it again! Jensen and Scott were the best chance we had for getting some real information on Pike."

"We offered to let them surrender. We told them to throw down their guns."

Eli snorted derisively. "They were dead men. Once we had 'em cornered, they were dead. Dead from our guns, or dead from hangin'. We needed to play out the string on 'em just a little farther."

"No! They might've gotten away. And then if they robbed someone, killed them—how could I sleep at night?"

"Do you sleep now?" he asked, his eyes probing hers a little too keenly.

"I sleep just fine," she gritted, turning her back on him.

Eli sighed. "I don't mean to torment you. It's just that I don't like your bein' a party to any of this. It ain't right. I only come along on this mad hunt of yours, because if'n I didn't, you woulda done it on your own. And I couldn't have that on my conscience." He gave his head a tired shake. "It would break your pa's heart to see you like this."

"Pa's dead."

"Lisbeth isn't."

"Don't. Just don't."

"You can't keep this up, girl. What them animals done to you and your kin, you're letting 'em do over and over again every day of your life."

"Don't call me *girl*," she spat out. "It's *Vic*. You can't slip up, even when we're alone, or you might do it when we're not."

"Dammit all"—his breath caught as a spasm of pain gripped him—"you're not even hearin' what I'm saying."

"I hear you," Torey said. "But I'm not listening. There are still four to go, Eli. Four. When they're dead or in jail, that's when I'll stop. And not one minute before."

He muttered a quiet oath. "I was wrong to take you this far. Wrong to bring you to Cuttersville. I should've locked you in the attic at your Aunt Ruby's in Denver. And I sure as hell never should have sent for—" He stopped.

Her eyes narrowed. "Sent for who?" she demanded. "What are you talking about?"

Eli shifted painfully. "Leg hurts. You'd best get started on that travois."

"Sent for who?" she pressed again. But Eli's mouth was set in a grim, stubborn line. He obviously regretted saying as much as he had. She knew it was useless to prod him when he got like this.

Angrily, she tromped away from him and headed for the horses. She was tired of arguing anyway. And she certainly didn't want to hold any debates on the right or wrong of what she was doing out here, chasing after murderers. To do so was to give a toehold to the doubts and fears she fought to keep at bay every minute of every day. And that she couldn't do. She had made a promise. And nothing was going to stop her from fulfilling that promise. If that meant she had to constantly fuel the fires of her own hate, then so be it.

From Eli's bay, she retrieved his canteen and brought it down to him.

"Rather have whiskey," he grumbled.

She managed a slight smile. He was obviously as tired of arguing as she was. "I'll see what I can do when we get to Cuttersville. You rest easy now. I won't be long."

Mounting Galahad, she rode over to the stand of aspen. Using a small ax from her saddlebags, she went to work on stripping down two sturdy but flexible saplings to use as poles for a makeshift stretcher. Two hours later she was dripping with sweat, but she had herself a serviceable travois.

She glanced skyward. There was still plenty of hours of daylight left. She should have Eli settled into a bed in Cuttersville well before dusk.

She paused before heading back, taking a quick drink from her canteen. She dumped some of the water into her palm and smoothed it over her grime-covered cheeks and forehead. The water refreshed her, but she made no real effort to clean her face. It was another price she paid to maintain her guise as a man. She needed the dirt to cover the fact that Vic Langley never had any occasion to shave.

"How about you, Gally?" she asked, patting her black gelding's silky neck. "You thirsty?"

The horse snorted.

Torey poured some of the water from her canteen into her hat, then let the horse drink from it. "That's a good boy," she said, giving the gelding another pat. "You're going to stay in a real stable tonight, you know that? I'll even buy you a bucket of oats."

The horse nuzzled her neck, and Torey managed a shaky smile. Galahad was her only real connection to a life that didn't exist anymore. She glanced around at the rolling hills, the tree-studded slopes, the precursors to the awesome snow-capped peaks of the Rockies visible in the distance. Not exactly the wide open prairies of Kansas.

Back home right now, the corn would be as tall as she was, taller, if Eli had ever had the chance to plant it, while over in the south forty the spring wheat would be a sea of yellow undulating in the breeze.

Lisbeth would be in the kitchen, bustling about making lemonade.

Her father would . . .

Torey closed her eyes.

It did no good to think about what should have been. She needed to concentrate on what was. Muttering to herself, she gripped the travois and mounted Galahad. Eli needed her. She'd best get back to him.

She was alarmed to find him barely conscious. His leg injury was evidently worse than he had let on. Fighting down a surge of panic, Torey secured the makeshift stretcher to Eli's gelding; then as gently as she could she dragged Eli to the top of the embankment. His lips were pale, his eyes shut tight. She cursed inwardly. Cuttersville had better have a doctor.

"Hang on," she told him. "You're going to be all right."

He opened his eyes. Torey winced at the pain she saw there as she settled him on the travois.

"Don't forget Jensen and Scott," he said. "You can't leave their bodies here."

"They're not important now. We need to get you to a doctor."

"If you leave 'em, the buzzards will get to 'em. There won't be anything left to identify."

Torey's stomach lurched. "I don't care."

"We need the money. We've got eleven dollars between us. That won't buy much information. And I doubt the doctor works for free."

"But . . ."

"Get the bodies. Now."

Torey relented. She didn't want to upset Eli any more than he already was. Hurrying, she led Galahad and the outlaws' horses up the slope. Flies rose in a thick swarm as she approached the corpses. Torey steeled herself, suddenly certain that Eli had had more than a monetary motive in mind for wanting her to handle the bodies.

Breathing through her mouth and averting her eyes as best she could, she looped a rope under Jensen's arms, then tied it off to Galahad's pommel. Using the gelding, she hauled Jensen onto the back of his horse, then tied him to the saddle. She repeated the procedure for Scott. When she'd finished, she was unnerved to note that the two men now resembled nothing so much as deer carcasses.

Despite her efforts to feel nothing, Torey trembled. She wanted to scream, run, vomit. But mostly, she wanted to take a bath, scour her own flesh to rid it of the feel of two dead men.

She did none of those things. Stiffening her spine, she took up the lead rope she'd attached to the horses and led them back to Eli. She was not surprised to find him watching her. She met his gaze levelly. "We can go now," she said. "I've got our eight hundred dollars trussed up and ready to travel."

His lips thinned, but he said nothing.

They headed out then, Torey choosing their trail carefully, guiding the horses along the smoothest path. She didn't want to jostle Eli any more than absolutely necessary.

It was early evening when they rode into Cuttersville. Torey eyed the settlement with a vague irritation, wondering how it had dared work up the nerve to call itself a town. It might once have hoped to be one, but nothing she could see suggested that it had ever succeeded.

Several half-finished structures lay like bleached bones, weather-beaten and rotting along the main thoroughfare. She ignored them, reining Galahad over to one of the few establishments that actually seemed to be open for business. MORTUARY AND CARPENTRY, the flyspecked window proclaimed. SILAS BERTRAM, PROPRIETOR. At least she supposed it was open. The door was ajar, obliged to remain so by a triangle of wood wedged beneath it.

Boarded-over buildings abutted the undertaker's on both sides. From farther up the street, however, Torey now caught the tinkling sounds of piano music. Evidently one of the saloons was still open. And perhaps a few other businesses as well. Across the street and down, she saw a man with a broom come out of what she guessed to be a mercantile and begin to sweep the boardwalk. She didn't bother to investigate further. Getting Eli to a doctor was her first priority. It seemed logical that an undertaker could tell her where she might find one.

Dismounting, she tied off all four horses to the hitch rail, then checked on Eli. He was either asleep or unconscious. She touched his forehead. It seemed warm, but not overly so. She started for the undertaker's open front door.

"Hold up there!" a voice called.

Torey turned to see a burly, bowlegged lawman striding

toward her. The tin star he wore pinned to his blue-striped shirt glinted in the slanting rays of the afternoon sun.

"Sheriff Hank Pritchard," he announced tersely. He was looking at the bodies, his fingers toying with the butt of the .44 Smith & Wesson he wore strapped to his right thigh. "You mind telling me what this is all about, mister?"

"Be glad to," Torey said, making certain to keep her voice husky, low, more so than she did when she was alone with Eli. "But first I need to get my friend here to a doctor."

"Uh-uh, first you tell me about the bodies."

Torey bristled, but held her temper. This was no time for a battle of wills. Quickly she handed Pritchard the reward dodger.

A new contempt showed in his watery blue eyes. "Bounty hunters," he sneered. "I shoulda known by the stink."

"The stink is coming from Jensen and Scott," Torey gritted, the challenge in her voice daring the lawman to press the issue.

He didn't. Pritchard's lips tightened, but he made no more derisive comments. Not that it would have mattered. Torey had gotten used to them. She had yet to meet an official lawman who didn't despise bounty hunters. Maybe because bounty hunters did the jobs lawmen failed to do.

She returned to Eli's side. "What about that doctor, Pritchard?"

"Don't have one. Not since the mine played out. Moses Johnson over to the livery doctors up animals pretty good. I suppose he could do all right by a human. You get your friend over to Miss Mamie's Boarding House and I'll get word to ol' Mose."

"I'd be obliged."

"Don't be." Pritchard strode over to the bodies of Jensen and Scott and none too gently grabbed each in turn by his hair to compare his face to the poster.

He grunted. "I had a couple of run-ins with these two

hombres myself a few years back. I was sheriff over to Abilene then."

Torey was curious why a man would leave Abilene for a hole-in-the-wall like Cuttersville, but she didn't ask. She'd learned it was better not to inquire too closely about a man's past out here. Her only exceptions were the men she trailed.

"My partner and I will want the reward," she said.

Pritchard shrugged. "I'll have to wire for it. It might take a few days. We don't have too much money in town on a good day, and then two weeks ago the bank was robbed."

Torey perked up. "A bank robbery? Any idea who did it? Did they get away?"

"Damn bastards killed a teller and a customer. No one else had a clear look." Pritchard's eyes were hard. "Only satisfaction to come of it was that the scum that did it hardly got more than three hundred dollars for their trouble."

Torey didn't dwell on whether it might have been Varney and Pike. Not yet. She would ask more questions later. Right now she had Eli to consider. She took up the reins to his mount. "I'm going to take my friend over to Miss Mamie's," she said. "You think you can get the undertaker to take care of these bodies for me?"

"Town ain't payin' for their burial."

"Their gear should be enough to pay for digging a couple of holes, don't you think?"

"Maybe."

She swallowed a curse. "Tell the undertaker I'll be by to settle up with him later."

Miss Mamie's was a two-story clapboard structure that had seen better days. But then, Torey discovered, that was only fitting because so had Miss Mamie. A plump orange-haired woman in her middle fifties, Torey had the distinct impression that Miss Mamie LaRue had once practiced a far less reputable profession than operating a boardinghouse. Thick rouge, thicker makeup, and false eyelashes that Torey feared could snare a small animal turned what might have been a kindly face into one more likely to frighten small children on All Hallows' Eve. But Torey was in no position to be choosy.

"I'll need a separate room for myself," Torey said as she and Miss Mamie helped ease a semiconscious Eli onto a surprisingly clean and comfortable featherbed.

"Happy to accommodate you, Mr. Langley," Mamie said, bustling about the second-floor room, throwing open curtains and shutters. "Most business I've had in a month of Sundays. I'll be sure to freshen up your room too. It's just down the hall. I like to keep things closed up when they're not in use. Less sun damage."

Torey handed the woman a silver dollar, which she promptly attempted to take a bite out of. "Guess it's real enough. You can stay." With that she was gone.

Torey leaned over Eli and touched his shoulder, gently trying to rouse him. He only groaned.

A knock sounded on the door. Thinking Mamie could be of help, Torey hurried to answer it. She opened the door to find herself peering up at the largest human being she'd ever seen in her life—a huge black man who towered over her own considerable height by at least a foot. The sleeves of his calico print shirt were missing. Torey was certain they had been cut away to accommodate the bulging muscles of the man's arms. His chest was no less formidable, and his hands . . . Torey had never seen such hands. Bear paws were smaller. Torey could feel her mouth gaping open, but she couldn't seem to summon the sense to close it.

"I'm Moses Johnson," he said, his mouth curving into an amiable smile. Apparently he was used to such reactions. "Sheriff tol' me you might could use some doctorin'?"

"Yes, please," Torey squeaked, then remembered herself. Clearing her throat and pretending to cough, she added more robustly, "I mean, come in. I'm Vic Langley."

She showed him to Eli's bed. "His leg's broken."

Moses knelt beside the injured mountain man, his hands moving over Eli's leg with a skill and grace that belied their size. "It needs to be set so the bones can mend. If you could fetch me some strips of cloth for bandages and some splints . . . ?"

"Right away." Torey hurried from the room.

She was back in less than ten minutes, but in that time Moses had managed to set the leg. Eli was even sitting up. He looked haggard and pale, but surprisingly better. Moses accepted the items Torey handed him and he quickly bound up the leg so that it wouldn't move out of line.

Eli clucked his admiration. "I've seen men with medical papers sayin' they've been through so much schoolin' they could be doctors three times over. I never met one with a better touch than you, Moses Johnson."

"Glad to help," Moses said, washing his hands in the porcelain basin Miss Mamie had brought in.

"We're mighty grateful," Torey said, reaching into the pocket of her vest. "How much do I owe you?"

"No money," he said.

"But . . . "

"I take money for blacksmithing, not for helping a fellow human being."

Torey smiled. "Thank you."

Moses headed for the door. Torey caught his arm. "I don't know how much the sheriff told you about Eli and myself."

"Said you was bounty hunters."

Moses said the words without inflection. Torey considered it a moral victory. "Would you mind if I asked you a couple of questions?"

"About what?"

"About the bank being robbed here two weeks ago. Did you see anyone, any strangers, during that time? The sheriff seems to think no one who saw anything lived to tell about it."

Moses scratched his chin thoughtfully. "I think one of the

robbers may have boarded his horse in my livery overnight. To me, it was like he was here ahead of the others to check things out."

"Varney," Torey muttered.

She then described Varney to Johnson and was rewarded by the liveryman's nod. "That's him, though that ain't the name I heard him use. I tried to tell 'im his horse could use a new shoe on the right front but . . . " Moses gentle eyes turned hard. "Lemme just say he wasn't too interested in what a man like me had to say. I wish you luck catchin' this particular fella, which is not somethin' I'd wish to most bounty men."

"Why's that?"

"Was bounty men who hunted runaway slaves."

"Never done that," Torey said. "Never would have. My pa taught me a man should take pride in himself, his family, and his land. And he taught me every man deserves that right."

"Your pa sounds like a fine man."

"He was." Torey turned away.

"My master was a pretty fine man too, in his way. He used to let me take care of his horses. Beautiful animals. One day he up and give me his prize stallion. That was the day he got word that the Yankees had won the war. I said he'd be needing that horse to start over. But he tol' me no, he wouldn't be startin' over.

"He burned his plantation to the ground. He shot his wife, then shot hisself. He'd already lost three sons to the war. He just give up. But not me. As long as a body's got a breath left in it, well, I just think the good Lord means you can't give in to hate and misery."

Torey chafed under the homespun philosophy, or maybe it was the memory of having helped kill two men today.

"Is there anything I should know about tending Eli's leg?" she asked abruptly.

"Just make him lie still. Bones need knittin' time."

"How long?" Torey asked, a new worry lancing through her.

"Should stay in bed at least three weeks. After that, he could maybe get around some with a crutch for another few weeks."

"What about sitting ahorse?"

Moses shook his head. "Not unless you want the leg to get busted again, get infected, and have to be cut off . . ."

Torey paced to the window, unable to meet the gaze she knew Eli was drilling her way. He must have known what she was thinking. How could she interrupt her search for Varney and Pike for upward of six weeks? Especially when she was now certain they were only two weeks ahead of her.

She turned. "I'm grateful for your help, Mr. Johnson," she said. "I'd be grateful too if you could see to our horses. Give them a ration of oats. The two men we brought in had animals that need tending as well."

"I'll see that it's done."

"You're very kind." She extended her hand.

It was engulfed by his much larger one. "You two take care," he said, and left.

Torey came over to fluff Eli's pillow. Too cheerily she said, "I think I'm going to go out and see if this town has a bathhouse. It seems Mamie is using her tub for planting petunias. What that says about her bathing habits, I don't want to—"

"You're not leaving this town by yourself," Eli cut in. "Don't even think about it."

"I don't know what you mean."

"The hell you don't."

"I'm going to go have a bath, then I'll find you a bottle of whiskey, and—"

"Stop it, *Vic*." He emphasized the name to annoy her. He succeeded.

"All right, fine!" she snapped. "I can't stay here for six weeks and wait for you to heal. Are you satisfied? You heard

Moses. Varney was here. That means Pike was likely here. And maybe Cal Grady and that other son of a—"

"God bless it!" Eli roared. "Stop swearing! Your papa is going to up and haunt me for what I've let you turn into."

Eli looked so serious that Torey swallowed the next epithet that rose in her throat. "Take it easy," she soothed. "We don't want to undo all of Moses's fine work on your leg." She rubbed a hand through her hair. "You get some rest. We'll talk about this in the morning."

"We'll talk about it now. For all I know, you won't be here in the morning." He winced, sucking in a deep lungful of air.

"Eli, please . . . "

It was his turn to swear. "I had decided not to tell you about this, to just let it go. Not even meet up with him, even though I told him to meet us in Cuttersville. He could just think we never showed up. But now . . . "

"Meet who?" Torey demanded. "What in the hell"—her jaw clenched—"I mean, what in the blazes are you talking about?"

"I wanted to tell you weeks ago, but I didn't know how you'd take it. I just kept putting it off and heading us in this direction."

"We were following Jensen and Scott," she said. "Not maneuvering for some meeting."

"We would've come through Cuttersville regardless."

"Why?"

"Because I'm an old man. And having another gun along would help us even out the odds with Pike and Varney."

Torey swore explosively. "How dare you involve someone else in my personal business!"

"I dare because I care about you. I don't want to see you dead." He didn't look at her, embarrassed, she knew, by the sentiment. She should have said something, reassured him, but she was simply too angry.

"Promise me, you're not going to just ride off," Eli went on. "Promise me."

She considered storming from the room and just letting him stew. But she was afraid he would leap from the bed, broken leg and all, and come after her. Injure himself further on her account. She relented. "All right. I promise. Now who is this man? How do you even know he's here?"

"I don't know. I never heard back from him. I just gave him a time period to be here. If'n he got my letter, he'll come. It's the kind of man he is. That's why I need you to go to the hotel and see if he's registered."

"Me? I don't want to meet him alone."

"Then leave a message, tell him to come here."

She straightened, a sudden thought occurring to her. "Just how much did you tell him in this letter."

"Not much. That I needed his help. That it was important."

"Good. I don't want him to know I'm a woman. Not right off anyway. I want to meet him first."

"Why?"

"Because he might be like you. He might not believe a woman could get away with what I've been doing for over three months now. The only way to convince him is not to have his opinion biased one way or the other when I walk into the room. If I can fool him, then I figure he'll buy that I can fool other people too."

Eli didn't look wholly convinced, but he didn't argue either. "I'll just tell him you're a bounty hunter tracking John Pike. He hates John Pike almost as much as you do. Maybe more."

Tory hooked her thumbs into the waistband of her trousers. "Good. Maybe he can be useful. Who is he?"

"His name is Noah Killian."

The name brought her up short. "The war hero? What connection does he have to Pike?"

"I told you it was a friend of Killian's who shot him in the back during the war. That *friend*"—Eli fairly spat the word—"was John Pike."

Torey gasped, stunned. "My God . . ."

"Noah and I both thought Pike got what was coming to him three years ago. If he's alive, I can't begin to tell you the can of worms we're going to be pryin' open. I figured Noah had a right to know."

Considering what Pike had done to Killian, Torey could hardly dispute that. And now with Eli's broken leg, Killian's arrival, if indeed he was here, could prove damned fortunate. "I'll stop by the hotel. Leave word. Now can I go out for that bath?"

Eli shoved both of his hands through the tangled gray of his hair. "I might as well tell you the whole of it before you hear it somewhere else."

"What do you mean?"

Eli seemed to be wrestling with his conscience. "Somehow it don't seem fair that you should know the truth about Noah, when he can't know the truth about you."

"What truth? What about Killian?"

"I told you he was assigned to Fort Laramie after the war."

"So? He'll know the territory. That's good."

"He ain't in the army anymore."

Torey waited. That couldn't be what Eli seemed so reluctant to tell her.

"Three years ago, there was some trouble. Noah left the army, but it wasn't voluntary. He was court-martialed."

"But he was a hero. You told me so." Torey didn't like the look on Eli's face, didn't like it at all. "What were the charges?" she asked softly, a little warily.

"I never believed a word of it, mind you."

"The charges, Eli. What did he do?"

Eli said the words quickly as though to lessen their effect. It didn't work. "He was leading a patrol that was attacked by a Sioux war party. The patrol was massacred. Seventeen men dead. Noah was the only survivor."

"My God. How horrible for him. But why did the army blame him? Surely he did his best."

Eli shifted uncomfortably.

"Why did the army blame him?" she repeated. "Had he gone against orders to engage the Sioux?"

"He was ambushed."

"Then I don't see—"

"Noah wasn't found with his patrol. He was found three miles away. Seventeen men dead. Noah didn't have a scratch on him."

The full implications of such a statement took a moment to sink in. "He ran away?" she whispered. "He deserted his men?"

"He was found guilty on three charges. Dereliction of duty, desertion, and extreme cowardice under fire."

4

Torey gaped at Eli, wide-eyed, disbelieving. "You want me to ride trail with a coward?" she exclaimed.

"I said Noah was *found* guilty. I didn't say he was guilty. Noah Killian is no coward."

Torey paced the limited confines of Eli's room, trying hard to control her temper. "You can't be serious. You and I have talked to twenty men these past three months, twenty men in a dozen different jails, trying to find out what we can about Varney and Pike. And to hear those jailbirds tell it, every damned one of 'em is as innocent as a newborn lamb! What makes Killian any different?"

"What makes him different," Eli said slowly, "is that Noah Killian is a friend of mine. I know him. I know the kind of man he is."

"People can hide who they really are," Torey said bitterly, recalling the surface charm of Cole Varney.

"I've known Noah for years. A man can't hide the core of who he is for that long. Noah Killian is not a coward."

Torey knew she should just let this drop. At least for now. Eli was tired and his leg probably hurt like hell. But this was too important. "The United States Army said he's guilty."

"The United States Army is wrong."

"*That* wrong? You said he was found three miles from his troops. How could that be?"

"I don't know. Noah never said a word in his own defense at his court-martial."

"Maybe he didn't have anything to say."

Eli scowled. "We're not going to get anywhere with this. I'll just have to ask you to trust me."

"I have no problem trusting you, it's Killian I have my doubts about."

"I'd stake my life on Noah Killian."

"And mine?"

"And yours," Eli answered without hesitation.

Torey had no response to that. She rubbed a hand over her short mop of hair. "All right"—she sighed—"if he's at the hotel, I'll leave word where he can find you. But just so we understand each other, when I meet him it's going to be as Vic Langley. He is absolutely not to know about me or Lisbeth."

"Whatever you say, *Vic*."

Torey's jaw clenched, but she was more frustrated than angry. She knew Eli had meant well to send for Killian. She settled her Stetson on her head and started for the door. "You get some rest. I'm going to see to Jensen and Scott's burial, then take that bath."

"I'd appreciate the whiskey, if you can swing it. This leg is going to be a bother for a few days."

"I'll be back soon."

Outside, dusk was settling over the strikingly unimpressive town of Cuttersville, Colorado. The day's heat, however, had yet to surrender to the setting sun. Torey swiped the grime from her forehead with the back of her hand. Lord above, how she wanted that bath! But first, she would deal with the undertaker.

As she walked, she thought again of the day's unsettling turn of events. What was she going to do? As much as she'd like to, she didn't dare wait around for Eli's leg to heal, not if it meant giving Pike and Varney a two-month head start. This was the closest they'd been to the outlaw leaders since they began their hunt three months ago. But to continue on without Eli was to open herself up to two equally distasteful choices. Go on alone. Or go on with a man of dubious character and reputation.

Unbidden, Torey recalled the tale Eli had spun out for her of Noah Killian's heroic exploits during the war. She had felt fanciful enough about the story and about Killian to allow that the Yankee officer might even have saved her life by keeping Quantrill from attacking Boden.

What could have happened to such a man that he would turn into the sort of craven coward who would desert his own troops under fire? Leave them to be massacred? The very notion sent a chill rippling along her spine. And yet she had to remind herself that Eli was absolutely convinced of Killian's innocence.

She supposed the only fair thing she could do was wait, muster up courage enough to meet the man, and make her own judgment. That is, if he had even bothered to respond to Eli's letter. Part of her was already praying that he had not.

She was so caught up in her concerns about Killian that it took her a minute to notice that she had reached the undertaker's. Blessedly, Jensen and Scott were no longer out front. Their horses were gone as well, no doubt released to the capable hands of Moses Johnson. She didn't have any real interest in the current whereabouts of the two dead outlaws, but she did want to make certain things had been settled up with the undertaker. She headed toward the shop's open front door.

Stepping into Silas Bertram's Mortuary and Carpentry Shop was like stepping into a maze. Nearly every available square inch of the place was taken up with furniture in various stages of completion. Torey had to zigzag her way around desks, tables, chairs, cabinets, and étagères. Caskets—thankfully unoccupied—were mixed right in among cradles and rocking chairs. The smell of sawdust and varnish hung in the air like a mist, a feature Torey deemed fortunate. It helped mask more unpleasant odors from Bertram's other line of work.

A squinty-eyed man in black that Torey presumed to be Silas Bertram emerged from a back room and shuffled toward her.

"You the fellow that brought in them two stiffs?" Bertram asked.

Torey nodded. "Name's Vic Langley."

"Don't care what your name is," the man grunted, "less'n I'm obliged to carve it on a tombstone."

"Did the sheriff square things with you about burying Jensen and Scott?"

"He tol' me I could have their gear, but I got no use for saddles and such. Never been on a horse. Scared of 'em. I'd rather have cash anyway."

"Meaning?"

"If I don't get paid, your friends don't get buried."

"Fine by me," she said. "I'd just as soon feed 'em to the buzzards."

A hint of alarm showed on Bertram's face. That was not what he wanted to hear. Torey supposed a man had to make his money where he could, even squinty-eyed little undertakers. She pulled a five-dollar gold piece from her vest pocket and handed it to Bertram.

"Tell me," she said, affecting her best bounty hunter's demeanor, "did you see anything of that bank robbery that happened here a couple of weeks back?"

"If'n I did, why would I tell you?" Bertram sneered.

"Maybe because I'm good for your business." Torey had to swallow the bile that rose in her throat. She could still scarcely believe that she had been party to a killing. Coldly, firmly, she reminded herself of the vow she had made to her father, her sister. Reminded herself too that Jensen and Scott had been trying to kill her.

Bertram obliged her by describing two men that could well have been Cal Grady and Cole Varney. "Mean sons of bitches," Bertram said. "Won't be long before I—or somebody—buries them two."

But Bertram recalled no one who fit the description of John Pike.

Torey thanked the undertaker and turned to leave. She could only hope that with the bank job a bust here, the outlaws were already swarming to hit again somewhere else. Maybe she'd get lucky, as Sheriff Hutchins had hoped, and the law really would take care of the bastards.

But just in case the law wasn't fast enough, Torey thought grimly, adjusting the Colt nestled in her holster—she would continue the hunt.

She paused on her way out of Bertram's, unable to resist trailing her fingers over the satin-smooth rosewood surface of a nearly finished rolltop desk. "Not much call for beautiful furniture in a dying town, is there?"

Bertram's face lit up. "You think it's beautiful?"

"You're an artist, Mr. Bertram. I've never seen better. My father would have loved . . . " She stopped.

Bertram smiled, a shy, pleased smile that was almost comical in his wizened face. "Thanks, mister." He handed back the money.

Her brows furrowed.

"This one's on the house."

Torey didn't argue. It was the last money she had. "Bury 'em deep," she said. "It'll make where they're goin' that much easier for 'em to get to."

Her next stop was the hotel. The clerk balked at first about letting her look at the register, but she made a show of spinning the cylinder on her Colt and he had a sudden change of heart. Torey regretted the theatrics, but she couldn't spare the dollar it would have taken to bribe the kid.

Only three people had registered at the hotel in the last seven days. None of them was named Noah Killian. Torey wasn't sure which emotion she felt more keenly—relief or disappointment. In the unlikely event he rode in overnight, Torey wrote out a message telling Killian where to find Eli. It seemed she wasn't going to have to worry about passing judgment on the man, after all. She was never going to meet him.

Back outside on the boardwalk, she paused, debating whether or not she should take the time for that bath. It was getting late. Maybe she should just duck into a saloon, buy Eli his whiskey, and get herself back to Miss Mamie's. But the idea of climbing between clean sheets with her trail-dusty body was more than she could stand.

What difference could twenty minutes make? That's all the bath would take, if she hurried. Just the thought of feeling clean again buoyed her spirits as she strode across the wheel-rutted street. She headed for a dilapidated one-story building with a message scrawled in whitewash across its false front: BATH 25¢.

The door's rust-coated hinges protested loudly as Torey pushed her way inside. The main room was dank and dimly lit, reeking of lye soap and sweat. But Torey wasn't looking for atmosphere. Neither was she looking for the complications other customers might present—like being led to a roomful of male bathers. She was thus pleased to find only one other person in the building, a disheveled-looking washerwoman scrubbing dispiritedly at a tubful of laundry. Torey had to resist the impulse to nudge the woman aside and finish the washing for her. The poor thing looked dead on her feet.

It was little wonder, considering the exertion the work itself required. On top of that, the place was a virtual sweatbox, at least in this outer room. A huge cauldron of water simmered in the fieldstone hearth in the corner. Near the cauldron was a bucket. No doubt to carry hot water back to customers whose bathwater was too tepid for their liking.

"I want a bath," Torey said. "A hot one. But I don't want any company. Do you have a private room?"

The woman raised tired eyes. "Two bits."

Torey tossed her five-dollar gold piece on the counter.

The woman grimaced. "I only got four dollars change."

"How much to wash my clothes?"

The woman managed a weary smile. "Special today only, mister. Six bits."

"Done." Torey collected her change and followed the woman to a small room in the back of the building. To the clean water already sitting in the wooden tub, the woman added three bucketfuls of hot water from the cauldron. Then she went back to her washing.

Inside the room, Torey quickly made certain the door was affixed with a bolt. If it hadn't been, she might have changed her mind about the bath, no matter how much she was looking forward to it. It would simply have been too dangerous. She couldn't chance anyone stumbling in on her. Naked, she would have no way to shield the fact that she was a woman.

But with the bolt thrown Torey could dare to feel safe. For a few minutes at least this tiny room would be her sanctuary, her haven from the deception that ruled her life.

She stared at the battered old washtub in the center of the room, brimful of steaming hot water. It was as appealing to her as a sun-dappled lake.

She hung her hat on a peg behind the door, then shrugged out of her vest and started to unbutton her shirt. This was going to be wonderful.

Abruptly she stopped, her gaze snared by a cracked shaving mirror hanging aslant on the wall to her left. It was set at such a height that the only part of her body she could see was her face. Torey winced, scarcely recognizing her own image. If she hadn't known better, she would have believed the sweaty, grime-covered countenance in the mirror actually did belong to a man.

She should have found the thought comforting, even reassuring, that her deception was so complete she could almost fool herself. But she was not comforted. She was stingingly, achingly hurt.

She was hideous, a freak. She looked so ugly she feared that even scrubbed up and dressed in the finest taffeta no one would be able to tell anymore that she was a woman.

With trembling fingers she reached up to touch her scraggly hair. It had been so lush, so beautiful. Her pride and joy. She remembered the feel of it down her naked back. Like strands of midnight-hued silk caressing her flesh.

She cursed. Enough! She'd been through this a thousand times before. She needed to look shabby and unkempt. It was all part of her disguise. If she was well groomed, even dressed as a man, someone might look too close—notice fingers too slender, a complexion too flawless, a form too willowy. Feminine.

Still, she flinched when she peeled off her shirt and felt the sweat-stained fabric cling to her skin, save for the band of fabric she used to bind her breasts. Shabby and unkempt? 'Disgusting' would be more precise. But necessary! she thought fiercely. More than necessary. Deserved.

With an oath she yanked off the rest of her clothes and tossed them out to be cleaned, then stepped toward the washtub. She wanted to think about nothing, no one. But while four walls could shield her body, they were no haven from the torment of her own thoughts.

She sank into the steaming water, and against her will, she remembered that awful, despairing night four weeks after the attack on her family. The night the plan had come to her . . .

She had been sitting in her bedroom, knowing that the next day Eli would be taking her and Lisbeth away from the farm forever. The land was to be sold, the money used by their aunt Ruby for whatever care Lisbeth would need when they reached Denver.

Torey shuddered, her eyes burning. And Lisbeth would need care, constant care. She had shown no improvement. If anything she had retreated even farther into her dream world, a pain-free world where nothing unpleasant was permitted entry. To Torey, it was as if her sister had died in the attack, after all. What was left was an empty shell that looked like Lisbeth, even sounded like her, but the spirit, the essence of Lisbeth was gone, lost. And Torey despaired that it was lost forever.

She reached for the wanted poster of Cleve Jensen and Wade Scott that lay on her bedside table and stared at the line drawings of the two killers with cold, unadulterated hate. Four weeks, four weeks and they were still out there somewhere, free to rob, to rape, to murder. Her vow to make them and the others pay for what they had done seemed more and more empty, meaningless. Try as she might to come up with a scheme that would bring them to justice, she was stymied time and again by the one reality she could not circumvent—she was a woman, and what could a lone woman do against a band of killers? No matter how proficient she was becoming with Eli's spare six-gun.

Hire yourself a bounty hunter, Sheriff Hutchins had told her sarcastically. Torey had been pondering the advice as a real option for over a week now. Maybe it wasn't all that outrageous an idea. Gripping the poster, she headed out for the barn. Perhaps Eli could offer some advice on how she could go about employing such a person.

She found him mending a harness, a harness that would no doubt be used by the farm's new owners, strangers who would build their own dreams on the ashes of her family's dream. "I want to hire a bounty hunter," she gritted. "Do you know where I can find one?"

He dropped the harness. "You want to do what?"

"You heard me."

"Have you gone plum loco, girl?" he shouted. "Some bounty hunters are worse than the scum they're chasin'."

"All the better. I want Varney and his friends dead, Eli. They can't get away with what they've done."

"The law'll get 'em. Scum like that will end up on the wrong end of a bullet eventually."

"But how many more innocent people will they kill in the meantime? How many more women will they . . . ?" She couldn't finish.

He touched her arm. "I know how you feel."

She pulled away. "No, you don't," she said sharply. "No one can know. Don't you see? I can never get past this being my fault. Cole Varney never would have come here but for me. He and his friends would have tried to rob the bank in Boden. You and the sheriff and his extra deputies would have sent them all to hell where they belong!" Her voice quavered, broke. "Oh, God, Eli, I have to find a way to make them pay. I have to."

"I wish it could be different, girl. I really do. But a lady can't go marchin' into jails and saloons, asking questions after Pike and Varney. A lady can't call a man out into the street for a gunfight." He scratched at his beard. "If you could wait a mite though. Be patient, there might be someone I know who could—"

"I'm out of patience! Tomorrow we start for Denver. And those men are no closer to a rope than the night they killed my father."

She turned and ran back to the house, fearful that if she continued her railings at Eli she would begin to cry. And that if she ever again allowed herself the luxury of tears, she would never stop.

Inside the house she headed for her room, pausing first to check on Lisbeth. Her sister was huddled up almost in a ball atop the coverlets on her bed. Every minute of every day Torey prayed for some kind of change. Every minute of every day she was disappointed. Lisbeth lay as ever, oblivious, sucking contentedly on her thumb. Against her breast, she cuddled a rag-stuffed doll, one she'd had as a little girl.

Torey reached out to tuck a stray tendril of hair away from Lisbeth's face. "I miss you so much," she murmured. "Can't you come home, Lissa? Can't you please come home?"

Lisbeth smiled, a vacant smile that never failed to chill Torey's blood. "Pretty dolly," Lisbeth crooned. "Such a pretty dolly."

Torey fled to her own room.

She sat on her bed, still gripping the wanted dodger, trembling now with a fury such as she'd never known. Fury and an impotent frustration. It wasn't fair. It just wasn't fair. If she were a man she wouldn't be constrained by custom and expectation. If she were a man, she could ride out of here tomorrow, track Varney and Pike to the ends of the earth, and when she found them, she could call them out, gun them down, and no one would so much as raise an eyebrow.

If she were a man . . .

The thought hit her like a thunderbolt. *A man.*

Scrambling off her bed, Torey rushed over to her vanity. Perching on the bench seat in front of her mirror, Torey gave her looks a swift but critical appraisal. Could it work? Could such an outrageous idea possibly work? A strange excitement began to pulse through her.

Reaching up, she pushed her hair away from her face. Her features were strong, attractive enough, but not delicate. Never delicate. She turned sideways. She had never been the most voluptuous woman. In fact, for years she'd envied the more womanly curves of her sister's body. Tonight she was glad for her own slimmer build. And her height . . . Oh, God, how she'd always loathed her height.

Until now.

Torey's heart thudded. It might work. It just might work. There was only one feminine attribute she could not disguise. Rushing to the kitchen, she grabbed up a butcher knife, then returned to her room. Standing in front of her mirror, she took a long, last look at those waves of spun midnight; then she raised the knife. Her hand shook, and for a moment she hesitated. As she did so, Cole Varney's words echoed through her mind. *Never seen such hair. You must be some kind of an angel.*

Torey hacked the silken strands off almost to the roots. When the deed was done, she stared into the mirror for long minutes, assuring herself that the strange hurt she was feeling had nothing to do with her shorn hair. Still, she spun abruptly from her reflection, quickly busying herself with the rest of her plan. She rushed about the house fetching first a pair of her father's trousers, a shirt, and a vest, then grabbing up Eli's spare six-gun and a holster. She even went outside briefly for a little dirt from the front yard.

When she finished changing her clothes, she stepped back in front of the mirror. The transformation stunned her. If she hadn't known better . . . But then she cautioned herself. It could just be wishful thinking on her part. She went back out into the parlor. She would wait for Eli, see what he thought.

Nervous, unwilling to credit just how much was riding on this, she began to pace, hefting the Colt from its holster. Almost reluctantly, she acknowledged the strange sense of power the weapon seemed to give her. This would work. It had to work.

She would ask Eli for his honest opinion. Once he stopped swearing maybe he would even—

The front door opened and Eli walked in. In the space of a heartbeat he was bringing his rifle to bear. Only Torey's shout prevented him from dropping her where she stood.

Eli had resolved her doubts. Her transformation was complete.

Vic Langley was born.

The next day she and Eli had begun the trip to Denver with Lisbeth. Over every mile by stage and by rail, Eli had tried to talk her out of her plan. Over every mile Torey had only become more resolved. For Lisbeth's sake—and because Torey continued to hope against hope—she had dressed in her usual feminine manner for the journey, wearing a bonnet to cover her shorn locks. By the time they reached Aunt Ruby's, however, Torey was out of patience and determined to implement her plan.

Blessedly, Aunt Ruby proved to be a delight, as well as a strong and resourceful woman. Torey had no trouble telling her aunt the truth about what had happened in Kansas. Her only lie had been that she and Eli would be leaving at once to scout out land for a new homestead.

Torey then issued an ultimatum to Eli—come with her or stay behind. Either way, she was going after Pike and Varney. In effect, she wagered her life that Eli would not permit her to pursue a band of outlaws alone. She had won.

On the trail, she astonished even herself at how quickly she adapted to her role as a man. It was downright emancipating to have the freedom to come and go as she pleased. Other liberties were soon evident as well. Little things, big things. Like walking into saloons free of harassment. Not needing a chaperone everywhere she went. Leaning back in a chair and putting her boots up on a table.

"It's amazing what you men can get away with," she complained to Eli over a campfire one night. "You can spit, curse, scratch, and otherwise behave like an ass and no one turns a hair. As a woman, I can't even hiccup without feeling like I have to blush and offer six different kinds of apologies."

Eli's lips thinned. "Don't you think you're getting just a mite carried away with all this? Especially when you're out here in the middle of nowhere alone with me? It wouldn't hurt you to wash your face a little more often."

Torey ignored the sting of his words. "You just don't like how damned good I am at this. Don't worry, I'm only focusing on character traits that seem to be the most universal. The spitting, the cursing—"

"You mean the ones you see as the most vulgar," he cut in.

She cursed, then managed to call up a deep belch to drive home her point—and hopefully irritate Eli all the more. "It's a man's world," she gritted. "To win in a man's world, I've got to play by a man's rules."

"Dammit, all men are not beasts." Eli actually looked hurt.

"All right," she allowed, "I know not all men are beasts. But I have to be careful. I can't let the woman in me get in the way. I can't afford any slipups. I've got murderers to find."

"Are you sure that's the whole of it?" Eli asked, those keen eyes studying her too closely. "Or maybe you got that woman in you buried for other reasons too, reasons you don't even want to know about."

Torey scoffed, refusing even to listen to such foolishness. Eli was just worried about her getting hurt, that was all. It was natural for him to use any weapon he could to try and get her to call a halt to her chase. Bury the woman in her? Nonsense. Why ever would she do such a thing? She had loved being a woman. Loved brushing out her long, lush hair, loved wearing her mother's forest-green velvet dress, loved . . .

I'm going to show you how it's done, honey. When I'm through with you, you'll know what it is to be a woman. . . .

Torey gasped, jerking awake in the tiny wooden washtub in the Cuttersville bathhouse. For long seconds she sat there, trembling, terrified.

Then she berated herself for falling asleep. Of all the careless . . . Picking up a washcloth, she pressed the now tepid wetness to her face. She didn't regret the price she was paying to bring Varney and his ilk to justice. And she wasn't going to sit there and dwell on any imaginary price Eli was trying to convince her she was paying.

With a tired sigh, she pushed to her feet. Thinking of Eli had brought with it a stab of guilt. She had left him without his whiskey long enough. Sloshing out of the tub, Torey grabbed up a towel and dried herself off. She'd best get dressed and get herself back to Miss Mamie's as quickly as she could. She tossed aside the towel and reached for her clothes.

Her eyes widened. Where were they? Oh, God! She had thrown them out to be washed but forgotten to bring a fresh set of clothes with her. How could she have been so stupid?

Wrapping herself in the towel, Torey padded over to the door, unlatched it, and very cautiously peered out. When she saw no one, she dared call out to the washerwoman. She received no response.

She called again, louder. Nothing.

Torey stood there listening for voices, movements, anything, but the place was almost ominously silent. Even the crackling of the fire in the hearth had been stilled. She crept into the outer room, her heart thundering in her chest. She was terrified that at any second the door would burst open.

If a man should come in here . . . find her in such a state . . . Torey trembled.

There was no sign of the washerwoman anywhere. What was worse, there was no sign of Torey's clothes. The woman must have gotten them mixed in with some others she'd taken for deliveries.

Desperate, Torey searched the rest of the room. She would have to settle for whatever she could find. She opened drawers, even fished through two water-filled washtubs. There wasn't a stitch of clothing to be found anywhere.

Save one.

Torey gaped at the only garment in the entire bathhouse. It was a dress, dangling from a peg in one of the rear bathing rooms. But this was no ordinary dress. Torey stared at it as though it were a living thing. A gaudy red silk with a black feather-boa neckline. A saloon-woman's dress. Torey's face grew hot just looking at it.

She couldn't wear *that*. She just couldn't. If it had been any other sort of dress, a simple calico, a modest gingham, she assured herself she wouldn't be feeling this unsettling panic. She would have snatched it up in a heartbeat. Though, of course, even with a properly chaste dress, she would have had to worry about being seen. The chances were remote, but some townsman might wonder later about a tall woman, a stranger, with close-cropped hair and blue-green eyes who would seem to vanish into thin air, and the coincidental presence in town of a medium-height bounty hunter with similar features.

Frantic, Torey made another search of the bathhouse but found nothing. She couldn't just sit here and wait, on the off chance the washerwoman would return. For all Torey knew, the woman had forgotten about her, closed up shop for the night. God knew, as exhausted as the woman had looked, Torey wouldn't have been surprised.

Again Torey looked at the garish red silk. What choice did she have? She could hardly scurry up the street in her flour-sack towel! Allowing herself no more time to think about it, Torey yanked the crimson atrocity over her head.

It was even worse than she had imagined. She stood there shivering violently. It was the most outrageous garment she'd ever had on in her life. Because of her height, the hem barely reached her knees. A bow caught up one edge of that already indecent hemline, scooping it upward, exposing the creamy white column of her left leg all the way to her hip. And the neckline! Merciful heaven, half of her breasts were spilling out over the bodice. The towel, at least, she could have clutched to her throat.

Enough! It was the dress or nothing. It wasn't as if she would have to wear the thing the rest of her life. She would rush to Miss Mamie's, dash up the backstairs, and rid herself of the vulgar silk as swiftly as humanly possible.

She started for the door, then stopped abruptly, gazing down at her bare feet. Torey cursed. Her search of the premises had already confirmed that the owner of the dress hadn't been foresighted enough to leave a pair of dance-hall shoes behind. What was she going to do?

But she already knew. What choice did she have? Swiftly, she shoved into her own trail-scuffed boots, which the washerwoman had blessedly left behind.

Torey completed her odd ensemble by plucking some of the feathers from the dress's neckline and arranging them amidst the strands of her close-cropped hair. She would just have to hope that anyone looking at her would think her hair was merely pinned up beneath the plumage.

With great trepidation she then snuck out the back door of the bathhouse. As inconspicuously as possible—considering her attire—she made her way along the back alleys of Cuttersville. Thankfully, the sun was gone and it was fully dark. She was certain she could make it to Miss Mamie's undetected.

But her conscience niggled at her. She thought about Eli waiting patiently for the whiskey she had promised him. She did have her four dollars with her. Maybe she could duck into a saloon and buy him a bottle. She'd been in many a saloon since she and Eli had left Denver. She'd never had any problems. Of course, she'd had the security of being dressed as a man. . . .

Her senses on alert, she peeked over the batwing doors of a saloon with the ironic name of Take Your Chances. She breathed a little easier. The place wasn't exactly rollicking. In fact, it was nearly deserted. Promising herself she would be in and out in a heartbeat, she pushed through the swinging doors and went inside.

As she made her way toward the bar, she took in every nuance of her surroundings. She wanted no surprises. At one end of the bar, a couple old-timers and a younger man stood nursing beers. At the other end, a red-bearded man was making quicker work of a glass of whiskey. To her right, a card dealer played solitaire at a table with no takers. The only other patron was a man she passed on her left. He was sitting at a table near the batwing doors, his head lolling forward. He was either drunk or asleep or both.

Stiffening her spine, Torey marched up to the bar. "A bottle of whiskey, please."

"You're new here, ain't ya?" the bartender asked. "Belle hire you on my day off yesterday?"

"Uh, yes," Torey blurted out, rather than come up with any other explanation. She laid a dollar on the bar, then picked up the bottle.

The red-bearded man sidled close. "Buy you a drink, little lady?"

"M-maybe later." She held up the bottle. "I've, uh, got a customer waiting for me."

"Don't see any such customer." His breath stank of stale beer and cigar smoke, his body stank of days-old sweat. "Something you don't like about me?"

"No. Of course not."

"Then let me buy you a drink." He ran his fingers along the flesh of her forearm. "You'll like ol' Farley." His other hand went to his crotch. "You'll like ol' Farley just fine."

Torey had to bite the inside of her cheek to keep from screaming. "Like I said . . . my evening is already spoken, er, paid for. He—he asked me to meet him here. I . . . oh, there he is . . ."

Torey bolted for the table near the batwing doors, taking the chair next to the lone man sitting there. The one that was either drunk or asleep. His head still lolled forward, his chin resting on his chest. His dusty black Stetson was at such an angle that it all but obscured his face. All Torey could really tell about him was that he had longish dark hair that trailed in shaggy waves over the collar of his shirt.

"There you are, handsome," she said softly. She would sit here for just a moment, wait for Mr. Redbeard to lose interest. "I've been looking for you." She praised God when he didn't move. Her heart hammered against her ribs. It thrummed so loudly in her own ears, she feared the sound of it might actually rouse him. Her hands were clammy. She couldn't seem to catch her breath.

She leaned toward him. "Oh, my"—she giggled in a stage whisper—"go to your hotel room? All right. I can do that." Lord above, were these words actually coming from her lips?

She gripped her bottle of whiskey and started to get up.

The man stirred and groaned slightly. Oh, God. He raised his head, tipping his hat back.

She noticed his eyes first. They were gray, a stormy, fathomless gray, that for the briefest instant were filled with a soul-deep pain that she knew had nothing to do with physical hurt. But then the pain was gone and she was left to note that those same eyes were also bloodshot and unfocused, set in a face so hard-edged it could have been carved from a block of granite. A three-or-four-day-old growth of dark beard stubbled his cheeks and neck, and the hair that skimmed his nape was shot through with gray at his temples. Still, she would have guessed his age at no older than thirty-four or thirty-five.

As she continued to gape at him, a lazy grin came slowly to a mouth that was full and generous, a grin that somehow managed to soften the harsh angles of his face, a face she unwillingly perceived for all of its untidiness to be a strikingly handsome one.

"I've been waiting for you too, sweetheart," he said, his dark brows furrowing as he made a sloe-eyed assessment of her attributes. Torey wanted to die. "Belle said she'd send me her very best, and I can see she wasn't exaggerating."

The polished timbre of his voice belied his unkempt appearance. He was, it seemed, a well-educated drunk. But that hardly mattered. What mattered was her getting away from him.

"You said you'd meet me in my room?" he drawled.

"Of course. Just tell me the room number."

"I'll take you there."

"No. I mean, please, don't bother. Let me get there ahead of you. Get—get ready for you." Torey could feel bile rising in her throat.

His hand circled her waist, pulling her into him. He leaned forward to plant a warm kiss on what would have been her mouth, except that at the last instant Torey averted her head and his kiss landed on her cheek, then trailed a path of fire to her throat.

She wanted to cry out at this terrifying bit of intimacy, but she didn't dare. To do so would be to alert the man at the bar that she had lied to him. Besides, she had to be safer with this shaggy-haired drunk. The man was all but passed out. If she could just hurry him on his way to oblivion, she could get herself out of here.

"Thirsty, honey?" she managed. "Maybe you need another drink."

The man nuzzled her neck, mumbling softly. Torey expected the words to be crude, disgusting. But surprisingly they were not. If she hadn't been so terrified, she might even have considered them tender. She had the strangest suspicion that for a moment at least he was in another time, another place. Talking to another woman . . .

Then he seemed to shake himself, attempt to focus on the here and now. "I'll make it worth your while, lovely lady," he murmured. "I promise. Maybe we can both forget our troubles, just for one night."

There was a strange wistfulness in his voice that she doubted he was even aware of. "I wish it was that easy to make the fear go away," she murmured, then berated herself. What was she saying?

The man pushed back his chair and started to get up.

The fear returned full force. "Let me go," she begged. "Please."

He frowned, obviously trying hard to concentrate. "It's all right," he said. "I'm not going to hurt you."

Torey froze at this unexpected echo of John Pike's words. All pretenses were gone. The abject terror she felt at that moment must have shown on her face.

Abruptly, the man released her. His gray eyes narrowed with curiosity, and for a moment he almost seemed sober.

"I'm sorry."

That was all she heard him say as she stumbled away from him and ran from the saloon.

She bolted for a back alley, cursing herself again and again for ever having gone into the saloon in the first place. She could only count her blessings that the consequences of her foolhardiness hadn't been any worse than a kiss.

When she reached Mamie's she drew in a desperate breath, praying that no one was about. For once luck was with her. She raced up the backstairs to her room. Inside, she wasted no time ripping off the dress; then she went to her saddlebags and yanked out her spare clothes. Like a madwoman she threw them on, not feeling safe again until she was fully dressed in her guise as a man.

Then she sat on her bed and trembled. Despite her terror, despite everything, what she found herself remembering was the feel of the dark-haired man's lips on her throat, the pain-edged sweetness of his words—even though she knew most of those words hadn't been meant for her at all.

But he'd called her "lovely lady." *Lovely*. And for the tiniest instant she had been pleased that he had found her attractive. And for that, most especially for that, she sat there now and was violently ashamed.

The man was a drunk, and God only knew what else. What kind of a person was she to be flattered by such a man? Hadn't she done enough harm flaunting herself at Cole Varney? Hadn't she learned in the cruelest way possible the ways of such men?

She had made another vow the night she had cut off her

hair, a vow more desperate than the one she had made to her father and sister. A vow she intended just as fervently to keep. No man was ever going to touch her again.

Noah Killian stared after the fleeing woman through bloodshot eyes, trying hard to shake loose some of the cobwebs from his brain. He was not successful. Try as he might, he could make no sense out of what had just happened.

The woman had obviously been one of Belle's girls. She had certainly dressed the part. And yet something had set her off, scared the living hell out of her, a terror so real, so genuine that it had even managed to penetrate the haze of oblivion he had so carefully woven around himself tonight.

Lurching slightly, Noah reached for the nearly empty bottle of whiskey sitting in the middle of the spur-scarred table. What did he expect? A woman, even a saloon woman, didn't need a drunken lout pawing at her. He chuckled mirthlessly. Not exactly proper behavior for West Point graduate and former U.S. Cavalry officer Noah Killian.

He drew the bottle to him. Not bothering with the glass the bartender had set out for him earlier that afternoon, he brought the bottle to his lips and upended it, draining down the last of the amber liquid.

It didn't even burn this time. It didn't do anything.

Because he didn't feel anything.

Well, maybe one thing. He felt vaguely irritated. The woman shouldn't have run off like that. She should have stayed. Hell, that's what she got paid for, wasn't it? Accommodating men. He couldn't have done anything to her she hadn't had to put up with plenty of times before. And maybe he would have done it better. He'd meant what he said about the two of them helping each other forget their troubles.

Sweet Lord above, her skin had been soft, so damned soft . . .

Noah swore viciously, shoving the empty bottle away and pushing to his feet. He didn't need the woman. He didn't need anybody. He stood beside the table and swayed unsteadily. Maybe he'd had a little more to drink than he should have. He laughed again. Nah, trouble was, he hadn't had enough. If he had, he wouldn't be paying any attention to what was happening behind him at the bar. Someone was talking to him. Some red-bearded man he didn't know.

Or rather, the man was talking *about* him. Loud whisperings he was meant to overhear. And then the man moved away from the bar and stepped directly behind Noah.

"The lady didn't want your company after all, did she, *Captain*?" The man said the rank derisively. "I guess even Belle's women have their limits as to who they'll spread their legs for."

Noah sighed wearily. Not tonight. Please, God. Not tonight.

"Killian, ain't it?" the man said. "Captain Noah Killian. Thought I saw a yella streak runnin' down your back earlier, but I wasn't sure 'til you pushed that Stetson off your face. I was passin' through Fort Laramie three years ago when they were nailin' your hide to the wall." The man leaned close, though he spoke loud enough for all to hear. "I still say they shoulda hanged you for what you done."

Noah put his hands on the table. He didn't want to fight. It never did any good.

"Did you hear me, coward?" the red-bearded man taunted.

"You tell him, Farley!" someone shouted from the bar. "You tell him how we don't want his kind in Cuttersville."

Noah pushed himself away from the table. It was time to leave. "I guess you're all entitled to your opinion."

"My *opinion*," sneered Farley, "is that you're a yellow-bellied coward!" He was laughing, his gaze shifting about the room for moral support from the other patrons. They eagerly egged him on, hollering out more epithets of their own.

"I've got no quarrel with you, mister," Noah said evenly, though his head pounded and he felt as if he was going to throw up. He needed a bed. He smiled slightly. One with the woman in the red dress would do nicely . . .

Perhaps Farley misunderstood the smile. Or perhaps he didn't. In any event, he hauled back his fist and slugged Noah square in the face, sending him reeling backward onto the hard planked floor.

Noah saw stars. He shook his head in a vain attempt to clear it. Gasping, he levered himself up onto one elbow, gingerly testing the location of his teeth. His lower lip was split and his hand came away bloody.

Farley was laughing. So was most everyone else in the saloon. Farley was also standing splay-legged, his fists raised, waiting for Noah to make the next move. Three other men from the bar had joined him, their fists clenching and unclenching at their sides, eager, ready to join the fray—now that the victim was already half-unconscious.

Groggily, Noah considered his options. Stay on the floor and get the hell *kicked* out of him. Or stand up and get the hell *beat* out of him.

He shifted sideways and began to push himself up, careful to seem to take no notice of his four adversaries. He gained his feet, hunched nearly in two.

Without warning he launched himself at Farley, driving his shoulder like a battering ram into the man's midsection. A whoosh of air escaped Farley along with a cry of surprise and pain as Noah drove him all the way to the wall. Then Noah's fists came up and connected solidly, first his right, then his left with the man's jaw.

The man flailed wildly at Noah, striking a glancing blow to his right eye.

Noah hit him in the stomach, then landed a fearsome uppercut to Farley's chin. The man went down as if poleaxed.

Noah rounded on the others. "Next?"

He watched their eyes, three brave men deciding whether or not they could take down one coward. They looked at the crumpled form of their friend, then looked at one another.

The three brave men then slunk back over to the bar, muttering among themselves that it hadn't really been their fight anyway.

"All right, Killian," the bartender grumbled, coming out from behind the bar, carrying a pitcher of water, "you've had your fun." He walked over to where Farley still lay slumped on the floor and dumped the contents of the pitcher onto the man's head. Farley coughed and sputtered and slowly opened his eyes.

"Farley was right," the bartender went on. "We don't need your kind in Cuttersville, Killian. If I'd've known who you were, I never would've served you."

Farley turned a sullen gaze toward Noah, but he made no move to get up.

Noah reached into his vest pocket and pulled out a dollar.

"I don't want your money," the barkeep said.

Noah flipped the coin on the bar. "I always pay what I owe." Stiff, bone weary, he walked toward the batwing doors and pushed them open.

Behind him, Farley couldn't resist a parting shot. "Just how much does a man owe for seventeen dead men?"

Noah sighed, more disgusted with himself than with the men in the saloon. Why did he let bastards like that get to him anyway? After three years, he should know better. Giving his head a tired shake, he started up the street toward his hotel.

He'd been in town for three days and had managed to get progressively drunker each day. Today, he decided, he was even drunk enough to reregister at the hotel under his own name. Ignoring the goggle-eyed young clerk at the front desk, Noah picked up the pen lying next to the registration book and crossed out the false name he'd used when he'd first signed in. With a shaky flourish he inscribed the next line down: Noah J. Killian.

"Not too many people passing through your bustling little

metropolis, are there?" Noah asked, wondering if his words sounded as slurred to the clerk as they did to his own ears.

"No, sir," the clerk said, keeping as far away from Noah as the pigeonhole room key and message slots at his back would allow.

Noah pulled his key from his pocket and trudged up the creaky, bare wood stairs to his second-floor room. Inside, he crossed to the window and pulled down the moth-eaten shade. Only then did he take off his hat and gunbelt. He didn't credit Farley with the grit to come after him again face-to-face, but he wouldn't put it past the little ferret to draw a bead on him from the rooftop across the street. It wouldn't be the first time some brave back-shooter had tried to take out that infamous coward Noah Killian.

Noah snorted cynically. Not that it would necessarily be a bad thing.

Striking a match, he fumbled with the grease-smudged chimney of the room's only lamp and lit the wick. The light cast dancing shadows across the drab room's even drabber furnishings. At the washstand—an off-level table with a chipped pitcher and a tin basin—Noah unknotted the blue bandanna at his throat and dipped it into the water he hadn't bothered to use for a shave that morning. He took a couple of desultory swipes at his cut lip, then used the wet cloth to smear away the sweat-damp grime from the back of his neck.

He could use a bath, but he was too tired, too drunk to bother. Maybe in the morning.

Exhausted, he flopped on his back atop the threadbare quilt on the bed, the straw-stuffed mattress affording him about as much comfort as a rock quarry. He closed his eyes. Damn, what the hell had ever brought him to this flea-bitten excuse for a town in the first place?

Then he remembered.

The letter. He fumbled in his shirt pocket and withdrew the crumpled missive. He didn't bother to read it. He knew what it said by heart. And it didn't say much. *Come to Cuttersville . . . Urgent . . . a chance to get your life back. I swear.*

And so Noah had come. Not because of the letter, but because Eli had once been a good friend. And even though facing that friend meant facing . . .

Noah swore. He was in no mood to dredge up old memories.

He pushed himself up long enough to blow out the light and pull off his clothes. Clad only in his drawers, he lay back down. The night was hot, sultry. Sweat beaded on his exposed flesh. There wasn't a breeze to be had anywhere. His head throbbed. His lip hurt. His right eye would likely swell by morning. If the night could be any more miserable, he didn't know how. And then a mosquito buzzed by his ear.

He swatted at it. Missed. He raked his hand through the sweat-damp strands of his dark hair.

Three years. Had it really been three years? Years of panning for gold, punching cattle, and riding fence, anything that could earn him a few dollars and didn't require much, if any, contact with his fellow man.

Or woman.

Woman. His loins tightened. Damn, he wished Belle's whore hadn't run off. It would have felt good to lose himself in the wet, welcoming folds of a female body tonight. She had been a pretty one too. Hadn't she? Her image was murky in his mind. He hadn't been seeing things too clearly at the time.

Dark hair. She'd had dark hair.

And soft skin. Very soft skin.

He remembered that much. But when he tried to picture her face, he failed.

Oh, well, she couldn't be that difficult to track down. He would stop by Belle's tomorrow. Ask about her.

After all, it wasn't as if he had anything else to do. He had heard no more from Eli. Truth be told, he was pretty damned irritated by the cryptic tone of the old man's message. Eli could have at least hinted at what he wanted. There was the chance too that the ex-scout had changed his mind about coming, or sent another letter that had never reached Noah, detailing some change in their rendezvous point.

Noah would give Eli another day or two at most; then he would ride on.

For now he should close his eyes, sleep. But he resisted. The dreams had been coming again. As they always did whenever he thought too much about what happened three years ago. He considered getting up, retrieving the bottle of whiskey in his saddlebags. But no matter how drunk he got, it never stopped the dreams. He closed his eyes.

He dreamed of faces, faces of dead men.

And a woman's face filled with scorn. Katherine.

But just before he woke Katherine's face changed, melded into the image of another woman. A woman he didn't know, but who seemed to be afraid of him. Terrified. She tried to run away, but he wouldn't let her go.

She began to struggle, scream. . . .

Noah woke at dawn, and it was as if he hadn't slept at all. He sat up, pushed his hair out of his face, and cursed. His head hurt. Every muscle in his body ached. He grimaced and was rewarded with his split lip threatening to tear open again.

Maybe he'd be better off spending the day in bed. The life of an army deserter wasn't exactly crammed full with responsibilities anyway. No reveille. No troop inspections. No council with Red Cloud to discuss the chance of peace between their two peoples.

But nature prodded him. His body had demands, even if his mind didn't. The damned room didn't have a commode.

Staggering out of bed, he found the clothes he'd worn yesterday and pulled them on. He let out a humorless laugh. The clothes he'd worn for quite a few yesterdays.

Crossing to the washstand, he splashed water on his face,

but he couldn't bring himself to shave. He did make a half-hearted attempt to tuck in his shirttail, but gave it up after the second attempt failed. His head still felt as if someone were pressing it between two boulders. He considered taking a drink but decided against it.

It was then he noticed the folded piece of paper on the floor near the door. Frowning, he walked over and picked it up. It was a message telling him Eli was at a place called Mamie's Boarding House. Noah crumpled the paper in his fist. He should ignore it, ride out of this godforsaken town. Hell, he never should have come here in the first place, certain now that nothing good was going to come of it. But he owed the old man. . . .

Ten minutes later Noah was knocking on the door to Eli Burkett's room. Despite his aches and pains, he was suddenly nervous, making a futile attempt to smooth the untamed waves of his hair. Maybe he should've shaved. Ah, hell. Maybe he should've had that drink.

When a familiar gravelly voice hollered out, "Come in," Noah shoved open the door.

The old man hadn't changed much. That was what Noah noticed first. Big, ugly, and as alert as a hungry bear, despite being flat on his back in bed. Noah would have thought he'd be prepared for Eli's reaction at seeing him again. He wasn't. He winced at the obvious disappointment in the big man's face.

"Not exactly spit and polish, eh?" he said, a shade defensively.

"What you look like don't matter so much as that you're here," Eli said, pushing himself to a sitting position and extending his right hand. "It's good to see you again, son."

Noah accepted the handshake, then took a step back, shoving his hands into the rear pockets of his jeans. He should probably opt for some innocuous amenities to bridge the three years that they hadn't seen each other, but he was in no mood. "You sent for me. Why?"

Eli gestured toward a chair. "Have a seat. We can talk about it."

Noah dragged over a ladder-back chair, spun it around, and straddled it backward, his arms folded across the top of the chairback. "Talk."

But Eli had never been a man to take a straight road when a more roundabout one might prove more interesting. "Three years been kinda rough on you, I see. Or at least last night was, from the looks of that shiner."

"I didn't come here to talk about me. You're the one who sent the letter, remember?"

Eli shifted his body slightly, evidently seeking a more comfortable position. He nodded toward a bottle on his bedside table. "Pour me a whiskey, would ya?"

Noah looked at the bottle. As he reached for it, his hand trembled slightly. Picking it up, he uncorked it with his teeth and managed to pour Eli a glass. The scent of the amber liquid seemed to permeate his every pore. It was all he could do to hand the glass to Eli. Distracting himself, he asked, "What happened to your leg?"

"Took a fall."

"That's too bad." Noah was still looking at the half full bottle of whiskey.

Eli's next words snapped his head around. "Just how far of a fall have you taken, old friend?"

"That's not your business," Noah gritted.

" 'Fraid it is. At least some." Eli took a drink. "Got some information I thought you'd be interested in, but now I'm not so sure I should tell you."

"Suit yourself." Noah started to rise. He didn't need this. He judged himself harshly enough without the censure so evident in Eli's gaze. His instincts had been right. He should have just ridden out of town.

Eli raised a staying hand. "Still don't remember anything about that day, do you?"

Noah's jaw clenched. "I don't need to remember. I've

been told often enough what happened. Those men were my responsibility. They're dead because I wasn't fit for command."

"Even if that were true, don't you think you've punished yourself enough?"

Noah swore.

"I was supposed to be with you on patrol that day, remember?" Eli prodded.

"You were sick."

"I'd never been sick like that before or since."

"It happens. Are you going to tell me why you sent for me or not?"

"I'm getting there. There was a civilian along on that patrol, as you'll recall."

"He wasn't *along*," Noah corrected testily. "He was my prisoner, and you damn well know it. I was taking him to Cheyenne to face charges of robbery and fraud." Noah's mouth was grim. "Those were the only charges I could pin on him, though God knows he was guilty of plenty of others. Including putting a .44 slug in my back."

Eli nodded. "Pike."

"So are you going to tell me what the hell this is all about?"

"I just did. It's about John Pike."

"Pike is dead. That's the only good thing that came out of that day. The Sioux killed Pike the same as they killed my men."

Eli hesitated a long minute, then said slowly, "But what if they didn't."

Noah's eyes narrowed dangerously. "What?"

"What if John Pike is alive?"

"What are you talking about? He's dead, dead like all the others. His body was mutilated, but . . ." Noah swallowed. "But there was enough left for an identification." He paced to the door. "If this insanity is why you sent me that letter . . ."

"I sent you the letter because I need you to act as a guide for a friend of mine. A bounty hunter named Vic Langley."

Noah pressed his hands to his temples. "You'll have to forgive me," he said slowly, "I've got a bit of a headache. If this is making any sense at all, I'm missing it. Why in the name of hell would you expect me to be a trail guide for a bounty hunter?"

"One of the men Vic is after is John Pike."

Noah stalked back over to Eli. "I told you, Pike is dead."

"I have a witness," Eli said calmly. "A witness who saw Pike at the scene of a murder five months ago. The murderer had a crossed-saber tattoo on his right forearm and a scar across his right cheek."

Noah was still unconvinced, but his heart was thudding. "I don't believe it."

"Neither did I."

"But now you do?"

"I'm about as certain as I can be for not having seen him with my own eyes. Think about it," Eli urged. "At least open your mind to the possibility. If Pike is alive, you have a survivor who knows what really happened that day."

But Noah didn't dare let in even a flicker of hope. To do so was to risk its being crushed, just as it had been the day Katherine had—"So where is this witness who saw Pike alive?" he snarled. "What's his name?"

"It's Langley. And he's plum set on revenge. But I don't want him facin' down Pike alone. Vic's young, hotheaded, liable to get himself killed."

"I heard talk around town that a bounty hunter brought in two dead men yesterday. He doesn't sound like a man who needs his hand held."

"Pike's nothing like the two we got yesterday."

"How'd you get to be such good friends with a bounty hunter anyway?"

"It's a long story."

Noah snorted his disgust. "That you're not going to tell me, right?"

"Right."

"I'll look for Pike myself." Noah stalked toward the door. "If he's out there, I'll find him." He started to turn the knob, but Eli's next words stopped him.

"I thought we were friends."

Noah looked back over his shoulder. "I haven't had any friends for three years."

"Katherine still cuts deep, doesn't she?"

"Shut up."

"She didn't believe in you," Eli said quietly. "You're well rid of her."

Noah let go of the knob. "I said shut up."

Eli had enough sense to let the subject drop. "That day wasn't your fault, son. I'll never believe it, even if you do. Find Pike and maybe you'll get the answers you need so you can sleep nights without . . . " He flushed, stopping himself.

Noah's voice was savage. "Without hearing my men screaming?"

Eli said nothing.

"I'm not buying a word of this, Eli. Not one word."

"Talk to Vic. You'll believe it then." Eli's keen eyes narrowed. "Or maybe you already do. Just a little?"

Noah didn't answer. Seventeen bodies had been accounted for at the massacre. Sixteen troopers and Pike. If Pike had survived, how could the body count match?

"What have you got to lose, Noah?" Eli prodded, not ungently. "That you haven't lost already?"

Despite Eli's caring tone, Noah stiffened with rage. "If you weren't lying in that bed, old man . . . "

Eli took another sip of his whiskey, a hard light coming into his craggy face. "If I wasn't in this bed, maybe I wouldn't have let this talk go on as long as it has. Vic Langley deserves better than what I'm seein'."

Noah decided he'd put off having a drink long enough.

"I'll be back this afternoon at two. Have Langley here." With that he opened the door.

Eli sniffed the air. "No offense, but between now and then I'd suggest you take a bath."

Noah's jaw tightened. But rather than be offended, he felt a sudden, stinging bite of shame. He really had let himself go to hell. "I'll see what I can do." With that, he was gone.

Eli sagged back against his pillow, wondering if he'd just made the biggest mistake of his life. He wouldn't have thought a man could change that much in three years. Not at his core. But Noah had changed. He was bitter, cynical, eaten alive with guilt. To hook up such a man with Torey, who was hurting so much herself . . .

Maybe if he told Noah the truth about Torey, made him promise not to let on he knew. No. Instinct warned him that Noah would've backed off from the meeting at once, never buying the idea that a woman could pass herself off as a man. Torey was right. She needed to present herself to Noah as Vic Langley first. Prove to Noah that her impersonation of a man was an uncannily accurate one. Eli grimaced. Despite her occasional excesses toward the negative.

But even seeing how good she was, Noah could still balk. No matter what Katherine had done to him, Noah Killian was a breed of man that would never deliberately use a woman, put her life in danger. Not even to get John Pike.

Eli cursed the fates that had left him with a broken leg. If Noah left Torey behind, she would never wait for Eli to mend. She would go after Pike alone.

Eli had to make damned sure that didn't happen, make damned sure that Noah was there to protect her. No matter what he might have to say to Noah to get him to do it. It was the best chance Torey had. Maybe the best chance she and Noah both had. And even it might not be enough. Even with Noah's gun along, they could still both be killed.

5

Torey paced the limited confines of her room at Mamie's Boarding House, trying hard to slow the trip-hammer beat of her heart. It was well past midnight, and she was exhausted. But she was afraid to lie down, afraid to sleep. Each of the previous three times she had dared close her eyes tonight it had only been to find herself snared in the web of the same horrible dream.

He had been there. In her dream. The dark-haired stranger. With his pain-edged words and whisper-soft kisses. Beckoning her to come to him. His generous mouth had curved into a lazy, sensual smile, while his eyes, those fathomless gray eyes, caressed her, teased her, lulled her. Made her trust. His voice, too, had been soft, so soft. Mesmerizing. *I'll make it worth your while, lovely lady. I promise. Maybe we can both forget our troubles, for just one night.*

He'd come toward her then, his smile never wavering. But his eyes. Oh, God, his eyes. They had changed. From gentle and warm to cruel and cold as ice.

"Stay away from me!" Torey cried. "Stay away!"

"What's the matter?" he asked silkily as he stepped closer

still. "Don't you trust me? Don't worry, sweet lady, I'm not going to hurt you."

He lunged for her then. Torey screamed, desperate, despairing. She tried to turn, run, but his arms snapped around her like the jaws of a trap. With a savage twist he had her on the ground, pinioned beneath his superior weight. He was laughing, laughing. "You never learn, do you, sweet thing? You just never learn. Pike didn't teach you. Varney didn't teach you. But I'll teach you. I'll teach you so you never forget . . ."

He brought his mouth down on hers.

For just an instant she was aware of something different, something . . . an emotion she couldn't name. But she quickly shuttered the feeling away. She didn't want to know, didn't dare know. Her mind whirled in a paroxysm of terror. Like a wild animal, she struggled, fought. He was suffocating her. He was destroying her.

Somehow she worked one arm free.

Her gun. She remembered she was wearing her gun. She reached for it, felt the cold steel against her palm. He wouldn't teach her. She would teach him. She drew the gun . . .

Torey sat bolt upright in bed, clamping her hand over her mouth, stopping the scream that threatened to tear from her throat. She was shivering violently, though her whole body was drenched with sweat. Heart hammering, her eyes cut to the heavily shadowed door. Had her screams been only in her mind? Or had she been screaming aloud? She sagged back against her pillow. Merciful heaven, when had she even gone back to bed?

She sat there gasping, her pulses thrumming so loudly in her ears, it took her a moment before she could catch any other sounds at all. Blessedly they were the normal sounds of the night. Crickets chirruping, a coyote howling, a dog barking, a rider setting his horse into a lazy, loping gait northward out of town.

Using the bandanna knotted at her throat, Torey wiped the sweat from her brow, vaguely aggravated with herself that on such a humid night she was still fully dressed. But she knew why. She had been unable tonight to shed her guise as Vic Langley even to go to sleep, so distressed was she by what had happened in the saloon. The singular catalyst of the night's events—the red silk dress—lay in a wadded-up heap in the far corner of her room, only because she'd been afraid to risk burning it. Miss Mamie would just have to deal with the thing as she saw fit.

Torey threaded her fingers through the perspiration-damp strands of her hair. Only now was her heartbeat beginning to slow, return to a more natural rhythm.

Reaching for a half full glass of water she'd left on the night table earlier, she drank it down. It was warm, but it was wet. She tipped the last few droplets into her palm and smoothed them over her face.

How could she have had the same nightmare four times in a row? More to the point, why?

Pike didn't teach you. Varney didn't teach you. But I'll teach you. I'll teach you so you never forget . . .

Teach her what? Torey shoved to her feet and paced. Teach her what? That a man could heap pain and degradation on a woman anytime he chose, simply because he was stronger than she was? Torey was already too hellishly aware of that fact.

And yet she'd left herself vulnerable to exactly that sort of treatment last night by going into that saloon dressed as she'd been. It had been a stupid, dangerous mistake. One she would not repeat. In the space of five minutes she'd all but destroyed the gossamer thin veil of security she'd managed to weave around herself since leaving Denver. A security grounded in her masquerade as a bounty hunter. As a man.

In the dress she had felt vulnerable, defenseless, weak.

As Vic Langley she would never have fallen prey to such frailties.

I'll make it worth your while, lovely lady. I promise.

No. No more red silk dresses. No more whisper-soft kisses. No more sweet, tender lies.

She was safe only as Vic Langley. That's what the dream had taught her. That's why at the end of it she had been reaching for her gun.

With a weary sigh Torey crossed back to the bed and lay down, confident now the dream would not return. And yet before she drifted off to sleep her last conscious thoughts were once again taken up by fathomless gray eyes.

She woke to a thunderous pounding on her door. Groggily, she opened her eyes, then closed them, stung by the brightness of the room. She must have overslept. No wonder Lisbeth was angry. The pounding continued.

"All right, Lissa," she mumbled. "I know the chickens need to be fed. I'm up. I'm up."

For the tiniest instant everything was set right again, her world was as it had been. And then Torey came truly awake. The pain, when it hit her, was almost beyond bearing.

She was grateful then for the pounding. It gave her a moment to gather herself. Too, it had obscured the sound of her words.

"Mr. Langley?" trilled Miss Mamie from outside the room. "Mr. Langley, are you decent?"

Torey shoved herself up on one elbow. Bright light streamed through the open windows that faced east and south here at the rear of the house. Good grief, what time was it? It had to be nearly noon. She snatched up the windup clock by her bed. Make that two o'clock.

Pushing to her feet, Torey staggered to the door, taking time to pull on her hat. Unlatching the bolt, she eased the door open a crack, blinking again, for Miss Mamie LaRue's made-up face and bright orange hair had the same effect on her as the sun. "Is Eli all right?" Torey asked.

"Mr. Burkett is doing just fine," Mamie said, sidling past Torey and ambling into the room. "I picked up his lunch tray about an hour ago. He seemed quite chipper. Which is more than I can say for you."

"What do mean?"

"I mean you had a helluva night, didn't you?" Mamie's bright blue eyes were shrewd, probing.

Torey turned away. "I had a nightmare. I hope I didn't disturb anyone."

"No one at all, Mr. Langley, don't worry. I was up only 'cause my rheumatiz' was troublin' me. Mr. Burkett made good use of the whiskey you brought him. Slept like the dead."

Chalking up the unease she was feeling to the aftereffects of her nightmares, Torey strode over to the washstand. Why did Mamie LaRue have to choose this morning to be so chatty? Maybe the woman would take a hint. "I didn't mean to sleep so late myself. I . . . if you don't mind, Miss Mamie, I need to get ready for what's left of the day. Wash up." She cleared her throat. "Shave."

"Don't let me keep you. If you want, I could whip up the lather for you. I've had three husbands, I'm pretty good at it."

"No. No, I'll do it."

Torey picked up the straight razor she carried around in her saddlebags for show. Short of tossing Miss Mamie out bodily, there didn't seem to be a whole lot she could do about the woman's continued presence in the room. It was Miss Mamie's house, after all. Torey would just have to go through with this. She only prayed she still had a face left when she finished.

Mamie stepped over to the basin and took the razor from Torey's trembling hand. "You know"—the woman clucked softly—"I've been wondering since the minute you walked into my place, what in blazes would ever make such a pretty girl hide herself under all those god-awful clothes. Must be one powerful reason."

Torey blanched, then stiffened with what she hoped

seemed like outrage. "I beg your pardon?" she demanded. "How dare you . . . ?"

Miss Mamie chuckled, but her eyes were kind. "Give it up, honey. I've been around the block more times than a St. Louie postman. I don't mean to pry, but you were so restless last night . . . so afraid, I can't help askin' after you."

Torey turned away, uncertain whether to continue her bluff or to just beg the woman to say nothing to anyone.

"Mr. Burkett knows, doesn't he?" Mamie asked.

Torey's shoulders slumped. What was the use? "Yes, Eli knows, but Mamie, please, I . . . " How could Torey tell this woman that she'd just spent the better part of the night coming to the conclusion that she felt safe these days only as Vic Langley. The idea that her charade could be over sent a near crippling shaft of dread through her.

Mamie held up her hand. "Don't fret. I'm the one people in this town gossip *about*, not the one who spreads it. Like I said, I was worried. You seem like such a nice girl, ah . . . boy."

Torey managed a slight smile that quickly vanished. She walked over and sat on the bed. "It's a very long, very ugly story, I'm afraid."

"The why of it ain't my business. But I been told a time or two I'm a good listener."

Torey hadn't even told Aunt Ruby the whole truth, that Pike and Varney's descent onto the farm was Torey's own fault. But for reasons she couldn't fathom, she sat there now and told Mamie LaRue. Torey finished by saying, "You see? I promised my father, promised my sister. I owe them that much for what I did."

"I understand hate, honey. I understand hate real good. I've been there. I've felt that kind of pain, that kind of guilt. That's why you couldn't fool me, when you could fool most anybody else. I used to have that same look in my eyes."

"I thought I was pretty good at hiding it."

"Oh, you are. Real good. Maybe too good. You hide

it from yourself too. But like I said, I've been there. My first . . . introduction . . . to the ways of men, you might say"—a slight tremor coursed through her plump body—"was from my stepdaddy. I was twelve years old. I never thought I'd feel clean again. Never thought I'd want a man to touch me again."

"Please," Torey whispered. "Don't . . . like I told you, those men didn't . . . I mean, they mostly . . . they hurt Lisbeth."

"They hurt you both," Mamie said flatly, "don't ever think that they didn't. And don't ever be too sure which one of you got the worst of it. The one who had it done, or the one who seen it."

Hot tears stung Torey's eyes. She swiped them viciously away. Mamie just didn't understand. What had happened to Mamie was tragic, but it wasn't the same. Mamie had been an innocent. Like Lisbeth. "Mamie, I—"

"My, my," Mamie interrupted, hurrying over to the room's far corner. "What have we here?"

Torey felt her cheeks flame as Mamie stooped to pick up the red silk dress. "I know it's hard to picture," Mamie said, molding the crimson material against her bosomy frame, "but I once would've cut quite a figure in this dress. Red's my color, you know."

"You sound like you're proud of it." Torey flinched at the censure in her voice, following on Mamie's kindness, then quickly explained how she had come into possession of the dress.

"The dark-haired one sounds mighty tempting," Mamie said, giving Torey a wink. "I'd have kept him up all night. In more ways than one, I'll wager."

Memories of warm, moist lips sent Torey skittering for a glass of water.

"Gentle ones are hard to find," Mamie said. "Real rare." Her gaze took on a faraway look. "I never had much schoolin'. And when I run away from my stepdaddy, well, a saloon job just seemed to be all I was suited for. It was, you might say, my only talent." For the first time a hint of bitterness shaded Mamie's words. "Leastways, saloons taught me a few things. They taught me that some men are good at sex. And some aren't, but think they are. And some, well, they're just like my stepdaddy. Pure scum."

"Please . . ."

"I was wrong to let my stepdaddy run my life, even after I was a thousand miles away from him. Dead wrong. Like I didn't deserve anything decent and fine to touch my life ever again. My mother . . . "—Mamie's voice shook just a little—"my mother knew what my stepdaddy had done. She told me it was my fault, that I lured him into my bed, that I wanted him to . . ." Mamie shuddered. "It was a lotta years before I knew my mother was wrong. Before I saw her own weakness for what it was. That what happened with my stepdaddy was his fault, not mine.

"Anyway, one night in one of those saloons a man come in. Not handsome, not rich, just lonely. Him and me hit it off. We talked all night. Just talked, then along about dawn we started taking off our clothes. That man taught me something that I never knew before, not in twenty years' worth of nights in a saloon."

"And what was that?" Torey asked, not at all sure she wanted to know.

"That there's one more breed of man out there. One that doesn't just take for himself in bed—for good or for bad. But who spends time getting to know a woman, to care about her, to take his pleasure from pleasuring her. If you ever find one like that honey, latch on to him. Don't let him get away." Her eyes grew misty. "I let him get away."

"I assure you," Torey choked. "I am not looking."

"Oh, he'll find you, honey. I'm a great believer in fate. It's just that most people are blind to it. They're so wrapped up in their problems, the answers just plum pass 'em by.

"That's why you gotta have a care. When the right man

comes along, don't make him pay for what them others done. Be real careful. Don't make him pay."

Torey's mouth tightened. "I know you mean well, Mamie. But I can't bear to talk about this anymore. Please, go. Please."

"I understand." Mamie started toward the door, then stopped. "Can you believe it? I near forgot what brought me to your door in the first place. Got a message to give you from Mr. Burkett." She handed Torey a note.

"Thank you."

Again Mamie started out the door. "Remember, honey. Don't let him get away." With that she was gone.

Torey gripped the note and walked to one of the open windows, where a breeze was ruffling the lacy curtains. Torey let the gentle wind drift over her. To have such a hellacious night be followed by such an emotionally charged conversation was doubly unnerving. Torey could only pray the note from Eli was of no particular consequence. A request for a newspaper or beef jerky.

She unfolded the paper.

Vic,

Come to my room at two. It's time to keep your word. Killian will be here. Eli

Killian. Just like that. Right down the hallway. The mysterious war hero turned coward.

Torey surprised herself by laughing, if a trifle hysterically. The way things were going Killian would probably have two heads and only eat raw meat. She crumpled the note. Poor Mr. Killian. He didn't know it, but he was about to make up for the rest of this hideous day.

She looked at the clock. Two-thirty. A half hour late. Good. She could see first off how the man handled a little irritation.

After a quick check in the mirror to reassure herself that

she could still pass muster as Vic Langley even after a round of Mamie LaRue's devastatingly on-target perceptions, Torey headed out the door toward Eli's room. She deliberately gave herself no time to think or prepare as she traversed the narrow hallway toward her encounter with Mr. Noah Killian. If she did, she might well turn around and run.

She could hardly believe Killian was here. Had he ridden into town overnight? It was odd how she had such a clear picture of the man in her head. A grizzled old war-horse like Eli. Strong, likable, grandfatherly. A man Eli believed in, trusted. It might be a little discomfiting at first to tell someone new her secret, but it would free her a little too, allow her the rare luxury of being with a man and feeling safe as a woman.

No doubt Killian would try to be deferential toward her, paternal, like Eli. Torey would have to tactfully but firmly set the man straight. She wanted no special privileges accorded her for being female, beyond an occasional moment of privacy. As long as Killian understood that and understood who was in charge of this expedition, they would have no problems. Vic Langley was not riding with Noah Killian. Noah Killian was riding with Vic Langley.

As she approached Eli's door, Torey felt her equilibrium returning. Her encounter with the dark-haired stranger, she assured herself, was already a fading memory, as was her unsettling chat with Miss Mamie LaRue.

Marching up to Eli's door, Torey raised her fist and rapped sharply.

"Door's open!" Eli called.

She turned the knob and stepped into the room. "Afternoon, Eli," she said, nodding toward her injured friend, who was lying on his bed beneath a thin layering of sheet, arms folded across his massive chest. Mamie had described his mood as chipper. At the moment he looked anything but. Torey couldn't tell if he was annoyed by her apparent tardiness, or if she'd interrupted some sort of disagreement with the second man in the room, the one standing at the window with his back to her. In either case, Eli only managed a slight nod in her direction. Evidently for the moment at least she was on her own with Noah Killian.

Her gaze tracked to the man at the window. With his back to her she could guess nothing of what *his* mood might be. But the fact that he hadn't yet turned around to greet her certainly didn't go very far toward endearing him to her. As long as he was determined to be rude, she decided to let him. It would give her a chance to study him unobserved, perhaps develop some kind of intuitive sense of him. Not that she placed the highest value on her intuition.

She found his attire remarkable. Black hat, black shirt, black vest, black trousers, black boots. Even his gunbelt was black, as was the silk kerchief knotted around his neck. Had he been attending services at Silas Bertram's? she wondered sarcastically. What kind of color was black for the middle of August anyway? Didn't the man sweat?

At least his gun wasn't black. It was instead a .36 Navy model Colt, well used judging by its worn ivory handle. His shaggy hair—black, of course—trailed from under his Stetson to his shoulders. Torey's annoyance intensified. The man had longer hair than she did! Recently washed, it lay in soft waves against his neck.

A niggling unease rippled through her, which she ascribed to his continuing to ignore her. Yet other factors about this man disconcerted her as well. He was not old. He was not grizzled. And judging by the rigid set of that broad back, she had no reason to consider him deferential or paternal either. His hips were narrow, his thighs well muscled, and he was of a medium height. Maybe her own five ten, maybe not. But he seemed taller. Imposing, somehow. Even from the back.

And there was something else about him too—familiar, yet not. Her mouth tightened. Blast the man! How far was he going to take this silent act? How far was she going to let him? She had entered this room with the express purpose of making it clear to Killian, ex-officer or not, that *she* would be the one in charge of the search for Pike and Varney. It was time he got the message. "You expecting company through that window?" she asked irritably. "Or didn't your mama teach you any manners?"

The man turned. Torey's knees almost buckled. God in heaven! No. His fathomless gray eyes were no longer bloodshot and unfocused, though the cheek beneath his right eye sported a new, angry-looking bruise. His hard-edged face held no hint of the lazy, sensual smile of the night before. His growth of beard was gone and she caught the scent of lye soap and bay rum. The dark-haired stranger from the Take Your Chances Saloon had shaved, bathed, changed clothes, changed everything. Everything.

Everything but Torey's own excruciatingly vivid memories of being in this man's arms, feeling him touch her, hearing him whisper sweet, tender lies. *Maybe we can both forget our troubles, just for one night.* One night . . .

Torey coughed, choked, her eyes watering as she walked unsteadily over to the ladder-back chair beside Eli's bed. She sagged onto it and pressed her hand to her forehead, desperate to obscure her face, obscure the scarlet blush now staining her cheeks. Oh, God. Oh, dear God. How could the fates be so cruel? How could the fates in all the wide world of men deliver her this one?

"Something wrong, Vic?" Eli asked, concern edging his gravelly voice.

"I . . . I have a headache," she managed. "I didn't sleep too well."

"Miss Mamie said you had a rough night."

"Yes, a very rough night." Did Killian know her? Had he somehow realized who she was? Was that the reason for his silence? With no other choice, Torey dared look at him again.

Drunk, he'd had an air of vulnerability about him, a wistfulness that had touched her when she didn't want to be touched.

Sober, and he was most definitely sober, there was no softness in him. His eyes were flint hard, stone cold, seeming to stare right through her. But blessedly there was no hint of recognition in them, no acknowledgment that they had ever in their lives met before.

Her fists clenched and her gaze dropped to the floor. *Get hold of yourself, Vic,* she fumed inwardly. *Now!* To Killian's eyes she was Vic Langley, cold-blooded bounty hunter. Until and unless she made some stupid blunder and betrayed herself, he would have no reason to doubt her.

. . . I'll teach you so you never forget.

Torey's heart thudded, her head snapping in Killian's direction, certain he had spoken the words from her dream aloud. But those full, generous lips remained grimly silent. Apparently the man was just as he seemed, a rude son of a bitch. Her heartbeat slowed to a more agreeable rate. Vic Langley could handle a rude son of a bitch. To Eli, she snapped, "Can he talk or what?"

"I can talk," Killian said smoothly. "Can you tell time?"

Torey sprang to her feet, incredulous. "That's what this is about? You stare out the window for five minutes because I'm a little late?"

He didn't even blink. "I stared out the window for five minutes because I wanted to see how a man who might one day have my life in his hands reacted when things didn't go his way. I stared out the window for five minutes because I had to wonder if I told that man to be at a certain place at a certain time, if my ass would be in the fire because he couldn't tell when the big hand was on the twelve and the little hand was on the two. I stared out the window for five minutes because I don't have a very high opinion of bounty hunters, but I have a damned high opinion of Eli Burkett."

His lips curved into a disdainful smirk. "My opinion of bounty hunters hasn't changed."

Torey bristled. He could talk all right. Now she only wished he would shut up. How dare he be assessing her character, when she was supposed to be assessing his? At least his arrogant tone had accomplished one thing, it had oddly served to calm her, allow her to set aside for the moment their initial encounter last night in the saloon. That encounter had given her one other advantage Killian didn't have. It had let her see weakness in him, let her know that this flinty-eyed, cocksure bastard was not the only working version of Noah Killian.

She considered telling him that she had been late only because Miss Mamie had absentmindedly delayed delivery of Eli's note, but Torey decided not to give him the satisfaction. Despite her shock at discovering Noah Killian and the dark-haired stranger to be one and the same man, she was suddenly enjoying their exchange, the verbal battle of wits between them. After the night she'd had, any diversion was welcome. She was not yet ready to predict the outcome of this meeting. But it wouldn't be boring. And, she thought acidly, Killian wasn't going to win. Somehow she was going to pay him back for those nightmares.

"So you're not real fond of bounty hunters, eh, Killian?" Torey drawled. "Well, I'm not real fond of cow—"

"Now, Vic," Eli cut in sharply, cajolingly, "it ain't that Noah hates all bounty hunters. He just don't know you like I do. I'm sure he'd have a different opinion once he knows the *real* you."

Torey scowled at Eli, both for interrupting her fine insult and for reminding her that she was supposed to tell Killian at some point during this little rendezvous that she was not a he. Well, Eli was in for a long wait. Torey had no intentions of telling Killian she was a woman. Not today. Maybe not ever. She was not so rash that she didn't realize she needed his help in finding Pike. But Noah Killian would be riding with Vic Langley, not Victoria Lansford. Any notions she'd had of telling some grandfatherly friend of Eli Burkett's that she was a lady bounty hunter had been summarily canceled when Noah Killian had turned away from that window. Torey just hoped the glare she sent Eli was enough of a hint that he was not to take the matter into his own hands and tell Killian about her himself.

"Just how long have you been a bounty hunter, Langley?" Killian asked.

"Long enough."

"You don't look very old."

"I'm old enough."

She watched his mouth tick upward in mocking amusement. "If you go after John Pike, maybe you won't get any older."

"And maybe it'll be him who doesn't have any more birthdays," Torey shot back.

He actually chuckled. "You must figure you can handle that Colt on your hip pretty well, then?"

"You saying I can't?" Torey asked mildly, amused herself that he would challenge one of the few skills she had these days about which she had no doubts. Slowly she lifted the weapon from its holster, as though to study it more closely. Then just as slowly she leveled it in the direction of Killian's head. "I handle it well enough to part your hair down the middle of your skull."

Noah took a step toward her, that mocking amusement still in his gray eyes. "You forgot one thing, Vic."

"What's that?"

"Never point a gun at a man unless you're willing to use it." He took another step.

Torey eased back the hammer. "Who's to say I won't."

He took another step.

Torey quailed inwardly. What was he doing? She couldn't show weakness and let him disarm her, yet neither could she shoot the bloody fool. He took another step. He was barely four feet from her now.

With what she hoped was a convincing show of contempt

she let down the hammer and reholstered the gun. "No wanted dodgers on you, Killian. It's not worth the price of a bullet to kill you."

He let out a cold chuckle. "Just so I know the code of honor you operate under."

"At least I have one," she snapped.

The amusement went out of him. "Meaning?"

"Meaning seventeen men died because you cared more about your own skin than theirs."

A muscle in his jaw jumped.

"Blast it, Vic," Eli blustered, "what are you—?"

Killian cut him off with a wave of his hand. "No, Eli, let him have his say." He looked again at Torey. "So you got me all figured out then, eh, Langley?"

"I got you all figured out," Torey said coldly.

For a long minute he looked at her, the coldness in those eyes tinged with a pain so fierce it made her wince. And then he turned away, embarrassed she knew because he had failed to hide that pain from Vic Langley.

For a moment Torey experienced a surge of triumph. She had won. She had paid him back for last night. And then she felt a biting shame. What was she doing? Becoming? That she could be so deliberately cruel.

Unconsciously, she raised a hand as though to soothe him, then remembered herself and curled her fingers into her palm. "I'm sorry."

He swore viciously. "At least let's keep it honest between us, Langley. You don't think much of me, and I don't think much of you." He looked at Eli. "I'm sorry, old friend, but this isn't going to work. Not even to find Pike am I going to ride with this son of a bitch."

"And I'd rather ride with a rattlesnake," she shot back.

Eli looked from one to the other. "Are you finished? Are you both finished? I've been sitting here listening to the two of you snap and snarl and bite at each other until I'm ready to spit. But I kept my mouth shut, figurin' I'd let you draw a little blood, get it all said and done here, instead of out on the trail somewhere when one of you might need the other to stay alive."

Eli gave his head a weary shake. "I swear neither one of you got the sense God gave a prairie dog. It's John Pike who needs hurtin', not the two of you."

Torey flushed. "Eli's right, Killian," she said softly. "And I was wrong. I'm sorry. Truly. I don't know you, and you don't know me. But we both hate Pike. I say we do whatever it takes to find him."

She stepped toward Killian, extended her hand in the time-honored gesture of conciliation between men. For a moment she wasn't sure he would accept it. And then with a grimace, he did.

His grip was strong, firm, his flesh warm, the contact sending an unexpected bolt of electricity sizzling up her arm. She had meant the handshake as a courtesy. He had accepted it as such. But for her, it was more as if she'd shoved her hand into an invisible flame.

"Be at my hotel room at first light," Killian said. "We'll head out." He started for the door.

"Noah, wait," Eli said, looking at Torey. "Don't you have something else to tell Noah, *Vic*?"

"Not that I can think of," she said, being now deliberately obtuse.

"Dammit, Vic . . . "

Her lips thinned in a stubborn line.

Killian frowned. "If this has something to do with finding Pike, you'd best tell me now."

"It's nothing. Really. I . . . " Her mind raced. Damn Eli, anyway. This wasn't his call. She affected a chagrined look. "Eli thinks I should tell you, I . . . I'm deathly afraid of snakes."

Killian's eyebrows shot up. "What?"

"Eli was afraid you wouldn't think much of a bounty man who shimmied up a tree to get away from an eight-inch garter snake."

Killian snorted his disgust. "Be in my room at dawn." With that he left the room.

"What the hell was that?" Eli gritted. "I never seen a snake yet that could make you jump. Why didn't you tell him the truth?"

"I just changed my mind, that's all. It'll be better for both of us if he knows me strictly as Vic Langley."

"Why?"

Because he's not old and grizzled, because he held me in his arms and kissed me, because . . . because of a thousand reasons she couldn't even explain to herself let alone to Eli. "Because it will," she said lamely. "It doesn't matter why."

"You're going to be riding with that man twenty-four hours a day. And you expect him not to find out you're a woman? What are you going to do, blindfold him?"

"I'll manage."

"And what if you don't manage? What if he finds out when you're in the middle of nowhere? He'll wring your neck for deceiving him and then come and wring mine to boot."

"He's not going to find out," she repeated mulishly. "Now I'd best go to the livery and check on Galahad, make sure Moses has him ready to travel in the morning."

"Dammit, Vic, you tell Noah the truth."

"No! And you'd best not either."

"It's not my place. But I wish you luck the day he finds out. And he will. You mark my words. He will."

Torey walked out of the room and shut the door, then stood in the hallway, trembling. She'd pulled it off. Vic Langley had made it through her encounter with Killian. But she wasn't feeling much like Vic Langley right now.

Day in and day out with the dark-haired stranger? Over pitch-black nights and lonesome trails. *Pike didn't teach you.*

Varney didn't teach you. But I'll teach you. I'll teach you so you never forget . . .

She shuddered, her hand reflexively touching the walnut handle of her Colt. No. Whatever it took, she had to make certain that Noah Killian never found out she was a woman.

6

Noah lay sprawled on his stomach in his bed in the Cuttersville hotel. He was naked. And so was the woman lying next to him.

Exhausted, sated, he forced open one eye, his gaze trailing languorously over the lush curves of the still-sleeping Belle Whitley. She had promised him she was going to send him one of her very best. She finally had. Herself.

His mouth curved into a lazy grin. It had been one helluva night. Belle was good. Damn good. He had to give her that. But then—his grin grew positively scandalous—so was he. At one point during the night he had had her so hot, so eager, so ready that *she* had promised to pay *him*, if he would just bring her the release her body craved and stay with her forever. He chuckled, knowing what kind of response he would get were he to remind Belle of her erotic vows of faithfulness in the cold light of day.

Propping himself up onto one elbow, Noah began to trace feathery circles along the creamy white flesh of Belle's back and upward to her shoulder. He paused, frowning, noticing her blond hair. Odd, how in the darkness he'd forgotten she was blond. He'd spent the night thinking of her with dark hair, dark hair and wide, sad eyes, garbed in a red silk dress that didn't suit her, didn't suit her at all.

Noah muttered a curse, low, under his breath, not wanting to disturb Belle's sleep, but annoyed that his thoughts seemed to drift again and again to the raven-haired beauty who'd all but fallen into his lap at the Take Your Chances Saloon. She'd been a whore, for chrissakes. No different than Belle. Why did he find this particular whore so damned special, intriguing?

He closed his eyes, disgusted with his own attitude. Who was he to judge Belle or the woman in the red dress for what they did to survive? He tried to imagine such a life. Women who traded their bodies for money, who suffered the lustings of strangers to earn a living. What did Belle Whitley get out of a night like last night? Besides a few dollars. And a few transient moments of pleasure. If that. Most of her nights were no doubt spent in the throes of artificial ecstasy, performed artfully enough to appease the vanity of the men she serviced, and perhaps to gain an extra dollar or two for her purse. Belle herself likely felt nothing.

But she'd felt something last night with him. He'd seen to that. She'd felt the yearning, the hunger, the power of her own lust, her own passion. For Noah Killian was a man who took especial pleasure in pleasuring a woman who was above her own feelings, resisted them, denied them. For him, evoking cries of genuine rapture from such a woman was a challenge not to be resisted, but embraced. Awakening a woman to the wonder, the magic of her own body was a prize equal to his own release. He reveled in those moments, triumphed in them. Maybe because in some ways their release was his as well. They were alike, he and his faceless ladyloves, each of them with an affinity for the night, the anonymity of darkness.

Among the shadows he could dare to feel, to give himself up to emotions he kept shuttered tight under the scrutinizing glare of the real world. In the darkness he could dare a woman to touch his soul as he sought to touch hers.

Still, even in the darkness, there was an imaginary line he would not cross, a part of himself he always held back. He had almost crossed that line with Katherine. But she had taught him well. To never give everything. For to do so was to be left with nothing. To be nothing.

Noah groaned, annoyed at the fanciful direction of his thoughts, vaguely embarrassed as he always was when morning came and he found himself in bed with a woman about whom he knew nothing. Except where and how to touch her. Vaguely ashamed as well because he didn't want to know anything else about her, no real-world troubles to intrude on the night. Maybe she knew his name, maybe she didn't. It didn't matter.

What mattered was the few hours they spent together—without entanglements, without commitments, without obligations. He wanted no misunderstandings, no hurt feelings. The night was, for him, an agreeable diversion, a respite from unpleasant dreams. He enjoyed his partner's fervor, her delight, but he never failed to make it clear from the outset—before a single article of clothing was removed—that their lovemaking was a one-night-only affair, an entertainment to be savored, devoured, then forgotten like yesterday's dessert.

He wasn't worried that Belle would be a woman with any higher expectations. They had been of a kind, the two of them, giving, taking, until both of them had been exhausted. Noah had no complaints. Between the demands of her body and his, he hadn't had much chance to sleep, and therefore he hadn't had much chance to dream.

Leaning over, he kissed her lightly on the back of her neck. "Sweet dreams, Belle," he whispered. "Sweet dreams."

Noah rolled over and sat up, planting his feet on the floor. Had the woman in the red dress been with someone who cared about her last night? Or had her partner merely pawed her and poked her for his own selfish wants?

Noah cursed feelingly. What the hell did it matter? Why couldn't he get the woman out of his head?

Maybe because he'd scared the hell out of her. Maybe because he didn't even know what he had done to frighten her. But he had, and the fear in her eyes had even sliced through his drunken haze.

Last night he'd briefly considered asking Belle about the woman. If anyone would know about her, Belle would. But then he'd decided, diplomatically, that the question would best keep until this morning. He assured himself his interest was strictly altruistic. After his own part in upsetting her, he merely wanted to make certain the woman was all right. It wasn't as if he were trying to arrange an evening with her. After all, he was riding out of town today with that son of a bitch bounty hunter, Vic Langley.

Thoughts of Langley jarred him, forced him to think, something he'd been studiously avoiding last night in the arms of Belle Whitley. He still wasn't sure what the hell he'd gotten himself into with Eli and Langley. All he was sure of was that young Langley had one man-sized mouth for a kid who didn't look like he needed to shave more than once a week.

No wanted dodgers on you, Killian. It's not worth the price of a bullet to kill you.

But maybe it would be worth my knuckles to deck you, Noah thought acidly, then grimaced. The kid couldn't be all bad or Eli wouldn't practically dote on him. Besides, when Langley hadn't been strutting about like a peacock, Noah had sensed real hurt and anger in his blustery manner. Hurt and anger no doubt compliments of John Pike.

Pike. The name sent a chill through Noah, along with a long-dormant sense of fury, hate. Could the bastard truly be alive? If he was, he had more lives than a cat. But then,

Noah thought bitterly, Pike had always had an uncanny knack for landing on his feet.

Even from the first time they'd met, as new cadets at West Point, Pike had been a chameleon, adapting his personality to whatever a particular time and circumstance demanded of him, though Noah had not seen through the facade until it was too late. Instead he'd welcomed the friendship of the ingratiating preacher's son, the two becoming almost like brothers over their first years together at the academy. Since Pike's parents were deceased, Noah even took Pike along on holiday treks home to the Killian family estate in Vermont.

But even during those years, the good years, there had been signs that all was not right. Pike would become enraged over imagined slights by upperclassmen, a curt remark by an instructor; even a defeat in a game of chess with Noah would send him into a rage, for which he would later apologize with an almost obsequious contrition. Noah attributed Pike's occasional outbursts to the pressure of being at the Point.

To that pressure, Pike added the nearly impossible goal of finishing number one in his graduating class. Amazingly, toward the end of his senior year, Pike seemed in line to do just that. His chief competition for the spot was Noah.

Noah never denied his own ambitions, often crediting his competition with Pike for keeping him sharp, keeping them both jockeying for number one. And then a week before graduation, it had all come apart.

Noah discovered that Pike was cheating, stealing exams to remain on top. More than that, he'd tried to alter, lower some of Noah's scores. Noah planned to confront his friend and demand an explanation. But by then Pike had already been summoned before a board of inquiry.

Pike had slammed into Noah's room, crazed with fury, his dark eyes wild, murderous. "You turned me in, you bastard! You turned me in. They'll expel me. How could you do this to me? You ruined me." His fists clenched and unclenched at his sides. "Damn you, I should kill you for this!"

"You ruined yourself," Noah said quietly. "But I didn't turn you in, John. I wanted to talk to you first. Hear you out. I wanted to hear you tell me why you did it."

"Bastard! Liar! Always the perfect, the honorable Noah Killian. Do everything by the book, everything right. Never make a mistake. No, not the son of the great Colonel Marcus Killian. It was his pull that got you in here, while I had to scrape and beg for a congressman's handout.

"But I showed them. I showed them all who was best. In war strategies, in battle tactics, being a leader of men—me. And by God, you just couldn't stand it, could you?"

"John, you've put so much pressure on yourself. You don't know what you're doing, saying. Let me help you—"

"You've done enough, goddamn you! You and your privileged family. You've done enough. I despise you, Noah. I always have. Your money, your power, your position. You were born to it, had it handed to you by right of your birth, while I had to crawl on my belly to even get anyone to notice me. Well, I tried to play the game by your rules. But the deck is stacked. I should've known. To win, I've always needed my own rules. I won't forget it again."

Pike had left West Point in disgrace. Just before he did, Noah had tried once more to make contact with him, to offer his help.

"You won this one, Noah," Pike snarled. "But you won't always win. Someday, when you least expect it, I'll be there to help you lose. And I mean, lose everything, just like I have."

Pike had disappeared then, and for a time Noah had all but forgotten about him, especially with the advent of the War Between the States. A bullet that missed his spine by half an inch proved a grim reminder of his one-time friend's existence . . . and his threats. Until that bullet Noah had never suspected just how far John Pike would go to avenge himself, to achieve his own ends. Unfortunately for Noah, after the shooting, Pike once again disappeared.

And then, four years ago in Wyoming their paths had crossed again. Noah had been on assignment, stationed at Fort Laramie. That particular afternoon he'd been in the sutler's store on the outskirts of the fort, decked out in his best dress uniform for a party he was to attend within the hour. He was alone in the store, the sutler having gone off on an errand. In those waning minutes before the party Noah was still futilely trying to select a birthday bonnet for Katherine Dodd, daughter of his commanding officer, and, Noah hoped, soon to be his fiancée. Noah had just picked up a frothy sunflower-hued confection with trailing ribbons of pale rose silk, when a coldly familiar voice had spoken up from several feet behind him.

"It's not you," the voice drawled unpleasantly. "I think your color is more Yankee blue."

Noah wheeled, tossing the bonnet aside and instinctively going for his army pistol, but he let his hand drop when he saw that the black-eyed man standing in the shadowed entryway of the sutler's store was unarmed. Pike. It couldn't be. But it was. "I thought you were dead."

"Thought or hoped, old friend?" Pike asked smoothly, hooking his thumbs into the waistband of a pair of finely tailored gray trousers. A white silk shirt, black broadcloth coat, and string tie heightened the air of prosperity about the man. "If you're alluding to that nasty rumor that I drowned when the *Sultana* went down, well"—he spread his hands expansively—"I guess you just can't believe everything you hear, can you?"

The *Sultana*, Noah knew, was a Union steamer that had sunk in the Mississippi just after the war ended, claiming the lives of over fifteen hundred homeward-bound veterans. And yes, he had heard that Pike had been among the dead. Heard and been glad.

Pike stalked across the hard-packed earthen floor, stopping barely four feet from where Noah stood. "I knew you were . . . looking for me back then. The boat's sinking was very convenient. Almost poetic. I wish I had thought of it myself. But alas, I had something more mundane in mind until the boiler blew."

Noah studied those coal-black eyes, eyes that seemed only to reflect back on themselves, offering no glimpse of the man behind them. How had he ever been fooled by this man for so long? The only noticeable difference in him was the angry red slash across his right cheek, a fairly recent wound that had healed badly. "I see someone got a piece of you at least."

Pike's smirk faded. "I got more of her. She's dead. Like you should be. Ah, well"—he brightened—"it's not often I have the pleasure of killing a man twice."

"You've got that turned around, Pike. I'm going to see you hang."

Pike chuckled, walking over to a table filled with buffalo hides and wolf pelts, running his hands over them as though to assess their quality. "Ah, Noah, you always did have delusions of grandeur. You know, it may surprise you, but I was even pleased to hear that you had survived my bullet. I thought about it later, and the bullet had been much too quick, too . . . merciful."

Noah sensed it then, an undercurrent, a feeling of something not right. He could almost believe that Pike had come to the fort deliberately, knowing he would find Noah here. The man seemed remarkably cool, at ease for someone who was wanted for a long list of crimes committed during the war. Noah had to resist the urge to draw his gun, take the man into custody at once. Instead, he forced himself to be patient, to wait for Pike to tip his hand.

"Tell me, Pike," Noah said, "have you finally acquired a conscience? Have you come to turn yourself in?"

"Turn myself in for what?" Pike asked blandly. "It was a war, Noah. You can't fault me for what I did. I was simply on the losing side."

"I'm not talking about what you did to me. There were other men, men who died."

"Like I said, it was war."

"Except that you weren't on either side. You even betrayed Quantrill. When I was in the hospital recovering from your bullet, I heard you went after a Rebel gold shipment. You ambushed the guards and stole the bullion. You killed eight men, Pike. You had them disarmed, bound and gagged, but you went from man to man and shot each one of them in the back of the head."

"Rumors, rumors," Pike demurred, waving a hand dismissively. "You can't arrest a man over rumors."

"I've heard other rumors that claim the four men who helped you rob that shipment have all died too—more lead poisoning."

"A heartbreaking condition, to be sure." Pike turned away from the animal skins. "But not one I'm likely to fall prey to. I've always been a most careful man, a very tidy man. I don't leave loose ends."

"You left me."

Pike's cool facade crumbled for just an instant. "A mistake that will one day be rectified, I assure you."

"There are other mistakes out there too. No one's that tidy, Pike. I'll find those mistakes, and you'll hang."

"I don't think so." The smirk was back. "You see, the government has a code of ethics all its own. It seems they were very interested in that gold bullion. And while I assured them I had no idea how it had come to be in my possession, they were more than willing to make a deal for its return."

"A deal?" Noah felt a sudden sick dread.

"Our dear government, it seems, was much more interested in the gold than in the eight poor fools who were safeguarding it." Pike spread his palms wide to show that he had no weapon, then reached carefully into the inside pocket of his jacket and withdrew a folded sheet of paper. "This is my freedom, Noah. My own personal Emancipation Proclamation. You can't touch me. No one can."

Noah stared at the paper, a very official, very authentic-looking document. Amnesty, a full pardon. Washington had traded eight lives for a few pounds of gold.

"My soul has been wiped clean, Noah. Uncle Sam has decreed that I am to go and sin no more." Pike laughed, almost giddily. "Go and sin no more. My pappy used to say that to me all the time when I was a boy. He was a preacher, you know. A real hellfire and brimstone proselytizer. He used to practice his sermons on me, did I ever tell you that? He'd beat me and scream that I was a terrible sinner, that I must repent or be damned. Some nights he'd even hit me with his Bible. One night I told *him* to go and sin no more—and I sent him to hell with a shotgun." There was an unholy light in Pike's eyes. "It's one of my fondest memories."

"What made you decide to sin no more at Fort Laramie, Pike?" Noah gritted.

"Why, I should think that would be obvious. I wanted to be near my best friend, Noah Killian. That's why I bought this very store. I'm the new sutler. We'll be seeing quite a lot of each other." He raised his hand and preened the greased-back layers of his hair. "No doubt I'll be seeing a lot of a Miss Katherine Dodd as well."

Noah stiffened. "You go near Katherine and I'll kill you. Your amnesty be damned."

"Now, now, is that any way to talk to one of Katherine's newest friends? I introduced myself to her not more than an hour ago and told her you and I were of long-standing acquaintance. She very graciously invited me to attend her birthday soiree tonight." His eyes glinted dangerously. "She even promised me a dance."

Noah gripped Pike's shirtfront, his face bare inches from Pike's own. "You heard me. You touch her and you're a dead man."

Pike only chuckled. "That's where we're different, you and I, *Captain Killian*. You'll choke on your code of honor first. You won't do anything to me as long as I'm . . . well behaved.

It's not in you. And I assure you, I'm going to be quite well behaved. Especially where Miss Dodd is concerned."

It had been all Noah could do not to rip the bastard's heart out. And if he had known what was to follow, he would have. Better that he be hanged himself for murder than to have let Pike live to spread his poison into every life he touched.

But Noah hadn't known, and when he'd finally gathered enough evidence to stop Pike legally for new crimes he'd committed, Pike had apparently gone to diabolical lengths to stop him.

Memories of the massacre pressed in on him, and Noah shoved them viciously away. He sat on his bed in the Cuttersville hotel and trembled, his body now drenched with sweat. His night of passion with Belle had gone for naught. He had not kept ugly memories at bay. But for the first time in a long time, he was glad.

In fact, Noah liked the budding sense of purpose he was feeling. He was suddenly anxious for Langley to be here. If Pike was alive, Noah would find him and once and for all send Pike to join his father in hell.

Crossing to the washstand, Noah gave himself a cursory sponge bath, then pulled on his denims and socks. His gaze traveled with a distracted affection to Belle Whitley, still sprawled across the bed in all of her naked loveliness. She was snoring softly. Noah crossed over to her and gently tugged the sheet up to cover her. He might as well let her sleep until he was actually ready to leave.

Returning from a quick trip downstairs, Noah was pouring fresh water into the basin for his shave when a knock sounded on the door. His mouth twisted ruefully. It was dawn. Maybe Vic Langley did know how to tell time after all.

Torey stood outside of Noah Killian's room and fought an almost overwhelming urge to flee. How was she going to face

Killian alone? How was he going to react to her without Eli as a buffer between them?

Somehow yesterday in Eli's room, she had managed to bluff her way through her first official encounter with Killian, even as her thoughts had time and again swept her back to their first unofficial encounter in the Take Your Chances Saloon. Unwanted memories of being in his arms, feeling his kiss, had driven her to say things to him yesterday that in retrospect horrified her.

One pronouncement in particular had haunted her long into the night . . . *seventeen men died because you cared more about your own skin than theirs.*

How could she have baited him like that? Taunted him with the deaths of his men?

She had spent many hours in her own room later wondering if she had finally taken Vic Langley too far. If her interpretation of being a man had become so twisted, it had given her a license to be cruel. But that wasn't it. Being brutally honest, she would not have behaved as she had yesterday with Killian if he had been as her mind had pictured him—a grizzled old war-horse, an ill-used veteran, wrongfully accused of a heinous offense.

Instead he had been the dark-haired stranger—the man from the saloon and the man from her nightmares. From that instant on, everything had changed. Noah Killian, the real Noah Killian, had had no chance.

She had treated him wretchedly because he had wrapped his arms around a saloon woman in a red silk dress, a saloon woman who had voluntarily whispered in his ear that she would meet him in his room. She had treated him wretchedly because her dreams had put him in the indefensible position of trying to rape her, and somehow she had made Noah Killian responsible for her dreams.

In neither instance had she been fair. In neither instance had she been right. And so, as she had strode over here this morning, she had had a short but firm talk with herself. No matter how difficult it was, she was going to march into Killian's room, greet him on level ground and treat him as she would have treated the grizzled old warhorse friend of Eli's that the man should have been. She would be straightforward, respectful, and tolerant of the man. Killian was a human being. He deserved that much. It wasn't his fault he was a good thirty years shy of being old. And as for grizzled . . . Well, maybe if he made it to the far side of one hundred.

Nor, she realized with a grudging reluctance, was it his fault he was so annoyingly handsome either. And solidly built. With those incredible storm-gray eyes . . .

Torey cursed, deciding on the spot that her first order of business was to stop thinking of Noah Killian as a man at all. She was Vic Langley. Enumerating another man's attributes was not a character trait she would ascribe to a tough bounty hunter, unless those attributes could help her in her search for Pike and the others. Attributes like strength, cunning, and quickness with a gun. The ability to track a sand flea in a dust storm. Now those were the worthwhile qualities she should be on the alert for in Noah Killian. Whether he looked like a tree stump or a Greek god didn't matter, she told herself. Finding Pike was what mattered.

That settled, Torey took a deep breath, raised her fist and knocked, hard.

"You don't have to bust it down," came the surly grunt from inside the room. "Come in. It's open."

Straightforward, respectful, and tolerant, she reminded herself firmly, and opened the door.

Her breath escaped her in a whoosh. Killian was standing bare-chested over his washstand, his denims riding low over his lean hips, a towel slung carelessly over one shoulder. He gave her a cursory glance and she noted the right side of his face was lathered with creamy white soap, while the left side was already clean-shaven perfection. His long hair hung in dark waves tinged with silver at his temples, skimming the tops of his shoulders to caress his sweat-damp flesh. At she continued to gape at him, he reached up to touch his hair in a gesture that was almost sheepish. "Not exactly a military cut, eh, Langley?"

Think grizzled old war-horse, Torey thought desperately. *Grizzled. Old.*

Like Adonis. Or Hercules. Or Lancelot.

Stop! "I . . . I thought you'd be ready," she said. "You told me to be here at dawn."

He shrugged. "Long night."

"So it's all right for you to be late, but it's not all right for me?" She made the comment solely as a defense because she was absolutely unable to take her eyes off him.

"Dawn is a more inexact time than two o'clock," Killian said in a slightly mocking tone. "But if it makes you happy, then yes, I'm late and we're even."

"I'm not looking to start another argument, Mr. Killian."

"Good. Because this time you wouldn't win."

His words suggested that he had conceded some sort of victory to her in yesterday's verbal battle. The thought was not comforting. She had already lambasted herself for her behavior yesterday. This further proof that she had indeed wounded him with her cruelty only added to her shame. Her only consolation was that she had been trying her damndest to erect some kind of barrier between them to ward off memories that wounded her as well. Not wanting to inadvertently start any new battles, she kept her mouth shut, but continued to watch as he scraped the razor in quick, rhythmic strokes along the corded muscles of his neck.

"Hoping I'll slit my throat?" he drawled, angling a glance at her, though he did not turn his head from the mirror.

Torey jumped, yanking her gaze away from him and riveting it on the floor. "Of course not, I . . . " She straightened. "I . . . I mean, I wouldn't want the maid to have to clean up the mess."

He chuckled. "That's some chip you got on that narrow shoulder, boy."

"I don't recall asking your opinion." She couldn't just concede the upper hand to the man. She had to seek some kind of balance between them. Her problem at the moment was how to maintain eye contact with him when he was half naked. Her gaze slid away from him only to collide with the rumpled sheets of his bed. She was appalled to find herself wondering if he slept in the raw.

Marching to the window, Torey tried looking out on the street below, but the glass hadn't been washed since the place was built. At least the window didn't have a rippling chest and gray eyes . . .

"So you ready to ride out with me?" Killian asked. "Sure you'll be safe?"

Torey couldn't suppress a tiny gasp. Safe? She looked at him. Did he know? Suspect? "I . . . what do you mean?"

"I mean you'll be riding with a coward, a deserter." His words had a false lightness to them, and there was a definite wariness in those wintry eyes.

Torey was only relieved that he'd been making no veiled reference to her being a woman. "Eli trusts you, Killian. That's good enough for me."

"You really like the old man, don't you?"

"He's been a good friend."

"He was a good friend to me too." For once there was no sarcasm in Killian's voice.

"Before we head out, I'll have to stop back at Miss Mamie's to say good-bye. Eli was still asleep when I left."

Killian made short work of the lather on his upper lip. "He told me you haven't been able to find out much about Pike's movements these past few months."

"No. It's like he vanished, like he doesn't exist."

The thought that he didn't was clearly etched on Killian's face, but he said only, "He always was a pretty crafty son of a bitch."

"Eli told me what he did to you in the war."

A muscle in Killian's jaw jumped, whether at the memory of Pike's bullet or the notion that Eli had been talking about it Torey couldn't have said. Either way, she couldn't let his anger deter her. Still, her voice was just a shade more tentative as she continued, "Eli also told me a little bit about . . . about Fort Laramie."

Killian's eyes glittered dangerously, but Torey plunged on. "Do you think . . . I mean, could we find any sort of clues to Pike's whereabouts if we went—"

"No!" he cut in. "Absolutely not. Pike's dead and buried as far as the army's concerned. A trip to Laramie would be pointless."

"But—"

"I said no."

"Look, Killian," Torey said, trying hard to sound placating, "I know a trip there would be difficult for you, but if it leads to—"

Killian was in Torey's face, so close that she instinctively shrank back. "I'll say it again, Langley." He spoke harshly. "In English. No trip to Fort Laramie. If that's where you're headed, you can make the ride by yourself."

"All right," she managed. "All right. I'm sorry."

"Don't bother," he snapped, spinning away from her and grabbing up the towel to wipe the remaining lather from his face. "Like I said yesterday, we don't have to like each other. We just have to find Pike."

Torey winced, stung by his censure. He'd misunderstood, but trying to explain that she had only felt empathy for him would, she was certain, just make things worse. "I need to talk to you about . . . about how we're going to go about this hunt. There are others of Pike's gang we need to go after too. Cole Varney. Cal Grady. And one other whose name I don't know."

"I just want Pike," Killian gritted. "I don't give a damn about the others."

"But they're murderers, ra—" she stopped herself before she said "rapists," uncertain why she had. "Rabid dogs," she finished. "They need to be brought to justice."

" 'Justice,' " Noah snorted. "Now there's a fine word."

"You don't believe in it?"

"I believe one thing about it. Justice is most certainly blind. Sometimes deaf and mute as well."

"Are you protesting your innocence, Mr. Killian?"

He straightened, his eyes hard. "I'm not protesting anything, Langley," he said. "And you'd do well to watch your mouth if you want to keep all of your teeth over the course of this little trek of ours."

Torey blanched, taking a step back. "I . . . " Damn, why was she forever provoking this man? "Eli said that you and Pike were fr-friends once," she stammered. "Did you know him well?"

"Obviously not. But at least now I know not to turn my back on him. Unless I want the scars to be symmetrical."

Torey ground her teeth, telling herself she was just going to have to get used to this man's ill temper and black sense of humor.

"That gun on your hip," he said, nodding toward it. "You can aim it, but can you shoot it?"

She stiffened, touching the walnut handle. "Anyplace you say, anytime you say."

"Fine. We'll check it out on the trail after—"

Torey nearly jumped out of her skin at the sound of a low moan coming from the direction of Killian's bed. Her jaw dropped as a blond woman pushed herself groggily up to a sitting position from underneath those rumpled sheets. "Noah, darling . . . " the woman murmured, "where are you?"

"Mornin', Belle." With a grin that was at least moderately embarrassed, Killian made the proper introductions between the sleepy woman and Vic Langley.

Torey could feel her eyes going wide as saucers.

Belle Whitley stretched and yawned, the sheet dropping away to reveal her more than ample bosom.

Noah ambled over to the bed and with seeming negligence drew up the sheet to cover her. The gesture seemed inconsequential, but Torey had the odd impression he had done it out of respect for the woman's privacy. Belle was not yet awake enough to fully comprehend that there was another "man" in the room. Torey was annoyed that such a trifling bit of kindness would affect her so.

"I—I didn't realize you had a guest," Torey stammered. "I'll go say good-bye to Eli while you and . . . your lady friend . . . do whatever it is you do of a morning."

Noah's grin grew more lascivious. "Jealous?"

"Certainly not!"

Noah chuckled. "Right. When's the last time you had the pleasure, Vic?"

Torey straightened to her full height, forcing down the heat that threatened to suffuse her cheeks. "Why, I'll have you know that I . . . I had company last night, thank you very much."

Noah laughed outright. "I'm sure."

"I did so," she insisted indignantly, for no reason she could fathom. "She . . . she was wearing a red silk dress. I didn't catch her name."

Killian stilled. "You were with her? You?"

"Yes. She was . . . she was very nice."

"Were you good to her?" His tone was unreadable.

"I don't wish to discuss it. It's . . . it's private." Oh, why had she ever stuck her foot into this one? But she'd only been trying to measure up to him, man-to-man. Damn. Those eyes of his were regarding her with a look that made her want to squirm, but she didn't dare.

"Did she seem . . . " Killian seemed curiously at a loss for words. "Did she seem all right?"

"Of course. Why wouldn't she be all right? Do you think

you're the only one who can do this . . . this . . . ?" She gestured helplessly toward Belle.

Noah stepped close to Torey, so close that she had to force her eyes not to focus on that broad expanse of chest, those dark hairs curling ever so enticingly across the upper half of his torso, then arrowing down into the waistband of his jeans to . . .

She dragged her eyes up to meet his. He was frowning, an odd look in his eyes. But then he seemed to shake himself. For no reason she could comprehend Torey took that moment to note that she and Killian were indeed the same height. Or she might even have him by half an inch. It was difficult to say for certain, since she was trying so hard to sink through the floor.

Belle was fully awake now, sitting up, fluffing her long, tangled mane of blond hair. She let the sheet slip from the breasts Noah had so considerately covered.

"Want to join us, boy?" Belle purred silkily, moistening the tips of her fingers and drawing wet circles around her tautening nipples. "Noah tells me you and him are going to be on the trail a long time. I can give you some good memories."

"No," Torey squeaked. "No, thank you." She had watched Killian's eyes darken with pleasure. Lust. Though he had the grace to look a trifle abashed at how brazenly the woman was behaving in front of an audience. Against her will Torey's gaze skittered to the front of his denims, where she didn't miss the all too obvious evidence of his physical response to Belle's erotic invitation.

To Torey, Belle gave an eloquent shrug. "Your loss, kid." Belle caught Killian's hand and urged him into the bed.

"What's a man to do, eh, Vic?" Killian chuckled. "Don't hurry your good-byes to Eli. I may be a while."

Torey fled the room, surprised that she didn't leave a trail of dust swirling in her wake. How could she have been such a fool? It wasn't just that she had to worry about Killian's *finding out* that she was a woman. With a man as blatantly male as Killian, as obviously active as he was in his sexual appetites, she was also going to be faced time and again with the equally distressing problems raised by the fact that he *didn't know*.

His behavior just now, while libidinous and disgraceful in Torey's mind, had nevertheless been prompted by the woman named Belle. Killian and Belle were consenting adults who could do whatever the hell they pleased. And quite frequently it would seem!

Torey stood outside on the boardwalk in front of the hotel and tried to collect her scattered wits. Had she been wrong to keep the truth from Killian? Should she have told him she was a woman, then done her best to convince him she was also a damned good bounty hunter?

No. Telling him would have presented two potentially disastrous complications. One, that he wouldn't take her at all. And two, that he might one day look at her the same way he had just looked at Belle Whitley.

Torey was certain she had done the right thing. She would just have to learn to avoid situations like the one upstairs, or at least extricate herself from them as quickly as possible. Because there had been a third unforeseen complication sparked by the events in Killian's room. One that left her mortified, terrified.

It had been her own body's response to that sinfully sensual look in those storm-gray eyes.

She had thought she couldn't trust Killian. Truth to tell, Torey was no longer certain she could trust herself.

7

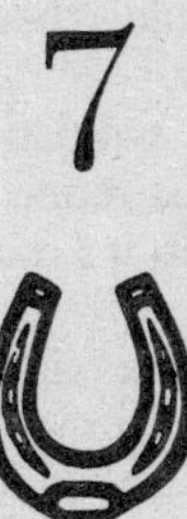

Torey sat on the ladder-back chair next to Eli's bed, her hands twisting nervously in her lap. She should have been concentrating on Eli, telling him how much she was going to miss him. Instead all she could think about was Killian and the heat in those gray eyes as Belle Whitley had pulled him into bed. "He's scary, Eli," she whispered. "He's so scary."

Eli's eyes narrowed. "Noah? Scary? Did he say something to you? I can't believe—"

"No, nothing. It's . . . it's hard to explain." She stared at her hands. "You wouldn't understand."

"Oh." He nodded in mock agreement. "I wouldn't understand. Well, let's see, that must mean it has something to do with his being a man, and your being a woman. Except that he doesn't know you're a woman."

Torey blinked, startled. "How could you—?"

Eli's mouth ticked upward amidst his bushy beard. "I'm not that old, Vic."

"I'm sorry."

"You are still a woman under all that muck you wear,

whether you try to deny it or not. And Noah Killian was quite the man with the ladies as I recall."

"He still is," Torey said, then caught herself. "I . . . I mean . . . I wouldn't know."

Eli's brown eyes grew sympathetic. "Noah had a guest, didn't he? Overnight in his room?"

Torey's lips thinned. "So it's that much of a long-standing habit, is it?"

"No. I have a feeling it's a fairly recent habit, taken up by a man whose whole world turned to ashes three years ago. Even more than you know. But before that?" Eli shook his head in wonder. "Before that Noah Killian had himself a way with the ladies, let me tell you. It was something to behold. They'd go all fluttery around him, like bees on a honey pot. Where most men get tongue-tied and stupid, Noah would be the Pied Piper, knowin' just what to say, what to do to make a woman feel pretty, feel special."

"In other words, he'd butter them up so he could have his way with them," Torey interjected.

Eli's mouth twisted. "Them clothes are goin' to your head, girl. With Noah it weren't no lies. He really cared about women. It was like he had the magic touch with 'em."

Beneath her shirt a sudden shiver skittered along the flesh of Torey's arms, and her heart skipped a beat . . . *magic touch.* Eli hadn't meant the words literally, but she wouldn't know it by the reaction of her body . . . *magic touch.* She rubbed her arms and cursed inwardly, assuring herself that there was no way she wanted that man to touch her. Ever.

"Noah could've had his pick of any woman, anywhere. I never understood why the blazes he picked one who—" Eli stopped abruptly. "I'm sorry, Miss Torey. Sometimes I forget myself with you in that outfit. This ain't no fittin' subject for me to be talking to a lady about."

"It's all right, Eli," Torey said, though she was still recovering from her ridiculous interpretation of Eli's whimsically meant *magic touch.* "Please. Killian and I are going to be spending"—she swallowed hard—"spending a lot of time together. I need to know this man as well as it's possible to know him. But he seems . . . he seems so very guarded, closed off. It makes me nervous not to be able to read his moods better."

She stood and paced. "I know I didn't help matters any yesterday with my big mouth. I'm surprised he's even agreed to ride with me. He's probably only doing it because of his high regard for you. He certainly doesn't have any regard for Vic Langley."

"It'll be all right, girl," Eli said gently. "Noah can be tough, but I've never known him not to be fair."

"That's not enough, Eli." She returned to the chair and sat down, leaning forward, her elbows on her knees. "I need to know more than that. And Killian's certainly not going to tell me . . . tell Vic anything about himself." Her eyes burned and her heart pounded. "You're right about my being scared to be a woman sometimes. I never even realized how right you were until . . . until a couple of nights ago."

Slowly, haltingly she told Eli of her humiliating encounter with Killian in the saloon, finishing with, "Most of the time, I don't even think about . . . about what I wear or how I look or how I feel about . . . about certain things anymore. But . . . oh, God . . . with Killian I don't seem to think about anything else."

Eli reached out and gave her hand an awkward pat. "He must have scared the living hell out of you, after what you went through at the farm."

She nodded, a tear tracking down her cheek. She couldn't tell Eli that what frightened her more was the part of her that had responded to the pain in those winter-gray eyes.

"All right," Eli conceded. "Maybe it's fittin' that I tell you what I know. If anyone can understand Noah and what drives him, I would think it would be you."

"Why?"

"Because," Eli said slowly, "Noah blames himself for what

happened to his men. Just like you blame yourself for bringing Pike and Varney down onto your family."

Torey bit her lip. She had never thought of it that way. "What was he like before the massacre, Eli?"

"He was a helluva proud man, arrogant some would say. But he had a right to be. Because he was good, damned good at what he did. In the war, he would've brought down Quantrill if not for Pike. Out in the West, though, things weren't so clear-cut. He wasn't sure anymore he was on the right side. He seen how hard the Sioux were fightin' for what had been theirs for a thousand years. He did his damndest to work for peace, but he was an army officer. He had a job to do. A job that was making him sick to his stomach sometimes. He was walking a helluva fine line, tryin' to stay within the army's rules and still get justice for the Indians. Noah Killian is a man who cuts himself no slack for mistakes. None at all. That's why the massacre was so hard on him."

"If he was working to get the army to see the Indian side of things, why would the Sioux attack him?"

"That's one of the things that's never made any sense to me about that day. Red Cloud was Noah's friend." Eli's brown eyes glittered angrily. "But Pike wasn't. I was always of a mind that those renegades attacked the patrol to get to Pike. Noah doesn't remember any of it. That whole day is a blank in his head."

"Kind of convenient, don't you think?"

"No, it isn't. Noah would sell his soul to remember what happened. That way he could get on with his life."

"And maybe Pike knows?"

Eli nodded. "I'd bet my eyes that bastard knows. I pray to God it was really him you saw that night . . . "

"But what if it wasn't? What if this Pike really is dead and Killian has his hopes up for . . . for nothing."

"Maybe helping you will at least give him something to grab on to. God knows, he can't go on the way he was when he first walked into my room two days ago."

Torey studied the pained look in Eli's craggy face. "Why do you care about him so much, Eli? There has to be more to it than his just being a good man. It's more like . . . " She faltered.

"Like he's my son?" he finished.

She nodded.

"I'd be mighty proud if'n he was. I never told you why I left the mountains, did I?" Those brown eyes took on a far-away look. "It was eight years ago. I lived in the foothills of the Rockies, near the Wind River range with my Blackfoot wife and two sons. Eight and nine, they were. I always called 'em my little men. When I was off trappin' and such, I'd tell 'em how they was to watch out for their mama, take care of her.

"I took 'em to visit her people one day, a small band camped just west of Fort Laramie. I left her there, her and the boys, while I went out hunting buffalo with some of the braves. The boys begged me to let 'em go along, said they were old enough to hunt buffalo with their father. But Morning Star—that was her name—she would've been awful lonely without 'em. So I made 'em stay." His voice shook. "I made 'em stay.

"While me and about five braves were gone, it happened. A young Blackfoot boy the army had took prisoner for stealin' a goat was sent home." Eli's massive body shuddered. "Sent home infected with smallpox."

Torey gasped. In that instant she knew where this story was going and she didn't want to hear any more, didn't want to know. But she had started this. She had no right to interrupt.

"Indians got no defense against the pox," Eli went on. "None. When we got back they were all dead. All of 'em. The whole band. Forty-three people. My wife had been one of the last to go. I found her by their graves." He paused, then continued, "She'd buried the boys with her bare hands.

"I hated God, hated everything and everyone. And then I

found out that an army surgeon passing through at the fort had deliberately inoculated the boy with the pox before the army sent him back. Deliberately given an Indian boy smallpox."

Torey made no attempt to wipe away the tears trailing down her cheeks.

"The army murdered them," Eli said. "Old men, women, children. My children. My boys.

"I went to the fort, looking for blood. I would've killed them all. Noah stopped me. Noah had just come to the fort. He hadn't heard what happened. He had no part in it. When I told him, he thought about joining me in killing them. But he said we had to do it right, so it would never happen again. He was so angry. He tried to have that army surgeon brought up on charges. Forty-three counts of cold-blooded murder. But the top brass wouldn't listen. They didn't believe him. More than that, they didn't care.

"Noah went over their heads. To Washington. To a couple of senators he knew. None of those responsible were ever court-martialed. But a couple were demoted, a couple others were killed in a raid by a band of renegade Sioux. The surgeon who inoculated the boy and sent him back to the tribe put a gun to his head and pulled the trigger. It's a good thing. He was the one man Noah couldn't have talked me out of killing."

"I'm glad Killian got you some justice at least," Torey said.

"But the fuss he kicked up made it awful easy for them bastards to take him down the first chance they got. It was their revenge for his goin' against his own kind." He drew in a shaky breath. "You can trust Noah, Miss Torey. He's in a lot of pain over them dead soldiers. But he's a good man. I swear it. On the graves of my boys, I swear it."

"I know this was very hard for you to talk about, Eli. Thank you." She leaned over and kissed him on the forehead, then stood. "I guess . . . I guess I'd better go."

Eli collected himself. "Yeah, you'd better. You don't need Noah giving you another lecture on tellin' time."

Torey managed a slight smile. "I love you, Eli Burkett. I'll write you when I think you've gotten to Denver, tell you what progress Killian and I are making."

"You'd best do more than write to me, girl. I expect to see you in Denver. You need to see Lisbeth. She needs to see you."

"If Pike's trail takes us that way," Torey hedged, "then of course we'll stop by."

Eli frowned, but reached for the saddlebags that lay on his bedside table. "Sheriff brought by the bounty for Jensen and Scott." He pulled out a handful of greenbacks.

Torey only stared at the money.

"Second thoughts about how we earned it?" Eli prodded.

Torey had indeed been thinking exactly that, but Eli's transparent motive rankled. She snatched the money from his hand. "They weren't men. They were animals. And I don't intend to stop until I've found them all."

"Whatever you say, girl."

She held out some of the money. "You'll need it to get to Denver."

Eli took only a few dollars, then shoved the rest back to her. "Noah didn't look too flush in the pocket. Don't want you comin' up short." He stuck out his hand. "Good luck to you, girl."

Torey bent over and gave him a swift hug. "I'll see you soon. You take care." She started for the door.

Eli's voice stopped her. "One more thing—"

She looked at him.

"If Noah should happen to find out you're . . . you're not who he thinks you are . . . "

Torey tensed.

"I didn't mean what I said about him wringin' your neck. I was just tryin' to get you to be honest with him. If he finds out, you'll be fine. He might be mad, but he won't hurt you.

Not ever. He's a man a woman can feel safe with, safe being a woman."

She nodded her understanding and left.

Outside Eli's door, Torey paused, trembling, uncertain if the mountain man's stories about Killian had made things better for her, or worse. Maybe she should have clung to her harsher earlier judgment of the man, when she'd heard of his conviction for cowardice and desertion. This sympathy, this empathy—heaven save her—this *admiration* she was feeling after hearing what he had done for Eli, only added to the terrible sense of confusion the man stirred in her whenever she went near him.

She had to get her focus back, remember what had brought her and Killian together in the first place—a mutual hatred for a man named John Pike. She had to remind herself, too, that as long as she maintained her guise as Vic Langley, she was indeed safe from Killian, safe from herself. As Vic Langley she would never have to deal with any absurd or imprudent notions that might cross her mind about Killian as a man. She assured herself that was exactly the way she wanted it.

Feeling calmer, more resolute, she collected her saddlebags from her room, then headed for the livery to fetch her horse and Killian's. Once there, she thanked Moses Johnson again for his help with Eli. Then she went looking for Killian.

She found him on the boardwalk in front of the hotel, Belle Whitley's arms draped over his shoulder much like his towel had been earlier. They were both laughing, both walking just a little unsteadily. Killian was at least fully dressed now, as was Belle, if Torey could call what the woman was wearing a dress. It must have been stitched up by the same lecherous degenerate who created the red silk monstrosity that Torey had been subjected to. The woman's bosoms were practically spilling out all over Killian's shirtfront. The heroic images Torey had been conjuring about the man just minutes before vanished in a haze of disgust. Her mouth grim, she marched over to them.

"You come back anytime you want, Noah Killian," Belle purred, trailing her fingers between two closed buttons on Killian's gray cotton shirt. "You're always welcome in my bed."

Noah squeezed several dollars into Belle's palm. "I'll do that, lovely lady."

Torey's insides twisted. *Lovely lady*. So it was just a meaningless pet phrase he used for all of his bought and paid for whores. Torey dug her fingernails into her palms, telling herself it didn't matter, that she didn't care.

But she did care. Damn his hide. She did care.

"Let's get going, Killian," Torey snapped.

"Don't rush a man when he's making love to a beautiful lady," Killian said, feathering kisses along the delicate curve of Belle's jaw.

"I wouldn't. Except I don't see any ladies around here."

Killian's head snapped up. "Watch your mouth, Langley."

"Maybe I should," Torey shot back. "You sure as hell aren't watching yours."

Killian stiffened.

"It's all right, Noah," Belle said soothingly. "I can handle a wet behind the ears pup like this one any day." She gave Torey such a long, hard look that Torey feared for just an instant she might somehow have aroused the woman's suspicions. But then Belle merely sniffed disdainfully in Torey's direction. "I don't need no bounty hunter passing judgment on my virtue."

"No," Torey allowed, "I think you've pretty much done that for yourself."

"That's enough, Langley," Killian gritted. "I mean it." He gave Belle another nuzzle on her neck and Torey felt her own flesh grow hot. Unconsciously, she reached up to touch the spot where Killian's lips had once brushed against her own throat.

"You're in an all-fired hurry to mount up, Langley," Killian said with his usual sarcasm. "You got any notions which way we're headed?"

"As a matter of fact, I do. I talked to Moses Johnson over at the livery, when I picked up the horses. Moses thinks Varney was headed north. He remembered seeing one of the others, too, a man who talked with Varney a couple of times. From the description I'd say it was Grady. Moses even thinks Varney may have forced Grady to trade mounts with him. Varney's horse had a stone bruise on its right front hoof that needed rest, which might put Grady within reach."

Torey grinned. "Moses was also foresighted enough to put a little triangle-shaped nick in that horseshoe. 'Just in case somebody wanted to follow that fella,' Moses said. The only other information I have on Cal Grady was that he robbed a church up in Rimrock last summer. Maybe he's on his way back to make another collection."

"Did you say *Cal* Grady?" Belle asked, a sudden nervousness shading her blue eyes. "What do you want with that bastard?"

"Do you know him?" Torey demanded, the possibility of getting information on Grady instantly allowing her to set aside any animosity she felt toward the woman.

"Nothing I'd tell you about, bounty man."

Killian pulled her close. "Would you tell me?"

Belle smiled. "I'd turn in my sainted mother for you, Noah." Her smiled faded. "Grady was a son of a bitch. He slapped me around. I told him to leave, but that only made him madder." Her voice grew whisper soft. "He . . . he raped me."

For just an instant Belle's haughty facade slipped, and the fear and humiliation in her blue eyes reflected exactly the emotions that had been in Lisbeth's eyes that horrible night five months ago.

"I'm sorry," Torey said, and meant it.

Killian had not let go of Belle. The look in his eyes was

flint hard, dangerous, yet with an undercurrent of compassion for Belle so real, so fierce that Torey had to look away.

"Grady said I could count myself lucky I was still breathing," Belle said. "If you catch him, put an extra bullet in him for me, will you?"

"Maybe you might want to consider a new line of work, Miss Whitley," Torey said.

"Right, mister. I'll get me a job as a schoolmarm next term." She laughed shakily. "What I'm doin' isn't so bad when I get me a customer like this one." She traced a finger along Killian's jaw then over to those full, generous lips. "He knows how to treat a woman. Oh, my, does he ever."

"You take care, Belle," Killian murmured. "One day I might be back."

Belle's eyes misted. "No. You won't be back. Some fine, upstanding lady is going to snatch you up soon, and she'll never let you go." Belle smiled a tremulous smile. "I know I sure wouldn't."

Killian's grin had an edging of pain to it. "There aren't many fine, upstanding ladies who would have me. I'm not exactly a prize catch, you know."

"Oh, you're a prize, Noah Killian. You are a prize indeed. Any woman that wouldn't have you is the biggest fool God ever made."

"Spare me," Torey spat. "Both of you." She said the words harshly, fearing that if she didn't she was going to start bawling, so touched was she by this hard-edged woman's obvious affection for Killian. "If you two are finished slobbering all over one another, you might even consider getting your butt up on your horse, Killian. We've got a job to do." With an oath, she mounted Galahad and spurred the gelding northward out of town.

In minutes she heard the thunder of hoofbeats behind her along with a string of curses, blessedly snatched away by the wind. She considered urging Galahad into a run, but decided she and Killian had best have this out now. She reined the gelding to a halt.

"What the hell's the rush?" Killian shouted, reining in beside her, his bay gelding bumping haunches with Galahad's. "I had a good mind to just let you ride off to bloody blazes by yourself."

"I'd have muddled through somehow."

His mouth tightened. "You are one stubborn cuss, you know that, Langley?"

"I've heard."

"What the hell is eating you anyway?" His voice almost grew cajoling. "It's going to be long time between towns. And Belle Whitley is a woman who knows how to keep a man's nights stocked full with memories."

"You mean she gets paid to know," Torey said, unwilling to let any new sympathy for the woman get in the way of setting a few things straight with Killian.

Noah shrugged. "So?"

"So a decent woman would never offer her favors in exchange for money!"

Noah laughed harshly. "Maybe Belle's just more forthright than a *decent* woman. But all women have a price of one kind or another for their . . . favors."

"You're a real cynical bastard, you know that?"

"What's the matter, Vic," Noah taunted. "You only do it . . . *for love*?"

"I don't do it at all!" she snapped indignantly.

Noah's dark brows shot up in astonishment. "So the truth comes out, does it? I thought that story you told about you and the woman in the red dress sounded a bit farfetched. She didn't seem like your type."

"What does that mean?"

"She'd want a man, not a boy."

Torey squirmed in the saddle. They were talking about her! This was crazy. "I don't need your advice in that area, Mr. Killian."

"Sure you don't." Those gray eyes regarded her much too closely, and then he grinned. "You're a virgin, aren't you, Vic?"

Torey turned away, but not before she felt color rise in her cheeks.

"Well, I'll be damned." He slapped his knee, chortling. "Why didn't you say something? Belle would have been happy to . . . initiate you. Your rites of passage, so to speak. But don't you worry, we'll get that little inconvenience taken care of in the next town we come to. There's nothing to be ashamed of."

"I'm not ashamed," she hissed. "And just how much of a man does it take to do what . . . ?" She bit off the words, terrified she'd already said too much. "Leave it be, Killian! I mean it."

His eyes narrowed with a sudden curiosity. "Whatever you say, Vic." Shifting in the saddle, he reached behind him and flipped open one of his saddlebags. From it he extracted a half full bottle of whiskey. Torey watched as he yanked out the cork with his teeth. In a mock salute, he hefted the bottle in her direction. "Breakfast."

With lightning swiftness Torey snatched the bottle away and heaved it toward a boulder some dozen feet from the edge of the trail. The bottle hit its mark, shattering into a thousand pieces, its amber contents runneling across the rock face like so many tears. "You work for me, you work sober," she said, her thoughts ricocheting to the drunken attentions of a dark-haired stranger.

But Killian was not burdened by such memories. His gray eyes glittered with murderous fury. His bay gelding snorted, sidestepped under the savage grip Killian now had on the reins, the savage grip Torey suspected he also had on his temper.

"Let's get one thing straight, Langley," he snarled. "Right here and right now. You don't tell me what to do. Ever. I don't work for you, and you don't work for me. We're both after Pike. That's all. You ever cross me like that again, and I'm gone. I'll ride out and you won't see me for the dust. You got it?"

Long minutes passed as they sat astride their fidgeting horses and glared at one another. Finally, it was Torey who relented. "I'm sorry. I should have asked you not to drink. I had no right to throw it away."

Her words seemed to mollify him somewhat. The anger in his eyes abated, if just a little. "Just so we understand each other."

With that they began riding again, setting the horses into a ground-eating lope. Killian rode ahead of her, but not too far.

"Whiskey's not good for you, you know," Torey called out to him.

He looked back over his shoulder, his eyes unreadable beneath the dark brim of his Stetson. "I don't need any temperance lectures, thanks."

Torey let the subject drop. She had to be careful that she didn't arouse the man's suspicions regarding her gender. It wasn't as if she believed in the abolition of spirits. She'd even taken a nip or two of her father's homemade brew on occasion herself but found she didn't much care for it. In fact, it gave her a headache. Maybe Killian didn't get headaches. Or maybe he considered them worth the price. She supposed he did have some memories to drown.

They rode in silence for a while, Torey taking the time to study the surrounding terrain for the first time since leaving Cuttersville. They were on a north-northwest heading, angling toward Rimrock. In actual distance the town was nearly two hundred miles from Cuttersville, and the profile of the land made the going difficult at times for horse and rider alike. Forests of pine, spruce, fir, and silver-stemmed aspen blanketed the higher elevations into which she and Killian rode, the trees broken up here and there by grassy mountain meadows. The air was a delight—clear, crisp, heavy with the scent of pine—and pleasantly cooler than Cuttersville. She guessed, at their present pace, it would likely take up to ten days or more to reach Rimrock.

Torey sighed, pondering how abysmal those days could be, if the first hours of the journey were any indication. Hopefully, she and Killian would settle into some sort of routine fairly quickly and not get on each other's nerves any more than absolutely necessary. Most of the compromising and conciliation, she was certain, would be up to her. Partly because as a onetime army officer Killian was a man used to giving orders. And partly because she was the one who desperately needed to maintain her deception.

Toward noon they reined in beside a tiny rill and dismounted to rest and water the horses. Torey too was grateful for the respite. Killian had kept them to a faster pace than she was used to and she was tired, though she'd rather die than tell him that.

She took a long drink from her canteen, then refilled it with the cool, bracing water from the mountain-fed stream. Hobbling Galahad to let him graze, Torey was thinking about retrieving a hunk of beef jerky from her saddlebags to appease her rumbling stomach, when it hit her—one more unforeseen complication of riding trail with Killian, one that sent a real alarm ripping through her. She shifted uncomfortably, realizing she needed to answer a call of nature.

Worrying her lower lip, she shot a covert glance at Killian. How in the world was she going to—?

To her horror, Killian was obviously feeling a similar urge. The man was unbuttoning his fly! With a barely suppressed squeak of panic, Torey wheeled toward her horse and made an elaborate pretense of rummaging through her saddlebags, all the while humming as loudly as she could, because she didn't want to hear anything! Lord above, this arrangement was never going to work. It was only natural that Killian would have no modesty about his bodily functions. To his mind, he was a man on a hunt with another man.

Oh, Eli, what have I done? Torey thought miserably, leaning forlornly against Galahad. Already Killian had demonstrated in a half dozen wildly different but equally distressing ways that riding trail with him was not going to be at all the same as it had been with Eli. Eli had been paternal, deferring, considerate. More important, Eli had known she was a woman and had behaved accordingly.

Noah Killian was a dangerous, unpredictable man. Irritable one minute, amused the next. And he was laboring under an almost indefensible handicap. He did not know he was traveling with a woman.

Torey recalled his reaction to her snide remarks to Belle Whitley, and how quickly Killian had come to the woman's defense. This was a man who could be crass, even vulgar in the more relaxed company of other men. But in the presence of a woman Noah Killian operated under a different set of rules. Sober at least, he was a gentleman, a gentleman with standards of conduct he would not compromise with a member of the opposite sex.

How would he react if he ever found out the truth about her? Torey could only cringe, imagining the poor man thinking back to all of the things he had said and done in front of her. Embarrassed wouldn't begin to encompass what he would feel. He would kill her. He would simply toss her off the nearest cliff and be done with her. And Torey wasn't entirely sure she could blame him.

But she'd been through all that, and her position hadn't changed. Her duplicity was necessary. In fact, she was more convinced than ever that she'd made the right decision. Killian's sensibilities be damned. With a resigned sigh, Torey marched toward a stand of trees. Let him think whatever he pleased about her prudish habits. It was better than having him learn the truth.

When she returned a few minutes later, she was delighted to see that he had built a fire and was making coffee. Maybe she had been fretting over nothing. Maybe he hadn't paid the least bit of attention to her brief absence. She sat across from him at the fire and reached for a coffee cup. She made the mistake of making eye contact with him. One look in those eyes and her notion of not having been missed vanished. The man was pure eaten alive with curiosity.

"You are one persnickety bounty hunter," Killian mused, pouring himself a cup of coffee. "Or were you just afraid you wouldn't *measure up* to a real man?" His smirk left no doubt as to his meaning.

"That isn't your business," Torey snapped, outraged.

"I wouldn't have laughed," he assured her in that infuriatingly sarcastic tone of his.

"Maybe I'd be the one laughing," she spat back, the look in his eyes assuring her that *no, she wouldn't*. "Besides," she added hotly, "for all I know you fancy boys."

This time Killian threw back his head and roared with laughter. It was a full minute before he recovered himself enough to speak. "If I did fancy boys, Vic," he managed, grinning from ear to ear, "I guarantee you—I still wouldn't fancy you."

"And why not?" Torey demanded, unaccountably insulted.

Killian was still chortling. "For one thing, you're a bit too scrawny for my taste. For another, you're too damned bossy." He gave her one of his lazy, killer smiles. "You see, I like to run the show in the bedroom."

"Meaning the woman doesn't have anything to say about it?"

"Oh, she has plenty to say. Allow me to quote . . ."—he affected an enraptured look—" 'Don't stop. More, more.' " He was laughing again. "Why, I remember one time down in Waco there was this little redhead with a body that—"

"Stop it!" Torey's cheeks were burning. Hell, her whole body was on fire. Killian was doing it on purpose now.

He seemed to sense, however, that she'd had enough. "Don't worry, Langley," he drawled, "I don't really give away my bedroom secrets. I just like watching you twitch. I don't know what it is about you, kid. You're like an itch I can't reach, and you're driving me loco." His smile softened. "If you ever do want any pointers about how to . . . encourage a woman to enjoy her own body, you let me know."

Torey scrambled to her feet and stalked off. She was going to drop dead. Drop dead from sheer embarrassment, she was certain of it. For long minutes she tromped along the edge of the stream, just trying to work off the effects of her mortifying conversation. Is this how men really talked to one another? If it was, she was never going to survive this journey, not unless her ears turned to rawhide. At least, she reasoned, she'd managed to parry his words for a little while. She just had to get better at it. And now was as good a time as any. Drawing in a steadying breath, she headed back to the horses and Killian.

The fire was out, and he'd packed up the coffeepot and cups. He was sitting on a boulder, apparently waiting for Langley's return. He looked up at her, his eyes unreadable.

"Sorry," he said. "I went too far. I didn't mean to make fun of you. It's just been a helluva long time since I . . . " He shook his head. "Never mind."

"Since you had a good laugh?" she prodded ruefully.

He looked sheepish, but nodded.

"I'm glad I serve some purpose for you," she said loftily, but she was grateful for the apology.

As they made ready to mount and head out again, she felt his eyes on her. She looked up sharply, expecting him to turn away. Instead he regarded her with an uneasy intensity.

"You are one curious puzzle, Vic," he said. "Prissy as a girl on some subjects. Yet cold as ice on others. Like John Pike. I get the impression you could put a bullet in his skull without batting an eye."

"And maybe I've got my reasons."

"Want to tell me about 'em?"

"No."

He shrugged. "Suit yourself."

They traveled steadily after their noon stop, only pausing for inevitable bodily needs. Thankfully, there was always enough cover about for Torey's purposes. If Killian had any further thoughts about her prissy behavior, he kept them to himself. She must have spooked him just enough though, because he made certain he found at least a boulder to duck behind whenever it was his turn, for which Torey was silently, but fervently, grateful.

Finally toward dusk he called a halt to their travels for the day. Among the tree-studded foothills, the sun would disappear quickly. As soon as the light had started to fade Killian scouted out a suitable campsite—a small clearing amidst a grove of aspen some hundred yards from an underground spring.

Torey could only gape at it. The tiny meadow amidst its natural cathedral of towering aspens was breathtaking, glorious. And in a different time, under different circumstances, she would have found it almost ethereally serene.

But Torey was not feeling serene. Even as she dismounted, her thoughts were roiling with images of the coming night, her first on the trail with Killian. How could she lie down, close her eyes, dare to sleep within arm's reach of the man? What if he—?

She jumped, startled, as he stepped up behind her. He was carrying his rifle. "You set up camp, Langley. Take care of the horses, start the fire, the coffee. I'm not in the mood for jerky again. I'm going to get us some real meat. I'll be back in an hour."

Torey managed a weak nod. The man could move like a stalking panther. She watched him check the load on his Winchester, then stalk off into the trees.

Quickly, she set about doing everything he'd told her to do, if only because the activity kept her mind occupied. It wasn't long before she heard a single report from his rifle. Her stomach growled, and she hoped whatever he'd caught had enough meat on it to feed them both. As she waited for his return, she finished getting the camp ready by tossing his bedroll on one side of the fire, while her own she unrolled on the opposite side. She would manufacture as much distance between them as she could and still benefit from the heat and protection of the fire. With the advent of darkness, the temperature would drop considerably.

Rubbing her arms, Torey glanced toward the thick growth of trees into which Killian had disappeared. Mr. Punctuality was nowhere in sight, and it had been at least half an hour since she'd heard the rifle shot, over an hour since he'd left camp. Had he only wounded some beast and been forced to track it to make the kill? She frowned. It was getting too dark to track anything.

The sheltering canopy of trees seemed suddenly not so sheltering. Her thoughts, no longer occupied with readying the camp, were doing her peace of mind no favors. She sat on a fallen tree and stared into the writhing flames. What if Killian was playing some sort of trick on her? What if he had figured out she was a woman and was merely waiting for full darkness to let her know what he thought of her deception? He could come pouncing out of the trees without warning. Or, God forbid, he could disable her with that rifle anytime he—

A twig snapped somewhere behind her. Torey dove in front of the tree fall, using the dead aspen as a barricade between herself and the forest beyond. Heart pounding, she yanked her Colt from her holster and tried to pick up the precise direction of the noise she'd heard, furious with herself for having been so witless as to stare into the fire. It took several dangerous seconds for her eyes to grow accustomed to the inky darkness of the forest.

"Yo, the camp!" came a shout from somewhere off to her left. Torey thumbed back the hammer of the Colt. "It's me, Langley," the voice gritted. "Killian."

Torey wasn't reassured. She kept her gun trained on the sound of the approaching footsteps. Only when she saw that he was carrying his rifle under his left arm did she let down the hammer on the Colt. In his right hand he carried the carcass of some furry beast she couldn't yet make out.

He tromped over to her and tossed it at her feet. "I killed it, you clean it and cook it."

Torey made a face. Not at the prospect of cleaning the dead rabbit. She'd cleaned her share over the years. But cook it? Killian didn't know what he was asking. If only Lisbeth were . . .

Torey gasped, overwhelmed by the sudden, unexpected image of her sister bustling about her kitchen, smiling, dishing out a plateful of bacon and eggs for their father, an extra corn muffin for Torey, three extra corn muffins for Eli. Torey all but fell to her knees. Only Killian's curse kept her on her feet. Her head snapped up and she looked at him blankly, then forced herself to focus on that heavily shadowed face now awash with disgust.

"Don't tell me you're a squeamish son of a bitch too," he demanded.

Torey shook herself. "No," she rasped. "No. I'm not. I'll . . . I'll take care of it."

He continued to glower at her as she drew her skinning knife from a sheath in her boot. The man was testing her, and she'd best not fail. She'd already raised too many questions in those gray eyes today.

With a sniff of disdain she picked up the dead rabbit. "This should be enough for me to eat. What are you planning to do, Killian? Gnaw on the bones?"

His eyes narrowed, evidently wondering if she was baiting him. He must have decided she was, because he gave her a dismissive grunt and walked over to his bedroll.

Torey would show him. At least as far as she was able. She carried the rabbit and a lit torch from the camp fire to a place several hundred yards away. She didn't dare clean the carcass too close to camp, lest she tempt some other four-footed creatures to invite themselves in for dessert. By rights, Torey thought, they should eat at one fire, then make camp at another. But who was she to question the wilderness experience of Noah Killian? Besides, she was too exhausted to even think about moving the camp now. As long as they kept the fire going, they should be able to discourage unwanted guests.

She made short work of skinning and gutting the rabbit, then returned to camp. Killian was watching her from beneath the brim of his Stetson. He wasn't doing it overtly, but she knew his eyes were on her just the same. She resisted the impulse to toss the dressed-out rabbit into his lap.

As Eli had showed her many times, she arranged forked sticks on either side of the fire, then slid another, thicker stick through the carcass and hung it over the flames. She frowned. This was always the place where Eli had taken over, especially after his half dozen more-than-patient attempts to teach her to make something edible out of their catch of the day had failed miserably. Should she warn Killian? The man was likely as hungry as she was. To take a chance on cremating the poor rabbit, after it had so nobly given its life . . .

"I'm not much on the cooking end of things," she said.

He levered himself up and stepped over beside her, hunkering down bare inches away. She was aware of the musky man scent of him, all leather and woodsmoke. She watched his hands adjust the sticks and shift the rabbit from where she'd had it to a couple of inches farther above the flames. Her breath seemed to catch in her throat. She couldn't seem to drag her eyes away from those hands—strong hands, capable hands . . . gentle hands?

Hands that possessed a magic touch. Eli had told her so. *Magic* . . .

What would it be like to feel those hands on her? To have him touch her? To have him . . .

Torey bolted to her feet and ran blindly into the night.

"Did you burn yourself?" Killian called, a real concern

threading that husky voice. "Dammit, Vic, answer me." He rose and strode toward her.

Torey backed away. She couldn't look at him, couldn't let him see her face. No clothes, no trail dust, nothing could hide the shameful thoughts skittering through her mind just now. "I—I'm fine," she stammered. "Just a cinder. It . . . caught me on the cheek. Don't worry about it. You'd best keep an eye on the rabbit."

He stopped, still some ten feet from her. "You sure you're all right?"

"Fine. I . . . uh, I just need to . . . I need a little privacy."

That got him. Killian swore. "Maybe you should see a doctor the next town we come to, Langley. Your kidneys work too hard." With that he turned and stomped back to the fire.

Torey hurried into the trees, making her way through several yards of dense undergrowth before she found a tiny clear spot and sank to her knees. What was the matter with her? How could she be having such shameful thoughts about Noah Killian? She barely knew the man. And most of what she did know scared her half to death. To imagine his hands on her, imagine him touching her, wanting her . . .

She cursed under her breath. Hadn't she learned her lesson with Cole Varney and Jim Buckley? Hadn't she herself seen Killian in action with Belle Whitley? Whispering words of endearment to a woman that meant nothing to him. Nothing at all.

Just as Noah Killian meant nothing to Torey. He was a means to an end, she assured herself fiercely. A weapon to use in her revenge against John Pike. And that's all he was. If she had to remind herself of that cold, hard fact a hundred times a day, then so be it.

Torey pushed to her feet and looked back through the trees at the faint orange-yellow glow of their campfire. She needed to get back out there. She didn't want Killian traipsing through the woods looking for her.

Besides, she really was hungry.

Killian was slicing off chunks of rabbit meat and tossing them into a tin plate when she returned to the fire. Torey's mouth watered. It smelled delicious. She and Killian said nothing to one another as she sat down and helped herself to some of the meat, sucking in her breath when it burned her fingers. Gingerly, she bit into a fair-sized hunk. It tasted as heavenly as it smelled.

"You're a good cook, Killian," she acknowledged grudgingly.

"You should see me over a real stove. I make a helluva venison stew."

His voice was light, and Torey decided that perhaps he too had had enough of their bickering for one day. Instead of making her feel better, his friendly tone only added to her unease. She did not want to like this man, not as Vic Langley, and certainly not as Victoria Lansford.

She made no further effort to draw him into a conversation as they ate their meal together. And he seemed content keeping his thoughts to himself. When she'd finished eating, Torey forced an exaggerated yawn. "I think I'll turn in."

"Sounds good."

Suppressing her nervousness, Torey lay down and quickly cocooned herself in her blankets, then drew her Colt and settled it beside her head.

"Expecting trouble?" Killian drawled.

"You never know." She kept one eye on him as he crossed to his own bedroll and sat down. He took off his hat and raked a hand through the tousled mane of his hair. The flames from the campfire cast eerie shadows across that hard-angled face, making him seem somehow mysterious, menacing. Torey's pulses tripped and she chided herself for letting her imagination get the better of her. Killian might be a bad-tempered grouch, but he'd done nothing to threaten or alarm her.

She watched as he rolled up an extra blanket and propped it at the head of his bedroll to use as a pillow. But he did not lie down. Instead he dragged his saddlebags onto his lap and flipped one of them open. He reached inside, then hesitated, looking briefly toward Torey. She feigned indifference though she did not look away. With an annoyed grunt, Killian closed the saddlebags and lay down.

For long minutes Torey watched him through slitted lids, not daring to relax until she heard the deep, even breathing that told her he had fallen asleep. That he did so with relative ease surprised her. But then, why should he have trouble sleeping? He wasn't hiding anything. He wasn't deceiving her at every turn. And though he too had memories that haunted him, it was just possible that the trail they followed could eventually free him of those memories. There would be no such freedom for Torey.

She snuggled closer to the fire, but even the warmth of the flames did not heat the sudden chill in her soul. Memories. Nights on the open trail had always been the worst, the times when she too often relived the attack on the farm, wondering time and again what she could have done to prevent it, or once it started, what she could have done to alter its outcome. But it was only wishful thinking at its worst. Nothing could change what happened. Her father was dead. Lisbeth . . . Dear God, had Lisbeth made any progress at all in these weeks since Torey had left her with Aunt Ruby?

Torey had sent her aunt only a couple of letters in all this time, and then merely to report that her and Eli's search for a new homestead was proceeding more slowly than expected. Because of the nomadic nature of their quest, Torey had told Ruby not to try to write back. Nevertheless, Eli had more than once attempted to get Torey to send a wire to Ruby and wait for a reply. The last town they'd been in with a telegraph office some two weeks ago, he had pressed his point home harder than ever.

"You need to know how Lisbeth is doing," he insisted.

"I need to find the men that hurt her."

Eli snorted in disgust. "Sometimes I think you don't want

to know if Lisbeth's gotten better. Because then you might find out she's been asking for you, crying for you. And that would mean you'd have to give up this insanity of yours."

"Stop it!" Torey hissed. "Lisbeth isn't better. She'll never get better. Don't you understand that? And it's my fault. But I made her a promise, Eli. The day I fulfill that promise, that's the day I can face my sister again. And not before."

Eli had been hurt, angry, and when Torey had stalked off to question the town's sheriff, he had sent a telegram anyway. The reply had come two hours later. *Eli: Lisbeth is happy, serene. There has been no change. I am dreadfully sorry. My love to Victoria. Please bring her home soon. Ruby.*

Torey had been vindicated—and devastated. Right or wrong, she would continue the hunt.

But with his broken leg Eli was done, finished. In a day or two he would leave Cuttersville by stage bound for a connecting point on the Kansas-Pacific Railroad and from there on to Denver and Lisbeth. Torey had assured him that she would stop by and see them if at all possible. But she knew she'd just said that to placate him, ease his mind. It would be so much less complicated not to see him, not to see Lisbeth. Torey touched the handle of her Colt. Maybe if luck was with her, and she and Killian caught up with Cal Grady soon, got some word on Pike and Varney, maybe then—

A sound out of sync with the night caught her ear. Torey froze, listening.

It was Killian tossing fitfully, mumbling in his sleep. Torey pushed to a sitting position, eyeing him warily. Should she wake him? His features contorted and he almost cried out. He was dreaming and the dream was not a pleasant one. Torey caught snatches of words, though none she could make out. Except one, a name. "Katherine . . . "

Torey was still debating whether or not she should try to rouse him, when he let out a searing curse, then sat bolt upright, flinging back his blankets. His hair straggled damply across his forehead, and he was breathing in harsh, ragged gulps. Torey wasn't certain but he seemed to be trembling. She worried her lower lip. Should she say something? Ask him if he was all right?

Without so much as a glance in her direction, he went for his saddlebags. This time there was no hesitation as he pulled out a full bottle of whiskey. He wrenched the cork free and upended the bottle, taking a swift gulp. He gasped, then swiped at his mouth with the back of his hand.

Torey's heart thudded. She didn't dare risk his getting drunk, risk any kind of repeat of his performance in the Take Your Chances Saloon. "Looking for your spine in that bottle, Killian?" she demanded shakily. "What about all those stored-up memories of Belle Whitley that were supposed to get you through the night? Did you use them up already?"

Killian glared at her. "Maybe I didn't make myself clear this morning, Langley. I don't need a conscience. I already have one that works too well."

"Does it?" she pressed, her own fear prodding her to be reckless, even as she gripped her Colt under her blanket. How far would this man's temper take him? "What would your conscience have to say if Pike came riding out of that timber right now? You'd be no use to me in a fight. I'd be one more dead body for you to dream about."

For an instant she feared she had gone too far. That past a certain point Killian's temper controlled him, rather than the other way around. His hands were balled into fists, and Torey was terrified that he was going to attack her. What terrified her even more was that if he did, she would shoot him. But then he let out a harsh laugh and took another drink. "I don't know what Eli ever saw in you, kid, besides one helluva big mouth."

"I could say the same about you. Eli would never hide in a bottle of whiskey or use women for his own selfish wants the way you do."

"I don't use women."

"The hell you don't. You use them the same way you use that bottle. To forget."

"You're quite the philosopher, aren't you, Langley? And what are you trying to forget, courtesy of Mr. John Pike?"

"That's none of your business."

He gave her a cold smile. "I thought so." He took another long pull on the bottle, some of its contents dribbling down his chin. He didn't bother to wipe it away. "It's really too bad you didn't get the name of the woman in the red dress, bounty man."

"Why?"

"Because I'd like to know her name. It would give me something to call her in my dreams."

Torey lay stock still. *Varney didn't teach you. Pike didn't teach you* . . . "You'd treat her like you treated Belle Whitley, wouldn't you?"

"She wouldn't complain if I did."

"How do you know? Not all women have the stomach for . . . for that sort of thing."

He gave her a drunken grin. "That's because they haven't been with Noah Killian."

"That's quite a boast. Does *Katherine* feel that way?"

Killian's eyes went stone cold, his voice deceptively soft. "Who told you about Katherine? Eli would never—"

"You told me. You called out her name in your sleep. Was she a woman not taken in by your . . . charms, Killian?"

He closed his eyes, the fight seeming to drain out of him. "No. No, she wasn't, as a matter of fact. She was going to marry me until my court-martial. Then she told me—and I'm paraphrasing here"—he gritted cynically—" . . . to go to hell."

Despite her fears, despite everything, Torey's heart twisted at the pain in Killian's voice. "I'm sorry."

He shoved the cork back into the bottle and lay down, facing away from her. "Yeah, so am I."

Torey lay on her back and stared into the star-studded sky.

She had been angry, disgusted by Killian's drinking. Her fears too had been aroused by his suggestive attitude toward the woman in the red silk dress. But once again he'd turned it all around on her. Torey could see only too clearly what drove him, savaged him. Memories as haunted, as brutal as her own. And now it seemed the massacre had cost him not only his men and his career but the woman he loved.

Torey closed her eyes, determined not to feel sorry for this man, not to care. She couldn't, wouldn't. Considering her own circumstances, it was simply too dangerous. And yet right before she drifted off to sleep one thought thrummed through her mind over and over again—that whoever Katherine was, she was a fool.

8

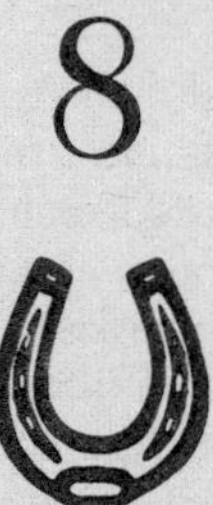

Noah let out a low curse, reining in his gelding at the edge of a rocky bluff. Beyond the steep ridge, forests of piñon, fir, and aspen spread out in an undulating wave of hills and valleys like some vast emerald ocean. Beautiful land. Magnificent land. And, Noah grimaced, very nearly impassable land. At least at any decent rate of travel.

It had been five days since he and Langley had left Cuttersville. Five days of grueling terrain for man and beast. And from what Noah could see, it wasn't going to get any easier.

He said as much to Langley when the young bounty hunter reined up beside him.

Langley swore. "There has to be a faster route. You're just not seeing it."

"We could fly," he drawled.

"Dammit, Killian—"

"Don't start." Noah hauled back on the bay's reins, turning the horse away from the ridge. He was in no mood for yet another lecture on their progress, or lack thereof.

Time and again he had tried to explain to Langley that Grady and Varney weren't making any better time than they were, but Langley wasn't listening. He was too busy haranguing Noah about everything from the lay of the land to the altitude, and when he wasn't doing that, he was haranguing him about his drinking.

This, even though Noah hadn't had a drop since that first night. Not out of any deference to the kid's tirades, but because he'd been so exhausted each night that he hadn't been plagued by his usual dreams about the massacre, and thus had felt no need for the whiskey.

He and the kid had fallen into a routine of sorts—eating, sleeping, and riding. The few conversations they had had usually wound up as an escalating exchange of insults, which Noah took more pleasure in than he wanted to admit. Bright, ornery, and opinionated, the kid could give as good as he got.

Noah cast a sidelong glance at his belligerent trail partner, noting that Langley had ridden his black gelding perilously close to the lip of the ridge. A slap to the gelding's rump and . . .

Noah chuckled, amused at his diabolical thoughts. He supposed he couldn't actually send the young bastard over the edge. After all, he didn't want to hurt the horse.

"What's so funny?" Langley demanded.

"You wouldn't want to know."

"Why are we stopping here? There's still a good hour of daylight left."

"I have this ridiculous custom," he drawled. "I like to know where the hell I'm going."

"What's to know? We're still heading for Rimrock, aren't we?"

"In general, yes."

"What does that mean?" the kid asked, his blue-green eyes blazing in his grime-covered face.

Incongruously, Noah found himself wondering if the kid had ever taken a bath in his life.

"You haven't gotten us lost, have you?" Langley went on.

"Rimrock's still out there," Noah said. "Three days, maybe

four. But I haven't been there for years. For all I know it may have dried up and blown away. It was never more than a handful of buildings, a played-out mine, a saloon, and a church."

"It has to be there."

"Grady could have been heading somewhere else."

"It's the only lead we have. We're going to Rimrock."

"Fine." Noah dismounted.

"Now what are you doing?"

"We'll camp here."

"But it isn't dark yet."

"An hour of daylight isn't enough to get us down this ridge. You want to break a leg or two, be my guest. I'm bedding down here."

Langley glared at him. "You really don't care if we catch up with them or not, do you?"

Noah briefly reconsidered sending the kid over the bluff. Instead, he sighed. "Rimrock's north and west. You want to go on alone, I won't stop you. If not, then take that rifle of yours and catch us some supper. It's about time you took a turn."

Langley bristled, evidently considering his options. Finally, he dismounted. "You're cooking whatever I catch."

"I wouldn't have it any other way. I prefer my food edible."

Muttering obscenities, Langley hefted his rifle from his saddle boot and stalked off into the timber.

Noah watched after him, shaking his head. Vic Langley had to be the most arrogant, pigheaded, obnoxious human being Noah had ever met in his life. Ill-tempered, rude, and possessed of a vocabulary as salty as Noah's own, Langley challenged every scrap of patience Noah had ever possessed. And yet there was something about him, something almost vulnerable, naive, that put the lie to much of the kid's swaggering bravado. It was a dichotomy that Noah had yet to figure out.

But then, there was still a key piece of the puzzle missing—the reason Vic Langley wanted John Pike dead.

Maybe in the next few days Noah would find that missing piece. Langley didn't know it yet, but they were closing the gap on one of the men from Cuttersville, the one riding the roan Moses Johnson had told Langley about. Noah's best guess would make that Cal Grady—the son of a bitch who had raped Belle Whitley.

Twice in the past couple of days Noah had cut sign that suggested Grady's mount was giving out. He hadn't told Langley, partly because the kid made him mad, and partly because he didn't want to get his hopes up. From the look of the tracks Grady was continuing to ride the horse rather than rest him long enough to let the animal heal. It was costing him dearly. His two-week lead had shrunk down to maybe three days.

When they caught up with the bastard, Noah intended first to have a talk with him about his treatment of Belle, and then, if the man was still breathing, Noah would happily let Langley have a turn with him. Until then—

A series of gunshots interrupted Noah's musings. Minutes later Langley returned to the camp carrying two dead rabbits.

Noah grimaced. "With all the shots I heard, I thought you brought down a dozen."

Langley colored under the grime on his face. "It's getting dark. Besides"—he tossed the carcasses at Noah's feet—"we're not going to starve."

"Not yet anyway. But now that I've seen how good you are with that rifle, I have to wonder what you can hit with that six-gun on your hip."

The kid touched the weapon's walnut handle. "Want to find out?"

"Don't tempt me on an empty stomach."

Noah set about preparing their supper, adding spices and wild onions to the rabbit for a more than tolerable stew.

Langley spent the time currying the horses, fussing and babying both of them as if they were overgrown pups. Another piece of a most curious puzzle.

"Food's on!" Noah called.

Langley gave each horse a final pat and headed toward the fire.

"You keep spoilin' my bay," Noah grumbled, "and he's going to want me to carry him, instead of the other way around."

"He's a good horse," Langley said. "What's his name? I never hear you call him anything."

"He doesn't have one."

Langley looked indignant. "How long have you had him?"

Noah frowned, trying to remember. "Couple years, I think."

"He should have a name." Langley gazed at the bay for a moment. "He's handsome. He can be Lancelot."

Noah snorted. "I'm not riding a horse named Lancelot."

"Why not?"

"It's too . . . too . . . " He groped for the right word, then gave up. "I don't like it."

"He should have a name," the kid insisted.

Noah rubbed his chin, looking at the gelding. "I don't suppose you'd settle for 'horse'?"

Langley actually looked hurt. Noah rolled his eyes. How had he gotten into this? "All right, all right. A name. How about . . . Bear? He's thick-chested and kind of brown-red. I saw a bear that color once."

Langley smiled, a warm, genuine smile. "I like it. *Bear* it is."

It occurred to Noah that that was the first real smile he'd ever seen on Langley. It made him look even younger than the eighteen or nineteen Noah guessed him to be. In fact, it almost made him look like . . .

No. Noah shook his head. Now he was being crazy. Maybe Langley had a point about his drinking.

They ate in silence, but for once it was congenial. As they were settling into their bedrolls for the night, Noah decided to use the rare tranquility to see if he could put any more of that puzzle together. "Okay, kid, I named my horse. Mind if I ask you a question?"

"What?"

"Why are you after Pike?"

Silence. No longer congenial.

"It might help to talk about it," Noah said.

"I don't need to talk about it," Langley snapped. "I eat it, live it, sleep it . . . " He clamped his jaw shut, then added brusquely, "I thank you for naming your horse. And now I'll thank you to mind your own business."

Noah considered pointing out that whether or not his horse had a name had been precisely Noah's business, but he held his tongue. Whatever memory Noah had pricked was obviously still pretty raw.

"Oh, and Killian," Langley said, "you'd best not be planning to drink tonight."

Noah's jaw tightened. So much for the lull in their hostilities. Noah resisted the urge to reach for the whiskey just to spite the ungrateful whelp.

He lay down and closed his eyes. The night sounds should have soothed him—a soughing wind, a preying owl, a distant, plaintive wolf. But they did not.

Damn Langley anyway.

The night pressed in, and so did the memories.

Memories of seventeen dead bodies. Tortured, savaged, mutilated.

As he had so many nights over the past three years, Noah tried to push the images away, but they persisted, intensified. The seventeen bodies had names.

Like Sergeant Shamus O'Reilly, fiery-tempered noncom, who could ride his men like a tyrant but be the first to hold their hands for everything from a broken bone to a broken heart. Noah identified him by the patch of red-orange hair that still clung to his crushed skull.

Corporal Ed Yates, a Reb still trying to win the war, only now his war was against Indians. He flaunted a Yankee bayonet scar like a medal of honor. It had still been visible on his arrow-riddled chest.

Private Billy Joe Brown.

Noah trembled. No more than eighteen, Billy Joe was a rebellious, smart-mouthed orphan who came to the army because he had nowhere else to go. The first day Noah met him, the kid—drunk and playing in a poker game for stakes way over his head—took a swing at him. Noah had not been in uniform.

"I thought you was the son of a bitch that tried to steal my horse last week in Cheyenne," the boy said, staggering slightly and running his fingers through a thick mane of white-blond hair.

"No," Noah said evenly. "I'm your captain."

"Oh," the boy said, "my mistake. I thought you was the son of a bitch *captain* that tried to steal my horse last week in Cheyenne."

Noah tossed him in the guardhouse.

And then Noah put him to work. He assigned Billy Joe to the worst details on the post—slopping hogs, mucking stalls, digging latrines. The kid took it all and came back for more.

Noah praised his work, and the kid beamed.

Noah upgraded Billy Joe's assignments and the kid thrived.

"Never seen the like," O'Reilly had said one day as Noah and the sergeant were watching Billy march smartly back and forth during a stint on sentry duty.

"What's that, Sergeant?" Noah asked.

"The change in that boy. I'd've pegged him for prison, for sure. He still gambles away his money every payday, but he's a good soldier, and he worships the ground you walk on."

"I just expect good work out of him."

"That's just it, sir. No one ever expected nothin' at all from him before. I swear, Cap'n, that boy would die for you, if'n you asked him to."

Noah shut his eyes. Billy Joe hadn't died *for* Noah, but because of him.

Billy Joe's face had been smashed, obliterated, his body disemboweled, emasculated.

Noah swallowed hard and tried not to think about the whiskey an arm's reach away in his saddlebags. "I'm sorry, Billy. So damned sorry."

Only now did Noah understand what it was about Vic Langley that had gotten to him. The same kind of "I dare you to give a damn" belligerence that had been in Billy Joe Brown—a bluff and bluster way of attacking life that masked the fears and hurts of a little boy lost in a grown man's body. Noah could only pray that Vic didn't meet a similar end.

God, what had happened that day? Why couldn't he remember?

He remembered too well the grief-stricken cries of the women when the patrol sent out to find Noah and his own patrol returned to the fort with only Noah.

He remembered too well the cold feel of the iron chains that shackled his ankles and wrists as he was led to the guardhouse.

He remembered too well the look of disillusionment and despair in Katherine Dodd's eyes as the court-martial rendered its verdict.

With a curse, Noah threw back his blankets and reached for the whiskey. He would take just one drink. Just one. He upended the bottle, feeling the amber liquid burn like fire all the way down to his belly.

But the memories didn't go away. They never did. What he really needed was a woman. For a few hours at least a woman would help him forget the faces and the names.

But not a woman like Katherine, who judged him and

found him wanting. And tonight, not a woman like Belle, a woman to be paid, pleasured, and forgotten.

What he wanted, needed in his life was a woman to love him, believe in him, even when the world did not. A woman to help him believe in himself again.

He laughed without humor. Did such a woman even exist?

Unbidden, he saw her then, in his mind's eye, as she had been that night in the Take Your Chances Saloon. His lady in red. She had been sad and lonely and frightened. Frightened even of him. Why?

She had not been one of Belle's women. He was sure of that now, though she had certainly dressed the part. If he hadn't been drunk, he could've followed her, helped her, found out what had made her so afraid.

He took another drink. Perhaps found out, too, what it would have been like to make love to her.

His loins tightened and he swore feelingly.

Throwing back his blankets, Noah cast a quick look in Langley's direction. The kid seemed to be asleep, but it was a fitful sleep. Noah rose, took his whiskey, and tromped off toward the trees. He had no idea where he was going. He only knew he needed to be alone.

A quarter mile into the stand of aspens, he found himself in the midst of a small clearing, a space where filtered starlight illuminated a patch of lush grasses. The grasses surrounded a shimmering pond maybe fifty yards in diameter, no doubt fed by an underground spring. Much of the greenery at the water's edge had been trampled or nibbled away by foraging animals.

Noah glanced back toward the camp, pleased to note it was no longer visible through the trees. He couldn't even make out the fire from here. Restless, pensive, he paced beside the water for long minutes, then finally forced himself to sit down. He picked up a stray pebble and tossed it into the still water, watching the concentric circles drift outward until they hit the mud at the pond's edge. He took another pull on his whiskey bottle.

He remembered taunting Langley about his last night in Cuttersville, telling the kid he'd spent the night with Belle to store up erotic memories, memories to get him through the long, lonely nights on the trail. Evidently, he'd used up his supply. Try as he might he couldn't even picture Belle's face.

Another face kept intruding, a face shrouded by misty, drunken recollection. His lady in red with her dark hair, full lips, and green eyes. He frowned. They had been green, hadn't they? He wasn't sure. But green would suffice.

God, her skin had been soft, so damned soft . . .

Muttering a quiet oath, Noah kneaded the tautening bulge beneath his denims, trying to ease the pressure, the ache, then he cursed and took another drink. The hunger, the longing were fierce in him. Staring into the dark water, he let his mind drift . . .

He lay in bed in the Cuttersville hotel, naked, a sheen of sweat dappling his taut, hard-muscled body. The room was dark, save for shimmering slivers of moonlight slanting through the open window.

Beside his bed, bathed in that moonlight, stood his lady in red. Her eyes were luminous, filled with passion and want. She had sought him out, found him, asked to be let into his room, asked too that he lie naked in his bed.

"Noah," she whispered, her voice husky, sweet, "Noah, I've waited all my life to be loved by you. All my life."

His body burned, ached. But he would wait, wait for her to touch him first.

Never taking her eyes from his, she reached behind her and worked the hooks on the back of her dress. Her face flushed, she let the material fall away, exposing her breasts to his heated gaze—small, high, firm, with coral-tipped nipples eager for his loving. She cupped her hands beneath the creamy mounds and offered them to him as though he were some pagan god and she were his virgin sacrifice.

He felt the bed give as she sank down beside him, guided one taut, erect nipple to his mouth. Greedily, he suckled, tasted, devoured, rejoicing in her whimpers of pleasure and delight. His hands roamed freely, wantonly. She was so exquisite, so perfectly made. He pushed the dress past her hips, let the garment slide to the floor. Gentle curves, long legs, a dark nest of curling hair at the apex of her legs—all enticed, excited, invited. He gloried in her nakedness, praised her, worshipped her with his hands, his mouth, his words.

"Teach me, Noah," she gasped. "Teach me to love you."

And he did. He guided her hand to the throbbing center of his manhood and tutored her in how to pleasure him. He cried out, his breath catching, and her eyes glistened with wonder and an answering need. "I want you, Noah. I want you to love me." Their mouths joined, and they kissed, long and hot and deep.

She writhed, moaned, begged. "Now, Noah, now. I can't bear it. Please . . . please . . ."

He raised himself above her, drove himself swift and hard inside her, felt her wet, welcoming folds envelop him, sheath him, consume him.

"All of you," he gasped hoarsely. "I want all of you."

She let her legs fall open wider, allowed him in deeper and deeper still.

"Your name, sweet angel," he whispered. "Please . . . tell me your name."

She said it then, but he didn't hear it. His whole body arched, convulsed, his release shuddering through him with a violence that rocked him to his soul.

She was his, his lady in red. She was his. For just an instant all was right with his world.

And then his world vanished. The room, the lady, everything was gone. And Noah was alone under a canopy of trees in the Colorado foothills, frustrated beyond bearing, stunned, scarcely able to credit the power of the fantasy he'd just lived through.

It had been so real, so real that for a moment he had been certain he could open his eyes and find her beside him.

But his eyes were open now, and she was not there.

Instead, there was an emptiness more profound than anything he had ever known.

Angry now, he stood up and abruptly, impulsively began to shed his clothes. The night air and the whiskey had failed to take the edge off of his passion, maybe a dip in the pond would.

The chill waters hit him like a fist. He gasped, sagging to his knees on the muddy bottom. The chill had indeed eased his lust, but it had done nothing to ease the ache in his soul.

Why? What had it been about the woman in red that had reached him, snared him, and refused to let go? Their encounter had ended in less than a minute, yet he had the oddest notion that it hadn't ended at all.

Where was she tonight? he wondered. Who was she with? Was she happy? Was she safe?

Or was she still sad and lonely and afraid?

If only he hadn't been drunk that night . . .

He cursed savagely. If he hadn't been drunk, what? Would he have followed her, cheered her, courted her, asked her to be his bride? Offered her a life with a convicted coward and deserter? No doubt she would have jumped at the chance. Noah Killian, answer to any woman's nightmares.

Son of a bitch. He should never have let his imagination roam free. He rose to his feet and waded out of the cool water. His reward for his night's efforts was to feel more empty and lost than ever.

Torey woke to the sound of Killian stalking away from the camp. At first she thought nothing of it, figuring he was just going off to relieve himself. But time passed, and he didn't return. Could he have gotten lost? Hurt? She considered both possibilities highly unlikely.

Her lips thinned. There was one possibility that wasn't unlikely at all. The man had gone off to get drunk, and he'd left the camp to avoid a confrontation with Vic Langley.

Damn him! He knew they were supposed to ride out after Grady at first light. Pushing back her blankets, Torey climbed to her feet. He wasn't going to get away with it this time.

Treading softly, not wanting to intrude on him just in case he really was answering a call of nature, Torey crept off in the direction he had gone.

She heard him before she saw him, a low curse that halted her in her tracks. Cautiously, she continued toward the sound.

He was sitting near the edge of a shimmering pond. Swiftly, Torey ducked behind the nearest aspen, some fifteen yards to the right of Killian's position. Better to know what he was doing rather than barge in and make a fool of herself. She watched and waited. A minute passed. Killian didn't move, and she began to wonder if for whatever reason he had merely taken up a new place to sleep.

And then suddenly, abruptly he stood. As she watched, astonished, the man began to unbutton first his shirt, then his trousers. In less than a minute Noah Killian was standing at the edge of that dark pond stark naked.

She told herself she needed to move, run, get away. Get back to camp at once. But even as she thought all of those things, she didn't move, nor did she turn away.

She couldn't breathe, couldn't think as she stared at the lean, hard perfection of Noah Killian's body. The moonlight only added to the sense of unreality that wove itself around her. It was as if she had turned to stone. Part of her was terrified, horrified, her mind slamming her back to the nightmare on the farm, when Varney, Pike, and the others had used their sex as a weapon to violate Lisbeth. But another part of her, a nameless, unidentifiable part was mesmerized, fascinated, transfixed by Noah Killian and that part of him that made him a man.

Torey felt her knees buckle, felt her bones seem to melt. Soundlessly, she sagged to the ground. She should leave. How dare she stay here, spy on him . . . But her muscles refused to obey her. She was trapped, snared, held by a force over which she had no control. She wanted to flee, to run, and yet she couldn't even bring herself to close her eyes.

Her own flesh grew warm, hot. There was a new moistness spreading between her legs, a strange, sweet ache at the very center of her being. He was apart from her, and yet in some ancient, primeval way they were not apart at all. What would it be like, she wondered, to touch . . .

Killian waded into the water.

Enough! How dare she? This was wrong. Dead wrong. What if the situation was reversed? What if he had come upon her in some private moment? She would never excuse his spying. Never.

Commanding herself to rise, Torey staggered back toward their camp, praying Killian would never know what she had done.

She collapsed near the fire, her body still shaking so badly she could barely function. But somehow she managed to cocoon herself in her blankets. *Please God, never let him find out. Please God* . . .

Minutes later she heard him returning, heard his footfalls halt near the fire. He was looking at her. She sensed it. And for a wild instant she thought he knew. But then he continued to his side of the fire and lay down. Only then did she start breathing again.

She was so confused, so lost. How could she have done such a thing? It had been almost as if she had suffered some brief insanity, a reaction to the ongoing denial of her own womanhood. For a moment out there tonight she had responded to Killian as a woman, allowed herself to feel a woman's feelings, to ache for the touch of a man.

Five months ago it would've all been so different if a man like Killian had come into her life. Five months ago she had been a normal, healthy woman, given to occasional longings she did not fully understand, dreaming of the day she would find the right man to help her explore those longings. But Cole Varney and his ilk had shut them all down. And that was, she assured herself, just as it should be. If she hadn't been flaunting herself, if she hadn't been so vain . . .

And yet, and yet . . .

To have been a woman in Killian's arms tonight, to have felt the power of his loving . . .

Torey shuddered. Enough!

Enough.

When was she going to admit it? Vic Langley was no transitory disguise to be discarded when Pike and the others were caught. Torey Lansford was dead. She never intended to be a woman again.

9

Noah winced, opening his eyes to a sun already well advanced in the eastern sky. Damn. Two hours of daylight wasted. He stretched tiredly, his head aching, his mouth dry as desert sand. It had been a helluva night. Even the bittersweet fantasy he'd enjoyed with his lady in red seemed a distant memory in the unforgiving glare of the morning sun. But maybe the night had had one benefit, he thought miserably. Maybe Vic Langley had been offended enough by Noah's latest ignoble bout of drinking to get on his horse and ride out.

Noah grimaced ruefully. No. The way his luck was running, he would turn around and find out instead that Langley had a twin.

"It's about time," came a cranky, raspy, annoyingly familiar voice from somewhere off to his left. "I was about ready to give up on you and head out on my own."

"I could pass out for another hour," Noah offered sarcastically, pushing himself to a sitting position but taking care not to look in Langley's direction, lest there really were two of him.

"Just get the hell up!" Langley gritted. "If you think I'm going to feel sorry for you, you're very much mistaken."

"Nobody asked you to," Noah countered churlishly, already regretting his attempt to engage in this verbal duel. Who had given anyone permission to use his head as a blacksmith's anvil anyway? "I need a cup of coffee."

"What's left of it is on the fire. In two minutes it'll be *in* the fire, unless you're ready to mount up."

"It's such a pleasure to be in your gracious company this morning, Vic," he sneered. "In fact, it was either wake up to your cheerful countenance or keep dreaming about the mutilated bodies of seventeen dead men. So I'm sure you can understand why I overslept."

"You're disgusting!"

Noah let out a harsh chuckle. "That I am, Vic. That I am. I'll give you credit for that much—you're one fine judge of character." He reached for the coffeepot, dropping it with a curse when the handle burned his fingers. "You could warn a person," he growled.

"Warn a grown man that a metal coffeepot sitting on burning hot coals might be hot? Never occurred to me."

Noah raised a hand in mock surrender, peering at Langley through heavy-lidded eyes. "Truce?"

Langley glowered at him, and Noah rolled his eyes. The kid was in a worse humor than usual. "What bee you got in your bonnet this time, boy? Mad because I didn't offer you a drink last night?"

"Most certainly not!"

Noah shook his head. "You know what you really need, kid? I swear, the next town we come to, you need to get yourself laid. Take the edge off."

Langley actually looked like he was going to faint. Noah frowned. He was never going to figure this kid out. And his head hurt too much to try.

"We need to leave," Langley said sharply. "Now!" The kid hunkered down beside the cook fire and with a gloved hand reached out and gripped the coffeepot. He poured out a cup of the steaming black liquid and shoved it in Noah's direction. "Drink it fast, then we ride."

Noah accepted the coffee gratefully, swallowing it down in two quick gulps. Then he made a face. "What the hell did you use for coffee beans, Langley? A pair of your dirty socks? Dammit to hell, can't you even make decent coffee?"

"It tasted decent enough two hours ago," Langley snapped. "But then you were too busy dreaming about dead bodies to bestir yourself, remember?"

With an oath Noah slammed down the coffee cup and pushed to his feet. An action he instantly regretted. His head reeled, and his stomach lurched. He shut his eyes in a vain effort to stop the world from spinning.

Behind him, Langley snorted derisively. Noah stiffened. He couldn't give the skinny son of a bitch the satisfaction of watching him be sick. Forcing one foot in front of the other, Noah staggered toward a stand of trees.

He didn't make it. Some six feet shy of the stand of aspens, Noah dropped to his knees and vomited.

Torey bit off a curse. She stared after Killian, her thoughts roiling with a mixture of disgust and despair. She had done her best to put the events of last night behind her, almost accepting Killian's drinking as punishment for her own unforgivable behavior. She had arisen this morning, determined only to press on in their hunt for Grady. But Killian, as usual, was being impossible. The man's late night drinking had now cost them precious hours of daylight. And his blasted hangover was squandering even more time. Maybe she damned well should just mount up, ride out, and not look back.

But she didn't. She was angry, furious, but she was no fool. She could survive in this wilderness. Eli had taught her that much and more. How to construct a shelter, hunt food, build a fire. But there was a difference between the raw skill of staying alive and the kind of knowledge men like Eli and Killian accumulated over a lifetime of wilderness experience.

Like how to follow a trail across terrain that appeared untouched by man or beast. Eli's uncanny knack for doing just that had kept so much pressure on Cleve Jensen and Wade Scott that the two outlaws had finally turned at bay to fight. Despite appearances to the contrary, Torey suspected Killian possessed a similar talent.

A sober Killian, that is.

Again she glanced toward the timber. She shook her head. At least the worst seemed to be over. Killian was still on his knees, but he was no longer retching.

As she watched, he lurched to his feet and turned in her direction, keeping the brim of his Stetson set low over his forehead. The attempt to avoid eye contact seemed deliberate as he made his way toward his gelding, his stride more than a little unsteady. Even beneath his deep tan, Torey didn't miss the dull red stain creeping up his neck.

Annoyed, she shrugged off a sudden pang of sympathy. He had gone four nights without drinking. Why had last night been any different? Had it been spurred on by his trip into the woods? She trembled. No, she wasn't going to allow herself to think about that! She had blundered in on a private moment. The more she dwelled on it, the more guilt-stricken she became. It was best not to think of it at all.

Besides, Killian's midnight swim was not the issue. Killian's drinking was the issue. She wasn't going to give a damn about his sensibilities. It had been his choice to get drunk. How many other mornings had his pride been a casualty to the excesses of the night before?

"Hurry up!" she snapped before any nigglings of compassion could get the better of her. "It's going to be sunset before you even get your horse saddled."

Killian glowered at her but said nothing as he stooped to collect his gear. Though Torey chafed at each passing minute, she made no move to help as Killian struggled with both his saddle and—judging from his expression—an apparently savage headache.

His first attempt to heft the saddle onto the gelding's back failed miserably. The second attempt succeeded, but he had to lean heavily against the horse for a long minute afterward. When he flicked a glance her way, she gave him a carefully crafted smirk. A fair response, she reasoned, considering his abominable behavior. Killian must have thought so too. He didn't even swear.

Maybe the man had actually learned something, she thought acidly. Maybe now they could be on their way and—

And then Killian flipped open his saddlebags and pulled out his whiskey bottle. Something inside her snapped. In a heartbeat Torey was hurtling across the dozen feet that separated them. "Damn it to hell!" she cried. "Not again!" Fists flailing, she slammed into him, tearing at him, grappling vainly for the whiskey that he held at arm's length.

For an instant she saw his gray eyes widen, startled and oddly perplexed, and then they narrowed with an icy fury that terrified her. But she did not let go of him. Her sole focus was that half full bottle of whiskey.

"God damn it, Langley!" he roared. "It's not what you—"

She pummeled him with her fists, one blow glancing across his jaw.

With a strength and swiftness that astonished her, he threw her off him, then whirled and backhanded her across the face. The blow stunned her, sent her reeling to the grass-covered earth. Torey touched her lip, tasted the salty sweetness of her own blood. Desperately she fought off the dizziness that threatened to overwhelm her. She dared not pass out. If she did, Killian would learn the truth, and she would be lost.

But even staying conscious didn't guarantee her safety. She had loosed a dragon. On her knees she tried to scramble away, but Killian advanced on her, his face a mask of rage. Terror pulsed through her. In her mind's eye she was suddenly back on the Lansford farm, her father's body crumpled, lifeless, her sister brutalized, John Pike coming at her, his black eyes Satan's own. Torey went for her gun.

With a savage curse Killian's boot flashed out, connecting solidly with her wrist, sending the Colt flying. Torey bit back a cry of pain, even as she felt Killian's hands on her, felt him haul her to her feet, saw his fist arch back. "You're going to pay for that one, boy."

Instinctively she closed her eyes, as much against the bitter knowledge of her defeat as against the blow itself. But the blow did not fall. Instead, with another oath, Killian released her, shoving her violently away from him.

Torey stumbled back, awkwardly managing to stay on her feet. Out of the corner of one eye she spied her Colt lying in the grass some ten feet away, but she made no move to reclaim it. She was still trying to digest what had just happened. Killian had had every chance to overpower her, beat her senseless if he so chose, but he had let her go.

Expelling a shaky breath, Torey straightened and canted a glance in Killian's direction. His eyes were closed. His chest heaved. His fists clenched and unclenched at his sides. He was obviously still waging an all-out war with his temper, but his temper, she now knew, would not win. Even half-drunk Killian maintained a measure of control that surprised her. And somehow comforted her as well. She took a step toward him.

"Killian, I . . . I'm sorry. I shouldn't have . . . "

"Shut up! I don't want to hear it." He pressed a hand against his forehead. "Christ, you were actually going to shoot me."

"No! No. I just didn't want you beating me up."

"But it was all right for you to attack me."

She looked at the ground. "No," she said softly. "No, it wasn't. I don't know what got into me. I can only say I'm sorry."

He straightened, drilling her a look that chilled her blood.

"You ever come at me like that again, and you'll be even sorrier. Let's get something straight between us, Langley. Once and for all. You and I are riding together because we both want to find John Pike. But that doesn't mean either one of us has any say-so in the other man's life—not what he eats, what he drinks, who he sleeps with, or whether or not he goes to church on Sunday. You got that?"

She nodded meekly, though she cringed at his mention of bed partners, the words conjuring up all too vividly the image of a voluptuous Belle Whitley and the woman's seductive summons to a sleep-tousled Killian that he rejoin her in his bed.

She forced her mind from the thought. She might rail at Killian about his drinking habits, but he needn't worry that she would ever counsel him on his sleeping arrangements. She assured herself that the very subject repulsed her, that that was why her skin tingled, her mouth felt dry.

Momentarily distracted, she couldn't summon the energy to continue their battle of words. She could only watch as Killian yanked the cork from the whiskey bottle.

"Not that it's any of your business, Langley," he said, "but I wasn't planning to take a drink."

She grimaced, wincing when the movement aggravated her split lip. "Sure."

But Killian only swished a small amount of whiskey in his mouth, then spat it out.

"What was that for?" she asked.

"If you threw up before breakfast, you might want to get the taste out of your mouth too."

Torey closed her eyes. "Why didn't you say something? Explain."

"Before or after you tried to knock my teeth down my throat?"

She looked away.

He managed a mirthless chuckle. "At least I returned the

favor." He stepped close to her. "Here"—he offered her the whiskey—"dab some on that lip before it swells."

She took the bottle, but instantly wished she hadn't. She was now close enough and aware enough to see the beard stubble on that carved-granite jaw. She hadn't noticed it earlier when she'd been so angry. But she couldn't seem to take her eyes off it now. Her hand trembled slightly as she pulled a clean kerchief from her rear pocket. It trembled harder when she upended the whiskey bottle onto the blue cotton cloth.

Killian muttered a mild oath. "Let me do that."

Before she could stop him, he had the kerchief in his hand and was dabbing at the tiny gash on her lip. Reflexively, Torey jumped, sucking in her breath at the alcohol's biting sting. But it wasn't the pain that made her want to pull away. It was the sudden, intense curiosity in those wolf-gray eyes.

When he raised his hand as though to catch her chin, steady it, Torey panicked. It was one thing to be a young man and have precious little beard stubble; it was quite another to have none at all. She didn't dare let him touch her face. She snatched the kerchief from him. "I can manage myself, thanks."

Killian shrugged. "Suit yourself."

His nonchalance relieved her. Obviously, he still had no notion of her gender. But his next words started her heart thudding all over again.

"Who taught you how to fight, Langley?" he asked.

"Why?" she managed.

"I've never seen worse. I don't know where Eli ever came by you, kid, but you fight like a damned girl."

Torey coughed, choked, pretending the whiskey was to blame. "You won fair and square, Killian," she said, shoving the bottle at him. "But that doesn't mean you have to be insulting."

He snorted. "Right. God forbid I insult a bounty hunter."

Torey retrieved her Colt, the heavy pistol giving her a

measure of security as she jammed it into the holster on her hip. Was the man toying with her? Did he suspect the truth?

No, she assured herself. He couldn't. If he'd figured out that she was a woman, there was no way he wouldn't confront her, at the very least demand an explanation.

And yet . . .

He could be waiting for the right time, the right place.

To do what?

Torey shivered, forcing the thoughts away. She gathered up Galahad's reins and gave Killian what she hoped was an icy glare. "You can insult me all you want, mister, if it makes you happy. Just as long as you help me find John Pike."

The mention of Pike's name drove the humor from Killian's gray eyes. "Let's ride."

They both mounted, and Torey reined Galahad into step behind Killian's bay. No, she amended her thoughts, smiling slightly, behind Bear. At least Killian wasn't totally reprehensible.

She was so grateful to be on the trail again that she offered no objection when Killian veered them away from the game trail they had been following yesterday and instead led them down a boulder-strewn slope that appeared to have no particular passage to the bottom. Time and again Killian's attention seemed drawn to the sweeping grasses and rainbow-hued wildflowers that were the slope's primary ground cover.

Torey couldn't imagine what he was looking for. They couldn't expect to cut Grady and Varney's trail. Not after a two-week head start. To her mind she and Killian should just be heading for Rimrock at the fastest pace possible. They might not find the outlaws there either, but Grady's past connection to the town offered at least the possibility of picking up a lead.

Killian, though, kept their pace maddeningly slow. Even when they topped a rise and started down the other side, he held Bear to a walk. Time and again he would lean down, practically inspecting each blade of grass as they rode past. Torey grew frustrated, irritated. At this rate they wouldn't reach Rimrock before the first snowfall.

And then Killian reined in the bay and dismounted, stopping their progress altogether. Wincing slightly, he hunkered down beside the nearest boulder.

"God bless it, Killian," she snapped, "if you're going to be sick again—"

"Shut up!"

"I will not!"

"Are you interested in Cal Grady's trail or not?"

She frowned. "What are you talking about? Even Eli couldn't pick up a trail after two weeks. There can't be any sign left."

"It hasn't been two weeks since Grady was here. Come and look."

Torey clambered off Galahad and hurried over to Killian's side.

"Watch where you're walking," he said.

Torey looked down. All she saw was grass and a patch of larkspur. She shook her head. "I think you're still drunk."

"And I think you've still got a big mouth. But that doesn't change this." He swept aside a tuft of thick grass to point to a horseshoe-shaped depression in the dried earth. "This print was made maybe three days ago. It was muddy. The sun dried it out and left an impression just like a mold."

Torey felt a stirring of hope, which she quickly tempered. She and Eli had suffered dozens of false leads and mistaken trails before they'd been able to pin down Jensen and Scott's true course. "That print could have been made by any drifter passing through."

"The print was made by a horse favoring his right front hoof."

Torey squatted down to study the print more closely.

"That's why the impression is only half formed and shallow," Killian went on. "I saw a few similar tracks a couple days back. But the right front wasn't as clear as this one."

Torey worried her lower lip. "Anyone can have a lame horse."

"One with a triangular nick in the right front shoe, compliments of Moses Johnson?"

Torey finally allowed herself to smile, but still played devil's advocate. "Grady wasn't traveling alone. He left town with a man matching Cole Varney's description."

"There's no honor among thieves, Langley. Varney could have left Grady behind if he couldn't keep up."

"Especially if they had some planned rendezvous with Pike," Torey mused aloud. She stood up, unconsciously adjusting the Colt on her hip. She was excited now. "We have to catch up to whoever left this print. If it is Grady, and he's alone, he'll be that much easier to take."

"One step at a time," Killian warned. "We're still talking about a three-day lead. He could be anywhere."

"Three days on a lame horse? How far could he get?"

"Far enough to change horses. At some ranch house maybe. Or he could've even made it to Rimrock by now."

Torey's jaw clenched. Now that she had allowed herself to think that Grady could be within their grasp, she didn't appreciate Killian's negative remarks, no matter how much sense they made. She gathered up Galahad's reins. "Let's ride."

For just an instant she had the strangest notion that Killian was about to object, but then she dismissed the thought as nonsense. He had to be just as anxious as she was to find someone that could lead them to Pike.

"Remember," she said, mounting. "I want Grady alive. I want to talk to him."

Killian quirked an eyebrow at her. "Like you talked to Jensen and Scott?"

She didn't answer.

"Sorry," Killian said. "That wasn't fair."

"Forget it." Torey kneed Galahad forward. Killian's anger was disconcerting enough. But his sympathy? That she couldn't bear.

Blessedly, they rode in near silence the remainder of the morning, stopping only rarely to let the horses rest. At noon, they built no fire, settling for a meal of beef jerky and tepid water from their canteens.

It was midafternoon when Killian again stopped them. This time it was to inspect a trampled section of grasses a hundred yards east of a tumbling mountain-fed stream. Killian quickly surmised the area had been Grady's camp.

"My guess is he holed up here for at least two days," he told her, "finally trying to rest the roan."

"Did it work?"

Killian marched off several paces, hunkering down frequently to check the ground. In spite of their volatile relationship, Torey couldn't help but admire the man's talent, how he could so easily "read" the very earth itself. Grady—she would no longer allow herself to believe the man they trailed could be anyone else—might as well have left a map.

Killian rose and strode back to her. "The horse improved a little," he said. "But not enough. If he rode him very far, he likely broke down again."

Torey began to pace. "The fact that he keeps trying to ride a lame horse has to mean something, that he has a prearranged rendezvous with someone. If not Pike, then Varney."

"Seems logical."

"How far ahead of us is he now?"

Killian shrugged. "Not more than a day."

Torey made no effort to suppress a surge of sheer joy. A day! And a mount that could give out on him at any time. It was more than she could have hoped. *We'll get him, Lisbeth,* she vowed silently. *We'll get him, and he'll tell us where to find Pike and Varney. And then those two bastards will pay, pay for what they did to you, what they did to Papa.*

To Killian she said, "What are we waiting for? We have a chance, a real chance now. With three hours of daylight left we shouldn't be wasting a single minute."

To her astonishment, Killian shook his head. "I say we camp here for the night. There's plenty of good grass for the horses. Good water. We can get an early start in the morning."

"Are you out of your mind?" she gasped. "We could catch him. Maybe this very night."

Killian shoved his hands into the back pockets of his jeans. "We can't just go off pell-mell after a killer. We need a plan. We need to figure out how to go in, if and when we come across him. That is, if we don't want the tables turned."

"What are you talking about?"

"If he gets wind that we're tailing him, he could choose a spot, pick us both off before we knew what hit us."

Torey gave her head a violent shake. "Absolutely not. That son of a bitch can't outsmart the two of us. With your tracking skill we could come up on him before he even—"

"We stay the night here," Killian cut in. "And that's final. From here on out it just makes sense to be cautious."

Torey was so angry, she was shaking. "Cautious?" she choked. "I'm not making this ride to be cautious, Killian. I'm hunting murderers, beasts. And I'll do whatever it takes to find them. I thought that was the one thing you and I agreed on. That finding Pike was your goal too."

"It is."

"Then I don't understand."

"Maybe I don't either."

She shot him a quick glance and was surprised to see a flash of real misery in those gray eyes, misery that she perceived had nothing to do with the remnants of his hangover. Despite her almost overwhelming need to be after Grady, she found herself backing off. "What's wrong, Killian?" she asked, more concerned about this man and his troubles than she would have liked to admit.

"It's not your business."

She grimaced. It was the answer she expected. But she was not put off by it. "You might as well tell me," she said, careful to keep her voice at least moderately terse, lest he grow curious about the all too real compassion she was feeling toward him right now. "I can be one stubborn son of a bitch, remember? And I'm going to keep asking until you do."

He sighed wearily. "You would, wouldn't you?"

She nodded.

For a long minute he said nothing, and she wondered if perhaps he was going to try and out-stubborn her, then finally, haltingly, he said, "I don't remember what happened the day of the massacre."

She frowned. "Eli told me that. But I don't see—"

"What if I find Pike . . . " Killian began, then stopped. He cleared his throat, but the threading of pain was still there when he spoke again, a pain so deep it burrowed its way straight into her heart. "What if I find Pike, and instead of clearing my name, he only confirms the judgment of my court-martial? What if what John Pike knows proves I really am a coward?"

10

Torey paced in front of the fallen aspen on which Killian sat. "You're not a coward," she said fiercely. "That's absurd. You took on Quantrill during the war. You took on the army to get justice for Eli."

If she had expected him to be grateful for her sudden burst of support, she was quickly disappointed.

Killian's mouth curved into an all too familiar smirk. "Where were you during my court-martial?" he drawled. "I could've used a character witness with that much fervor. Who knows? With an outstanding citizen like a bounty hunter on my side, instead of settling for my dishonorable discharge, they could have just hanged us both."

Torey blushed and turned away, unaccountably hurt by his caustic set-down. Why had she been so quick to defend him anyway? she wondered. She'd practically sounded like some blasted zealot. Which was absurd. She couldn't answer the question he'd posed, any more than he could. *What if what John Pike knows proves I really am a coward?* "Dammit, Killian," she muttered stubbornly, "Eli would never have partnered me up with a man who couldn't stand up to a fight."

"That's quite an about-face, don't you think?"

"What do you mean?"

"Now let me see"—he rubbed a hand over his beard-stubbled jaw—"how did you put it back in Eli's hotel room? '*Seventeen men died because you cared more about your own skin than theirs*.' Is that about right?"

Torey blushed again. "I didn't know you then."

His voice was ice. "You don't know me now."

"Maybe I do, better than you think."

Killian stood and paced. "I don't need this bullshit. And I sure as hell don't need any phony consideration from you."

Torey stuffed her hands into her pockets. Damn his hide! She wasn't being phony. For a minute there, she had actually allowed herself to care about this man and his feelings. But she'd be damned if she'd tell him that. "Eli said we were of a kind, you and me."

Killian snorted. "Do I thank him for that or punch him in the jaw?"

She shrugged, her voice tight. "I was just wondering the same thing."

For an instant they just glared at one another, then Killian shook his head and laughed. "You're a spunky bastard," he said. "I'll give you credit for that. Not many men would have the balls to stand up to me the way you do."

Torey coughed, sputtered, the casual vulgarity catching her off guard. "Damned straight, I've got the balls," she managed, then when he shot her a quizzical look wished to God she'd said nothing.

Stomping over to Galahad, she made an elaborate display of getting herself a drink of water from her canteen, even as she tried desperately to slow the mad beating of her heart. Blast! How was it that time and again she and Killian could seem to converse, argue, even fight on level ground and then *wham!* a word, a phrase—a trip to the woods—and it would all come crashing down again, reminding her all too crudely that they were not on level ground at all. And it was she who had to constantly struggle to maintain her balance.

Hooking her canteen to her saddle horn, she shot him a wary glance. He had again perched himself on the fallen aspen, but, though he was looking her way, nothing in his manner suggested he had given any more than passing notice to her comment. Torey steeled her spine, forced herself to return his gaze.

His tone was wry when he spoke again. "How the hell did I ever get mixed up with a smart-aleck son of a bitch like you, Langley?"

Torey strode back over to him. "Lucky?"

His mouth twisted. "The same kind of luck I had the day I met John Pike, no doubt."

Her heart skipped a beat. It was an opening she had not expected. A chance to restore the balance. The better she knew this man, she assured herself, the better she could handle her reactions to him. Taking a deep breath, she sat down beside him on the fallen tree. "How did you meet Pike?"

At first she thought he wasn't going to answer, and then he surprised her. His voice was even, matter-of-fact, as he told her about West Point, about Pike's pretense at friendship, about his duplicity, his threats. The details were sparse—"We were in class together," "He panicked; he cheated," "He shot me in the back"—but Torey found herself filling in the gaps, and more than that, filling in Killian's emotions.

She hadn't known Killian long but she'd already seen for herself the fierce regard he held for loyalty, a steadfast—even bullheaded—allegiance to anyone lucky enough to be called his friend. It was, she suspected, what had made him a good soldier. It was also the very quality that had not allowed him to turn his back on Eli, no matter how much he might have wanted to when he discovered Eli's objective to be John Pike.

Killian went on to tell her of his postwar encounter with Pike at Fort Laramie and how the man had taunted him with his governmental amnesty. Killian's voice was now laced with disgust. "He paid for the lives of eight men with a wagonload of gold."

"I can't believe that," Torey said.

"It made me sick. I wanted to cut his heart out. But of course, I didn't." His disgust was self-directed now. "Not me. Not duty-bound Captain Noah Killian. I played by the rules. I accepted the will of my superiors and let him off scot-free."

"You had no choice."

"I had a gun."

"But you're not the judge and jur—" Torey stopped. That was not a direction she wanted this conversation to take. Thankfully, Killian went on.

"I knew Pike. I knew it wouldn't be long before he started a whole new list of crimes. I intended to be ready."

Torey realized she was holding her breath now, waiting to hear of the events that led up to the day of the massacre. But Killian's body had grown rigid, and as his recounting approached that fateful day he brought an abrupt end to his tale, finishing instead by telling her of Pike's proud confession that he had killed his own father.

"Why doesn't that surprise me?" she asked.

Killian tugged free a foot-long blade of grass and absently twined it about his fingers. "This is going to sound strange coming from me, and I know it doesn't excuse what Pike's done, but apparently his father spent most of his time beating the hell out of Pike."

Torey was not impressed. "He didn't succeed, did he?"

"No." Killian's voice grew thoughtful. "I think what his father did instead was to beat hell *into* John Pike."

Torey stared at him. "You're an amazing man, Noah Killian. And a much more compassionate one than I am."

He gave her a half smile. "Don't be so hard on yourself,

Langley. I've just lived longer." He looked past her then, his gaze sad, almost melancholy.

Torey was unnerved at how appealing he looked to her at that moment, how endearing. A strange heat threaded through her, and she had to drag her gaze away from his face. She told herself to get up, get away from him, but she couldn't seem to summon the will to move. He was so close, so damned close. What on earth had possessed her to sit next to him?

He was leaning forward, his arms resting lightly on his knees. His shirtsleeves were rolled up, and she found herself staring at the dark hair stippling his powerful forearms. From there her gaze trailed inexorably to his hands.

He was still toying with the blade of grass, idly twisting it about his long, tapered fingers. On any other man such hands might once have been considered elegant, a pianist's hands. But Killian's cultured Eastern upbringing had long since been overwhelmed by the physical nature of a life spent out West. His sun-bronzed fingers were marred by numerous tiny scars and his palms bore the calluses of a man who spent more time in the saddle than out of it.

Against her will, Torey remembered the feel of those hands as Killian had brushed his palm against her cheek in the Take Your Chances Saloon. Magic touch indeed . . . What would it have been like if those hands had been allowed to linger? What would it have been like if—

With a squeak of terror, Torey leaped to her feet and stumbled off several paces. What was she doing, thinking? When was she ever going to learn? She could not indulge the womanly feelings Killian was somehow stirring to life inside her. Not now. Not ever.

"What the hell's the matter, Langley?" Killian grumbled with surprising good humor. "Sit on a bug? Or are your overactive kidneys at work again?"

"Stay on the subject, Killian!" she snapped, wishing to

heaven she had taken her own advice. "You've stalled long enough. We need to get after Grady."

He shrugged. "Tomorrow's soon enough."

"No, it isn't!" she cried. *Not after I've been sitting here imagining what it would be like to have you touch me, feel your hands . . .* "We need to go *now*!" she said, barely managing to swallow a very un-bounty-hunter-like "please." "You want Pike as badly as I do, and you know it. Finding out what happened the day of the massacre has to be better than spending the rest of your life not knowing."

He seemed to consider her words, but said only, "We camp here tonight."

"Damn you—"

He cut her off with a wave of his hand. "You're right, Langley. I want Grady. But his tracks show he's close."

"All the more reason to—"

"All the more reason to stop. To think. We could stumble into Grady's camp tomorrow. Maybe it's the ex-soldier in me, but I need to know my enemy, and"—he looked straight at her—"I need to know my own troops, such as they are. Like just how good are you with that gun on your hip?"

"Good enough for this *trooper* to shoot rings around you, mister."

He grinned. "That's what I like about you, Langley. You're so humble. But somehow I can't picture you in a uniform. Not even the army could be that desperate."

"No, they'd rather have soldiers like you!" The words were out before she could stop them. She had meant no more than her usual insult, but the grin that had been on his lips vanished, and the look that flashed through those gray eyes reminded her of nothing so much as a once-proud stallion who had felt the bite of a quirt one too many times. She took a step toward him. "Killian, I . . . didn't mean . . . "

"Save it!" he snarled. "I knew that little speech about believing me innocent was just so much smoke."

"But it wasn't, I—"

"I said, save it. We both talk too much anyway." He rose and began tromping about their campsite, stopping here and there to heft stones of varying sizes, from mere pebbles to fist-sized rocks. When he'd gathered as many as he wanted, he returned to the fallen aspen and settled the stones in a haphazard line along its trunk. "It's time you let your gun do the talking, Langley."

Torey's shoulders sagged. She could accept his anger. She was used to it. It was his hurt she was having trouble with. Blast it all, she hadn't meant the words the way he'd taken them.

Or had she?

She thought about it, forced herself to be brutally honest. While Killian had been sharing his memories with her, she'd been unsettled yet again by an all too womanly reaction to the man. Her image of him as a drunken, cynical bastard had been turned on its ear. Yes, he drank too much. And he was as cynical as hell. But he was also tormented by a past as painful as her own. Time and again she found herself drawn to him, responding to him as a woman responds to a man. She had wanted to do more than have him touch her. She had wanted to touch him back.

And the thought, as ever, scared her to death. Better that he hate her than run the risk of exposing her charade. And yet . . . and yet . . . what would Killian think, if he knew?

"You going to stand there all day?" he asked.

Torey shook herself, only now noticing that Killian was waiting for her to follow him. She would think about her problems later. Quickly, she fell into step behind him.

When they were about fifty yards from the fallen tree, Killian turned. "You take the three stones on the left," he said. "I'll take the three on the right." As he said the words, he loaded a sixth bullet into the cylinder of his Colt. Just as she rode with the hammer over an empty chamber, so apparently did Killian.

Torey straightened, determined to get things back to some

semblance of normalcy between them. "Say when," she told him.

Instead Killian dove for the ground, rolled, and came up firing.

For an instant Torey was too startled to do anything; then belatedly she drew her pistol, but Killian had already fired off six rounds, hitting all but one of the stones.

"That wasn't a fair test," Torey choked, wrinkling her nose at the acrid stench of gunsmoke that now clung to the air all around her. "You didn't tell me you were going to—"

"That one stone I missed just emptied his gun into you, Langley," Killian drawled, already reloading his pistol. "I sincerely doubt Grady or Pike will trouble themselves to tell you before they start shooting."

"You lied." She shoved a sixth cartridge into her colt and reholstered it.

"You think Pike wouldn't?"

The smugness in Killian's gaze bored through her jangled nerves. "Cleve Jensen and Wade Scott didn't make any announcement before they started shooting at me," she gritted. "And I won that one, didn't I?"

"How do I know Eli didn't get them both?"

"Because I'm a better shot than Eli. I—" She stopped, suddenly sickened, appalled. What was she saying? Was she actually squabbling over bragging rights in the deaths of the two outlaws? Yes, they had tried to kill her. And yes, they deserved to be brought to justice for what they had done to her father, to Lisbeth. But to boast about it? Torey shivered, recalling how swiftly she'd veered away from any discussion of Killian's ambition to be John Pike's judge and jury. "They're dead," she finished tersely. "And I'm not."

Killian marched over to set up six more stones. "This time we'll do it your way," he said, reholstering his Colt. "On the count of three."

Torey stood beside him, heart thudding, determined now to prove herself.

"One," Killian began. "Two . . . "

Torey drew, fired, pulverizing one stone after the other. She didn't stop until she had dispatched all six.

Killian whistled his appreciation. Torey felt a ridiculous surge of pleasure.

"But I didn't say three," he said.

"Neither would Grady," she countered.

Killian nodded his approval. "You may be a son of a bitch, Langley, but you learn fast. And you're damned good with that gun."

Torey smiled, both at the insult and the compliment. Killian was obviously still smarting over her earlier remark about soldiers, but she sensed that he was softening, even giving her the benefit of the doubt. A prospect she found remarkable considering his sensitivity on the subject. She almost wished she had the courage to bring it up again, clear the air between them.

But that would hardly be prudent. She had come to recognize the value of a bit of lingering animosity between them. When she and Killian got along too well, she seemed bent on getting herself into trouble, jeopardizing her identity as Vic Langley. She would think about things she had no right to think about—like long, rein-callused fingers . . .

With an oath, she began shoving new cartridges into the cylinder of her Colt. "All right, I've proved I can shoot. Can we go now?"

"No."

"Why not?"

"We're not going to find a better spot to camp than right here."

"Dammit, Killian, Grady could be in Rimrock by now."

"And he could be holed up over the next rise."

Torey's jaw dropped. "Then we may have just given ourselves away!"

"Exactly."

"You thought of that?" She was flabbergasted. "Are you out of your mind?"

"If you heard all that shooting and were desperate for a fresh horse, what would you do?"

Her eyes widened, realization dawning. "I'd come and see who fired the shots and try to steal myself a horse."

"You're catching on, Langley. And since we have no idea whether or not we're about to have a guest, I suggest we get ready for one just in case."

Quickly Killian laid out his plan, even as they both set to work carrying it out. In short order, they had tethered the horses, built a fire, and arranged their bedrolls to look as though they were curled up inside them, asleep. They finished just as the sun began to disappear behind the mountains to the west.

Swiping at the sweat on her brow with her shirtsleeve, Torey stood back and surveyed their handiwork. She had to admit Killian's strategy was sound. In the flickering firelight Grady would have to get awfully close to realize the blankets were a ruse.

"You do good work, kid," Killian said. "Now all we have to do is get into position and wait." He started toward the cluster of boulders he had picked out as their sleeping quarters for the night.

Suppressing a flutter of alarm, Torey followed. She wasn't at all keen on the part of the plan that called for them to sleep away from the fire. But they were in Killian's field of expertise now, his expertise as a soldier, a tactician. She didn't consciously remember making the decision, but they were still a good twenty feet from the boulders when she suddenly reached out and caught his arm.

He stopped and looked down at where her hand rested on his sleeve. His expression was unreadable. "What is it?"

"I . . . nothing. Never mind."

He frowned. "Are you all right?"

"I'm fine, I . . . " She noticed she was still touching him

and abruptly snatched her hand away. "Let's get to those rocks, shall we?"

"What's wrong, kid?" Killian pressed, more concerned about Vic Langley than Torey would have liked him to be.

"Nothing." *Don't do it. Don't say it.* "I . . . oh, hell, I just wanted to apologize again for what I said earlier."

"Oh. Forget it." He was annoyed, but not as annoyed as she would have predicted he would be by her bringing up the subject again.

"No, I don't want to forget it. I want you to believe me when I say I didn't mean to hurt you."

He said nothing, his gray eyes seeming almost to be looking through her now.

Torey bit her lip. Why was she doing this? Hadn't she made up her mind that it was better for Killian to hate her than risk giving herself away? And her reference to hurting him. Was that a comment one man would make to another? For five months she'd stayed focused within herself as Vic Langley. And then she'd met Noah Killian. At every turn now she felt she was losing another little piece of Vic, that despite her protestations to the contrary, she wanted—needed—Killian to find out the truth. Which only made it all the more imperative that he did not.

"I'm sorry. I'm just sorry. All right?"

"All right." He was still regarding her much too curiously. Finally, he seemed to shake himself. "Come on, we'd best get settled in."

Torey's distress was not eased by what she found when they reached the rocks. She stared, panic-stricken, at the spot Killian had chosen for their overnight vigil. At the base of the haphazard arrangement of stone was a shallow depression that might once have been a den to some now long-absent wild creature. The depression faced squarely into their camp. It couldn't have measured more than six feet by four feet with a depth of barely a foot.

"Home sweet home," Killian pronounced.

"You can't be serious."

"It's perfect," Killian said. "Complete cover along with a direct view of the camp, including the horses."

"There has to be a bigger—I mean better—place."

"Not one that lets us see the whole camp and still not be seen ourselves."

"But—"

"Look, Langley," Killian said, obviously running out of patience. "I know it's cramped, but we need to stay together. If Grady shows up, I want to know where you are. We don't want to catch each other in a cross fire. As tempted as I might be at times, I really don't want to shoot you." With that he scrunched into the small opening and lay down. "I'm bushed. You take the first watch. Wake me in about four hours."

Torey swallowed hard. Just like that? Just like that, she was supposed to ease herself in beside him? She stared at the tiny space. No matter how hard she would try to melt into the sidewall of the den, there would be no room to spare. She would have to touch him, feel him against her, hard-muscled, warm, and dangerous . . . so dangerous. She shivered. Noah Killian, sensitive and caring, with a crooked smile that mocked the world but mostly mocked himself, could be far more dangerous to her this night than Grady or Pike.

But what could she say? How could she explain her reluctance to join him?

She gave herself an inward shake. She couldn't. Yet if she waited much longer, she was going to have to.

Gritting her teeth, Torey willed herself to crouch down. She would slide her left leg in first, then—

Her boot slipped on a loose stone. With a surprised cry she skidded forward and down, slamming full-length into Killian.

She heard the air explode from his lungs, heard him curse, but all Torey was aware of was the hard-muscled length of his body against her own. With a yelp of dismay she skittered as far away from him as their cramped quarters would allow. But still parts of her were pressed all too intimately against parts of him.

"For chrissakes, Langley," Killian snapped, rolling over to glare at her in the waning light. "You look as if you expect me to eat you alive. Believe me, I'm not that hungry. And the mountain lion that likely lived here is long gone. But I might try fetching him back, if you don't settle down."

"Go to sleep!"

"I'd be glad to, if you'd stop wiggling around like a dust devil in a windstorm."

Torey's fists clenched. He thought he had it bad? She was the one who was sleeping with the devil, a devil with wolf-gray eyes and a sensual mouth, a devil who smelled of wood-smoke and raw masculinity, strength and tenderness and passion. A devil whose heat seeped from the thin cotton layering of his shirt into her jean-clad thigh, sending spirals of something foreign, unnameable to her center, to lay there, heavy and frightening, seductive and impossible.

"Go to sleep!" she rasped again. "Please."

He sent her another unreadable look, then with an oath he shifted onto his left side, again facing away from her. This time he angled his hat down to cover his eyes.

For long minutes Torey didn't move, scarcely dared breathe. All she wanted in the world was for Killian to fall asleep, to end the awareness roiling inside her. If he would just sleep, she could calm herself, think clearly again.

More minutes ticked by, or was it hours? She didn't know. As much as she wanted to capture Cal Grady, she prayed the outlaw had been out of range of their gunfire, after all. As scattered as she felt, she would be no use to herself or Killian if Grady showed up now. If she didn't regain some measure of composure, she could even get them both killed.

She made herself take in long, deep lungfuls of air and concentrate on the tranquility of the night sky. The moon had come out and millions of stars twinkled overhead. Gradually, her pulses began to slow. She began to relax. And then Killian's voice nearly made her jump out of her skin.

"Heard anything?" he asked.

"You're still awake?" she squeaked. "How are you going to spell me if you don't sleep?"

"I need a drink."

"Oh, for God's sake . . . "

"Don't start. I said I needed one, not that I was going to have one." He paused, then came a quiet, "Ever been afraid to dream, Langley?"

"All the time." She said the words without thinking.

She could feel his eyes on her in the darkness, curious, intense. "What did Pike do to you, kid? And don't tell me it's not my business. I told you things about myself today I never told anyone. For some reason I decided it was important that you understand what drives me. I want to understand what makes a kid like you pick up a gun and go after a man like Pike."

"I don't want to talk about it."

"Might help if you did."

Would it? Would talking to Killian help her? Help rid her of the guilt, the hate, the deceit? She looked out into the darkness, their campfire flickering against the night like the faintest of hopes. She wanted to believe in Killian's soft voice, in the concern she heard there. Maybe if he knew why Vic Langley hated John Pike, he would be less inclined to wonder about Langley's occasionally unmasculine behavior, and more inclined to simply concentrate on helping Langley find Pike.

The words were slow, halting, agonized. "Pike and his men attacked my family's farm in Kansas. They killed my father, and they raped my sister, left her for dead."

"My God. I'm sorry. How long ago was this?"

"Five months."

"Stays raw a long time, doesn't it?"

She nodded, then realizing he couldn't see her in the dark, whispered, "Yes. Yes, it does."

"Too bad Lady Justice hasn't figured out how to hang a man more than once. You said they left your sister for dead. Did she . . . is she alive?"

"Yes, but Eli thought it best that Pike didn't know he'd left any witnesses. She's in Denver with an aunt. Eli should be there by now himself."

"You should have said something. We could have drifted toward Denver. It would've only cost us a day or two. You could have seen her."

"No. No, getting Grady's the important thing." She couldn't tell him that she couldn't yet face Lisbeth.

"Eli told me that you saw Pike, that you were a witness to what he looked like. But Pike thinks no one survived. Did they shoot you too?"

"No. No, I . . ." She had to be careful here, very careful. "I rode in afterward, when they were getting ready to ride out. I saw them. I saw them all. But they didn't see me, not clearly. They didn't know who started shooting at them."

"And you remembered them all?"

"I had seen them in town earlier. It was my fault they even knew about the farm."

"How do you figure that?"

"I . . . I had met Varney in town. I was with my other sister, Torey. She didn't mean it, but . . . but she kind of flirted with Varney. They must have followed her home. I stayed in town. I should've guessed what they would do." Torey felt herself shaking against Killian, and knew she should move away, even if it meant she was half in, half out of the den. But she didn't. Reliving the horror of what happened on the farm, she drew comfort from the strength of this man lying next to her. "I should've known."

"How could you know that Varney was an animal? Christ, you're hardly more than a boy."

"Torey didn't mean to hurt anybody. She didn't mean it."

"Your sister had no part in the blame. A woman flirting with a man doesn't give him license to attack her."

Torey shut her eyes so tight they hurt. If she didn't, she was going to start bawling like a baby. And then Killian would know that she wasn't Torey's avenging brother. She was a lost and confused young woman who didn't know who she was anymore, a woman bound by a vow to her brutalized sister and dead father to exact revenge for what had been done to them. Bound too by a vow that she would never again allow any man to touch her. And yet here tonight, right now, what she wanted more than anything in the world was to feel Noah Killian touch her, pull her into his strong arms and hold on tight, make all the hurting go away.

"You only mentioned one sister in Denver," Killian probed gently. "Where's Torey?"

She trembled, her voice aching, barren, lost. "Torey's dead. She died that day along with my father."

"I'm really sorry, Vic. No wonder you want Pike so badly."

"I want him dead, Killian. I want him dead like I've never wanted anything in my life."

He squeezed her shoulder. "We'll get him."

"What if . . . what if when we do, you get the wrong answer to your question about what happened the day your troops were killed?"

"I'll worry about that when the time comes. For now all I care about is finding the bastard, stopping him from hurting anyone else."

Her throat constricted. "Eli was right."

"About what?"

"You're a good man to have as a friend, Noah Killian. Thank you."

She wouldn't have been surprised if he'd deflected the compliment with a wisecrack. Instead he said quietly, "You're welcome."

He again settled down to try and sleep, but her feelings about his being so close were different now. She took a fierce comfort in his presence, a warmth she never thought she would feel toward any man. Minutes later, she smiled when she heard the deep, even breathing that told her he had fallen asleep.

Gently, tenderly she dared for just an instant to lay her hand on his chest, feel the strong, measured beating of his heart. "Sweet dreams, Noah Killian," she murmured. "This night for you, I wish only sweet dreams."

11

Torey stretched tiredly, taking care not to disturb Killian, who was still sleeping peacefully beside her. It was past midnight, and she had been on watch in their cramped quarters for hours. Every muscle in her body ached. She longed to stand up, take a walk, if only for a minute or two. But she didn't dare. Not because she feared Grady. She had long since decided the outlaw wasn't going to show up. But because leaving the den would almost certainly awaken Killian. And that she didn't want to do, even though it was well past his turn to stand guard.

She tried to tell herself she was just being considerate. That Killian had had a rough night last night, and she was merely allowing him to catch up on his sleep. But that wasn't it, and she knew it. She didn't wake him because she was afraid. Not of Killian. But of herself.

Time and again she had tried to rein in her feelings for this man. Time and again she had failed.

And tonight had been the worst. First, she had apologized to him, after swearing that she would not. And then she had poured out her soul to him about Pike's attack on the farm. He'd reacted to her modified truth with compassion and sympathy, not only for Vic Langley, but for "Torey" as well. *Your sister had no part in the blame. A woman flirting with a man doesn't give him license to attack her.*

Torey wished it was as easy to absolve herself. And yet it was Killian's absolution that had nearly pushed her into finishing her story, telling him the whole of it. Only one thing had stopped her. And that was Killian himself. Not because he wouldn't have understood, but because he would have, only too well. Understood her deceiving him, understood her need to hide behind Vic, understood her need for revenge. And that very understanding would have been her undoing.

Her eyes brimmed with unshed tears. As much as she might want his empathy, his kindness, she didn't dare allow herself the luxury. She couldn't.

She had thought it was because of her growing awareness of Killian as a man. But it went deeper than that, far deeper. It was more than her fear of being Torey Lansford; it was her fear of *not* being Vic Langley.

She needed to maintain her charade, needed it desperately. To lose Vic was to forfeit her edge, her advantage in going after Pike. To lose Vic was to surrender the strength and power that came with moving freely in a man's world. Worst of all, to lose Vic was to renege on her promise to her father and Lisbeth.

And yet day in and day out with Killian, she felt herself losing, felt herself wanting to give in, give up. Not quit exactly, but give over the hurt. Share it. Ask Killian to help make it go away.

And she despised herself for it. How could she be so weak? Her father was dead. Her sister? God only knew if Lisbeth would ever recover from what those animals had done to her. And what was Torey doing about it? For five months she had focused on bringing those responsible to justice. Five months.

And then she had met Noah Killian. Now what she seemed most to be thinking about was herself. *Her* hate, *her* guilt, *her* pain. She needed to refocus. Get inside Vic Langley's skin once again. Stop this nonsense of looking to Killian to save her, protect her, care about her.

You're a good man to have as a friend, Noah Killian.

Torey closed her eyes. She had said the words, meant them. But she hadn't counted the cost. She couldn't be Killian's friend, not and maintain her identity as Vic Langley. The price was simply too high. But she could hardly announce they were at each other's throat again either. As for being neutral, it was impossible. With Killian, her emotions only seemed to come in extremes. And sometimes exact opposites. There had been times she hated him. Other times—she swallowed hard—other times she could almost think she—

Enough! She knew what she had to do. And it was Killian who had unwittingly given her the idea. Earlier tonight, he had mentioned drifting toward Denver to see her sister. Torey had wanted no part of it. But now she would insist that they do just that. After they'd captured Grady, of course.

She would tell Killian she had changed her mind about seeing Lisbeth. Once there, Torey would use the city's size to give Killian the slip. Somehow she would find another guide—some horse-faced, tobacco-chewing lout who would join her quest only for the money. And then she'd be safe, safe to be Vic Langley forever, if necessary.

Forever.

And that was exactly the way she wanted it, she assured herself fiercely. To be free of Killian. Free of feelings she wanted no part of.

Free to never see him again? She trembled. Is that what she really—

A twig snapped, the noise crackling like gunfire through the tranquil clearing.

Torey stiffened, her troubled musings forgotten, her every sense alert. The sound had come from somewhere off to the left of the counterfeit camp she and Killian had rigged out as bait some fifty yards in front of them. Her ears strained against the night, but the sound was not repeated.

Even so, she drew her gun. The paw of a stalking animal would not snap a twig.

She lay there, tense, anxious, debating whether or not to rouse Killian. What if it was a false alarm? Then she would be in exactly the predicament she had wanted to avoid. The two of them awake in the darkness. But if someone was out there, she could be putting both of their lives in jeopardy by hesitating.

Grimacing, she decided she had no choice. In the darkness she found his shoulders and feathered her hand ever so lightly over his neck, his jaw, trying hard to ignore the bitingly sensual feel of a day's growth of beard. Her plan was to press her fingers to his lips, prevent any sleep-hazed questions. But before her hand ever reached his mouth, Killian's own hand shot out, snaring her wrist like an iron band.

Startled out of her wits, Torey almost cried out. But no sound escaped her. Killian's hand was already covering her mouth. Frantically, Torey gestured toward the camp, as much to divert his attention from the feel of her face as to alert him to possible danger.

His hand dropped away, and Torey shuddered with relief. Soundlessly, Killian shifted onto his stomach and slid his Colt from its holster.

Long minutes passed. Nothing happened. Nothing but a renewed, nerve-jangling awareness of Killian on her part. Lord above, his whole body had practically been on top of hers! Every hard-muscled inch of him pressed intimately against her own softer frame. Had he noticed that softness? Had he wondered? She lay there, trying to gather her scattered wits, trying to convince herself that Killian's attention had been locked on a possible intruder, not on her. In the shadows of the rock overhang, she couldn't even see him. Nor could he see her. But she could most certainly feel him. With every strung-taut fiber of her being, she could feel him.

Oh, God, why hadn't she just let him sle—

She saw it then, a shadowy figure creeping toward the near-dead embers of what had been their campfire. Torey's breath caught. No friendly visitor would approach the camp with such stealth. Even if it wasn't Grady, whoever it was, was up to no good. He was staying downwind of the horses, obviously not wanting to give himself away. He halted some three feet from the first of the two blanket-wrapped forms. Only then did Torey note the faintest glint of moonlight off something metallic the man gripped in his hand.

Correction. Gripped in *each* hand.

Six-guns. Two of them. Her heart thudded. He must intend to get the drop—

The roar of gunfire shattered the quiet. Torey gasped, stunned, disbelieving, as the silhouette pumped round after round into both blanket-wrapped figures. If she and Killian had actually been out there, asleep . . .

Her stomach heaved and she had to fight down the urge to be sick. Belatedly, she brought up her Colt. Killian caught the barrel, eased it down.

"I'll take him," he whispered. "You cover me."

Fine, she thought wildly. *When?*

The silhouette let out a cry of unholy glee and stomped over to their bullet-riddled blankets. Laughing crazily, he kicked at them both. The laughing stopped. "What the—?"

Killian was already out of the den and on his feet. "Drop the guns!" he shouted. "Now!"

Instead the man whirled, fired, the bullet gouging a chunk of rock from the boulder above Torey's head. Killian fired back. Torey heard a grunt of pain, saw the silhouetted form crumple.

"Don't kill him!" she cried.

Killian cursed. "Drop the guns!" he shouted again. "Or I'll cut you down where you stand."

Two dull thuds hit the grassy turf.

"Get the fire up, Langley," Killian snapped.

When she didn't move, he nudged her with his boot. "Now!"

To the shooter, Killian said, "Keep your hands where I can see them."

"I'm hit!"

"You'll be dead, if I can't see your hands."

The man tried to straighten, but failed. "Help me. I'm bleedin' bad!"

"The fire, Langley," Killian repeated tersely.

Still gripping her Colt, Torey scrabbled out of the den and hurried over to the camp, careful to give their visitor a wide berth. Quickly she stoked up the fire's fading embers. In seconds she had the flames glowing brightly again. The orange-red blaze cast a six-foot circle of light that flickered eerily over the hunched form of their murderous guest.

Meanwhile, Killian collected the intruder's weapons, handing the two pistols, plus his own, over to Torey. "Watch him."

Torey kept her Colt trained on the wounded outlaw as Killian none too gently searched the man for any hidden weapons. He found a knife in a sheath in the man's boot and tossed it Torey's way.

"Please, mister," the man choked, his face obscured by the brim of his hat. "You've got to help me."

Killian snorted contemptuously. "The kind of help you gave me and my partner? What was it? Five slugs in each of us. That's more help than either one of us can stand."

"I thought you were"—the man's breath caught and he gasped—"I thought you were some men who were trailing me, meanin' me harm."

Killian retrieved his rope from his gear and swiftly hogtied the man. "Mister, you don't know the meaning of harm. Not yet." He gave the section of rope that bound the man's hands behind his back an extra yank. The man groaned piteously.

Torey winced but did not interfere.

"Come over here, Vic," Killian snapped. "Take a good look at this polecat. See if we won ourselves a prize."

Torey hesitated. The man's hat was still tilted at such at angle that she could not make out his face. But she was suddenly not so sure she wanted to see it anyway. Maybe she didn't want to know.

She trembled. Didn't want to know if this was one of the men who had destroyed her family? How could she explain that to Killian? She pressed a hand to her forehead. How could she explain it to herself? Reluctantly, she crossed the camp to Killian's side. He was studying her curiously again. Steeling herself, Torey reached for the wounded man's hat and snatched it off his head.

The shock of recognition nearly sent her to her knees. In a single blinding instant she was back on the farm. Her father lay sprawled on his back, broken, lifeless, beneath one of his beloved oaks. Her sister lay nearby, naked, bloodied, unmoving.

And all around her there were men laughing, laughing . . .

In the blink of an eye, Torey's gun was in her hand. She couldn't think. She could only hate. "We meet again, Grady," she gritted, pressing the barrel of her gun to the man's chin. "Tell Lucifer to get your room ready." She levered back the hammer on the Colt.

Grady shrieked with terror, tried to curl himself into an even smaller ball. "No, no, no, please!"

"Vic!"

Killian's voice sliced through her like a knife. But she didn't pull back, didn't uncock the gun. "It's him. One of the bastards who killed my family."

"I know. Put the gun down."

"No! You don't know. You weren't there."

"Put the gun down. Talk to me."

Her hand flexed on the walnut handle of the Colt, her palm sweating, a red haze seeming to swim before her eyes.

Answers didn't matter. Nothing mattered but exterminating a piece of vermin that didn't deserve to live.

"Talk to me," Killian repeated softly.

"Leave me alone."

"No. You can kill him. You can even enjoy it. But you'll pay for it the rest of your life."

"You weren't there. You didn't see it."

"I don't have to see it to know that he's the murderer, Vic. Not you."

"He belongs in hell. I want to send him there."

"You want Pike there with him, don't you?"

Her hand trembled. "Yes."

"Then ease off. The whole point of catching this bastard alive was to get answers. You can't get answers from a dead man."

Long seconds ticked by, before finally, Torey let her hand fall to her side. "Damn you."

Gently, Killian caught her wrist, eased the gun away from her, uncocked it. At her feet, Grady blubbered like a baby.

Torey was certain she was going to collapse.

Killian led her over to a log beside the fire and sat her down, then he brought her some whiskey. "Have a drink."

She shook her head.

"I mean it. It'll help calm you down."

"I don't want to calm down. That bastard raped my sister, killed my father."

For an instant Killian looked puzzled.

"What?" she demanded. "You don't believe me?"

"I believe you. But what about Torey? Didn't you forget Torey?"

"I never forget Torey!" she cried. "Never!" She heaved the bottle toward a rock, smashed it. "There, now neither one of us can get drunk tonight."

A muscle in his jaw jumped. "You about finished?"

"With what?"

"With taking out on me what you wanted to do to Grady."

She lifted her Stetson, raking her hand through her sweat-damp curls. "I'm sorry." Her shoulders sagged. "Truly. I don't mean to be such a bastard to you, Killian. I don't know what gets into me."

Killian snorted, his mouth ticking upward in that mocking grin she liked too well. "Yes, you do. It's what I like best about you, Vic. Like I said before, you've got balls."

Torey cringed. Not more balls. Then she laughed, albeit a trifle hysterically. If ever Killian did find out she was a woman, she was going to get her proper revenge. The man would purely die when he remembered some of the things he'd said to her. Then she sobered. He was never going to find out. They had Grady now. She would get Killian to take her to Denver. From there, she would hire a new guide or go after Pike alone. Either way, she and Killian were finished. She attributed the strange ache that accompanied the thought to the fact that she hadn't gotten any sleep tonight, assuring herself she was simply exhausted.

"Would you have shot him?" Killian prodded gently.

"I don't know."

"I think you do."

She closed her eyes, knowing what he was doing. He wanted her to answer the question, if not for him, for herself. She hadn't realized it until now, but Jensen and Scott had actually made things easier for her. By shooting it out, by dying, she'd never had to know what she would have done if she'd caught one of them alive. She hadn't wanted to know.

No, she wouldn't have shot Grady. But it scared hell out of her to realize just how much she'd wanted to. She let out a watery sigh and pushed to her feet. "Let's see if we can get some answers out of this bastard, shall we?"

Together they approached the trussed-up Grady. This time Killian hunkered down to check the man's wound.

"How bad is it?" Torey asked.

"Took some meat off him, that's all."

Torey strode over to her saddlebags and retrieved a fresh

shirt, which she promptly tore into strips. Though it repulsed her to touch him, she returned to Grady's side and fashioned a makeshift bandage for the man. "That should keep you from bleeding to death long enough to answer a few questions."

"Who are you?" the man whined. "What do you want with me?"

"Name's Vic Langley. This is Noah Killian."

"Never heard of you."

"Oh, but we've heard of you," Torey said. "And Cole Varney and Wade Scott and Cleve Jensen and John Pike."

"You got the wrong man. I don't know them either."

"Here's a name you might know," Killian said silkily. "Belle Whitley. I understand you recently spent the night with the lady."

"Lady?" Grady snorted. "Is that what this is about? What the hell should it matter to you what I did with that whore?"

Without warning Killian drove his fist into Grady's face. The man's nose collapsed, disintegrated, blood spurting over his already blood-soaked shirt. Grady yowled in pain.

"I think you might want to put that another way," Killian said, rubbing his knuckles and surveying his handiwork with grim satisfaction.

"I'm sorry, I'm sorry. I didn't mean nothin'. It'll never happen again."

Killian picked up Grady's knife, twisting the tip of the eight-inch blade between his thumb and forefinger. "I don't know what it is, Grady," he mused. "But I just don't feel comfortable taking your word for it. Maybe you can help me think of a way that would make me believe you."

"I won't touch her. I'll never touch her again. I swear!"

Killian shook his head. "Not good enough, I'm afraid. In fact, I can think of only one way to make sure you never rape another woman, Grady. Can't you?" With the tip of the knife Killian popped off the first button on Grady's trousers.

The man was a quivering mass of dread. He couldn't even

speak. Torey thought he was going to pass out. She glanced at Killian, noted the cold, feral light in those gray eyes. It occurred to her that he wasn't making his threat to impress anyone. As far as he knew he was in this clearing with a bounty hunter and a killer. He was championing Belle Whitley's honor because Noah Killian was an honorable man.

Torey took a guilty pleasure in realizing how far he would go to protect a woman he cared about. Then it occurred to her that Killian would have done the same for any woman.

Torey closed her eyes. That was exactly the problem. She could feel herself wanting to give herself up to that kind of protector, a black-garbed knight in shining armor who would shield her from a world of darkness. But if she ever did, Vic Langley would be lost. And so would her promise.

"Enough about Belle," she snapped. "We have other questions that need answers." She told herself she didn't need Killian's protection, didn't want it. She could damn well take care of herself. "If you're finished with your little show, Killian, maybe we can continue."

Killian glowered at her, but lowered the knife. "Spoilsport."

Torey took a long, deep breath, praying she wouldn't pass out herself.

To Grady, Killian went on, "I wouldn't go mute, if I were you. I've still got the knife. I suggest you listen real carefully to my friend's questions. He's no candidate for sainthood himself. There aren't many bounty hunters who are."

"Bounty hunter?" Grady sputtered. "I'm not wanted for nothin'."

"Oh, but you are," Torey said. "Maybe not officially. Yet. But on one of your little crime sprees with John Pike, you got a little careless. You left a witness."

"I don't know no Pike."

"Allow me to refresh your memory," Torey said. "Five months ago you were with Pike and seven other sons of Satan when you rode down on a farm outside of Boden, Kansas.

You killed a man." Her voice shook. "You raped and killed his two daughters." She still told the story the way Eli wanted her to tell it.

"It weren't me, I tell you!"

"You know," Torey said smoothly, "Jensen and Scott didn't talk either."

"Never heard of 'em," Grady said, his eyes betraying the lie.

"You know where they are now? They're buried in a Cuttersville cemetery."

Grady blanched. "Liar! Wade and Cleve ain't . . . " He coughed. "I mean . . . "

Torey smiled. She prayed it was a most unpleasant smile.

"They ain't dead," Grady insisted. "They can't be. They were fast. The fastest I ever saw."

"Not anymore."

The man shuddered. What spark of defiance he might have had left in him vanished. "What do you want to know?"

"First, where's Varney?"

"He left me behind when my horse went lame. Damned bastard."

"Where were you headed?"

"North."

"To Rimrock?" Killian asked.

He shook his head. "Farther. To Laramie, the fort."

Killian paled, turned away. Torey thought she heard him utter a barely audible "No."

"Why Laramie?" she demanded.

"I don't know. Varney never tells me nothing 'cept where to be and when to be there."

"Does he still expect you?"

Grady nodded. "Ten days. That's why I needed a horse."

"If Varney's on his way to Laramie," Torey reasoned, "Pike must be on his way too."

"Unless he's already there," Killian said, more to himself than to her.

"Listen, Grady," Torey said, "I know Varney doesn't give the orders. He has a boss, doesn't he?"

Grady nodded. "The boss plans everything." His mouth twisted. "And he keeps too much of the money for himself too, if you ask me."

Torey described Pike to Grady.

"That's him. But he don't go by the name Pike."

"What do you call him?"

"It's the craziest thing, but he makes everybody call him Ghost. He thinks that's real funny. I don't know why."

Torey and Killian exchanged glances. Grady had just all but sealed it. John Pike was alive.

Killian rose, his jaw set hard, his voice resolved. "Sounds like you're taking us to Laramie, Grady."

Grady gave his head a violent shake. "They'll kill me. Let me go. I'll head to California. You'll never see me again, I swear."

Killian gripped Grady's shirtfront and hauled him to his feet. The outlaw cried out as the movement aggravated his wound. "That wasn't a request. It was an order. You're the cheese that's going to catch us a whole nestful of rats." He shoved the outlaw away from him then, letting him sag back to the ground.

Torey stood beside Killian. "I'm sorry. The idea of going to Laramie can't be easy for you."

"To get to Pike, I'd ride through hell."

Torey well knew hell might be an apt description for what Killian would go through should he return to the fort. But there was no help for it. It was his best chance to find Pike.

In the east the sun was rising. The long night was over. Torey worried her lower lip. It was time to move on.

"We could stay here for a few hours," Killian said, as though reading her mind. "I know you didn't get any sleep."

"No, I'm fine. In fact . . . " She straightened, forced herself to say the words. "I want . . . I'd like to go to Denver. See my sister, after all. If that's all right?" She held her breath, unwilling to admit how much she was hoping, praying he would say no, refuse. And it had nothing to do with her fear of seeing Lisbeth.

But Killian read no hidden meaning into her words. "Fine. Denver it is. We could be there in two days now that we don't have to follow a trail. And we'll still have plenty of time to make it to Laramie before Grady's ten days are up."

"Sounds good." Her voice cracked, and she made an elaborate display of clearing her throat. She assured herself that, more than ever, she needed to hire that new guide. Logically, though, she would be hard pressed to escape Killian. The man would now be heading for Laramie with or without her.

Weary more in spirit than in body, Torey sank down onto a log beside the fire. She supposed she should be keeping an eye on Grady, but her gaze roamed time and again to Killian, who was busily saddling their horses. She watched him, memorized him, knowing that too soon all she would have left of this man was her memories.

She assured herself that would be enough.

But how did one memorize a man like Noah Killian? He had to be the most complex human being she'd ever met. Fiercely proud, yet humble and self-mocking. Noble and honorable, yet capable of being almost arrogantly vulgar. Passionate, petty. Gentle, strong. Tender, savage.

A man with whom if she wasn't very careful, she might even begin to think she was falling—

"Vic?"

She turned, startled. "What?"

"You coming?"

He had the horses ready.

"Of course," she said, curling her fingers into her palms, lest he notice her hands were trembling.

"Time to head out, Grady," Killian said, once again dragging the outlaw to his feet.

"Don't do this," Grady pleaded. "If you do, I'm a dead man."

Killian paid him no heed. Instead he hoisted Grady onto Galahad's back, then lashed the outlaw's feet together with a rope strung beneath the gelding's belly.

Torey frowned, a niggling of alarm spreading through her. "What are you doing, Killian? What am I supposed to ride?"

"You're a lightweight, kid," Killian said. "We can ride double for a while."

Torey took an unconscious step back. "No."

Killian rolled his eyes. "Now what the hell—?"

Without warning Grady dug his spurs into Galahad's sides. The gelding let out a piercing whinny, then bolted, tearing away from the camp in a headlong gallop.

Killian swore viciously, even as he swung aboard Bear and urged the bay into a dead run.

Torey could only watch in horror. Grady had no control of Galahad. The man's hands were still bound behind his back. The panicked horse was running for the sake of running, and Grady could not have chosen a worse direction. They were barreling hell-for-leather toward the swirling current of the mountain-fed stream that skirted their camp some two hundred yards distant. Killian would never reach them in time.

Torey broke into a run, never taking her eyes off the scene in front of her.

She watched as Galahad plunged into the shallow but swiftly moving water. She could tell Grady was trying desperately to guide the horse with his knees. But Galahad was not used to such rough handling. The horse was in a frenzy.

In midstream the gelding had had enough. He began to buck and writhe in a futile effort to rid himself of the bizarre burden attached to his back. With a shriek of terror Grady slid from the saddle and tumbled into the churning water. The stream was no more than four feet deep. But Grady's hands were tied. Worse, his feet were still lashed to Galahad's barrel.

Torey saw his head come up once, twice, each time gulping desperately for air. Then Galahad bucked again. His front hoof collided with a sickening thud against Grady's chest. Torey's stomach lurched as the man again disappeared beneath the surface of the water.

Killian was almost there. Astride Bear in the roiling water, he battled to maneuver the bay toward Galahad. But the current fought him every step of the way. Long minutes went by before Killian could finally pull close enough to grab on to Galahad's bridle.

By then Torey was at the water's edge. Without thinking, she plunged in, boots and all, wanting only to reach her horse, certain Galahad was going to break a leg in his frantic struggles. The water nearly stopped her in her tracks. It was ice cold. Determined, she shook off the effects and slogged on. Time and again she fell, the water closing over her head. Each time she grappled her way back to her feet. She heard Killian shouting something, but she paid no attention.

Only when he pulled his gun and fired a shot into the air did she stop. She straightened, gaping at him, while the water swirled up past her waist.

"Get the hell out of the water, Langley!" he shouted. "I've got both horses. I'm coming back to that side!"

When she saw that he indeed had both mounts under control, she retreated, noting oddly that each step toward shore seemed more difficult than the one before. Soaked to the skin, she staggered onto the grassy bank and collapsed, then turned to watch Killian. She winced as he used his knife to cut the limp body of Cal Grady free of Galahad. Catching up Galahad's reins, Killian remounted the bay and guided both horses back across the stream. Water cascaded freely from horses and rider alike as Killian rode up onto the bank beside her.

"Grady's dead?" she asked unnecessarily.

He nodded, dismounting.

She wasn't glad. But she wasn't sad either.

"Probably a damn sight warmer where he is right now," Killian muttered, "than either one of us."

She blinked, uncomprehending.

"That water's not much more than melted snow. We've got to get out of these clothes. Now."

Torey didn't move.

Killian hopped out of first one boot, then the other, flinging them to the ground. "Dammit, Langley. Did you hear me?" His shirt went next, and then he unbuttoned his pants.

Torey tried to stand, failed.

Killian stripped off his jeans, shedding them like a second skin. He was now dressed only in his drawers. The wet material outlined every ripple, every . . .

Torey staggered to her feet.

"It's about time," he groused. "What the hell's the matter with you?" He started gathering wood for a fire. "Hurry up. We don't get warm, we're dead."

Torey trembled violently, but whether from the cold or Killian's state of undress she couldn't have said.

"Dammit, Langley," Killian pressed.

"I'm fine," she lied, her teeth chattering.

Killian straightened, studying her closely. "You get out of those clothes, or I'm going to do it for you. I don't need to play nursemaid to a bounty hunter with pneumonia."

He crossed to their campsite and retrieved a dry blanket. One with several bullet holes. "It's a good thing we hadn't packed up yet before Grady took off. Here!" He tossed it at her.

She managed to snag it, though it nearly slipped from her numb fingers. Nervously, she reached for the top button of her shirt. But she didn't unbutton it. How could she? Helplessly, she looked around. She was just in time to see Killian peel off his drawers. She caught a flash of firm white buttock before she whirled to face the other way. With a cry just short of hysteria, she stumbled toward the boulders. Killian cursed, but otherwise ignored her.

In a narrow crevice between two massive boulders, Torey released the blanket and trembled. Her clothes were plastered to her skin. If it weren't for her vest Killian would already have guessed the truth. Yet somehow she was supposed to strip herself naked, wrap herself in that blanket, go out to the fire, and spend the next hour or two trying to warm herself without his becoming even remotely suspicious.

Terror pulsed through her. How was she ever going to pull this off? The cold was making it hard to think clearly. Fear made her already numb fingers clumsier still.

Time was her enemy. Shuddering, shivering, quivering, she fumbled out of her clothing, one article at a time. Her vest, her shirt, her pants. Each button she encountered became a major ordeal. It was taking too long, too long. Minutes seemed like hours. Killian would wonder what was keeping her. He would call out, he would . . .

Hurry! Hurry! You have to hurry! Her underwear and the binding that shielded her breasts went next. A vagrant breeze drifted over the rocks, raising gooseflesh on every square inch of her body. But Torey no longer felt the cold. It was panic that controlled her now.

Hurry.

She was naked. The blanket lay on the ground beside her. All she had to do was stoop down, retrieve it. Oh, God, she was cold. So very cold. And so very afraid.

From beyond the rocks she heard the crunch of bootfalls on the hard-packed earth. *Too late. Too late.*

Hurry!

Before she could react, cry out, Killian sauntered around the far edge of the boulders, carrying with him a dry set of clothes. "Thought you might want to put these on, Langley. I—"

The words stopped.

They both froze.

For long seconds Torey just stood there, stark naked, unable to summon the wits even to cover herself with her hands. Her only awareness was of Killian's strangled voice.

"My God," he whispered. "Oh my God."

12

Noah stood stock-still. If he had stepped around the face of the boulder and Vic Langley had shot him square between the eyes he could not have been more stunned. A woman. Vic Langley—rude, foul-mouthed, gun-toting son of a bitch Vic Langley—was a woman!

It couldn't be, couldn't be. But it was. In the space of a heartbeat his eyes took in what his mind refused to accept—smooth ivory skin; high, firm breasts; and long, willowy legs. God above, Vic Langley was not only a woman, she was a damned beautiful woman.

A beautiful woman who was trembling violently and making a futile attempt to shield her nakedness from him with her arms, her hands. Noah cursed low, under his breath. How dare he just stand there and gape at her? Swiftly, he moved toward her, stooping to retrieve the blanket that lay at her feet. Scooping it up, he settled it shawllike about her shoulders.

"I'm sorry," he murmured, pinching the two sides of the blanket together at her throat. "I didn't mean . . . "

She cringed away from him, catching the blanket sides in her own two hands and holding on tight.

He winced at the terror in her blue-green eyes. She was scared to death, scared to death of *him*.

That's when it hit him, slammed into his gut like a fist. He had seen that look before. That same fear in those same blue-green eyes. "Merciful God," he said wonderingly. "It was you! You in that Cuttersville saloon."

Her fear deepened, her eyes wild. "No. No, please." She shrank farther into the rocky crevice, halting only when her back came up against a wall of stone. "No."

"It's all right," Noah said, desperate to soothe her, ease the terror in those eyes, as he had not eased it that night in the saloon. "What happened that night doesn't matter." It mattered a helluva lot, but he wasn't going to press the issue now. "I want you to come out by the fire. You need to get warm. We need to talk."

She shook her head. "Leave me alone. Go away. Please . . ."

It was her voice. *Hers*. He was sure of it now. Quivery, nervous, just as it had been that night. His lady in red. Not at all the husky, lower-pitched tones he'd come to associate with Vic Langley.

"Don't hurt me," she whispered.

Noah felt an unexpected ache deep in his vitals that she could even think that he would. "I won't hurt you," he said. "I swear."

A tear tracked down her cheek, and he knew the thousand questions jumbling through his mind would have to wait. He needed to calm her down, reassure her yet again that he meant her no harm. "I tell you what, I'm going to go out by the fire myself and let you stay here and get dressed." He glanced toward the fresh change of clothes that had been his reason for coming back here in the first place. They lay in a heap on the ground near the edge of the boulders. He didn't even remember dropping them. Quickly, he snatched them up and brought them over to her. "Here."

She made no attempt to take them. To do so would have meant letting go of the blanket.

Awkwardly, Noah laid them near her feet. "You come out when you're ready. All right?"

She nodded quickly, too quickly. He had the impression she would have agreed to anything to have him gone. But he didn't have much choice in the matter.

He left her alone then. Though his legs felt like rubber, he traversed the fifty yards back to their campsite and sagged down in front of the flames. The chill from the water that had seemed to permeate even his bones was gone. He felt nothing now, nothing but a mind-numbing shock.

A woman. He could still scarcely comprehend it. Not only a woman but this particular woman, a woman who had haunted his thoughts since the moment he'd met her. His lady in red.

He'd thought about her, worried about her, wished to God he hadn't been drunk that night so he could've gone after her, helped her. And all along she'd been right here beside him. A shudder coursed through him as he recalled the too vivid fantasy his mind had conjured about her the other night, how real it had seemed when he'd made love to her. How precisely his imagination had sculpted her body for him—the dark aureoles of her nipples, the delicate mounds of her breasts, the long, tapered perfection of her legs. My God, she was as tall as he was. To think of those legs wrapped around him, holding him inside her . . .

Noah swore viciously. What the hell was he doing? She was already terrified. Was he trying to finish the job? If she even suspected he'd entertained such carnal thoughts about her, she would get on her horse and ride and not look back.

With another oath he stood and paced, anxious to work off the sudden tension in his loins, anxious too about what was taking her so long. Surely, she should be dressed by now. He tried to tell himself she was just embarrassed about facing him. And she was likely worried about his reaction to finding out about her.

He glanced toward the rocks. She wouldn't be foolhardy enough to run away, would she? He shook his head, dismissing the notion. Both horses were here, picketed in front of him. Even her boots were here. They'd been wet, so he had not taken them back to her.

She would come out when she was ready. She probably just needed a little time alone to gather her courage. Not that she didn't already have her fair share. She had to in order to have pulled off such a risky masquerade. She was scared now, of course, disconcerted, but there wasn't a doubt in his mind—that was one helluva woman back there.

Dammit, how he had not known? Suspected? Felt it in some core part of him? He had heard of women dressing up as soldiers during the war and going undetected. But he'd never really believed it, certain that any officer who couldn't ferret out a woman in his ranks would have to be pretty damned stupid or blind drunk or both.

Drunk.

Noah raked a hand over his head. Had he been in his cups so much that he hadn't seen the signs?

No. He'd been drunk, but not that drunk. And not that often.

She'd fooled him because her charade as a man had been virtually flawless. The few minor nigglings he might have entertained—like her prudish habits regarding her bodily functions—were hardly any dead giveaway. He had known men, real flesh and blood men, who went behind a tree when the opportunity presented itself.

Her clothes were oversized. She was slender and tall, damned tall. And then there was that ever-present dirt on her face. Not to mention the fact that she'd outcussed, outspit, and outshot him at every turn. Why the hell would he ever have suspected he was keeping company with a woman?

Once he had her settled down he would have to congratulate her. He had a feeling she would appreciate the compliment.

He grimaced. Unless it was her nature to spit, cuss, and shoot.

He remembered the look in her eyes, the vulnerability, and knew that wasn't true. At least it hadn't always been. Before John Pike had come into her life.

Damn, how much longer was she going to be? Noah felt his patience deteriorating. He wanted to get her out here, talk to her. He wanted desperately to understand. But instead he forced himself to again sit in front of the fire. He would wait. He owed it to her to wait.

He found himself wishing he knew her name. It was silly, inconsequential in the face of everything else that was happening. But he wanted more than anything to know her name.

He tried to recall all the things she'd told him about herself this past week, ever since Eli had first introduced the two of them in his room.

Eli.

Had Eli known?

Noah's jaw clenched. Of course Eli had known. The cagey old bastard. No wonder he'd given Noah the big speech about watching out for Vic. That Vic was a youngster who needed looking after. Noah should have suspected something was amiss then.

But something like this? It wouldn't have entered his head in a thousand years.

He remembered Vic's telling him about Pike's attack on the farm. How Vic's father had been murdered. One sister had been raped, the other killed.

Torey didn't mean it. She didn't mean it.

Torey. Vic. He frowned. Victoria?

It made sense. Eli had spoken of the farm on which he worked. A father, two daughters, nice people. But there had been no mention of a son.

So how much of what Vic had told him was truth, and how much fiction had been required to advance his charade? Had Torey been there the night of the attack? Had Torey seen what had happened to her sister? Noah shuddered. Had Torey been raped as well?

He shot a glance across the stream. Cal Grady's body still lay where it had fallen. It had been bad enough when he'd thought about Grady raping Belle, raping Vic's sister, but now . . . but now . . .

"Be glad you're dead, you son of a bitch," Noah gritted, reaching down to touch the hilt of the knife he carried in his boot. "Be very glad you're dead."

He pushed to his feet and looked toward the rocks. It had been too damned long. Maybe she was just too afraid to come out.

You're a good man to have as a friend, Noah Killian.

From Vic, Noah had considered the words high praise. From Torey? Had they just been part of her charade? Part of her need to use him to get to Pike? Had she ever been going to tell him the truth?

Eli had wanted her to tell him. Noah remembered that now. Instead she'd told him some nonsense about being afraid of snakes. Why?

He grimaced. Probably because Noah Killian was not high on her trustworthiness list. He was a convicted coward and deserter. She must have been just thrilled with Eli's choice of a replacement. So what was she thinking now? Now that he knew the truth. What was Torey's true opinion of Noah Killian? His lips thinned. Did he really want to know?

And what about his own behavior this past week? What if he had known from the first she was a woman? Would he have—

He stiffened. Jesus. Oh, sweet Jesus. He'd been thinking about *her* prudish habits. What about his own habits? He had just spent a week with a person he assumed to be a man. Spent a week without the checks and balances on his behavior that would have been in place if he'd known he was with a woman.

You've got balls, Langley, I'll say that for you. Noah's cheeks burned. Maybe the earth would just open up and swallow him. It might prove easier than facing her again.

What else had he done to humiliate himself this past week? He cringed. He didn't have to think too long and too hard to come up with a half dozen ignominious occasions, starting with Belle Whitley in Cuttersville. Christ, Torey had been in his room when Belle was lounging around naked, beckoning Noah to come back to bed! He'd even been half-embarrassed to have Vic in his room. And now . . .

Damn.

He'd put no constraints on his behaviors. None. Not for calls of nature, or language, or . . .

He trembled.

Or for backhanding a smart-aleck bounty hunter right in the mouth!

Noah sagged to his knees. God in heaven, he'd hit a woman. He could feel the blood drain from his face, feel his stomach twist as though he were going to be physically sick. He'd hit her. "Oh, God," he whispered, "Oh, my God."

He lurched to his feet. That was it. The last straw. He had to talk to her. He had to talk to her right now. No wonder she was terrified of him.

Noah marched toward the boulders, making sure to make as much noise as possible. He didn't want to startle her again.

When he reached the rocks he announced his presence, but received no response.

He waited.

Nothing.

Taking a deep breath, he averted his gaze and rounded the last curve in the boulders. "Miss?"

Nothing. Not a sound. Noah took a chance and looked.

She wasn't there.

A sudden dread gripped him. He raced back to the fire and stopped cold. Everything was just as he had left it.

With one exception.

Both horses were gone.

Torey urged Galahad into a gallop, even as she held on to the lead rope that guided Killian's bay behind her. She had no idea where she was going. She only knew she had to put distance between herself and Killian. Only when she'd gone at least five miles did she rein in and attempt to take stock of her situation.

Dismounting, she took a long drink from her canteen and surveyed her surroundings. She was on a rocky outcropping in the midst of an impressive stand of lodgepole, the scent of pine so pervasive it was almost suffocating. She found herself mildly surprised that she was not afraid—not of the mountains, the altitude, the wildlife, or even of being alone. She was Vic Langley again, and as Vic she wasn't even particularly afraid of John Pike at the moment, convinced she could handle him and the others just as she'd handled Jensen, Scott, and Grady.

Not kill them. Despite the raw hatred that still pulsed through her with every beat of her heart that wasn't what she had in mind anymore. Thanks to Killian. He had stopped her from pulling the trigger on Grady. He had helped her see that she couldn't fight evil by becoming evil herself. Jensen, Scott, and Grady had brought their fates on themselves. What she wanted now was Pike, Varney, and their still unidentified confederate. And she would do her best to capture them alive, bring them to justice. Alone or with a new hired gun.

When she thought about being afraid, truly afraid, there was only one thing that came to mind—and that was a man named Noah Killian. Not fear for her life, but a whole different kind of fear. Because now Noah Killian knew she was a woman. Worse, he knew she was the woman in the red silk dress.

And just that quickly the morning came rushing back to her in humiliatingly minute detail. She had been stark naked, defenseless in front of a man whose sexual appetites she had seen with her own eyes to be formidable. He could have overpowered her in seconds. But he had not. Instead he had been flustered and embarrassed *for her*, responding to her plight with tenderness and compassion. He had apologized for his intrusion, shielded her with a blanket and then left her alone, giving her the freedom, the privacy to dress. Giving her too the opportunity to escape.

And so she had slipped around the opposite side of the rocks and waited. She knew Killian would eventually become impatient enough to check on her. She used the word "impatient" deliberately, refusing to acknowledge that he might have become concerned.

From her perch in the rocks she'd watched him pace, fret and fume. She told herself he was likely furious over being made to feel a fool. She wanted him angry with her. She wanted him to hate her. It would make her choices so much simpler. But he didn't hate her. And she knew it. Nor did she hate him.

She'd wanted nothing so much as to walk into that camp, sit down in front of that fire and pour out her heart and soul to him, let him pull her into his arms, make all the hurting go away. She'd wanted it since the day she'd first laid eyes on him. And for that very reason, she knew she had to leave, run.

She had debated taking Bear, vacillating over more than the act of being a horse thief. The idea of leaving Killian afoot bothered her greatly. But in the end she decided she couldn't risk his following her. When he'd headed for the boulders, she'd headed for the horses.

And now here she was some two hours later standing on a ridge, consumed by guilt, both for not having the guts to face him and for abandoning him. She lifted her Stetson, rubbing her hand over her sweat-damp crop of curly dark hair. Truth to tell, she didn't have far to look to know which of the two of them was the true coward and deserter.

Damnation! She slapped her hat against her thigh. She owed Killian better than this. She owed herself better than this. She would ride back, confront him, make it clear that their partnership was ended, but do it face-to-face. She had no doubt he'd be agreeable. After today, he probably couldn't get rid of her fast enough.

She would give him back his horse, thank him for his time, and wish him well. Then she would be on her way to Denver. Alone.

That decided, she remounted Galahad and headed back.

The sun was high in a painfully blue sky when she reached their campsite. What she found there almost made her turn around and ride out again. Killian was naked from the waist up, covered with dirt and sweat. He was in the process of digging out a grave for Cal Grady and hadn't yet noticed her return. Torey could scarcely drag her eyes away from the rivulets of perspiration that trailed down the muscles of Killian's back to disappear beneath the waistband of his denims. As she rode closer she noticed a jagged five-inch whitened scar just to the right of his spine, halfway down his back. She shuddered at the violent legacy of Pike's betrayal.

"You should've let the coyotes eat Grady," she said, reining in Galahad.

Killian whirled, diving for his six-gun, then cursed when he saw who it was. "Goddammit, don't you know better than to—" He halted in midharangue, nearly biting off his tongue in the process. "I'm sorry," he muttered, scrambling out of the shallow hole and grabbing up his shirt, which he quickly shrugged into. "I'm really sorry. I didn't mean to . . . I, uh, I'm glad you came back."

"Are you?"

"Of course." He was working the buttons of his shirt by

feel, almost as though he didn't want to acknowledge that it was unbuttoned in her presence. "I figured you'd come to your senses. It must have been pretty scary when you realized how alone you were."

His voice was almost comically nonchalant, as though there was nothing at all out of the ordinary going on between them. Vaguely irritated, Torey dismounted. "I stole your horse."

He shrugged. "You brought him back."

"Here." She held Bear's reins out to him. He accepted them, being careful it seemed to touch only the leather straps, not her hand.

"I had no right to leave you afoot," she went on.

"I appreciate that."

Torey ground her teeth together so hard her jaw hurt. Did he have to be so blasted polite? The man must be pure eaten alive with curiosity, yet he was being almost nauseatingly solicitous of her. What was the matter with him anyway? She sighed inwardly. It would be best, she decided, not to ask. "I'd better go," she said, turning back to Galahad. "I'd appreciate it if you wouldn't follow me."

He straightened, his voice no longer diffident. "Go? What do you mean, go?"

"It's for the best."

"Are you out of your mind? I can't let a woman ride off by herself in the middle of nowhere."

"You would've let Vic Langley."

"You're not Vic Langley."

"Yes I am!" She was startled by her own vehemence.

Killian held up his hands in a peacemaking gesture. "All right, let's not get excited. We need to talk about this. Don't you think I deserve that much?"

"There's nothing to say. I'm leaving for both our sakes."

"You want to explain that?"

"No."

His lips thinned. He was getting angry. Torey considered

it a victory. She wanted him to treat her no differently than he had treated "Vic." But again Killian drew rein on his temper. "Just a few answers," he said. "I think that's fair. If you still want to leave after I get them, I won't stop you."

"Promise?"

Exasperated, he nodded. "I promise."

Torey followed him toward the creek. Only now was she beginning to understand the full scope of how rattled he was by all this. He had no idea what to do, say. And Torey wasn't about to make it any easier for him.

They found a grassy slope beside the tumbling water. Torey sat down first because Killian seemed determined to stand until she did. But when he seated himself barely three feet away from her, she quickly got up again and moved off another three feet. Thankfully, he took the hint and stayed put. "All right," she said, "ask away." She hoped her voice sounded more blasé than she felt.

"I don't know where to start," Killian said, "Miss . . . is it Langley?"

"Lansford. Victoria Lansford. You can call me Vic."

He closed his eyes, and she wondered if he was counting to ten. When he opened them again, she was taken aback by the pain she saw there. "Miss Lansford," he began haltingly, "I would first like to sincerely apologize for blundering in on you this morning."

"You didn't know. It wasn't your fault." She wanted to change the subject. If there were apologies owed for blundering in on another's privacy, she owed him a hell of an apology herself from the other night. And she wasn't about to own up to that one.

"Please, there's more." He plucked a blade of grass free from the turf and curled it around his fingers. "I'd like to just get this said, if I could. My behavior this past week—"

"Has been perfectly natural," she interrupted. "No apologies are necessary."

"It has not been perfectly natural. Not . . . not for the way

I behave around . . . " He raked his hand over his hair, a now familiar gesture that confirmed he was frustrated and ill at ease. "Have you any idea what it's been doing to me to remember, for example, that I hit you?"

"Vic Langley deserved a pop in the mouth at that particular moment." She hoped to defuse some of his embarrassment with humor. She did not succeed.

"I hit a woman," he said. "I'm not sure my court-martial was as hard on me as realizing I did that."

"I was never in this to bring any hurt or embarrassment to you, Mr. Killian. But I desperately needed your cooperation. Vic Langley was the only means I had to get it. If you'd known the truth, you wouldn't have come with me, would you?"

"No," he answered without hesitation.

"Then you see, I had no choice. And given the same circumstances, I'd do it all over again the same way. For that, Mr. Killian, I should apologize to you."

"Why did you have to do it at all? Eli sent for me. He and I would would've gone after Pike in a heartbeat."

"Pike killed my father. He raped my sister. I wasn't going to hire others to avenge my family. Especially . . . "—her voice broke a little and she tried to mask it by clearing her throat—"especially since I was the one responsible for bringing him down onto my family in the first place."

"You're a woman. A woman doesn't—"

She swore viciously and his eyes went wide.

She shook her head in disgust. "Vic Langley could've said those same words and you wouldn't have turned a hair. A woman says them and you're apoplectic. That isn't fair, Mr. Killian. That's exactly why I dressed myself up as a man. Because as a woman I could never have gotten away with the things I've needed to do in order to track Pike."

She didn't tell him that as Victoria Lansford she felt weak, victimized. That as Vic Langley she felt just the opposite. Her problem with dealing with Killian at the moment was that she was dressed as Vic Langley but feeling like Victoria Lansford, a vulnerability she hadn't experienced since the night she'd stared into Killian's pain-edged gray eyes in the Take Your Chances Saloon. His next question made her wonder just how often he thought about that night himself.

"What was the red dress all about?"

"That was an accident," she managed, hating how defensive she sounded. "I was making use of a bathhouse, and the washerwoman wandered off with my clothes. The damned dress was the only thing in the place to wear. And then Eli wanted a bottle of whiskey, and . . . " She let her voice trail off.

A corner of Killian's mouth twitched, ticked upward.

"What's so funny?" she demanded, hurt that he would choose a subject about which she was most raw to become suddenly insensitive.

"I was just thinking what it would have been like if I had been the one taking the bath and found only a red silk dress to wear . . . " He shook his head. "Never mind."

He was still grinning as he leaned back on his elbows and hooked his thumbs in the waistband of his jeans, an action that had the unfortunate consequence of drawing her gaze to the quiescent bulge beneath his worn denims, a bulge now framed by those long, rein-scarred fingers. With a squeak of dismay Torey forced her attention back to his face. Thankfully, he seemed to take no notice of her scandalous scrutiny.

To cover her feelings she snapped at him. "I'll tell you what you would've done in that bathhouse. You would have marched out of the place stark naked, straight up the main street and not thought a thing about it. You're a man, Mr. Killian. Men get away with whatever the hell they want."

His grin vanished. "You've got it all figured out, don't you? Men don't have a problem in the world. We just wander through life and do what the hell we please and everybody else be damned. Is that about right?"

"Right."

A muscle in his jaw worked, and Torey took a savage delight in it. If she couldn't win him over to her side, then she would settle for irritating the hell out of him.

"Miss Lansford," he continued with forced patience. "I hardly think—"

"It's *Vic,*" she corrected.

Killian took a long, slow breath. "You've got to give me a chance here."

"None of this is your lookout anymore."

"Yes, it is. I've got a responsibility to you. That's the way we men are. Some of us, at least."

"I release you from your responsibility."

"That isn't good enough. I know you don't think much of my code of honor—"

"It isn't that," she cut in, anxious to make sure they were clear on this point at least. "I meant what I said about believing you're no coward. I'm just telling you, you're not responsible for me."

"And I say I am."

"So what do you intend to do? Force me? Go back on your word? You promised if I chose to ride out of here, you'd let me go."

"What I'd like to do to you, Miss Lansford," Killian said, "is tie you up, take you back to Eli, and knock the old coot clean to California. But I'm trying hard not to do anything to frighten you any more than you already are."

"I'm not afraid of you!"

"You're scared to death of me, Miss Lansford. I wish you weren't. But Lord knows I haven't been behaving in a way to inspire confidence. I'm not letting you ride off alone, and that's final. I have enough on my conscience."

"If I leave anyway?"

"I'll follow you. Every step of the way."

"Why?"

"Because if I hadn't come around those boulders, you'd

still feel safe. It's because of me you don't feel safe anymore."

That he had homed in on the precise reason for her unease rocked her. He had even used the right word. *Safe*. How could he know that time and again she retreated inside the skin of Vic Langley in order to feel safe? Safe from men like Pike and Varney. Safe even from men like Noah Killian.

"You don't owe me your protection," she insisted. "I can ride out of here as Vic Langley and be accepted in your male world anytime, anyplace."

"And I say your role in this is finished. You need to face that. I'm taking you to Denver, then I'm going after Pike alone."

Torey felt her temper slip another notch. His whole manner since he'd discovered she was a woman had become precisely what she had been most afraid of. At every turn she was being patronized, humored, and condescended to—all because of her gender. How could she help but feel weak and defenseless as a woman, when that was precisely the way he was treating her? Like some fragile china doll. Without a brain, without power, without choices. "I'm still the same person who outshot you yesterday afternoon. The only thing that's changed is your attitude, Mr. Killian."

"Everything's changed." Killian shifted restlessly. "The story you told me about Pike attacking your farm . . ."

"Was true," she said. "Except that I don't have a brother, and I obviously didn't die."

"What did happen that night?"

Torey looked away, knowing what he was fishing for, uncertain if she really wanted to tell him. Finally, she decided it didn't matter. "They didn't rape me," she said coldly, "if that makes you happy."

He winced as though she'd slapped him, but she didn't stop.

"Lisbeth pushed me into the root cellar and locked the

door. I got to hear what they were doing to my sister. Until one of them let me out, that is. Then I got to see it."

"I'm sorry."

She was shaking. "I have to be Vic Langley, Killian. I can't explain it to you. I can't make you understand. But Vic Langley is the only chance I have of getting to Pike."

"Then how about a compromise? When we get to Denver, we'll ask Eli to settle it. If he convinces me that I should let you come along, then I will. I swear."

"Am I supposed to keel over with gratitude?" she snapped. "I'm the one that let *you* come along, remember? And just to set the record straight, I didn't want you to take me to Denver so that I could see Lisbeth or Eli. I wanted you to take me there because I intended to hire another guide."

He frowned, bewildered.

"I didn't want to ride trail with you anymore, Mr. Killian."

"Any particular reason?" he asked curtly.

"Not that I care to share with you, no." She could hardly tell him she was spending much too much time thinking about Killian the man, instead of Killian the hired gun. Though now that they would both be heading for Fort Laramie, she supposed her reasons for eluding him were moot.

"Let me get this straight. We find out where Pike is and you decide to leave me out of it? Ride off without me? What sense does that make?"

"I don't owe you any explanations."

"You owe me a helluva lot, Miss Lansford. But I'm not going to call in any markers. Not yet. Because maybe I owe you something too. Like I said before, I should have killed Pike a long time ago. Maybe you wouldn't have a dead father or a brutalized sister if I'd taken him out."

"I could hardly have expected you to murder the man."

"Maybe not. But I'll tell you this, this time he isn't getting away. This time, he's a dead man. And since you were kind enough to jettison me, I'll return the favor. I'm leaving you with Eli. It's done. Like it or not, you've been through enough."

"Why? Because I'm a fragile, delicate female?" She smacked the turf with her hand, irrationally annoyed. Wasn't this precisely what she'd wanted? To be rid of him? And yet to have him be the one abandoning her, instead of the other way around, was beyond infuriating. "Let me remind you of your own words, Mr. Killian." She spoke through clenched teeth. "What was that colorful little phrase you kept using? 'You've got balls, Langley, I'll say that for you.' Is that an accurate quote?"

His face suffused with such color, Torey almost felt guilty. Almost. But he was being so blasted patronizing, she could not bring herself to let up on him. "I have what it takes to go after Pike, Killian. Even you've got to admit that."

"And maybe I don't have what it takes to put a woman's life in jeopardy."

"It's *my* life."

"I can't have another life on my conscience, don't you see that? Especially not a woman's life."

She glared at him, hoping to burrow past the determination in those steel-gray eyes. But he wasn't about to budge. "Then I'll go to Fort Laramie alone. I'm sure I can find it."

His eyes narrowed. He was dangerously angry now, so angry he apparently didn't trust himself enough to continue their argument. Instead he said only, "You do what you feel you have to. We both will."

"Damned straight. And what I have to do is find John Pike."

Killian shoved to his feet and stomped back toward Grady's body. Torey scrambled after him. "When are we leaving?" she demanded.

"As soon as I get this vermin planted."

"I'll be ready."

Killian rolled Grady into the hole with his boot, then he looked her straight in the eye. "I wouldn't want to commit any more breaches of your special brand of etiquette," he said. "So let me see if I'm getting this. From now until Denver, I'm supposed to act like I don't even know you're a woman, is that right?"

"You're catching on."

"Fine." He took a step back from the grave. "Then you can finish burying this"—he paused meaningfully—"*son of a bitch.*"

"My pleasure."

He started to stalk off, then turned. "One last question, *Vic.*"

"What's that?"

"Are you still planning to sleep with your forty-five? I keep worrying the damned thing's going to go off and blow out what brains you've got left in that thick skull of yours."

Torey drew her gun and casually checked the cylinder. There was an undercurrent in his question that she couldn't quite get a handle on, but she wasn't about to take any chances. "The gun stays, Killian. Count on it. It's not that I don't trust you." She shrugged. "I even like you, after a fashion."

She had to look at the ground, lest he read in her eyes just how much she liked him. Her heart was thundering against her ribs. She had to say this, had to feel safe again, had to end any protective instincts he might yet harbor toward her. "But I've seen what men are capable of, and you're most definitely a man. You touch me, Killian—ever—and I'll kill you."

13

Torey would have preferred arriving at her aunt Ruby's in the middle of the night. There would have been less chance of creating an uproar in the household. Torey had wanted only to slip in, talk to Eli, then slip out again. Though she knew it was abominably rude, she had not even wanted to see her aunt, knowing that the well-meaning Ruby would only bombard her with questions. As for facing Lisbeth, Torey couldn't even bear the thought of it. Not with her promise still only half fulfilled. She had told all of these things to Killian, and he had listened politely—he did everything so blessedly politely these days. And then he had proceeded to time their arrival at Aunt Ruby's for high noon.

Torey dismounted in front of her aunt's imposing two-story Victorian home, a home set like a crown jewel—isolated, magnificent—on a pine-studded hill on the outskirts of Denver. The cream-colored house with its forest-green accents highlighting dormer windows on both levels would have been impressive in any setting. Here, with its backdrop of awesome snow-capped mountains, Ruby Adams's home seemed plucked straight from a portfolio of Currier and Ives. But Torey gave the house and its surroundings scant notice.

She was too intent on what was about to play out inside that house. Slapping at the dust on her shirt and trousers, she cast a baleful glare at her trail partner, glad at least that for once he was as scruffy-looking as she was. For reasons unknown to her—she wasn't about to ask—he'd stopped his ritual morning shave.

Killian feigned an innocent look, dismounting to stand beside her. "I guess I've been hanging around with you too long, *Vic*." He was forever giving her name a nasty twist these days, as though it left a sour taste in his mouth. "I can't tell time anymore either."

"You did this on purpose!"

"You could've camped out in the field down the road for ten hours," he said.

"Don't think I don't know what you're up to. You think if I see Lisbeth and my aunt that I'll get all teary-eyed and homesick, and I'll stay here instead of following you to Laramie."

"No," he said softly. "Personally, I can't imagine a hardcase bounty man like you getting teary-eyed over much of anything, *Vic*."

She turned her head, lest he see how much his words stung her. Damn his hide. It had been three days since he'd found out she was a woman, three days of his self-righteous, judgmental attitude toward her choice to continue after Pike as bounty hunter Vic Langley. What hurt more than anything was the cruelty that had accompanied that judgment.

Oh, he'd let her carry out her role as a man, all right—with a vengeance he'd let her. He'd let her gather her own wood for their campfires, shoot and clean and incinerate her own meals, spend eighteen hours a day in the saddle following him to Denver on a journey that should've taken only a day and a half. And all of this he had done with a studied politeness that had nearly driven her mad.

But she was determined that his attitude wouldn't matter. That only getting Pike mattered.

"You'd best be as good as your word," she snapped. "If Eli says you're to let me ride along, then—"

"Don't throw my words in my face, Vic. Or I'll start tossing a few of your own back at you. You were going to ride out without me, remember?"

"That was before you found out . . . Oh, never mind. Forget it." She stomped toward the front porch, Killian half a step behind her. She bit back an urge to scream. If the man had handpicked ways to provoke her, he couldn't have chosen better. He was never more than two feet away from her anymore. He never touched her. He never once touched her. But he didn't seem keen on giving her room to breathe either.

Still she held her temper. Eli would straighten this all out. She was certain of it. And as for Lisbeth, maybe this would work out for the best. Maybe Torey would find out that her sister really was getting better.

Before she'd even reached the bottom step, the front door to the house swung open.

A handsome woman in her late forties swept out onto the porch. Attired in a simply styled dove-gray bombazine dress, Ruby Adams cut an imposing figure. A tall woman—taller by an inch than Torey—with graying brown hair caught back in a single braid that trailed down the length of her back, Ruby's hazel eyes studied the two saddle bums in her front yard with a wary though imperious air. "Who are you, and what do you want?" she demanded in no-nonsense tones.

Torey tugged off her hat. "It's me, Aunt Ruby. Torey."

Ruby's jaw dropped. "Landsakes, child!" she cried, rushing down the steps to Torey's side. "What on earth—?" She stopped, a hand flying to her mouth. "I mean . . . "

"It's all right, Aunt Ruby. I know I look a sight."

"Oh, dear. I didn't mean . . . that is, Eli tried to warn . . . I mean, prepare . . . I . . . oh, my dear." She gave Torey a swift, heartfelt hug. "It's so good to see you home safe."

Torey managed a slight smile. "Thank you. How long has Eli been here?"

"He arrived by train four days ago."

"And just how much did he tell you?"

Ruby's mouth twisted, though her eyes remained kind. "If you mean did I continue to believe that preposterous story about the two of you looking for a homestead, then no, I didn't."

Torey flushed. "I'm sorry."

Ruby sighed. "I'm just grateful you're all right."

"I . . ." Torey's heart hammered. "Is Lisbeth . . . ?"

Ruby's gaze grew sad, sympathetic. "She seems content, dear."

Torey bit back bitter tears, oddly calling on Killian's rancorous remark about her being a hardcase bounty man to keep her emotions under tight rein. "And Eli?" she asked. "Is his leg mending properly?"

"He's doing very well," Ruby said. "So much so that when he got it into his head that for propriety's sake he should put himself up elsewhere, he and I had quite a spirited argument. I, of course, wouldn't hear of his staying anywhere else."

Torey noticed her aunt's attention had settled on Killian.

"Forgive my manners, Aunt Ruby," Torey said. "This is Noah Killian. A friend of Eli's."

Killian doffed his hat. "My pleasure, ma'am." Ruby's smile was gracious, though a shade disconcerted. Torey had never noticed before, but the way Killian's long, dark hair tumbled about his face and shoulders, the man looked more like an Indian than an ex-cavalry officer.

"Mr. Burkett has spoken of you frequently, Mr. Killian," Ruby managed. "And quite highly, I might add. But to be perfectly frank, you are not what I was expecting."

Torey snorted. "He wasn't what I expected either, Aunt Ruby." When the concern in her aunt's hazel eyes turned to alarm, Torey hastened to add, "But he's proven to be quite helpful, truly. And, I can promise you, his behavior toward me has been nothing short of exemplary. In fact," Torey said, drilling Killian a caustic look her aunt could not see, "I've never met a more perfect gentleman."

Killian's jaw tightened.

Torey smiled sweetly.

"My goodness!" Ruby exclaimed. "Do forgive me. The two of you must be exhausted, and here I am chattering on as though we were settled for tea in the parlor. Please, both of you, come inside this minute."

Killian didn't move. "If it's all the same to you, Miss Adams, I think I'll head for a hotel."

"Nonsense," Ruby said. "I wouldn't hear of it for Mr. Burkett. I won't hear of it for you either."

"Yes, Mr. Killian," Torey interjected, ever so agreeably, "I wouldn't want to hear of your heading to a hotel either, because if you do, you can be sure I'll be right behind you."

Killian scowled darkly but raised no further argument. "Lead the way, Miss Adams."

Torey let out a relieved sigh. If Killian truly had it in his head to elude her, there was precious little she could do about it. Her only hope was that he would continue to feel guilty enough, obligated enough to stay with her, at least until he'd talked to Eli.

Still, she felt anything but confident as she followed Killian and her aunt into the house. Inside, Ruby bustled ahead of them down a long, shadowed hallway replete with wall sconces, hat rack, mirror, and umbrella stand. Torey tossed her hat on an available peg but studiously ignored the mirror, concentrating instead on the walls on either side of her. They fairly teemed with photographs, most of them depicting scenes of an earlier, less settled Denver. Most, but not all.

Torey paused in front of one of the pictures. A gilt-framed black-and-white image of a rather stern-looking dark-haired man in an ill-fitting suit, his hand resting on the shoulder of the delicate, fine-featured woman seated in front of him. Torey's throat constricted. Emma and Abel Lansford on their wedding day.

"They were wonderful together, weren't they?" Ruby said wistfully. "My sister loved your father so."

"They were very happy," Torey agreed, twisting away from the painful image, only to have her gaze collide with Killian's. Those storm-gray eyes were regarding her with such a curious intensity that Torey felt her breath catch, her heart flutter strangely in her chest. Then just that quickly the look was gone, and Torey was left to wonder if it had been a trick of the light in the shadowed hallway. She was grateful when her aunt led them into the parlor.

"Please," Ruby said, "make yourselves comfortable, both of you. I'll get the cook to prepare some tea, and we'll—"

"I'd just like to see Eli, Aunt Ruby," Torey cut in. "Please."

"I'm afraid Mr. Burkett is napping, dear; otherwise I would have announced your arrival to him at once." She smiled. "He's going to be so tickled to know that you're all right. He's tried hard not to show it—for my sake, I'm sure—but he's been quite worried."

"Then I'm sure he wouldn't mind if you woke him up," Torey said. The sooner she saw Eli, the sooner she could be on her way again.

Ruby's smile faded. "Please, Victoria, you look so tired. Won't you sit down?"

Torey glanced at the two overstuffed chairs in front of the fireplace, but made no move toward either of them. Nothing had changed in the elaborately furnished parlor since her first visit to her aunt's three months before, but somehow today the sheer vitality of the room was proving a shock to her already rattled system. She stood there feeling grungy and awkward, amid some of the loveliest things she had ever seen—from the elegant grand piano to the Carrara marble fireplace to the whatnot shelves brimming with fine porcelain figurines. Vivid maroon accents in the floral carpet and striped wallpaper gave the room a cheery air that seemed only to exacerbate the bleakness of Torey's mood.

"You have a lovely home, Miss Adams," Killian said.

"You're very kind," Ruby said. "I've been quite fortunate. I started a small dry goods store when Denver was hardly a gleam in the first settler's eye. I now own that store, plus several others."

Killian quirked an eyebrow at her, clearly impressed.

"Surprised that a woman is capable of running a successful business?" Torey asked.

"These days, Vic," he said smoothly, "I'm not at all surprised by what a woman's capable of."

She didn't miss the undercurrent in his voice. Unfortunately, neither did her aunt.

"Is everything all right, Victoria?" she asked.

"Fine. But please, you need to call me Vic, Aunt Ruby."

Ruby looked doubtful. "I don't know if I can do that, dear. Vic seems so . . . so . . . "

"Masculine?" Killian put in.

Torey's lips thinned. Their verbal sparring was taking a higher toll on her nerves than usual today.

Thankfully, Ruby changed the subject. "Did you and Mr. Killian have any success in tracking down those horrible men who hurt Lisbeth?"

For an instant Torey considered telling her aunt about Cal Grady, then thought better of it. She wasn't certain just how much Eli had really told Ruby, and she had a sudden suspicion that Wade Scott and Cleve Jensen might have been glaring omissions in any bit of tale spinning Eli might have done. "We've heard they're planning something up by Fort Laramie. Mr. Killian and I are heading that way after we talk to Eli."

"Oh, surely not so soon!" Ruby exclaimed. "You've only just arrived. You need to rest, see your sister . . . "

"No!"

Ruby's eyes widened.

"You implied Lisbeth was no better," Torey explained hastily. "That means there's no point in my seeing her."

"Oh, but Victoria, you must want—"

"No."

Ruby twisted her hands in the folds of her skirt, clearly distressed.

Torey started to rake her fingers through her hair, then stopped, incensed to realize that she was imitating Killian's patented gesture of frustration. "I'm sorry, Aunt Ruby. Truly." She couldn't bring herself to explain yet again the guilt she felt over what had happened to Lisbeth. "I just can't face seeing her right now. Not with those men still out there somewhere. Please understand."

"Of course, dear." Ruby said, though she obviously didn't understand at all. "I'll go check on Mr. Burkett. I . . . perhaps the two of you would like to freshen up? There's a wash basin in the kitchen."

Reflexively, Torey touched her face, feeling the ever-present layering of trail dust.

Ruby winced. "I meant no insult, Victoria."

Torey crossed to her aunt and gave her hand a reassuring squeeze. "I know that. It's all right. And thank you. I would like very much to freshen up."

Ruby smiled gratefully and left the room.

Torey turned to Killian. "You coming?"

"Think I'm going to sneak out while you wash your face?"

"I wouldn't put it past you."

"Your unfailing trust moves me deeply, Vic."

She glowered at him, then headed for the kitchen, relieved when he followed. She made short work of washing her face and hands, uncomfortable somehow having Killian standing there watching her. Then she stepped aside to allow him to do the same.

"That's better, isn't it?" he rubbed a hand over his freshly scrubbed three-day-old growth of beard.

"I . . . I'm sure my aunt has a razor around somewhere."

"Why? You gonna shave, Vic?"

She ground her teeth together. "You're not funny. I just thought you might like to."

He feigned a wounded look. "You saying you don't like my new beard?"

"I'm saying you can grow a second head for all I care! I was just being polite."

He chuckled, then sobered. "The beard's just a little insurance. I know I'm going to be recognized at Fort Laramie. But why advertise?"

"Oh. I didn't think."

He shrugged. "No reason you should. You're not a convicted coward."

Torey flushed. "I wish you wouldn't talk like that."

"You know a prettier way to say it?"

"That isn't what I— Dammit, Killian, do you have to twist everything into a quarrel? Can't we just pretend to get along for ten minutes? If not for our own sakes, then for my aunt's? She has enough to worry about, without her having to worry about my being with you."

Something flickered in those gray eyes, but it was gone so quickly Torey had no time to decipher it.

Killian sighed. "You were a little hard on your aunt yourself, don't you think?"

His tone was thoughtful, so much so that Torey was taken aback by it. She stared at him, at those eyes that could be ice cold and fire hot, and saw in them a sudden unguarded empathy that made her want to weep. Instead, she stalked toward the nearest window and stared out at the snow-dusted peaks of the Rockies. "I don't want to talk about my aunt."

"She cares about you."

"Don't you think I know that?"

"Frankly, no. I don't think you give anybody credit for caring about you these days."

"Don't."

"Don't what?"

She leaned her forehead against the coolness of the window pane. "Just don't." She closed her eyes. "Oh, God, this was all a mistake. I never should have come here. Not with Pike and the others still out there free to do their worst. Aunt Ruby can't possibly understand why I can't stay here, why I can't bear to see Lisbeth."

She heard Killian's bootfalls as he crossed the kitchen's wooden floor to stand behind her. She did not turn around.

"I'm sorry," he said softly.

She trembled. "For what?"

"For a lot of things. That you're even in this whole mess. That you and your sister aren't back on your farm, milking cows and baking bread."

Torey let out a tiny laugh. "Lisbeth would be baking it. I'd be burning it." She turned, her smile vanishing as she accidentally brushed his chest with her arm. She had known he was close. She hadn't known he was *that* close. Pulses tripping, she swallowed hard, feigning a nonchalance she in no way felt. "Why the sudden change of heart?"

"It's not sudden." He shook himself, as though he'd said something he hadn't intended. "Look," he said, rubbing a hand across the back of his neck, "I know I've been pretty hard on you these past three days, harder even than I meant to be. But there was a reason for it."

His face wasn't ten inches from her own. She could see every tiny hair along his beard-bristled jaw.

"I made a fool of you," she said. "You wanted to pay me back." His lips were full, generous, his teeth white, perfect. There was the tiniest scar just below his left eye that she'd never noticed before.

"No, that isn't it. It might have started out that way . . ." He raked a hand through his tousled locks. "Ah, the hell with it. You want the truth? I've been deliberately trying to make you as miserable as possible."

"Why?"

"Because I'd do anything to make you stop this madness. Anything. I want you to stay here with your sister and your aunt and Eli, where I know you'll be safe. Let me go after Pike alone. Let me get him for both of us."

A warning bell went off inside Torey's head, but she paid it no heed. She was lost in those eyes. Those incredible eyes. The intensity was back. The heat. She had the strangest notion that he wanted to kiss her. But that was absurd. It made more sense that he'd want to throttle her. And yet . . . and yet . . . she could swear those eyes were regarding her with the same kind of heady danger latent in a gathering storm.

Enough! Torey gave herself a mental shake. If Killian had the slightest clue she was entertaining such nonsensical thoughts about him he'd be within his rights to leave her behind on the grounds that she'd lost her mind. "I'm going with you to Laramie," she managed. "That's all there is to it. I made a promise. I intend to keep it."

"Your sister would never hold you accountable to a promise that could cost you your life."

"I hold myself accountable."

Whatever bonds of restraint Killian had attached to himself snapped with a sudden violence. He swore explosively, catching her up by the arms and giving her a swift, hard shake. "Don't you understand me, woman?" he gritted, "I'm not going to have your blood on my hands. I'm not."

Wild, terrified, Torey jerked herself free. "I told you never to touch me!"

He only cursed more feelingly than ever. "Why? Because you're going to kill me? Bullshit. You don't want me dead. Without me, your little plan for revenge goes straight to hell."

"How dare you!"

"How dare I?" His gray eyes glittered dangerously. "Sweetheart, you don't want to know."

Her lips thinned, her heart pounded. How could he seem

so considerate one minute, so callous the next? And how could she ever have thought the emotions simmering in those gray eyes had anything to do with passion? It was all too obvious that the only feeling Killian had for her was fury. Could he really be that angry about her wanting to accompany him to Fort Laramie? Or was something else going on?

"Maybe this isn't about me, at all," she mused aloud. "Maybe it's not my life you're so concerned about, but your own. Or more precisely your own damnable pride."

He blinked, bewildered. "I beg your pardon?"

"You hinted at it yourself. At Fort Laramie we'd be riding straight into your nightmares. And you don't want me there to see your welcoming committee."

Cold fury radiated from every muscle of his body. "You've got it all figured out, don't you? Well, you're dead wrong, Vic. My damnable pride's got nothing to do with this. You know why?" He laughed, a haunted, sick laugh. "Because I don't have any pride left, that's why. The army stripped it from me the day they stripped off my epaulets in front of the entire regiment. The day Colonel Dodd broke my sword over his knee and threw it in the dirt at my feet."

He was trembling, trembling with memories of humiliation so raw, so deep that Torey could feel them too. And then he seemed to shake himself, realize he had revealed too much. With a feral snarl he twisted away from her and stalked to the opposite side of the kitchen.

For a long minute Torey didn't move. She was afraid to, certain that if she took so much as a step her knees would buckle out from under her. Never in her life had she felt so completely engulfed by another person's pain. Her every impulse was to go to him, talk to him, make him understand that it wasn't the army's judgment that had just savaged him, but his own.

And yet she knew instinctively that any show of sympathy from her right now would be misinterpreted as pity and rejected, no doubt with supreme contempt. And so she kept her mouth shut and waited. She would give him a chance to collect himself.

But she wanted it clear in her own mind that this conversation was far from over. Whatever the real issue, Killian was still obviously bent on leaving her behind. And that simply was not going to happen. Not when they were this close to Pike.

She cleared her throat. Killian stiffened, but did not turn around. He was probably expecting that sympathetic platitude.

"I don't know what's keeping my aunt," Torey said, the lightness of her voice sounding false even to her own ears. "Maybe we should go see for our—"

"Sorry to keep you waiting!" Ruby said, choosing that fortuitous moment to bustle into the room. "Mr. Burkett can't wait to see you both. But, naturally, he wanted to make himself presentable. He was in his nightshirt and . . ." Ruby went on chattering, but Torey wasn't listening. She was watching Killian.

He had turned around when Ruby entered the room. The humiliation was gone. In its place was a steel-cold resolve. And Torey knew with a sudden, sick certainty that Eli's opinion wasn't going to matter one whit and neither was her own. Noah Killian was going on to Fort Laramie, and he was going on without her.

14

Torey almost conceded the battle to Killian, even as her aunt led them up the stairs to Eli's room. What was the point of another emotionally charged confrontation? Killian had his mind made up. If the man was intent on going on without her, she could hardly coerce him into doing otherwise. As galling as it was, she had to face the prospect of finding another guide, after all. In a city the size of Denver, surely it couldn't be all that difficult.

And then she got mad. It could take hours, even days to find someone she could even half-trust to ride with her. A fact Killian was likely counting on to give him an insurmountable head start to Fort Laramie. More than that, how could she hope to find a stranger who would understand the depth of her need to find Pike? Especially a stranger who would of necessity be little more than a hired gun? Hardly the most scrupulous of individuals. And of course she would once again face the daunting challenge of riding with a man who didn't know she was a woman. A man who most likely would not abide by the same standards of conduct Noah Killian held himself to.

Torey cringed at the image of someone other than Killian

finding her naked and trembling amongst those rocks, some hired gun she had taken on to help her track down Pike. Just the thought of what might have happened sent an involuntary shudder through her.

Dammit anyway. That was the final truth of all this. She didn't want another guide. As loath as she was to admit it, she wanted Killian. Wanted him, she assured herself firmly, for only the most practical of reasons—he could handle a gun, he hated Pike, and he already knew that she was a woman.

And, she acknowledged with the barest trace of a smile, despite the volatility of their relationship, Killian offered something else no bought-and-paid-for stranger could. He was her friend. She liked the son of a bitch. Most of the time anyway.

She shot him a covert glance as they reached the closed door to Eli's bedroom. She just wasn't sure that this was one of those times. He was looking entirely too smug. No doubt he foresaw no problems in rallying Eli's support for his plan to leave her behind. *Well, he could just think again,* she thought grimly. She'd be damned if she was going to be bullied out of her goal at this late date, not after all she'd been through. If Killian thought he could intimidate her, he could go straight to hell—albeit in a benevolent kind of way. Straightening her spine, Torey waited as her aunt rapped softly on Eli's door.

"Come in," came a familiar, gravelly voice.

Even before Ruby had the door fully opened, Torey burst past her aunt and stormed into the room. For just an instant she was taken aback by the sight of the burly, bearded Eli Burkett ensconced in a huge four-poster maple bed, complete with satin canopy. Amazingly, the buckskin-clad ex-scout looked quite at home amidst the half dozen lace-trimmed pillows at his back and the other three that bolstered his still-splinted leg.

The rest of the room—with its dolls and doilies and wax

flowers under glass—seemed just as feminine, though Eli's presence added a distinct masculine counterpoint to it all.

But Torey wasted no time detailing the room's decor. Instead she marched straight over to the bed. "Good to see you, Eli," she said brusquely.

Eli grinned, his gaze shifting from her to Killian and back again, as though fully aware that a pair of lit fuses had just walked into his room. "The last time you had that look on your face, Vic, you'd just found a rattlesnake in your boot."

"How appropriate," she muttered.

Killian's tone was none too subtle either as he stalked to the foot of Eli's bed. "I don't think you'll be too surprised to hear that I want to talk to you alone, old man."

"Not likely!" Torey snapped, jabbing a finger in Killian's direction. "Anything you have to say to Eli, you can say to me."

"Well, I'll be dad-gummed!" Eli said, slapping the thigh on his good leg and chortling gleefully. "I knew you two would send some sparks flyin', but this? Oh, what I wouldn't have given to be a fly on Galahad's rump."

He continued to chuckle while Torey fumed.

"So how long did it take to figure out Vic's little secret, Noah?" Eli prodded. "Five minutes? Ten?"

"It took him nearly a week," Torey spat out, "and he only found out because of a hideous accident."

Eli let out a low whistle. "A week? The great ladies' man Noah Killian? Bet that didn't settle too well on the side of male conceit, did it, *compadre*?"

Killian scowled darkly. Torey made no attempt to warn Eli that he was poking a wounded bear with a stick.

"When we're alone, we'll talk, Eli," Killian repeated.

"Talk about leaving me behind!" Torey said bitterly. "Damn you, that is not going to hap—"

"Victoria, please," Ruby interrupted anxiously, "I don't understand what's happening here. I thought the three of you were . . . were colleagues of a sort."

Torey winced. She had forgotten Ruby was even in the room. Her aunt had remained by the door, evidently to give what she had assumed were three old friends a chance to visit.

"I'm sorry, Aunt Ruby, I . . . this is difficult to explain. We . . . that is, Mr. Killian and I—"

"Your niece and I are friends, Miss Adams," Killian interrupted, the words spoken with a quiet conviction that surprised Torey and touched her more deeply than she cared to admit. That is, until he continued. "It's simply that my *friend*"—why did the word suddenly sound like a curse?—"doesn't have the slightest idea what's best for her."

"And sometimes a friend doesn't know what the hell he's talking about," Torey shot back. "We wouldn't even be having this conversation if you still thought I was Vic Langley. If Cal Grady hadn't gotten himself killed, and I hadn't wound up in that creek, you would never—"

Ruby gasped. "Someone died?"

"Nice going, *Vic*," Killian said, doubtless figuring he'd just secured Ruby to his side of this debate.

Briefly, tersely, Torey told Ruby and Eli about their encounter with Grady, finishing with, "The man drowned. It wasn't anyone's fault."

Ruby turned accusing eyes on Eli. "Mr. Burkett, you told me my niece was in the company of a former cavalry officer, who would act as her guardian. And that *he* would be the one who sought out the men who killed my sister's husband and brutalized my niece."

Torey snorted. "Noah Killian is not my guardian."

"Amen to that," Killian said, sending her a blistering glare.

"I have to apologize, Miss Ruby," Eli said. "I just couldn't bring myself to tell you that your niece was packin' iron and traipsin' after killers. I thought it would be easier on your mind to think she was being taken care of."

"The fault isn't Eli's, Aunt Ruby," Torey said. "It's mine. It was my choice to pass myself off as a bounty hunter. I saw it as the only chance I had of getting close to the men I was after. I know this must be impossible for you to understand, but . . ."

"Maybe not," Ruby said gently. "My first three years in this town, I told everyone I had a husband who was back East sending me money and making decisions. It was the only way anyone would do business with me. I'm not saying your situation is even remotely like mine, Victoria, but believe me, I understand the temptation of resorting to a charade to get by in a world where sometimes it just seems easier to be a man."

"Thank you for that, Aunt Ruby," Torey said, shooting Killian a triumphant look. He only shook his head, seeming more disappointed than angry.

"Not so fast, dear," Ruby chided. "I said I understood the temptation. I didn't say I approved. You've already risked so much, lost so much. Surely, it would be best to leave the rest of this manhunt . . . to men."

Torey began to pace. "I can't do that, Aunt Ruby. I made a promise to Lisbeth. I intend to carry it out."

"You know," Ruby said softly, "one of the things in her life that your mother held most dear was the closeness of her two girls. It reminded Emma of our own childhood."

"Don't do this . . ."

"What becomes of Lisbeth, Victoria, if a promise you made in her name costs you your life?"

"She wouldn't know one way or the other!"

"She's going to get well, Victoria. She is. I know it. In fact, a surprise visit from you might be exactly—"

"No!"

Ruby sighed deeply. "Very well. I'll leave you to your friends. It's time I prepared Lisbeth something to eat anyway." Ruby started toward the door, then hesitated. "Just ask yourself one thing, Victoria, please. In your heart of hearts, which has become more important to you? Lisbeth's getting well? Or your need for revenge?"

Bitter tears stung Torey's eyes, but she swallowed the angry, defensive retort that sprang to her lips. Instead she turned her back on her aunt, saying nothing more until she heard Ruby leave the room.

"I guess I couldn't really expect her to understand," she said shakily, crossing back to Eli's side. "She wasn't there. But you understand, don't you, Eli? You saw it. You saw what those animals did to Lisbeth, to my father. Please. Tell Killian he can't leave me behind."

Eli gazed at her with sad, sympathetic eyes, then slowly shook his head.

Torey felt the first real nigglings of defeat. With an oath she stomped over to Killian. "This isn't going to happen," she said. "You've got no right. I proved myself to you time and again. I can outshoot you—"

"You can outcuss me too," he cut in. "But that isn't going to make me change my mind."

Torey felt the tears again, tears of rage and frustration, tears that she was certain would only look to Killian like feminine weakness. "Why are you doing this?"

"I told you"—there was something hard beneath the mockery in his voice—"I don't want another body on my conscience."

"And I say you're a liar! Vic Langley didn't prick your conscience. You're backing out of this because I'm a woman. And that's the only reason, isn't it? Isn't it?"

"Your part in this is over, Victoria. Finished. Stay here and burn cookies for your family. It's where you belong."

If he had slapped her, he could not have hurt her more. To hear the scorn in his voice, the dismissal after she had fought so hard and so long to show herself capable, competent was an agony beyond bearing. The confidence she'd so carefully built up these past five months crumbled to dust. "I'll never forgive you for this." With a half sob she ran from the room.

* * *

The silence in the room hung heavy, tense long minutes after Torey's departure. Noah did nothing to ease it. If he had any sense, he told himself, he'd get the hell out of here, mount his horse, ride and not look back. Instead he stalked to the nearest window and fixed his gaze on the mountains. Always before, the sight of the Rockies had moved him, touched him, a natural wonder to behold with awe, even reverence. This afternoon they seemed only isolated and forbidding.

Finally it was Eli who broke the silence. "You mind telling me what the hell that was all about?"

Noah did not turn around. "You saw for yourself."

"What I saw was you being a bastard to a girl who means a helluva lot to me."

"You hit on the key word, Eli. *Girl.*" He stalked over to Eli's bed. "Why in God's name didn't you tell me the truth about her?"

"She asked me not to."

"That's not good enough."

Eli fingered the lacy border on one of the pillows. "She was going to tell you herself, after she proved she could pull off the masquerade. But she changed her mind."

"Why?"

"I can't be positive, but I think it had something to do with what happened in that saloon between the two of you."

Noah felt something twist in his gut. "I scared the hell out of her."

"Maybe. And maybe you reminded her she was—" He stopped. "Never mind."

"What was she like, Eli? Before Pike?"

Eli smiled, a thoughtful smile tinged with melancholy. "You wouldn't know it to look at her, but she was a real proper and sweet young lady. Happy, easygoing, with a head full of romantic dreams."

"Romantic?"

"Typical young-lady dreams. Knights on white horses. And, oh my, was she pretty. She had hair like spun midnight that hung clean down to her waist. Broke my heart the night she hacked it off." He shook his head sadly. "You would've liked her, Noah."

"I like her now," he said without thinking. Her spirit, her temper, her courage. His mind flashed to long, ivory-smooth legs. With an oath he shoved the thought away.

"You've been with her over a week, Noah. You've got to know what that promise she made means to her."

"Three of the men are dead."

"Three more are still out there."

"You saying you approve of what she's doing?"

"I never approved of it. But I understood it. And I think you do too. She's come this far, it should be her choice to finish it. Is she right? Are you backing out of taking her because you found out she's a woman?"

"She's exactly right," Noah said. "Exactly right for all the wrong reasons." He began to pace. "It's got nothing to do with how she handles herself. Hell, I'd rather have her watching my back than half the men I know."

"Then what is it?"

"It's me."

Eli frowned, confused. Noah could hardly blame him. He was damned confused himself. He had yet to sort through the feelings that assaulted his every waking moment since he'd discovered Victoria Lansford's "little secret," since he'd discovered she was one and the same with the woman who had inexplicably touched his battered, cynical soul in that Cuttersville saloon.

"All I know, Eli," he said slowly, "is that if there's a showdown with Pike, and she's there, I'm not going to be able to think straight. I'm going to get us both killed."

Astonishment dawned on Eli's craggy face. "I'll be damned. I knew it was something, but I never figured on . . . My God, man, she's got you culled, roped, and branded, and she doesn't even know it."

"Like hell!" Noah snapped, something akin to fear jolting

through him. "That's the last thing I meant to imply. I just meant that because she's a woman, I'd be worried about her."

"So, let me get this straight. Her being a woman isn't the problem. But it is." Eli snorted. "Torey's right, old friend. You *are* a liar. 'Cept I can't quite figure out who you're lyin' to. Torey or yourself."

A muscle in Noah's jaw tightened. He wasn't getting through to Eli either. "All right," he snarled, "you want it blunt and ugly? I want her, Eli. I want her in my bed. It's nothing more mysterious than that."

Eli's brown eyes narrowed ominously. "Maybe I need my hearin' checked," he said. "I can't have heard what I just think I heard."

"I want her, Eli. I can't sleep at night for wanting her. And if she comes with me, I'm going to have her."

"You saying her opinion wouldn't matter?"

Noah didn't answer.

"You'd best be glad my leg is broke, Noah Killian," Eli gritted. "If I could get out of this bed, I'd break your bloody neck. How dare you talk about her like that, after what she's been through. My God, I thought I knew you, the kind of man you are. The kind of man who honors a woman, who honors a promise to a friend."

"Be *her* friend, Eli. Make damned sure she doesn't follow me." With that Noah stalked from the room, slamming the door behind him. He stood there in the deserted hallway shaking with what it had cost him to be such a bastard to Eli. But he assured himself he had no choice. If Torey was still entertaining thoughts about following him, Eli would make damned sure she thought again.

He started down the hallway, then stopped. Across from him was an open door, beyond which he heard voices, female voices. One of the voices belonged to Torey. The other he didn't recognize. It was soft, melodic, a woman's voice, yet strangely childlike.

Noah told himself to just keep walking. He didn't want another verbal battle with Victoria. If he left without seeing her again, he could make certain she would have no chance to follow. It was a ruthless choice, even cruel. But it was necessary. His years in the army had not been without tough decisions, tough decisions he'd never once shied away from.

But this one was different. This time the tough decision was not what he should do, but what he shouldn't. He should leave, spare Torey any further grief. But the thought of never seeing her again—and he was certain once he rode out of here that he never would—weighed heavily on him. He didn't want her to hate him.

Crossing to the doorway, he peered into the room. A band seemed to tighten around his chest. Torey was sitting on the edge of a canopied bed, her trail-dusty clothes as much a contrast to the delicate frills of the bedcoverings as Eli's buckskins had been in his room. Her back was to him, her head bowed, her short dark curls falling toward her face. A bittersweet image rose up to haunt him, an image of a lovely young woman with long, dark hair spilling across her shoulders to her waist, a woman adorned in satin and lace, a bewitching innocence shining in her blue-green eyes.

Her shoulders were trembling, and he knew that she was crying. She was holding the hand of the fragile-looking young woman in the bed, a woman in her midtwenties who appeared to be playing with a rag-stuffed doll.

"Such a pretty dolly," Lisbeth said.

Noah cleared his throat. Torey stiffened abruptly, her hand going to her face to dash away the tears he knew she didn't want him to see. She stood then and faced him, her eyes sparking with a belligerence that made his heart ache. "Forget some particular insult?" she demanded acidly.

He kept his face expressionless. "I'm heading out."

"You already made that pretty clear."

"I'll get Pike. Don't worry."

Her eyes glittered with unguarded contempt. "If you'll excuse me," she said, "I'm going down to see what's keeping Aunt Ruby with Lisbeth's dinner." She brushed past him.

"Victoria?"

She stopped.

"You . . . uh, you take care, all right?"

She glared at him. "Go to hell." With that she was gone.

Noah stood there, feeling like the wrong end of a horse, but assuring himself he was doing the right thing, the only thing. He could not, would not, risk her life. Nor would he torment himself with another night of her asleep in their camp, so close yet so infinitely beyond his reach.

"Pretty dolly," Lisbeth said again.

Noah blinked, dragging himself back to the reality of the moment. He was startled to realize that Lisbeth was holding her doll in his direction.

"That is a pretty doll," he said, looking uncertainly toward the door. Should he call Torey back?

"You can hold her," Lisbeth said shyly.

"I can, huh?" Awkwardly, Noah sat down on the bed and accepted the bedraggled-looking doll, a plaything that had obviously seen better days. Mismatched shoe-button eyes stared blankly up at him. "Such a pretty doll should have a name. What's her name, Lisbeth?"

"Gertrude," Lisbeth said, her own eyes regarding him with a kind of detached serenity.

"My name's Noah. I'm a . . . a friend of your sister's."

Lisbeth's eyes misted. "Torey's not home. Torey's lost."

"No. No, she's here. She went downstairs. She'll be right back."

"Torey's lost." A tear trailed down Lisbeth's cheek.

Noah's own eyes burned. Maybe Lisbeth had a point. "I don't want you to worry about Torey. She's going to stay here now and help you get well."

"Torey's sad."

"Yes, Torey's very sad. She's sad because you aren't getting better. She needs you to get better, Lisbeth." He picked up her hand and squeezed it gently. "Can you do that?"

"Bad men hurt Papa. Hurt me."

"I know. But they're never going to hurt you again, sweetheart. I swear." He laid the doll to one side and spoke earnestly. "You're not a little girl anymore, Lisbeth. And I don't think it's a good idea to treat you like one. Torey talked about you sometimes, when she wasn't mad at me about . . . "—he grimaced—"about just about anything. I know you were married, and you lost your husband."

Lisbeth's lower lip trembled.

"Life doesn't make much sense sometimes, does it?" He wondered if he was making a grave mistake to press her. But there seemed to be just the barest hint of awareness in those green eyes, and so he plunged on. "You've seen the best a man can be. And you've seen the worst. I promise you, Lisbeth, if I could make the hurt go away, I would. But I'm going to be selfish here. I want the hurt to go away for Torey too. She's in a lot of pain, Lisbeth. She feels responsible for what happened to you. That's why you have to do your best to get better. Do you understand?"

He was so intent on Lisbeth, he did not know he was no longer alone with her.

"Torey misses you, Lisbeth. She needs you in her life." His thoughts tumbled frantically as he searched his mind for something, anything that might get through to her. "Maybe you could teach her to cook. She tells me that you're a very good cook, that you can make an old boot taste like apple pie."

Lisbeth smiled ever so slightly.

"Torey can't cook at all, can she? If you don't get better, someday she's going to poison the man who's lucky enough"—he curled his fingers into his palm—"who's lucky enough to marry her."

"Torey . . . needs me."

"Yes." His voice shook. "Yes, she does."

Lisbeth's hand shifted slightly, coming over to rest on Noah's own.

"My God." Torey's voice.

Noah turned, startled, letting go of Lisbeth's hand. How long had Torey been standing there?

"She heard you," Torey said wonderingly. "She was talking to you."

He felt raw, exposed, and not a little desperate, afraid that everything he'd said in Eli's room to get Torey to stay behind was going to go for nothing. That Torey would see through what he had been trying to do. He couldn't let that happen. Geting to his feet, he said stiffly, "I just said what I thought she wanted to hear."

"Lissa?" Torey leaned close to her sister. "Lissa, honey . . . ?"

"Noah . . . nice."

"Yes." Tears slid down Torey's cheeks. "Yes, he is, isn't he?" She was staring at him with wide, vulnerable eyes.

"I'd better go," he said.

"Noah, please . . ."

"Don't call me that!" he snapped.

She blinked, bewildered. "Call you what?"

She'd never called him anything but Killian. How could he possibly explain that the way she had murmured Noah just now was as much a caress as any touch he'd ever known? That the way she was looking at him was turning his blood to fire. He had to get out of here. Get out of here now. "I'll send word if I find Pike." He started toward the door.

Torey caught his arm, and he stopped.

"I'm sorry about before," she said. "I know you're just scared for me."

"Don't flatter yourself." The words sounded hollow even to his own ears.

"I want to go with you."

"No."

"Please?" Her hand tightened on his arm, her gaze imploring him.

God, oh God. Could she possibly be that naive? Didn't she know what she was doing to him? All he wanted in the world at that moment was to drag her into his arms, kiss the living hell out of her, find a private, secluded place and make love to her. Make love to her with a passion and ferocity that terrified him.

And in that instant he knew why he had stayed. Not to make sure she didn't hate him, but to make sure she did. Hate him so completely she would never be foolish enough to come after him, never be foolish enough to let him . . .

"You follow me, Victoria, you'll regret it the rest of your life."

"I thought we were friends."

He laughed harshly. "We were friends when I thought you were Vic Langley. But friendship isn't what I have in mind anymore. You're a woman, Victoria. And I'm a man. There's only one kind of alliance I'm interested in now."

Her eyes widened with shock, betrayal. "Are you trying to scare me?"

"I'm trying to advise you of the facts of life."

"You're lying! You wouldn't hurt me. You're not like Pike and the others."

"Oh, it wouldn't hurt, Victoria." He grazed her cheek with the tips of his fingers. "It wouldn't hurt at all. I guarantee it."

With a cry of outrage she slapped his hand away. "How dare you? You're despicable!"

"Believe it," he said softly, then turned and stalked out the door.

15

For long minutes after Killian had gone Torey stood in the doorway of Lisbeth's room and trembled. What had just happened? One minute she had been fragilely awed that he had seemed to reach into some secret corner of her sister's mind. The next he'd looked Torey square in the face and leveled a barely veiled threat about what he had in mind for her should she dare follow him.

There's only one kind of alliance I'm interested in now.

She shivered. How could he say such a thing? It didn't even make any sense. She wasn't the sort of woman to rouse his sexual appetites. She'd seen a sampling of his women in Belle Whitley—a bosomy, petite, libidinous beauty. Torey fit none of those criteria.

But then there had been that tiny fraction of time in the Cuttersville saloon, when he had pulled her into his arms and murmured wistful, melancholy words about both of them forgetting their troubles, just for one night. He had all too obviously been attracted to her then. Or rather, attracted to the woman he had thought her to be—a saloon woman in Belle Whitley's employ.

It wouldn't hurt, Victoria. It wouldn't hurt at all. I guarantee it.

It already hurt. It hurt because she had dared consider him a friend. Damn his hide. He had to know what a remark like that would do to her. That he evidently didn't care cut even more deeply than the words themselves. With a weary sigh Torey crossed Lisbeth's room to the window that looked out toward the city. Her gaze snagged on the lone rider heading up the winding tree-flanked road. In the long minutes Torey watched him, he never once looked back.

Her heart gave a strange twist. She should be angry, outraged both by his parting words and by his attempt to keep her from Pike. Instead what she felt most was an almost overwhelming sense of loss. And she had yet to decide what she was going to do about it. Let him get away with it. Or go after him, consequences be damned.

Torey's gaze shifted to her sister, noting with a bittersweet ache that Lisbeth had resumed playing with her doll. "That world of yours looks awfully inviting today, Lissa," Torey murmured. "Where nothing and no one can hurt you."

What would it have been like if things had been different? If the attack on the farm had never happened. If the massacre had never happened. If Noah Killian had come into her life the way she'd always dreamed a man would one day come—a man to bring her flowers, take her to dances, read her poems, take her on picnics. A man who admired her wit and intelligence and even her height. Her skin tingled. A man to want her the way a man wants a woman.

Damn. What was it about Killian that mattered so much anyway? That made her hurt in places she had locked up tight that hideous spring night nearly six months ago?

But she knew. Though time and again she'd denied it, repressed it, she knew. She was in love with him. She'd known it since the night they spent huddled in the rocks together awaiting the arrival of Cal Grady.

You're a good man to have as a friend, Noah Killian.

It had taken every ounce of restraint she'd possessed that night not to tell him the truth about Vic Langley, not to give herself over to the tenderness and warmth she suspected would have been there for her, if she'd but asked.

And then the moment was gone. And Noah had found out the truth by accident. He'd been compassionate and kind, but he'd been wary as well—and hurt. Deep down he had to know that her leaving her trail partner in the dark about her masquerade could only have meant one thing—she didn't trust him.

And she hadn't. At first.

But she'd realized early on that she didn't trust herself either. Not with Noah Killian.

He was a man to whom she had felt irresistibly drawn ever since that first moment in the Take Your Chances Saloon. At the time she'd chalked up her reaction to fear. But fear didn't explain the flutter in her heart when he had touched her, or the strange heat in her veins when he had kissed her. Time and again she had rejected the truth of those feelings, because she had indeed been afraid—afraid of herself as a woman.

But more and more lately those feelings were clamoring to be set free. She didn't want to be Vic Langley anymore. She wanted to be Victoria Lansford. And the reason for those feelings was riding up that road, and out of her life.

The question remained—would she let him?

Torey closed her eyes. She had found the courage to go after killers, but she wasn't at all certain she had the courage to go after love.

More miserable than ever, Torey turned away from the window and wandered over to her sister's bedside. "I'm so confused, Lissa," she said, sagging onto the quilted coverlet. "I wish I had my big sister to talk to."

"Torey lost." Lisbeth stroked the bedraggled curls on Gertrude's head.

Torey stared at her sister, almost afraid to breathe. Had

Lisbeth actually been speaking to her? Or was she just parroting part of the conversation she'd had earlier with Noah? Not daring to hope, Torey continued, "Yes, Lissa, I feel very lost."

"I've been far away."

"Yes."

Lisbeth's lower lip quivered and tears trailed down her pale cheeks. "Papa's dead."

Torey's heard thudded. "Yes."

"I'm sorry, Victoria. I shouldn't have gone away. I should've taken care of you." Lisbeth was still looking at her doll.

"You did just fine."

"You took care of me, brought me here."

"You remember that?"

"The train ride. Aunt Ruby. She's tall, like you. And Papa. He's with Mama now. And Tom. They talk to me sometimes."

Torey worried her lower lip, but Lisbeth did not seem in the least alarmed by the notion that she'd been talking to spirits. In fact, the thought seemed to give her comfort. Torey did not challenge it.

"Those men," Lisbeth said suddenly, her voice breaking. "Those horrible men . . ."

Torey caught her sister's hand. "They'll never hurt you again. I promise."

Lisbeth relaxed a little, her brow furrowing in concentration. "That's what he said. That nice man."

"Noah?"

"Noah. Yes. He was very nice."

"Yes. Very nice." Torey's own voice shook.

"Is he your beau?"

Torey's eyes went wide. "Why would you think that?"

"Papa said you had a beau now. And that he wasn't a spineless ninny like Jim Buckley."

Torey's heart hammered so hard she was surprised

it didn't burst from her chest. How in the world—? "Noah . . . Noah is just helping me." It was all so eerie, the way Lisbeth continued to talk to her, yet seemed not to be talking to her at all. "He's a friend of Eli's."

"He's helping you catch those men, isn't he?"

Torey nodded, assuring herself that Lisbeth had simply been more aware of her surroundings than any of them had suspected.

"But now he's alone," Lisbeth said. Before Torey could reply, Lisbeth went on, her next words sending a chill skittering up Torey's spine. "I didn't want Tom to go hunting alone that morning, Torey. Do you remember that? I tried to stop him. I should have stopped him."

A foreboding as real and ominous as the one she had ignored the day of the attack on the farm clawed through Torey. *I should have stopped him.* Only she wasn't thinking about Tom. She was thinking about Noah.

I should have stopped him.

"Victoria, are you all right?" For the first time Lisbeth's pale green eyes seemed to focus. She was no longer looking at her doll. She was looking at Torey.

Torey was still reeling from the force of her premonition. "Yes, Lissa, I'm fine," she lied. "Fine."

"Your hair. What did you do to your hair?"

Torey blinked, disconcerted by the whipsaw change of subject. "I . . . I got tired of brushing it." She couldn't concentrate on what Lisbeth was saying. She couldn't think of anything but Noah. There was more at stake now than her feelings. More at stake than waiting to confront him after he'd taken care of Pike. She was suddenly, terrifyingly certain that if she didn't go after Noah now she would never see him again. Not because he would choose to ride out of her life.

But because he was going to die.

Not because Pike was faster, but because Noah didn't much give a damn about living.

"Torey," Lisbeth murmured, "I'm frightened."

"So am I, Lissa. So am I." Torey sat there, trembling. What was she going to do? She had to go after Noah. But how could she leave her sister? Especially now when Lisbeth was making real progress?

Ruby bustled into the room then, carrying a dinner tray. "I'm so sorry I took so long."

"Aunt Ruby," Lisbeth said.

Ruby stood stock-still. "Merciful God."

Over the next hour Lisbeth slowly emerged from the protective cocoon that had sheltered her for so long. Torey and Ruby were both stunned by the number of real events Lisbeth had absorbed despite the fantasy world she'd lived in.

"I remember now," Lisbeth said wonderingly, looking at Torey. "I remember the night you cut your hair and strapped on that gun. I tried so hard to get out, to talk to you. I knew you blamed yourself. And I knew you shouldn't. But I couldn't make you understand."

"You have nothing to be sorry about," Torey said. "This whole mess is my doing."

"Never say that!" Lissa cried. "Papa doesn't blame you and neither do I. Those men are to blame. Only them."

Torey knelt beside her sister's bed, the truth hitting her like a fist. "I ran away, Lissa. Don't you see that? The clothes, the guns, the bounty hunting. I ran away because I couldn't bear to look at you, to remember . . . "

"Hush, now," Lisbeth said, pulling Torey into her arms and hugging her close. "Hush, now. It's all right. Everything's going to be all right."

For long minutes Torey allowed her sister to hold her, but finally she drew away. "I'm so glad to have you back, Lissa." She felt as if she were being torn apart. So much joy on the one hand, and yet on the other—stark terror. "I want so much to stay here, to be with you. You have to know that."

"But you're afraid for Noah."

"He's in terrible danger."

"I understand, Torey. I would've done anything to save Tom."

"But, Victoria," Ruby put in, "you can't mean to go after him on your own."

"Noah's hurting, Aunt Ruby. He's hurting so badly. He won't even admit how much. I'm terrified that all the ugliness of being at the fort is going to keep him from being focused on Pike. That he's going to get himself killed."

"Have you thought that he might be even less focused if you're there?" Lisbeth asked gently.

"What do you mean?"

"I mean, the man adores you. I could hear it in his voice. Don't you think he'd rather have you here, where he knows you'll be safe?"

"I can think of a lot of words Noah might attach to how he feels about me," Torey said wanly, "but I don't think 'adore' . . . " She stopped, frowning.

Safe. Of course.

I'd do anything to make you stop this madness. Anything. I want you to stay here with your sister and your aunt and Eli, where I know you'll be safe . . .

Anything. Including being a son of a bitch and scaring her half to death. "Forgive me, Lissa, Aunt Ruby," Torey said, "but I need to see Eli. I need directions to Fort Laramie."

Torey muttered a curse and reined Galahad to a halt. It was near dusk and she was on a wide dirt road heading north out of Denver. Her best guess put Noah still two hours ahead of her, which left her with virtually no chance of overtaking him before nightfall. Not that she was in any hurry to do so. She didn't regret following him. She just wasn't sure when she wanted to catch up with him—as quickly as possible or just before he reached Fort Laramie.

Four hours ago she'd charged out of Lisbeth's room set to ride after him hell-for-leather. And then she'd talked to Eli. The ex–mountain man had been less than enthusiastic about her decision. In fact, for the first time since she'd known him, Eli had been genuinely angry with her.

"Noah's a man on the edge, Miss Torey," Eli had said, his big fists knotting in his bedcoverings. "I want you to stay away from him."

"I can't do that. He needs me."

"You have no idea what that man needs."

She swallowed hard, then looked Eli straight in the eye. "Maybe I do."

He stared at her. "I never should've sent for him. Blast it, girl, your sister needs you now. Let Noah handle Pike."

"This isn't about Pike, Eli. Not anymore. It's about Noah. And it's about me." She shoved her hands into the pockets of her denims. "I love him. And I think maybe he has feelings for me too."

"Yeah, and I know what those feelings are," Eli snapped. "That's why you need to leave him be."

"Noah would never hurt me."

"Maybe he wouldn't mean to, girl," Eli allowed. "But that boy's been through a helluva lot of misery these past three years. And to think of him headin' back to the fort . . . " Eli's lips thinned. "It scares hell out of me. You didn't see it. You can't know what it was like for him. The massacre, the court-martial. He was a proud man, Miss Torey. And they cut him down to nothin'. Nothin'."

"That's all the more reason he can't go back there alone."

"Damnation, girl! I'm scared for you. He's not the Noah Killian I knew."

"Neither one of us is the same. Thanks to Pike. But wasn't it you who said you can't change the core of who a man is?"

"Maybe I was wrong."

"I don't believe that, and I don't think you do either."

Eli seemed to be waging some inner war with himself, and Torey suspected that, despite his doubts, he still felt an abiding loyalty to Noah. It was for that reason that Torey dismissed his other worries. If Eli truly felt Noah capable of harming her, he wouldn't just be angry about her going after him, he would stop her. Somehow, some way, he would stop her, even if it meant hobbling after her himself.

She crossed to the bed and took one of his bear-paw hands in her own. "I want you to think back to why you sent for Noah in the first place. It was because you loved him like a son. Isn't that right?"

Eli didn't answer.

"And because you were hoping that finding Pike would give him back his life. Like he gave you back yours after the army killed your family."

Eli closed his eyes. "I do love 'im, Miss Torey. Maybe that's part of the reason I don't want you goin' after him. Maybe I'm tryin' to protect him from himself. Keep him from makin' a mistake he'd regret the rest of his life."

"And I'll regret it the rest of my life if I don't go after him." She leaned over and gave Eli a kiss on his bewhiskered cheek. "Help me, Eli. Help me help him. Please."

With supreme reluctance Eli laid out the route to Laramie. When he'd finished, Torey turned to leave, but paused when she caught Eli eyeing her critically. "Now what?"

"I was just noticin' that even in that get-up you don't look like a man anymore."

That jarred her. "What do you mean?"

"Just what I said. Your little charade isn't so foolproof these days."

Self-consciously Torey touched her face, her hair. "It's just that I don't have my hat on. I left it downstairs."

"Uh-uh. That's not it. There's something about you. Your eyes, maybe. They're not the same. The woman in you is trying to get out, girl."

Torey considered that, then said softly, so very softly, "And maybe it's Noah who can set her free."

And now here she was, dusk approaching, riding the road to Laramie and marveling at her own boldness. *Set her free.*

Her heart fluttered. Just how far was she prepared to go to be set free?

There's only one kind of alliance I'm interested in now.

Had Noah's words truly been a threat?

Or could they have been an invitation?

She thought about him, up ahead somewhere, alone. What was he thinking? Did he regret his words, no matter what their intent? Or was he grateful to have her gone?

Gone, because he didn't want her.

Or gone, because he did.

She remembered his heated gaze in her aunt's hallway, the certainty that he'd wanted to kiss her when they'd been alone in the kitchen.

Then why had he been so adamant about leaving her behind? Was it really to keep her safe from Pike? Or, she swallowed nervously, was Eli right? Was Noah trying to keep her safe from himself?

It was a question she couldn't answer. She told herself that was why she held back, why she didn't push Galahad into a dead run to try and catch up with him tonight. She wanted to find him, pinpoint his location, but maybe, just maybe, it would be best for both of them if she waited to confront him until just before they reached the fort.

As she rode, Torey took comfort in the fact that Noah had made no attempt to disguise his trail, nor had he veered off the main road. At least not yet. She was grateful too for the lack of other traffic. She'd passed a few riders and wagons, some heading into Denver, some heading out, but there hadn't been enough activity to obscure Bear's hoofprints. Which, barring a rainstorm, would have been difficult to obliterate in any case, given the fact that Noah had kept Bear to the road's edge, while most other traffic opted for its center. It was almost as if he were drawing a map for anyone following.

Her heart skipped a beat. Was he?

She made camp only when it was too dark to follow. She

didn't want to chance accidentally getting ahead of him. She built a fire and chewed on some beef jerky, figuring it was better than anything she could've cooked. Then she curled into her blankets for the night. She was lonely and, she admitted, a little frightened, but oddly exhilarated as well. She'd come a long way from being a terrified Kansas farm girl. Noah, she decided, would be proud of her. That thought dancing uppermost in her mind, Torey closed her eyes and slept.

She repeated the same process over the next four days, riding from dawn to dusk, never seeming to get close enough to Noah to catch up with him, yet never quite losing his trail either. It was almost as if the man were toying with her. Staying just out of reach. And yet, she fumed, taking care not to let her get lost either.

On the fifth day she'd had enough. By her reckoning they were close enough to the fort now that they could be there the next day. She wasn't going to let Noah ride in without her. Tonight, even after it grew dark, she would keep riding.

She was studying the ground as the sun set. He wasn't more than two hours ahead of her. Her heart hammered against her ribs. In two hours she intended to be standing in his camp.

Drawing in a determined breath, Torey remounted Galahad and nudged the gelding forward. Though she tried to keep her mind carefully blank, she couldn't seem to stop herself from imagining his reaction to seeing her. He would be furious, of course. Or at least pretend to be. She had little doubt of that. But after he'd gotten used to the idea of her being with him again, where would he go from there? Would he admit that he'd wanted her to follow him? That he'd missed her? That he cared about her? Would the heat in those gray eyes finally translate into a kiss? Because she wanted him to kiss her. Oh, God, did she want him to. Some part of her couldn't wait to compare the kiss of a man like Noah Killian to the boy she now knew Jim Buckley to be.

Two hours passed. Torey stopped frequently to strike a match and check the ground. Was the man going to ride all night? And then she found the spot where he'd veered east toward a stand of willows. The trees meandered along a creek that she could hear, but couldn't see. If she positioned herself just right she could make out the orange-red glow of a campfire among the trees.

Her heart thudded. Noah was less than two hundred yards from where she was standing. All she had to do was close the distance between them. Then why was she having such a hard time convincing her legs to move?

She glanced about and noted several places she could set up her own camp, minus a fire. Wouldn't it be better to face him in the morning? The cold light of day and all that. Maybe he would be more amenable then to just letting her ride along.

"Can they court-martial a civilian for cowardice?" she muttered aloud. Because she was certainly guilty of it.

Squaring her shoulders, Torey gathered up Galahad's reins and headed toward the fire. She made no attempt to go in quietly. She didn't want to startle him. A Cal Grady welcoming committee was not what she had in mind. But if Noah happened to miss the sounds of her bootfalls or the whinnying greeting of Galahad to Bear, he would surely be able to pick up the nervous pounding of her heart. To her own ears, it was as loud as cannon fire.

She was thus astonished when he offered no sign he was aware of her approach. None. This, even though she was practically on top of the camp.

Stopping just outside the circle of light, Torey tied off Galahad to a shrub, then stared into the camp, disbelieving. Her days of anticipation had prepared her for any number of possible receptions on Noah's part. But she had been a pure fool not to anticipate the most glaringly obvious reception of all. Her hands curled into fists at her sides.

Noah was on his back near the fire, arms splayed out beside him, snoring loudly, his hat brim tugged low to cover his eyes. Next to his right hand was a nearly empty bottle of whiskey.

He was drunk. Blind, stinking drunk. He reeked of it.

Torey stood there, gaping at him, trying vainly to suppress the disappointment that ripped through her. Damn him. With an oath she stomped over to where he lay and kicked him square in the bottom of one of his booted feet. "Drowning nightmares again?" she demanded.

He jerked awake, cursing, belatedly groping for his gun. He stopped only when he saw who it was. Wincing, he struggled to a sitting position, then pressed his fingertips to his temples. "What the hell are you doing here?"

"Looking for you."

"You found me. Now get the hell back to your aunt's."

"No."

He cursed vividly, but stopped when the effort seemed to be more than his head could bear. "Dammit, get out of here."

"I'm going with you to get Pike," she stated flatly, her tone, she hoped, leaving no room for argument. All of her earlier fantasies of an emotion-charged reunion where each would declare their undying love for the other had disappeared in a haze of disgust. She tried to convince herself that he'd turned to the whiskey because he'd missed her, because he'd felt badly about the way he'd treated her. But he'd been drunk too many times before. He was drunk, she realized miserably, because that was the way Noah Killian chose to spend his nights.

"I told you," he said, his words slurring slightly, "I'll get Pike. I'll bring you his head on a stake, if you like. But I'm doing it alone."

"You wouldn't even know he was alive, if not for me."

"Oh, I'd know, all right," he said cryptically. "Pike would make certain of it."

"It doesn't matter. I didn't follow you because of Pike. I came because of you."

His smile was not pleasant. "Lured by my promise of a different kind of alliance no doubt."

"Don't do this."

"A thousand pardons." He proffered the bottle in her direction in a mock salute. "To Vic!" he proclaimed sarcastically. "You'll pardon me if I don't get up. My manners aren't as polished as they used to be. Besides, you never liked it when I tried to treat you like a lady, did you, *Vic*?"

"Maybe I've changed my mind." Her heart hammered against her ribs. Didn't he know how hard this was for her? How much courage it had taken just to ride out here? Or was it that he was too busy using up his own courage? The rough growth of his beard reminded her that no matter what he said, he was not eager for this trip to Laramie, not even to find Pike.

He lurched to his feet then, swaying unsteadily, and drilled her a look with bloodshot eyes. "How many different ways can I say this?" he snarled. "I don't want you here. I want . . . " He stared at her and swallowed hard. "I want you out of my life," he finished hoarsely.

Torey trembled. Only now did she notice that his shirt was unbuttoned, the sides hanging loosely to reveal the broad expanse of his decidedly male chest. Dark hair stippled that chest, arrowing down to the flat plane of his belly. From the shadowed recess of his navel, her gaze dropped lower still. The top button of his fly was undone. Letting out a squeak of dismay, Torey dragged her gaze back to his face, where she ran smack into those unreadable gray eyes. "If you didn't want me to find you," she managed, "why did you make it so easy to follow?"

"I took the only trail north. If that makes it easy . . . " He shrugged.

He was lying, but she didn't press him. She had too many other emotions to contend with. She had wandered into the dragon's lair and was only now beginning to realize how dangerous and unpredictable this particular dragon could be. Drunk, surly, and vaguely aroused, he was certainly no longer her notion of a knight in shining armor, at least none she'd ever read about. And yet knight or dragon, she couldn't help pushing him. She had to know just how far he would go. In her heart of hearts she still wanted to believe that this was all an act designed to drive her away, to leave him on his own to face Pike—and the ghosts of Fort Laramie.

But hadn't she been wrong about Jim Buckley, about Cole Varney? Could her instincts about Noah be just another hideous mistake?

No, she reasoned desperately, she hadn't known Buckley or Varney the way she knew Noah. A dance and a chance encounter on the street were hardly soul-searching exchanges. But Noah had been different. She'd been spending day and night with the man, days and nights when they'd had to depend on each other for their very lives. She'd seen him angry, afraid, embarrassed, rude, sad, tender. She couldn't be mistaken about him. She just couldn't be.

She loved him. This time a mistake would break her heart.

"Noah?"

"I told you not to call me that."

"It's your name." She hunkered down and tossed a stray stick into the fire. "You want to know why I came?" She wanted to tell him it was because she loved him. Instead she said, "I'm worried about you. I'm afraid you're going to get your fool head blown off without me around to back you up."

He snorted derisively. "I've managed without you for over thirty years. I think I can manage the three seconds it'll take me to kill Pike."

"Dammit, Noah," she pressed, "you have to listen. The day the farm was attacked, I had a strange feeling, a feeling I ignored, dismissed. That feeling is back. I'm telling you, you're going to need my gun against Pike."

He looked at the ground. "I don't need you at all."

Her heart thudded. "Look me in the eye and say that."

He did.

Torey took a steadying breath and tossed another stick into the fire. So much for that approach. "Did you have something to eat, or did you just drink your supper?"

He laughed mirthlessly. "You offering to cook? No thank you. I'd gnaw on tree bark first."

She smiled a little. "You, uh, you told Lisbeth she needed to teach me how to cook."

The mention of Lisbeth's name softened the hard lines of his face. "How is your sister?"

"Much better, thanks to you."

"I didn't do anything."

"Maybe you were just in the right place at the right time, but you made a difference, Noah, and I'm grateful."

He shifted uncomfortably. "This isn't going to work. You can flatter me to hell and back, but I'm not letting you come with me. It's too dangerous."

She stood up. "It was dangerous before. The only difference was that you didn't know I was a woman."

"And maybe that's what's dangerous."

"My being a woman?"

"My knowing it."

Those eyes actually seemed to touch her, caress her. It took Torey a minute to find her voice, and when she did it didn't sound like her voice at all. "Why does my being a woman matter?"

"Even you aren't that naive, little girl."

"Maybe not," she allowed, not backing down from that now-searing gaze. "But I came anyway, didn't I? I came because I didn't want you to face Pike alone. But there was another reason too." She took a deep breath. "I came because . . . because I care about you. Is that wrong?"

He laughed, harsh, bitter. "Wrong? Oh, heavens no. I'm

just an army deserter and a convicted coward. What could be wrong?"

"You're neither of those things. I don't care what your court-martial said."

"Well, I care. I care too damned . . ." He stiffened abruptly. "God damn it, I don't want you here!"

"I think you do."

For the space of a heartbeat she thought she saw the truth of her words in his eyes, and then he shuttered it away, and when he looked at her again, those gray eyes had gone stone cold. With a contemptuous glare he stomped over to his saddlebags and retrieved a fresh bottle of whiskey. "Do you know what I want, Victoria?" he asked, his voice soft, too soft. "Well, I'm going to tell you, so that there won't be any more mistakes or misunderstandings between us." He jerked the cork from the bottle with his teeth, then spat it out. His gaze trailed insolently up and down her body.

Torey took an unconscious step back.

"I want you naked, Victoria. I want you naked and writhing underneath me."

Torey gasped, outraged, crushed. She could tolerate his being crude, but not now. Not about this.

"A hundred times a day I think about it, about what it would be like to be inside you. A hundred times a day." He took a drink. "That's what I want, Victoria. Sex. With you." He peeled off his shirt and let it fall to the ground. "Do you want sex with me, Victoria? Come and get it. It'll be a helluva night. I guarantee it."

If this was an act, it was a damned good one. "I'm not afraid of you, Noah."

"You should be, little girl. You should be."

"No. You just want me gone. You're trying to frighten me. And you're doing a splendid job. But . . . but it isn't going to work."

"Are you sure about that?" He took a menacing step toward her.

Torey held her ground. "Maybe . . . maybe I wouldn't mind if you . . . you wanted to kiss me."

"I'm not a man to settle for kisses."

"Maybe I don't want you to."

He stared at her, and she could see the hunger in him, feel it. "Be careful, Torey. Be very careful."

"I'm tired of being careful." She stuck her chin out defiantly. "I . . . I want you to kiss me, Noah."

He closed his eyes. This wasn't happening. He had known she was following, prayed every day that she would turn back. But now she was here, and she was driving him mad. He couldn't think, could scarcely breathe. He wanted her, wanted her so damned much. She was a dream. His dream. He had imagined this moment, fantasized about it, ached for it. His lady in red coming to him, wanting him, caring about him. A night with her, one night, and somehow everything in his life could be made right again. All he had to do was reach out and take it. But the cost, oh, God, the cost. He had no right. No right.

He called on what few shreds of decency and honor he still had left. If he couldn't frighten her away, maybe he could reason with her. "Torey, please, this is all wrong. You don't know what you're asking."

"You don't want me?"

"Hell, yes, I want you, but wanting and having are two different things. You're not a woman a man makes love to for one night . . ."

"I . . . I know I'm not like Belle."

He swore explosively, raking a hand through the tousled length of his hair. "You just don't understand, do you? Belle is the best a man like me can expect. And she wasn't getting any bargain, believe me."

"I thought . . . I thought you were good at . . ." She blushed furiously. "For a woman who makes her living taking men to her bed, Belle was certainly eager for an encore."

"You deserve better."

"Damned right," she said softly, coming close, too close. "I deserve the best. I deserve you, Noah."

"No." His voice was strangled.

"Yes." Shy, tentative, she trailed her fingers across his naked chest.

He groaned, gasped, her touch branding him, searing him. He didn't move as she feathered her hand across his burning flesh, swirled her fingertips over his nipples. He ground his teeth together so hard his jaw ached.

He would make love to her. She wanted it, needed it, was practically begging for it. Why the hell shouldn't he give in to her? Who elected him Mr. Nobility anyway? But he forced himself to offer her one last chance at a graceful exit. "I'll take you to Laramie—the town, not the fort," he told her. "You can wait for me there until I come for you. We'll forget this ever happened."

"I never want to forget. Those awful men who hurt my sister—they're the ones I want to forget. Show me what it really means to be a woman, Noah. Your woman. I don't want to be afraid anymore."

To hell with honor. With a curse he pulled her to him, crushed her against him. He heard her gasp, moan, felt the softness of her breasts swell against the hard wall of his chest. She leaned into him, seemed to melt against him as he plundered her mouth with his own. The kiss went on and on—hot, hungry, tender, sweet. His loins tightened, threatened to explode.

"Noah, oh, Noah. I knew you cared. I knew it."

His hand came up and skated past her throat to her hair, tangling in the soft, dark curls. "Let me taste you. Let me." He teased her mouth open, enticing her with his tongue to mate with him. He made love to her with his mouth. "So sweet, I knew you would be sweet."

The kiss was like a drug. He never wanted it to end. His body was on fire, and she was fuel to his flame. He reached between them to cup her breast, knead the pliant mound beneath her shirt. He expected her to pull away, and when she did not, he began to work the buttons of her shirt, hurriedly, feverishly, lest he wake up and find out it was all a dream. Together they sank to their knees on the grass covered ground.

His fingers trembled as he pushed back the sides of her shirt. He was shocked to find that she was wearing a chemise. He could see the rigid points of her nipples strain against the thin fabric. Then he looked into her eyes, stunned by the emotion he saw there, the trust, the hope, and something else.

"This is the way I wanted it, Noah, dreamed of it. Oh, Noah. I love you."

That stopped him. Like a bullet, it stopped him. Stopped everything. Of course she would think she loved him. A woman like Torey wouldn't give herself up to a man for a night of tawdry pleasures. Oh, God. Oh, sweet God. What a fool he'd been.

"This isn't about love, Victoria." He had to get her out of here. Now.

"I don't believe you. Those things you said . . . "

"Lies, sweet lies. The kind of lies women want to hear." He was desperate to regain control, desperate to have her gone.

"Lies?"

"Of course. Tell them they're special. Tell them they're pretty. Tell them you can't live without them."

"All lies?" she asked in a small voice.

"Those and any others you'd like to hear."

The look in her eyes was a lance to his heart, but he went on, ruthless, brutal. "You wanted to know what it's really about. It's about lust, Victoria. About my body wanting your body." He grabbed her hand, pressed it between his legs. "That's what it's about, Victoria."

She jerked her hand violently back. "How dare you?" she cried. "How dare you make what I feel for you cheap and degrading. All I wanted to do was love you. I thought you were different, thought . . ." She scrambled to her feet. "You're no different than Pike and Varney, no different at all."

His voice was silky soft. "I never said that I was. You did."

With an agonized cry, Torey bolted for Galahad and vaulted onto his back. Sobbing, she spurred the gelding into the night.

Behind her, Noah stayed on his knees. He was trembling violently.

He felt lower than the belly of a snake, but assured himself that he had done what needed to be done. He had tried everything else to make her go.

I love you, Noah.

He closed his eyes against the pain. Another time, another place and he would have reveled in those words, thanked God for them. But not now. And with Torey, not ever. She had been right. She did deserve the best. And the best was not Noah Killian.

He had lied to her, lied through his teeth. Lied even to himself. He had thought it was because he wanted to keep her safe. And he did. Ever since Cal Grady had told them Pike would be in Laramie, Noah had known he couldn't let Torey come with him. It was a setup. A trap. It had to be. It was the kind of irony Pike thrived on.

But Torey herself had hit on the other reason. He just hadn't wanted to admit it until now. *At Fort Laramie we'd be riding straight into your nightmares. And you don't want me there to see your welcoming committee.*

He couldn't risk the tiny scrap of pride he still had left. The pain of going to the fort again would be bad enough, but to have Torey be a witness to the kind of humiliation that awaited him there . . . Humiliation that would make the red-bearded Farley and his ilk in the Cuttersville saloon look like Sunday school picnickers. He would rather she despised him, than feel sorry for him.

And so he had used his last weapon, a weapon he had never used against a woman in his life. Sex. Even that had almost ended in disaster. He had tried to be cruel. But just holding her, touching her had been too much for him. He had wanted her, wanted to make love to her. Wanted to show her the wonder, the magic of her own body. It was the only gift he had to give her. But at the last instant he had reined in his selfish impulses and instead given her her life. What he'd done, said, would hurt her for a while, but the pain would go away.

She was safe now. Safe. Safe from him and the misery that was his life.

Then why did it hurt so damned much?

With an oath he heaved the whiskey bottle against a tree. The night of the massacre, alone in his cell in the guardhouse, the enormity of the loss of his troops had overwhelmed him. That pain now had an equal. For the first time since that haunted, godforsaken night, Noah Killian wept.

Torey urged Galahad faster, faster, paying no heed to the rugged cut of the terrain. She clung to the horse's warm neck, the mane slapping at her face.

She was sobbing, terrified. But even more than fear, the emotion that sliced deepest through her was betrayal. She had loved him, loved him, and he had thrown it in her face. He didn't care about her, didn't care about her at all.

In the darkness she missed the main trail, guiding Galahad as best she could amongst the thick growth of trees along the creek's edge. Low-hanging branches slapped at her face, her arms. Snarled vegetation clawed at her legs. Her pace slowed. Galahad balked, but time and again she forced him onward. More than anything, she wanted distance between herself and Noah Killian.

He had won. If this was the final battle, and victory was to have her gone, then he had won. But oh God, oh God, what he had lost.

She had dared trust him, dared care about him, dared—

Torey never saw the branch that hit her. One instant she was lunging forward, the next she was catapulted backward, a searing pain erupting on the side of her head. She felt the earth slam up to meet her, the air explode from her lungs. And then she felt nothing, nothing at all.

16

Torey awoke to the feel of a cold cloth being pressed against her forehead. She winced, but made no effort to escape the cool dampness. It felt good against the painful throbbing of her skull. She tried to remember how her head had come to hurt so badly in the first place but failed. Rather than dwell on her forgetfulness, she concentrated instead on opening her eyes. In this too she failed. A skittering of fear washed over her, but she pushed it away. Gingerly, she reached up to touch the cloth and discovered to her relief that it lay across her eyes as well. She started to pull it away.

"Don't. Lie still."

A voice. His voice. Gentle, concerned. Noah.

He was taking care of her. She smiled groggily. That was certainly kind of him. She would have to thank him. But first, there was something she needed to remember. Something important. About Noah.

Oh, yes. Her skin tingled despite the pain in her head. He had been kissing her, and it had been wondrous, magical, more magical even than she could have imagined. She had gloried in the need she felt in him, the passion. He was going to make all of her fears go away. She had even dared tell him she loved him. And then . . .

And then . . .

Oh, God. It all came back to her in a single, horrifying rush. She began to tremble, reflexively reaching for her gun. It wasn't there. Terrified, she yanked the cloth away, her eyes smarting at the intrusive glare of the sun high overhead. She tried to sit up.

"Lie still."

She felt his hand on her shoulder. He was behind her. Instinctively, she jerked away, the movement sending a slicing pain ripping through her head. "Don't touch me!" she snapped. "Don't you dare touch me!"

He flinched, but held up a calming hand. "I won't. I promise. Please, Victoria, lie still."

He came around to face her, hunkering down beside her. Incongruously, she noticed that he had shaved. Propped up on her elbows, Torey shrank back as far as her awkward position would allow. She would have started screaming, but the look in his eyes stopped her. Those gray eyes were regarding her with undisguised anguish.

He gestured toward the campfire. "I . . . uh, I made you some soup. Are you hungry?"

She shook her head, but stopped when the motion exacerbated her pain. "Just get away from me."

"You were unconscious all night, all morning. You need to eat."

"I need you to get away from me."

He ran his hands nervously along his denim-clad thighs. "How do you feel?"

Torey gritted her teeth. "Like I got hit in the head with a tree."

He smiled faintly, pleased it seemed that her sense of humor had remained intact. Torey wasn't yet certain about her head. But she began to calm down a little. As rattled as she was, things were beginning to make a strange kind of sense. Noah's hovering concern, the sick look in his eyes . . .

"Things didn't quite turn out the way you planned them last night, did they?" she asked.

He stood and walked over to the fire. Squatting beside it, he snapped a small branch in two and tossed it into the flames. "I don't know what you mean."

"I mean I was supposed to ride all the way back to my aunt's, instead of parting company with my horse." She forced herself into a sitting position, then had to take several steadying breaths to keep from passing out again. "I guess you're lucky I've got such a hard head. You didn't have to bury me."

Something flickered in those gray eyes, but she couldn't quite read it. "I never meant for you to be hurt," he said quietly.

"Not physically anyway."

He said nothing.

"You scared me last night, Noah. But then that was your intention, wasn't it? It's this hard head of mine. I just wouldn't get the message. So you upped the ante."

"You give me too much credit, Victoria. You're the expert at charades, remember?"

She grimaced. "You and I must be dead equals in the hard head department. You just don't want to admit you're not the reprehensible brute you pretend to be, do you?" She felt muzzy, woozy, yet oddly alert, more finely attuned to her feelings and somehow to his. He was raw, vulnerable, and very obviously agonized by what had happened last night. If she was ever going to get him to be honest with her, it was going to be now. Headache be damned.

"I was drunk," he said slowly. "I wanted you. I got carried away. I'm sorry."

"You expect me to believe that?"

"Believe whatever you like."

"I believe that you're not a man who would ever deliberately hurt a woman."

"Dammit, Torey, let it go."

"Why? Because I might stumble on the truth? You forget, Noah, I've seen your effect on the opposite sex first hand. And from my recollection Belle Whitley was hardly of a mind to run away from you."

He flushed. "I wish you'd stop bringing up my ill-advised tryst with Miss Whitley."

"It didn't seem ill-advised at the time, at least not to you or Miss Whitley."

Noah glowered at her, even as he managed to look acutely embarrassed. He pushed to his feet and began to pace. "You are the confoundest woman! Most of the *ladies* I've known who've inadvertently stumbled in on a . . . a delicate situation would have the good grace not to bring it up every five minutes."

"Well, that settles it then, doesn't it?"

"What?" he gritted.

"I'm not a lady. But then"—she shrugged—"you're no gentleman. If you were, you wouldn't be hollering at me with my head about to fall off my shoulders."

He closed his eyes and raked a hand through the shaggy mane of his hair. "I'm sorry," he snapped. Then more gently, he said it again. "I'm sorry. When Galahad raced in here last night without you, I nearly lost my mind. Yes, I wanted you gone, but I wanted . . . I wanted you safe too."

She smiled, her head seeming not to hurt so much all at once. "That's why I'm calling your bluff, Noah. I'm going with you to the fort."

He was angry all over again. "You'll rest here a couple of days, and then I'm personally escorting you back to your aunt's."

"What about Pike?"

"He'll wait."

"What does that mean?"

"Nothing. Dammit, Torey, I'm tired of arguing."

"Good. So am I."

A muscle in his jaw jumped. "You're not coming with me, and that's final."

She lifted her chin defiantly. "Eli told me how to get to the fort. I could find it in my sleep."

"Ah, hell." He blew out a disgusted breath. "Fine, have it your way. Come along, get yourself killed. I'm not going to try to stop you anymore." With that he turned away and headed toward the horses.

Torey watched as he resettled the geldings' picket pins in a fresh section of grass near the creek. She should have felt victorious. She had won. He was letting her come along. Instead she felt strangely hollow, bereft.

As the afternoon wore on, Noah continued to see to her needs, but he spoke little and otherwise kept his distance. She tried to attribute his aloofness to guilt about last night, but it was more than that. He seemed defeated, lost. Her attempts to draw him out failed. She was beginning to think she knew why. There was a point about last night that neither one of them had yet addressed.

They had talked of the evening's aftermath—her headlong flight, her fall, but neither of them had broached the subject of what had gone on before—the very real passion that had fired between them before Noah had used that passion to drive her away.

If pressed, she suspected he would deny that passion, claim it had all been part of his plot to frighten her. But Torey had sensed the hunger in him, the need. Surely, he couldn't have faked that. Nor had he faked the hard evidence of his arousal.

What she couldn't resolve in her own mind was whether that passion had been the kind of release he sought during a night of forgetfulness with the Belle Whitleys of the world, or whether Torey could dare hope for more.

It was her fear of his answer that kept her from asking.

But she would, she assured herself. She would muster her courage and remind this stubborn, hurt-filled man that she loved him—whether he liked it or not. But not just yet. Right now her head hurt. She decided it would be best for both of them if she lay down and closed her eyes, just for a little while. . . .

When Torey awoke again, it was nearly dark. She sat up and stretched, surprised that every muscle in her body didn't ache after so many hours of lying on the hard-packed ground. It was then she noticed that the ground wasn't so hard after all. With a frown she raised up the edge of her blanket, then blushed furiously. Several layerings of cut grasses had been strewn beneath her bedroll. Sometime in the past few hours Noah had managed to lift her up, lay out the grasses, then resettle her on her blanket, all so gently that he had not awakened her.

She stole a glance at him. He was hunkered down in front of the fire, busily stirring a panful of something Torey could not see. Whatever it was, it smelled heavenly. He must have felt her eyes on him, because he suddenly looked up.

"Thank you," she said shyly, patting her blanket.

"How are you feeling?" The words were stiff, but genuine.

She smiled. "Better." Her head still hurt, but it was more of a nuisance than anything else. Besides, she was thrilled just to have the man speaking to her again.

He spooned out a plateful of stew and handed it to her. Famished, Torey began to eat heartily. "This is fabulous," she managed between bites. "What's in it?"

He hesitated, then said, "Some herbs the Sioux taught me about. I found some growing by the creek."

Torey wondered if she'd rejoiced too soon about a tentative truce between them. How could the man be reluctant to discuss stew? "Lisbeth would be jealous. But what is this meat? It's so delicate."

He cleared his throat, and she had the oddest sensation

he was about to lie to her. But then he apparently thought better of it. "It's rattlesnake."

Torey halted in midchew.

Killian muttered a self-directed curse. "I shouldn't have told you. I didn't want to leave you . . . I mean, leave the camp unprotected. The damned snake was the only creature that happened by."

Torey somehow managed to resume chewing, at least enough to swallow what she had in her mouth. "It really is quite . . . tasty," she told him, determined not to disintegrate into a squeamish female.

"I thought you'd need something more substantial than beef jerky."

"Of course." She took a deep breath, then scooped up another forkful of stew. "But if there's any dessert, do me a favor."

"What's that?"

She grinned. "Lie."

He laughed, his eyes twinkling with genuine amusement. "I'll do that."

"Thank you." She paused, then added, "And thank you for letting me come with you to Laramie."

The humor went out of him. "I don't recall having a choice in the matter."

Torey grimaced. "I was hoping we could at least pretend to be amicable about this."

"Not likely. I've commanded whole regiments. I fought Quantrill, renegades. I was top of my class at West Point, but I've never in my life had to deal with the kind of insubordination I've gotten from one intractable female."

"I'll consider that a compliment."

He gave her a sour look. "It wasn't meant to be."

"It sounded like one to me."

"You're driving me mad, woman."

"Does that mean you like me again?"

"I never stop— Dammit to hell, how do you maneuver me into saying things I have no intention of saying?"

"I'm sorry."

He cursed feelingly. "Don't apologize to me. Ever. After what I did last night—"

"You were desperate. I forgive you."

"Well, I haven't forgiven myself. In my life, I've never done anything so deliberately contemptible. And to do it to you . . . " He didn't finish.

"This isn't about Pike, is it, Noah?" she prodded gently. "It's about you and Fort Laramie and a battlefield full of ghosts. It's why you shaved your beard, isn't it? You want them to know who you are, after all. You dare them to know."

He was trembling, and she knew in his mind he was back on the parade grounds in front of the entire population of the fort, having his whole world stripped away from him. It occurred to her then that the mysterious Katherine might well have been one of those who witnessed his humiliation that day.

"It's going to be ugly," was all he said.

"It can't be any worse than your court-martial."

"Yes, it can, because you'll be there to—" He stopped, and though she waited, he did not continue.

She suspected that he had again said more than he meant to, that he didn't want her knowing that it mattered to him that she would be a witness to the reception that awaited him at the fort. "What was the evidence against you at your trial?" she asked finally.

For a long minute he didn't answer, then he let out a weary sigh. "What's the use? You'll find out soon enough. The prosecution raised more than one pivotal question. Like why was I unhurt, when my troops were slaughtered to a man? Why was I found three miles from the massacre site?"

"You don't remember how you got there?"

"No. Nothing."

"You could've been hurt, struck in the head. Your horse could've bolted."

"All admirable excuses, I'm sure. But not for a captain in the United States Cavalry. Besides, they had another bit of damning evidence. The reason they claim I cut and ran. The reason I was derelict in my duty. The reason I don't remember what happened."

"Which was?"

He looked her straight in the eye, daring her to react. "They said I was drunk."

She gasped.

He stood and walked away several paces, but not before she had seen the hurt in those gray eyes. "Now it's not so hard to believe, is it?" he asked softly.

She was silent for a long time, and she worried that he would mistake her silence for agreement. But she wanted to phrase what she was going to say next just right. "You told me once that you drink because of your nightmares. Was that a lie, Noah? Did you always drink too much?"

If she'd offended him, he didn't show it. In fact, he seemed relieved by her candor. "I never drank to excess. I threw back a couple of beers now and again. But that month I was angry and frustrated about not being able to get Pike charged with a robbery I knew he had his hand in. And then there was the little matter of my fiancée"—he said the word with acid bitterness—"finding herself unable to resist Pike's charms."

Torey remembered thinking once that Katherine was a fool. Now she was certain of it.

"Twice in the month before the massacre I went on a royal bender. Neither time was I on duty, but . . . It was pretty damned stupid. And there weren't too many people at the fort who didn't know about it. But I didn't drink the day of massacre. My hand to God, I didn't."

"What do you remember about that day?"

"Nothing."

"Nothing at all? Not getting out of bed that morning? Nothing?"

"Leave it be."

"No."

"Whether I was a coward that day or not, I've been a coward ever since."

"I don't understand."

"Don't you? You're the one who's made me see just how far I've let myself fall."

"I would never—"

"Look at yourself, Victoria," he interrupted. "Pike attacked your family. Did you sit around feeling sorry for yourself? Did you dive into a bottle of whiskey? No, you strapped on a gun and went after him. You. A woman."

She climbed to her feet. "You thought Pike was dead."

"For God's sake, don't make excuses for me. I've made too many myself. I am a coward. I couldn't face up to my own life, couldn't face up to my dead troopers. No matter what else happened that day, nothing can change the fact that I was in command. I should've been there, I should've saved them."

"You would've only died too."

"Better to die with honor than live with the shame of what happened. Don't take this wrong, Victoria, but there are some things a woman just can't understand about being a man. Like what it means to be a soldier."

Torey crossed over to him, dared to touch his arm, wished there was a way to touch his pain. "I understand duty and loyalty and honor, Noah. And responsibility. And guilt. I've been wrestling with all of those things myself ever since Pike and his men rode down on my family."

His eyes burned her, seared her. "You are one helluva woman, Victoria Lansford."

"I have to be," she said gently. "It's the only way I know to get one helluva man to notice me."

For an instant their gazes held, and she was certain he

was going to sweep her into his arms and kiss her. And then abruptly he turned and stalked off several paces. "You're wrong, Victoria. Whatever I was once, I'm not anymore. The whole image of who I was, was wrapped up in that uniform. And I brought the worst kind of dishonor to it."

"You don't know that," she reasoned. "We have to talk to Pike."

But Noah was no longer listening. "I was an only child. Did you know that? My mother died when I was six. I became my father's whole world. He was a colonel, a hero in the Mexican War. He raised me to believe a man's honor is more precious than his life."

"Is he still alive?"

"No. He lived just long enough to see me disgrace his name."

"I'm sorry."

"He's the only reason I didn't hang. That and my war record. My father pulled strings, called in favors . . ." His voice shook. "Begged . . ."

"Did he . . . did he believe . . . ?"

"The charges? He always believed me innocent, that one day I'd prove them all wrong. But that didn't stop him from dying of a broken heart."

"We'll clear your name, Noah. I know we will."

"Even if Pike knows something, he'd never give any testimony that would exonerate me."

"His being alive is evidence enough to reopen the case."

"Maybe." Obviously he wasn't ready to hope yet.

"Noah?"

"What?"

"I believe you. That you didn't drink that day."

She expected sarcasm. Instead what she got was a heartfelt and barely audible "Thank you."

"You're welcome."

Their eyes met, and Torey made certain that every bit of the love she felt for him was there for him to see. He stepped close, and she didn't move as he reached up and ever so gently glided his fingertips along the curve of her jaw. It was fully dark now. Torey watched the flames of the campfire leap and dance in the gray depths of Noah Killian's eyes.

"You should get some sleep," he rasped.

"I've been sleeping all day." Her skin burned where he touched her. "I'm not tired. In fact, I'm pretty sure I could stay awake all night."

He didn't take his eyes from hers. "Don't do this, Torey."

"Why?"

"You know why."

"Tell me."

"No."

"Tell me."

He groaned. "I want you."

"I want you too, Noah."

"No. You want the man you think I am. A man wrongly convicted, misjudged, an innocent man. You don't understand. I might be guilty."

"I don't believe that."

"You weren't there."

"I didn't have to be. The same way I didn't have to look out the window of my house to know that my father was out in the yard defending his family with his life." Her voice quavered and a tear slid from the corner of her eye. "Eli said it best, you can't change the core of who a man is. I know you, Noah. I *feel* who you are in the center of my heart. You could no more have run away from that battle than you could've raped me last night. Drunk or sober, you would've stayed to fight. Drunk or sober, if I had stayed last night, you would've stopped. Unless," she murmured, "unless I asked you not to."

"Don't ask me this, Torey. Don't ask. Please. I don't want you to regret—"

She pressed her fingers to his lips. "The only thing I've regretted since the day I met you was not being honest. If

I'd told you the truth that night in the saloon, I could've saved us both a lot of heartache. But I was scared. Scared of being a woman with a man who made me glad I was a woman. I don't want to be afraid anymore, Noah. Teach me not to be afraid."

"I'm not the right man to do this."

"You're the perfect man." She laid her hand against his shirtfront, felt the pulsing beat of his heart. "Maybe you could show me how you'd kiss a woman? A woman you cared about, just a little? You don't have to really mean it."

His heart beat faster, and she could feel him tremble. "That's just the trouble. I would mean it."

"I love you, Noah."

He stared into her eyes, so trusting, so vulnerable, so filled with love for him that it made him ache, made him humble, made him want to believe again. In something, in someone. Maybe even in himself.

He wanted to lose himself in her, give himself up to her. Let her love him, let her heal him. He had hurt for so long, so very long.

She was sunshine in a world of darkness.

She was love in a world of hate and despair.

And for this night, this one night, she was his. His fantasy, his dream, his lady in red. He would commit the ultimate selfish act and take what she so unselfishly offered. And he would glory in it.

And he would do everything he could, everything he knew how to make this night magic for her as well.

"It's been a long time," she whispered, reaching up to fluff shyly at the short ebony waves of her hair, "but right now I wish I was pretty. I'd like to be pretty for you, Noah."

"You're beautiful," he said hoarsely.

Beside them, the fire was hot, hungry, blazing orange bright. With a fevered groan he pulled her to him and claimed her mouth with his own.

Torey had thought last night's kiss had been wondrous,

magical. But tonight he let down the walls, let go of the false pride that had made him keep his distance. Tonight Noah Killian went magic one better.

"I'll make it good for you, Torey. I promise."

"You make it heaven, just by being here." She twined her fingers through his hair, giving special attention to the feathering of gray at his temples, wondering if the silver streaks would be there if the last three years of his life hadn't been spent in hell. "Tell me something."

"Anything."

"Do you wish . . . do you wish I was dressed in red silk?"

"I wish," he growled huskily, kissing her nose, her cheeks, her eyes, "that you weren't dressed in anything at all."

She smiled, a one-hundred-percent Torey Lansford smile—a smile both shy and bold, innocent and sexy as hell. "And what do you propose we do about that?"

His hands went to the buttons of her shirt. "I'm about to show you."

"I love you, Noah"—she sighed dreamily—"I love you so much."

His fingers fumbled with the first button. It didn't open. He tried again. Her breath caught. He looked into her eyes, shining, eager, yet still just a little afraid. He couldn't fail her. He didn't dare fail her.

Again he bungled his attempt to open the first button of her shirt. His hands, ever skilled, ever proficient when it came to pleasing a woman seemed determined not to obey him. He had never been clumsy at lovemaking in his life. Not even the first time. And yet now that it meant the world to him, his every move was as awkward and incompetent as a schoolboy's.

He found himself apologizing over and over.

Torey silenced him with a kiss.

At last the confounded button gave way, as did the next, and the next. Slowly, as though unveiling the most precious of treasures, Noah parted the sides of her shirt. Heat flooded his loins as he gazed on the chemise-draped perfection of her breasts, the pebble-hard nipples already straining against the thin fabric. He swallowed hard and reached for the ribbon that secured the chemise.

Torey's hands slid over his. "Let me," she whispered, her voice tremulous, but her eyes shimmering with such trust and love that it made him hurt inside.

Blood pounding in his temples, Noah watched her tug free the satin ribbon, lay aside the delicate fabric, expose her breasts to his searing gaze.

"Touch me, Noah," she pleaded. "I need you to touch me."

Eyes burning, he cupped one coral-tipped mound with his rein-callused palm and bit back a groan of sheer ecstasy. His sex strained against the front of his denims so hard it hurt. But this wasn't a night for pleasuring himself, it was a night for pleasuring her. He would wait. If it killed him, he would wait.

Gently, gently, he eased her down to the grass-cushioned blanket of her bedroll, all the while he continued to worship her body with his hands, with his mouth, with his words.

Her breath caught and she dug her fingers into the shaggy length of his hair. "Noah, oh, Noah . . ." His name on her lips was like the sweetest of prayers. "Love me, Noah. Love me."

"I will." He swore it. "I will."

With excruciating slowness he finished undressing her, soothing her, petting her, praising her, reassuring her each time her shyness or her fear made her hesitate, made her want to draw back.

"Tell me to stop and I will," he rasped. "I don't want you to be sorry, Torey. I couldn't bear if in the morning you were sorry."

"I could never be sorry for this." A tear slid from the corner of her eye to dampen the blanket beneath her. "To be sorry for this would mean I was sorry for loving you. And that, my wounded knight," she whispered, trailing the back of her hand along his whisker-stubbled jaw, "will never happen."

He burrowed his face in the lee of her neck, knowing in that instant that if he didn't she was going to see his own tears. God, oh, God. How did it happen? When? He had not been going to let it. He had not been going to allow that kind of pain in his life again. But it was too late, far too late.

He loved her. Loved her as he'd never loved anything or anyone in his life. God above, she was his life.

But the fort was out there. Close, so close. Looming like the gates of hell. The ghosts of Laramie waiting to snatch it all away. He knew it. In his vitals, he knew it.

Torey gasped, and Noah cursed inwardly. How dare he feel sorry for himself. Not here, not now. Not when he was holding heaven in his hands. Torey was what mattered. She was all that mattered. His fingers traced downward to capture the downy softness between her legs. "Open for me," he said hoarsely.

At first she resisted, but he murmured tender words of encouragement against her ear. Slowly, shyly she responded.

He slipped a finger between her legs, reveling at her gasp of pleasure, smiling against her neck when she let her legs fall open wider still. His fingers probed gently, massaged, caressed, stroked.

"Feel it, Torey. Just feel it. Don't think. Don't think about anything but what your body wants, what your body needs."

Her breath came in tiny gasps. What she wanted, what she needed was Noah. What was this sorcery he was performing on her? How could he know her body more intimately than she knew it herself?

"Let it take you," he murmured. "Let it."

Her body shuddered, convulsed, wave after wave of indescribable pleasure washing over her, through her. Nothing mattered, nothing existed, but Noah, Noah and the shattering release he gave her with the masterful skill of his own hands.

And just when she thought it was over, that she would have to come back to the real world, he drove her back over the edge. Again and again she climaxed, Noah seeming always to know just where to touch her, how to touch her, when to touch her. Until finally her world spun away into the welcoming arms of oblivion.

When she opened her eyes again, it was to find him propped up on one elbow beside her. His expression was thoughtful, warm, and for a change, unguarded. "How do you feel?" he asked.

She felt heat rise in her cheeks, but managed to smile with what she hoped was a little lasciviousness at least. "Like maybe I know why some women do this for a living."

His eyebrows shot up. Evidently, he had been expecting a more demure response.

She grinned wickedly. "It's your own fault, you know. You shouldn't be so good at what you do."

"Is that a complaint?" he drawled.

"That, sir"—she sighed dreamily—"is gratitude." She levered herself up long enough to plant a swift kiss on the end of his nose. "All I asked is that you teach me not to be afraid anymore. But now maybe I'm more afraid than ever."

He frowned. "Of what?"

"Of never having enough of what you did to me." She laughed, then laid her hand along the side of his face. "Will I pass out every time?"

He snorted. "I certainly hope not. I thought I killed you."

"Ah, but what a way to die, Mr. Killian."

"Oh, we're back to that now. I think it's a little too late for formalities between us, madam."

"Kiss me."

"No. Go to sleep." He wasn't going to put himself through that torture again. He was still hard as a rock, but he wasn't about to let her know it.

"But you didn't . . . I mean . . . " She blushed prettily. "I know there has to be more."

"Nothing you need concern yourself with."

"But I want to. I mean, you deserve . . . " She bit her lower lip, her blue-green eyes regarding him solemnly. "I want"—she swallowed hard—"I want to know your body the way you seem to know mine."

He groaned, arching his head back. How could a virgin drive him to the brink of orgasm just by *talking* to him? "Torey," he said slowly, "I want you to listen to me. What I gave you was my gift to you. Consider it a debt from a member of the male species who does not consider women his property or receptacles for his genitalia because he doesn't have the guts to risk being turned down. But you are still a virgin, Torey. And I am not going to take that from you. You deserve"—he sucked in a deep breath—"you deserve to hold on to that. To save it as your gift to the man who's lucky enough to . . . to win your heart."

"But you already have my heart, Noah."

"We've been through all this." How could he be having this conversation? He wanted her so badly, he didn't even trust himself to move. But he was determined to talk her out of what he would consider the mistake of her life. She was infatuated with him, even grateful to him. But he wasn't about to take advantage of those feelings, not even to have what he wanted more than he wanted to breathe. And that was to make love to her, fully, completely, with all that he was. All that he wished he could be. For her. "Go to sleep, Torey. Please."

She laid her palm against his chest. "Not until I give you what you gave me. Unless . . . unless you don't want me that way."

He closed his eyes, forcing the words past his lips one syllable at a time. "I . . . don't . . . want . . . you . . . hurt."

"Then love me." She undid the first button of his shirt. "And let me love you." She undid another button.

"I need a drink." He had thought to make her angry. It didn't work.

"What you need is me. The whiskey can't give you what I can give you, Noah. It can't touch you." She pushed aside the fabric of her shirt, skating her fingers over his naked chest. "It can't feel you." She traced her fingers around his hardened nipples. "It can't love you." She bent to kiss one nipple, then the other, her tongue flicking out just as he had done to her.

The last fraying thread of his resistance snapped. With a guttural cry he gathered her to him, crushed her against him in a bone-melting embrace. He wasn't honorable. He wasn't honorable at all, he thought savagely. And his father had been wrong. Honor wasn't more precious than his life. Only Torey was. Only Torey.

In a frenzy of love and lust and need he tore off his clothes, his mouth never leaving hers. He would take her, take her hard and fast. He had asked her, begged her not to do this to him, do it to herself. If she wouldn't listen, then the hell with her, the hell with them both.

His body was on fire. He was insane with his need to be inside her.

But even then, even swearing he would give her no quarter, he slowed, hesitated, took one last look into her eyes. "God damn it, Torey. God damn it, are you sure you want this? Please . . . are you very, very sure?"

Her answer was to stroke his belly, her eyes wild, wanton. And then, and then . . . oh, God, her fingers trailed lower. White hot, raw, a rush of desire ripped through him, so fierce it left him gasping. And when her fingers closed over the pulsing length of him, he thought he would go mad.

Reckless, heedless he bore her down, some last shred of sanity prodding him to warn her. "It might hurt. Torey, I've never . . . " Jesus Christ, he had never had a virgin. Never in his life.

"Take me," she gasped. "Noah, take me now. Now!"

He rose above her, staked his arms on either side of her, teasing the silken entrance to her womanhood with the throbbing tip of his manhood.

"Now!" she cried again, her fingernails digging into his back. "Now, Noah, please."

He drove his hips forward, even as his mouth smothered her gasp of pain. For a long minute he held himself still, let her quiet, let her grow used to the size of him, the heat. And then he was moving, thrusting, driving his hips against her, taking, taking, taking all that was good and fine and right and letting it swallow him up, envelop him in a cocoon of warmth and light such as he'd never known.

She was an angel. His angel. God's gift to a man who for a long time hadn't believed in God at all.

His eyes burned, tears scalding his cheeks, and when Torey kissed his face, he knew she tasted their salty sweetness. He made no attempt to explain them away. *I love you, Torey.* He thought it, thought enough of her not to say it. But he held her, held her, never wanting to let go.

She had given him the single finest moment of his life. In a very real way, she had given him back his life. It was just too bad that it was too late.

He would rest for a little while, wait for the banked fires to grow hot inside him once again. Every hour with her was precious now. Every minute.

Though he would make certain Torey was safe, he had no false hopes about the outcome of his own rendezvous with the ghosts of his past. He would not be returning from Laramie alive.

But if he died tomorrow, he intended to love Torey a lifetime's worth tonight.

17

Dawn shimmered on the horizon, painted in billowing strokes of purple and gold. Torey smiled, stretching languorously beside the blackened remnants of their campfire. Her blanket fell away from her naked body and instinctively she snuggled toward Noah, seeking both the warmth of his body and the security of his presence. She found neither. He wasn't there.

Frowning, she clutched the blanket close and sat up, wincing as the movement reminded her all too painfully that her head was not yet one hundred percent recovered from its encounter with a tree, and that overnight she had acquired a marked tenderness in other less commonplace areas of her body as well.

"Are you all right?" Noah's voice. Concerned, and something else. Angry? Wary?

Torey got to her feet and settled the blanket shawllike about her shoulders. He was over by the horses, getting them saddled up and ready to ride. Stepping gingerly, Torey walked toward him. "I seem to be a little sore here and there," she said, feeling her cheeks heat.

He stared at her over Galahad's back. "Oh."

"It's all right," she said hurriedly. "I wasn't complaining or anything. I . . . it was more than worth it. I mean . . . " She faltered, stopped, wishing he would come to her, pull her into his arms, tell her that last night had meant the world to him too.

"Get dressed," he said. "We're heading out in ten minutes."

Torey grimaced. That wasn't the response she'd hoped for, but she supposed it was the one she could've expected. His eyes were bloodshot, weary. While she had slept, Noah had evidently spent the remainder of the night thinking, or more precisely, brooding. "Maybe I should be the one asking you if you're all right."

"Get dressed."

She sighed. "You're sorry, aren't you?" It wasn't really a question.

He leaned against the horse, his jaw tightening. "Sorry? Why should I be sorry? Just because I was the world's biggest son of a bitch last night with a woman I . . . " He clamped his jaw shut.

She stepped up beside him, still clutching the sides of her blanket. "I'm not sorry, Noah."

He swore bitterly. "Well, you damned well should be. Last night was a mistake, Torey. An unforgivable mistake. I had no right."

"I gave you the right," she protested.

He gripped her arms, his voice savage. "You had no rights to give. You were a virgin. It was up to me to protect you."

She jerked free of him. "You make it sound like I had no choice in the matter. Dammit, Noah, I wanted it as much as you did. Maybe more. What were you supposed to do, protect me from myself?" Beneath the cruel hurt she was beginning to feel a nudge of anger.

"Yes, I should've protected you, even from yourself. Did it ever occur to you that there could be consequences from a night like that?"

"Consequences?"

"You could be . . . " He dragged in a deep breath. "You could be carrying my child."

She gasped. She hadn't thought of that.

"Ahh, Miss Woman of the World. Maybe you don't know everything after all."

"So how would you . . . " She blushed. "How would you have done it . . . differently."

"There are ways. Do you think I'm totally irresponsible? I don't have my little trysts with women like Belle without making sure . . . " His jaw clenched. "What the hell am I explaining this to you for?"

"Because maybe next time we could . . . "

He yanked on Galahad's cinch so hard the gelding snorted and tried to shy. "There isn't going to be a next time." Muttering under his breath, he adjusted the cinch. "I'm sorry, Torey. It's not you I'm angry with, it's me. I knew better. You're young, inexperienced. I should've stopped it."

"Then why didn't you?" she demanded tremulously.

"Because I . . . " He shuddered. "Because I wanted you so damned much I couldn't think of anything but having you." He looked at her. "I still do."

"You make it sound so wrong." Tears rimmed her eyes. "Don't you understand even now, Noah? I love you."

He stepped away from the horse and looked her straight in the eye. "But I don't love you." His voice was soft, deadly. "I want you. There's a difference. You're here. You're convenient. Like Belle. Like any other willing woman."

"You're lying!"

"No." He shook his head. "I'm sorry. I'm not saying this to hurt you. I'm just trying to be honest with you. You deserve that much after what I've done."

Deserve that much? Deserve to have her heart torn from her chest? Torey stumbled back over to her bedroll and sank down onto it, trembling violently. She wouldn't cry. She wouldn't. He was right. He was so very right. It would seem that for loving a man like Noah Killian, she'd gotten exactly what she deserved.

Noah finished saddling the horses, trying hard not to look at Torey. She had no idea how vulnerable she'd looked with that blanket draped over her shoulders, how devastatingly desirable. It had been all he could do not to yank the blanket away and take her again, a possibility made all the more enticing because he knew, *knew* she would've been only too eager for him to do just that.

To cover his own feelings, he'd hurt her. Hell, he'd savaged her. But, he told himself, it had been necessary, right. In four hours they'd be at the fort. In four hours Noah Killian could start expecting a bullet in his back from just about any quarter. He didn't want Torey wasting her life mourning his loss.

His only goal was to stay alive long enough to flush out Pike. The irony was that one of the few enemies he could expect to square off against these days face-to-face was John Pike. At least until Pike had taken a full measure of enjoyment from what he'd put Noah through these past three years. Then Pike would shoot him in the back. Or stake him to an anthill, or whatever else might suit his twisted mind.

Adjusting his Stetson, Noah mounted Bear. Considering the night he'd just had, he was in one hellaciously bitter mood. He supposed he could chalk it up to knowing that he'd never have a night like it again. Knowing too that Torey really did love him. Just as he loved her. And that nothing could ever come of it, no matter what happened at Laramie.

He'd already accepted the fact that finding Pike didn't mean clearing his name. What Pike knew might only prove what Noah feared most, that the verdict at his court-martial had been right. Even if it didn't, Pike would rather stake himself to an anthill than do anything that would help vindicate Noah Killian.

But Noah was past caring about any of that. What mattered was helping Torey the best way he knew how, by doing what he should have done years ago. And that was rid the world of a piece of vermin named John Pike. If nothing else came of his visit to Laramie, women like Torey and her sister could sleep a little better at night.

Noah watched Torey mount up. She didn't look at him. He wished there was something he could say, do, that would make this easier for her. But there was nothing.

Together they rode out in grim silence.

They spotted the fort just past noon from atop a bluff about a mile from the military outpost. They both dismounted to give the horses a breather. Despite his resolve not to react, Noah felt his gut twist as he stared out at the icon of civilization where every ambition he'd ever had had crumbled to dust. Fort Laramie, bold, imposing, rose up on a wide, flat plain in the middle of nowhere. Set near the confluence of the Laramie and Platte rivers, the fort had for over a quarter of a century offered sanctuary, security, and hope to the thousands of emigrants who'd trekked past it as they made their way along the Oregon Trail, heading West to forge new dreams.

But for Noah the fort held only nightmares.

"Do you suppose they'll assemble a brass band?" he muttered, not really expecting an answer.

"Either that or a firing squad."

He winced. "We'll go in separately. You circle around, come in from the north. We don't want anyone suspecting that you know me."

"That shouldn't be too hard," she said acidly. "I don't."

Noah's fingers curled into his palms. He was reaping what he'd sown, but still her words cut him. "We'll rendezvous after sundown by the river." He described the exact spot.

She nodded.

"If you see any of Pike's men, don't be a hero. Understand?"

Her lips thinned into that stubborn line he knew too well.

"Dammit, Torey, we can call this whole thing off right here, right now. God knows, it's what I wish you would do."

"I made a promise. I've come this far; I've got no intention of backing out on it now. But I won't do anything stupid, if that's what you're afraid of."

"I'm afraid you're going to . . . " He didn't bother to finish. She wasn't interested in his fears for her life. His best bet was to let her think she was still in this all the way, then find Pike and take him down before Torey even knew what was happening.

"Why do you think Pike will have men at the fort?" she asked.

"He doesn't dare show his own face there, so he'll need someone to let him know I'm back."

She frowned. "What I don't understand is why Pike would even think you're after him. You're supposed to think he's dead. If you hadn't met me, you'd wouldn't have any idea about any of this. You'd probably be . . . " She straightened. "Never mind."

"In a saloon somewhere, drunk on my behind?" he supplied sarcastically.

"Something like that."

"I don't know how he knows," Noah admitted. "But he does. I feel it in my bones. And he's looking forward to our reunion. What he might not understand is just how much I'm looking forward to it myself." He remounted then and gave Torey a sardonic tip of his hat. "I hope you haven't forgotten how to be Vic Langley, *Miss Lansford*."

"You take care of your end of this, Killian," she snapped. "I'll take care of mine."

"Fine. But forget the bounty hunter business."

"Why?"

"Because a gang of outlaws might not take too kindly to a bounty man."

"So I should just present myself as an outlaw?" she demanded testily.

"You don't goddamned present yourself as anything at all," he snarled. "Not unless I'm there to back you."

"And since when are you giving the orders?"

He stared into those belligerent blue-green eyes. Given any other circumstances he would have admired the sheer grit of this remarkable woman, but at the moment all he wanted to do was wring her neck. "I give the orders, because if you cross me, I'll have you thrown in the guardhouse faster than you can blink. I'm not too popular down there already, remember? I can be the bounty hunter. A couple of dodgers you've picked up have descriptions vague enough to have you slapped in irons. Or"—he paused meaningfully—"I can tell the officer in charge that you're a woman. He'd throw you in the lockup for your own protection."

"You wouldn't dare."

I'd dare anything to keep you alive, he thought, but said only, "Try me."

She muttered an oath. "Have it your way, Killian. Anything to get this done. The sooner we end it the better."

"I couldn't agree more." He reined Bear toward the trail that led to the bottom of the bluff. As much as he claimed to want her to hate him, he sure didn't much like it when she did. He started the gelding down the trail.

He hadn't gone a dozen yards when her voice stopped him.

"Killian?"

He glanced back over his shoulder. "What?"

She was toeing the dirt with her boot, looking more like a pouty little girl than any hardcase bounty hunter. "Don't take this like I care or anything," she said, "but"—her voice softened—"keep your head down, okay?"

If possible, he wanted her more in that moment than he ever had, but he was very careful to keep his face expressionless. "I'll do my best," he said, and rode out.

The fort was just as he'd remembered it, almost eerily so. The two-story enlisted men's barracks, the officers' club, the sutler's store. Even Old Bedlam, the bachelor officers' quarters. Nothing had changed. Not even the smells. The tannery, the blacksmith shop, the stables, the laundry, the mess hall. Soldiers were about their duties—some performing drills, some mucking stalls, some on watch. A number of civilians moved freely about the fort as well. The only thing Noah might count as different was the atmosphere of the place. The fear of Indian attack that had been so pervasive three years ago was gone. Relations with the Sioux and the Cheyenne, he knew, were fairly stable at the moment.

The ride across the parade grounds was the worst. Noah could feel himself being swallowed up by memories. The droning beat of the drum as he was marched in chains to the center of the field, Colonel Dodd reciting aloud the charges he'd been convicted of, the look in Dodd's eyes when he'd been compelled by order of command to be the one who tore the epaulets from Noah's shoulders . . .

With an oath Noah forced the thoughts away. So far he'd been relatively ignored since he'd ridden through the main gate, but if he wasn't careful he was going to start drawing attention to himself. Reining Bear over to the hitch rail in front of command headquarters, he dismounted, tied off the gelding, and stepped onto the boardwalk. If Vernon Dodd was still in charge, he wanted to talk to him.

"Bang! Bang!" came a shrill little voice from somewhere behind him.

Noah turned in time to see a sandy-haired youngster of about six aim and fire a wooden rifle at him yet again. "You're dead, mister!"

"I am, am I?" Noah grinned, tucking his thumbs into the waistband of his denims.

"That's right! I'm the law in these here parts and you're Jesse James. And I just kilt you dead."

Noah hunkered down in front of the child. "And how do you know I'm Jesse James?"

" 'Cause you're wearing the biggest gun I ever seen! And you look like an outlaw!"

"Well, I guess that pretty much settles it. But shouldn't you put me in jail instead of just shooting me down?"

The kid's face scrunched up in deep thought. "We don't have a jail, just a guardhouse. Will that do?"

Noah flinched visibly, remembering the fort's guardhouse only too well. Thankfully the kid didn't notice. "That'll do just fine. But can it wait a little while? I've got to talk to the commander first."

"Colonel Dodd?"

So it was still Dodd. Noah wasn't sure whether he was relieved or disappointed. "Colonel Dodd and I are old friends."

"Colonel Dodd is a good friend of my ma's, too. He helped take care of me since my pa died. He even lets me call him Grandpa when no one is listening."

Vernon had always been good with children. How many times had he talked about being grandfather to Noah and Katherine's anticipated brood? Noah forced the thought away.

"I'll wait right here for you, Jesse," the boy pronounced, "so's I can arrest you after you talk to Grandpa."

"You do that. I'll—"

"I'm so sorry, mister," came a woman's voice. "I hope he isn't pestering you to death."

"Ma, you don't 'pologize to Jesse James!" the boy shrilled, indignant. "I got him under arrest."

"Now, Tyler, how many times have I told you not to—" The words clogged in the woman's throat as her gaze collided with Noah's.

"Killian!" she whispered. "My God, how dare you show your face here?"

Noah stared at Millie Yates. A raw-boned woman as tough as the land itself, her sass and vitality had been the perfect match for a hard-nosed corporal named Ed Yates. It was

Millie more than anyone who'd helped Yates put his Confederate war years behind him, helped him fit into a new life on the frontier. Enlisted men weren't normally allowed to have their spouses with them at the fort, but Millie had been the fort's seamstress, taking in all manner of mending and sewing, scolding everyone from the lowliest private to the colonel himself for any rents and tears in her handiwork that she deemed due to pure carelessness. She looked like she'd aged twelve years.

"Is that pity in your eyes, Captain?" she ground out. "What's the matter? You don't think doing the laundry for a fort full of soldiers for the past three years has been so good for my complexion?" She gave a bitter laugh. "With Ed gone, sewing just didn't bring in enough money to support Tyler and me."

"Ed was a good soldier, Millie. You have to know how sorry I am about what happened."

"Sorry you were a coward and a deserter?"

Noah felt his belly clench. It was one thing to be vilified by the Farleys of the world, quite another to be confronted by a grieving widow.

Drawn by the commotion, a crowd had started to gather. One of those on the periphery, Noah noticed, was Torey. She regarded him without expression. He prayed that no matter what happened, she would have the good sense to stay out of it.

"What's wrong, Miz Yates?" The question came from a gravel-voiced sergeant that Noah did not recognize.

"What's wrong, Jeb?" Millie echoed. "This here's Noah Killian. That's what's wrong."

The sergeant's face went stony. "*The* Noah Killian?"

"Who is he, Ma?" Tyler demanded, his blue eyes confused and just a little frightened. "Is he really an outlaw?"

"No, Tyler," Millie said shakily, "he's much worse than any outlaw. This is the man who . . . " She stopped. "Maybe you should tell him who you are, *Captain*," she said derisively.

Tyler was looking more and more frightened. "Please, Ma, who is he?"

"Millie, I don't think—" Noah began.

Millie silenced his next words with a stinging blow to his face.

Noah did not react.

Millie slapped him again, harder. "A man like you don't deserve to be alive," she said, "not when my Ed is dead in his grave. It should've been you feeding those buzzards, Noah Killian. It should've been you."

"I wish it had been, Millie," Noah said softly.

The sergeant named Jeb drew his service revolver. "Get back on your horse, Killian, or I won't be responsible for what happens."

Noah stiffened, his temper slipping a notch. Millie was within her rights. This son of a bitch was another story. "Last I heard," he said, "it was still a free country."

"Not for your kind, it ain't." The sergeant turned to Millie. "Maybe you'd best take the tyke home, ma'am. We'll take care of things here."

Millie gathered up her now distraught child. "I'd be obliged to you, Jeb."

Noah was looking at Torey. He didn't miss the pity in her blue-green eyes as she watched Millie's retreat, pity that remained in her eyes when she turned her gaze back to Noah.

A brown-haired civilian stepped onto the boardwalk and braced himself in front of Noah. "I know men who'd pay money to have you killed real slow, Killian."

"You one of 'em?" Things had deteriorated much faster than even he could've predicted. He'd handled his share of sons of bitches these past three years, opportunists who wanted to add to their own reputations by taking a loathsome coward down another peg or two. But seeing Millie Yates and her son had brought home all too painfully the unending ramifications of the deaths of the men on his patrol—wives without husbands, children without fathers. Noah felt a sudden blinding rage to take out the injustice of it on somebody. This big-mouthed bastard would do for starters. Noah drove his fist into the man's face.

The man yowled in pain and tumbled back. Cursing wildly, he clawed for the weapon in his holster. But before he could draw, Noah hauled him up by his shirtfront and hit him again.

Then all hell broke loose.

Noah felt himself being grabbed at from all sides, his arms pinned back, men shouting, swearing. Someone hit him in the jaw. He didn't know who. He cursed himself for a fool. He shouldn't have lost control. This mob was going to kill him. Torey would be left on her own with Pike still on the loose. Someone else drove his fist into Noah's stomach.

"Get a rope!" a man yelled.

Doubled over, Noah tried desperately to scan the crowd, locate Torey. She was making her way through the throng of angry men. He could tell by the look on her face that she was not going to let him fight this battle alone. But if she interfered now, she would only die with him. Noah let his body sag against his captors. "Let me go, Sergeant," he said, hating the begging tone he forced into his voice. "I'll ride out. I swear."

"Once a yellowbelly, always a yellowbelly," the sergeant sneered. "Well, you ain't gonna get off that easy, coward."

The sergeant reholstered his gun and drew back his fist. "This is gonna be a pleasure."

Noah saw Torey reaching for her gun. "No!"

The sergeant misunderstood Noah's plea and grinned wickedly. "Gonna beg, eh? That's just fine by—"

The door to the building behind them slammed open, a booming voice demanding, "What the hell is going on out here, Sergeant Wilson?"

Every soldier present snapped to attention, the two holding Noah releasing him so abruptly that he had to take a step to right himself.

"Colonel Dodd," the sergeant acknowledged, swallowing convulsively, "I'm sorry, sir. We was just—"

"Don't you and your men have duties to attend to, Sergeant? If you don't, I—" He stopped, his eyes going wide with disbelief. "Noah."

Noah gave a barely perceptible nod. "Vernon." Dodd's features were still hard-angled, his spine still ramrod straight, and his blue eyes, Noah suspected, could still stop a charging bull—or a disorderly recruit—at twenty paces. Maybe there was more silver in his dark hair, but otherwise Dodd seemed unaffected by the passage of three years.

He gestured toward the door. "Get inside, Noah," he said. "Now."

Noah stiffened.

"Please?"

Noah cast a quick look around for Torey, but she was nowhere to be seen. He swore inwardly but allowed himself no time to puzzle it out. He would have to trust her, trust that she wouldn't do anything reckless. Hell, he was the one who'd already endangered them both. But to have any chance at all at finding Pike, Noah needed Dodd's cooperation. Reluctantly, he stepped inside.

Dodd's office was just as Noah remembered it. The Spartan furnishings included a bookcase crammed full with books on military strategy and fronted by multipaned glass. Above it was a framed map of the territory. To his left was a fireplace, now superseded by a potbellied stove whose black exhaust pipe was connected to the chimney just above the mantel. Above the pipe two crossed flags gave the room a splash of color, one the red-white-and-blue of Old Glory, the other a deep purple, fringed with gold and emblazoned with the emblem of the 11th Cavalry.

Noah's gaze flicked from the company flag to Dodd, who had walked behind his huge mahogany desk. "Brings back memories, doesn't it?" Dodd prodded. "Not too many of them pleasant, I imagine."

Noah said nothing. He was feeling decidedly ill at ease all at once. His encounter with Millie Yates had been painful enough, but somehow Noah had expected a different reception from Dodd. The two had once been close friends. Though Dodd had gone along with the verdict of the court-martial, Noah had always held on to the belief that Dodd had never quite accepted it.

Dodd leaned forward, palms splayed on his desk. "Why the hell did you come back, Noah?"

Noah's jaw tightened. "Can't a man visit his own grave?"

"You know what I mean. It's damned near suicide for you to be here."

"I've got my reasons."

"Care to try them on me?"

Noah stepped over to a window and looked out across the parade grounds. Several men were still milling about, obviously agitated, their gazes drifting time and again toward Dodd's office. "John Pike brought me back, Vernon. He's not dead."

"Impossible!"

"Two months ago I would've said the same thing." He stalked back to the center of the room. "But since then I've heard a lot of evidence that says otherwise."

"The man is dead, Noah. I saw his body myself. Or what was left of it. The tattoo, the scar . . . "

"I'm not saying I know how he did it, but he's alive. I know it. I feel it."

"All right," Dodd conceded, "just for the sake of argument, let's say you're right. If John Pike is alive, don't you think this is the last place on God's earth he'd come to?"

"Not if he wants to finish it between us. What better place than the site of my ultimate disgrace? Where I lost the career I worked a lifetime to build, the career he could never have."

"And what do you expect from me?"

"I expect you to make sure I can go about my business without the kind of interference the good sergeant and his friends were about to indulge in before you interrupted."

"And if I don't?"

"Then you're going to need a new sergeant," Noah said coldly. "And maybe a few enlisted men as well."

"Is that a threat, Noah?"

"Take it any way you like, Vernon."

"I could have you clapped in irons."

"You could, but you won't."

"Why won't I?"

"Because, old friend," Noah said slowly, "you've always been more than a good soldier. You're a good man. A fair man. And if you think there's one chance in a thousand I could prove myself innocent, you'll give me that chance."

Dodd came around his desk to stand in front of Noah. "What I'll give you is two days. After that I won't be responsible."

"Fair enough." Noah stuck out his hand.

Dodd accepted the handshake. "Watch your back, Noah. I can issue orders that you're to have complete access to the fort, but I can't order a man not to hate."

"I know." Noah turned toward the door. Dodd's voice stopped him.

"Aren't you even going to ask about her?"

Noah did not turn around. "I didn't figure she was any of my business, not anymore."

"She's married, you know," Dodd said softly. "Just celebrated her second wedding anniversary last week. Married Major Oliver Duncan."

"I'm glad she's happy."

"I didn't say she was."

Noah twisted around and for the first time looked more closely into Dodd's sun-weathered features, noticing new lines around his mouth, his eyes, eyes that seemed suddenly world-weary and very old.

"I'm sorry," Dodd said. "I shouldn't have said that. I had no right."

Noah shifted uncomfortably. Odd, he was having a hard time even picturing what Katherine looked like. Hadn't he spent the better part of the last three years thinking about her? Thinking about what might have been, if only she'd believed in him, just a little? And then he'd met Torey Lansford, and for the first time in those three years he had dared to start to believe in himself. "I'd better go, Vernon."

Dodd nodded. "Good luck, Noah."

Noah stepped outside into the sunshine. He had hoped to spot Torey, but he was quickly disappointed. Again he assured himself that wherever she was, she was all right. She wanted Pike as badly as he did, but she was no fool. If she'd found out anything, she would wait, share it with him tonight at their rendezvous.

The thought of being alone with her tonight sent a surge of heat through his veins, which he quickly checked. His feelings for her were already well out of his control, but that didn't mean he was ever going to be selfish enough to act on them again. If by some miracle he did survive this mission of theirs, he would take her back to her aunt's in Denver, leave her to carve out the rich, full life she deserved—by herself, or with a man who could give her more than ghosts and heartache.

Untying Bear's reins, Noah led the gelding toward the stable. The horse could use a good rubdown and a bucket of oats. More than that, the livery would be the kind of shadowy, isolated spot where he hoped someone with a beleaguered conscience could seek him out. Of course, it was more likely that someone would use the gloom of the place to blow his head off, but that was a chance he had to take.

As he walked, the hair on the back of his neck prickled. He was being watched by a number of unfriendly eyes. He ignored them all and marched into the stable, grateful to find it deserted. Tying Bear to a post, Noah unsaddled him, then picked up a cloth and began to rub the gelding down. He hadn't been in the barn more than a few minutes when he heard soft footfalls behind him.

He let go of the cloth and wheeled, gun drawn.

The woman standing in the shadows gasped, her hand flying to her throat. "Noah, please. It's me. Katherine." She stepped into the slanting light of the sun that filtered through a window.

Noah stared at her, his body seeming to have gone numb for just an instant. She was as beautiful as ever, maybe more so—her auburn hair done up in a crown of curls that perfectly accented her oval face and green eyes, her tiny figure shown off to best advantage by the exquisite lines and daring décolletage of her emerald-green silk dress.

"Aren't you going to say anything?" she asked, when he continued to stare at her.

"I . . . " he managed, "it's been a long time."

"So long that you have to keep pointing that gun at me?" She tried to make her voice light but failed.

Noah looked at the gun in his hand and gave himself an inward shake. He hadn't even realized he was still holding it. "Sorry," he said, shoving the weapon back into his holster.

She smiled, stepping closer. "When Daddy told me you were here, I couldn't believe it. I knew I had to see you. You look . . . you look . . . " She faltered.

"Like hell?" he supplied grimly.

She blushed prettily. "Not at all. As a matter of fact, I was trying to decide if it was appropriate for a married woman to say that her former beau looks more handsome than ever."

Noah said nothing. His stomach was in knots. He'd always wondered what it would be like to see Katherine again. But now that it was happening, he wasn't at all sure just what he was feeling.

"Daddy told me you think John is still alive," Katherine went on.

His jaw clenched. "John? It was John, was it?"

"Oh, Noah, there was never anything . . . anything serious between John Pike and me. He was just . . . just trying to make you jealous."

"He did a damned fine job of it too."

"Noah, please . . . I was a fool. He turned my head. He could be so very charming."

"Like a snake."

"He fooled you once too, didn't he?"

Noah couldn't argue with that.

"I never realized how dangerous he was until, well, until it was too late."

"Forget it, Katherine. It's done. Over."

"What if . . . what if I don't want it to be over?"

He straightened. "There was a time that would've mattered a helluva lot."

"But not anymore?" she prompted.

He lifted his Stetson and raked a hand through his tousled mane of hair. "What do you want from me, Katherine?"

"Your forgiveness, perhaps?"

"Fine. Done. I forgive you."

A tear trickled down her cheek. "Do you hate me so much?"

He stared at her, almost willing himself to feel something, anything, for this woman who had once meant so much to him. But what he found himself feeling most was pity. "I don't hate you, Katherine. I've never hated you. But you're married now, remember?"

He wished the words back when a sudden hope flared in her eyes. He'd only meant to let her down gently.

"Is that why you're reluctant?" she asked. "You needn't be. Oliver doesn't love me. He only married me to gain favor with my father."

"Then why did you marry him?"

More tears fell. "I was so lonely, Noah. So very lonely. I missed you terribly."

"We shouldn't be talking about this. I'm sure your husband—"

"Oliver isn't even at the fort. He's on assignment. He's riding to meet a payroll wagon that's due in next week."

Noah was very careful to keep his expression neutral. A payroll wagon. Pike would find such a temptation irresistible. "If you'll excuse me, Katherine"—he took a step toward the door—"I need to talk to your father." He would convince Dodd to help him set a trap, just in case. With any luck at all Torey could still be kept out of this.

"After you see Daddy," Katherine said, catching his arm, "maybe you could come by our quarters? Join Daddy and me for dinner? Just like old times."

Noah eased his arm free. "I don't think that would be a very good idea. The gossip would be hell on your reputation."

"I'm willing to risk it. It would give me a chance to explain, apologize."

"There's no need."

"But there is. I was wrong not to stand behind you, even if . . ."

"Even if you believed I was guilty?" he said, surprised when the words didn't come out as bitterly as he thought they might. What kind of spell had Torey woven on him anyway? What kind of spell was she still weaving? "You only believed what everyone at my court-martial believed."

"Oh, Noah, I've made so many mistakes." Katherine touched his chest, looked up at him with those luminous green eyes. "I don't care what you've done. I love you, Noah. I've never stopped loving you."

She curved her hands behind his neck and brought her mouth to his.

Torey backed away from the scene in the barn, her heart breaking. Damn him. Damn him to hell. She had all but convinced herself that Noah had been lying this morning.

That his assertion about one willing woman being the same as any other had been a defense against the passion they'd set free in one another last night.

But it would seem the man had been brutally honest, after all.

Torey staggered to the corral beside the barn, dimly aware of the curious stares she had roused in a small group of soldiers on the opposite side of the enclosure, where they had been working a few head of horses. Resolutely, she straightened. Somehow she had to get past the pain that was threatening to split her in two.

How could she have been so stupid? She had seen Noah heading for the barn and thought it would be a perfect place for a private meeting, even before their set rendezvous. Now she'd be damned if she'd include him in what she'd found out—Varney was here. In the fort.

She had noticed something ominously familiar about the voice of the brown-haired civilian who had accosted Noah earlier. But she hadn't been able to get a look at his face until after the colonel had emerged from his office. It had been all she could do not to pull her gun and blow the bastard's brains out right there on the boardwalk.

But she'd promised Noah that she wouldn't do anything crazy. And so she had waited.

Well, she wasn't waiting anymore.

She found Varney leaning up against a support post in front of the sutler's store, his indolent stance belying the watchfulness she sensed in him. He reminded her of nothing so much as a coiled snake. It took every ounce of discipline she possessed not to follow through on her earlier wish to kill him where he stood. She was still reeling from Noah's betrayal, and just seeing Varney again taunted her with agonizing images of what he had done to her father, her sister.

But Cole Varney was a flesh-and-blood link to Pike. She wasn't going to botch her chances to end her chase once and for all. Not when she was this close. Unwillingly, she looked back toward the livery stable, hating the way she wished Noah was here, not even wanting to think what he was doing right now.

She was taking a terrible risk to confront Varney on her own. If there was any man who could see through her masquerade, it would be this one. *Bet them legs of yours go on forever.*

Heart thudding, she strode up to him. "You and your friends give up on teaching that coward Killian a lesson?"

He looked at her, his brown eyes sullen. His left cheek was already taking on a purplish hue from the punch Noah had landed. "Head soldier boy stuck his nose in. Stopped us. Even issued a damned order about letting that yellowbelly walk free and tall in the fort. But there'll be another time."

"When?"

Varney grimaced. "Soon. Damned soon."

"You said you knew people who'd pay money to have Killian killed."

The man stiffened. "Do I know you, mister?"

"Nope. Name's Langley. Vic Langley." Torey kept the brim of her hat tugged low over her eyes.

"Well, Vic Langley, you're beginnin' to irritate me. So why don't you just beat it."

"Because I want to know who'd pay for Killian's head. And how much would he pay?"

Varney's gaze trailed curiously up and down Torey's lanky frame. For a long, frightening moment she had to remind herself to breathe. Then Varney snorted dismissively. "You sayin' you'd kill him, boy?"

"I'm saying I'm always open to easy money."

Varney laughed. "Even a coward like Killian wouldn't be afraid of a wet-nosed pup like you, kid."

"You'd be surprised," Torey drawled.

"Yeah? How many men you killed, boy?"

"Lost count."

"Uh-huh." Varney started to walk away.

"One of 'em I killed was a son of a bitch named Cal Grady."

For the space of a heartbeat Varney hesitated. Then he whirled, clawing for his gun.

Torey was faster. She shoved the barrel of her Colt in Varney's face, terrified by how much she still wanted to squeeze the trigger.

Varney swallowed hard and let his gun fall back into his holster. "My God, mister," he muttered. "I thought lightning was fast."

"Lightning doesn't concern itself with staying alive. Now"—she thumbed back the hammer—"you going to listen to me, or are you going to keep making cracks?"

Varney spread his hands wide. "I'm listenin'."

"Good." She glared back a number of curious onlookers who were sidling too close. "I think we need a little more privacy," she said, gesturing toward a stack of crates beside the sutler's store.

Varney ambled meekly ahead of her. She was surprised by how compliant he was all at once, recalling too well his merciless attitude toward her family. But then it occurred to her that he had the guts to be a tyrant only when his opponent was weaker and slower and had no gun. She stopped him when they reached the heavy afternoon shadows behind the crates.

"First off," she said, "about Grady—"

Varney shrugged, interrupting. "Knowin' Cal, he likely give you good reason for killin' him."

"He tried to steal my horse."

"That's Cal. He was always hard on horseflesh, always needing a fresh mount." Varney fished in his shirt pocket and pulled out the makings. "So how'd you come to find me?"

"He didn't want a second bullet. He and I had a little chat. Tried to cut a deal so I wouldn't shoot him again. But it turned out the first bullet was enough." Torey decided a little embellishment on the tale wasn't out of order. It didn't sound nearly as menacing to tell Varney that Grady had fallen off his horse and drowned.

"Grady always did have a big mouth," Varney said, rolling himself a cigarette. "Just what exactly did he tell you?"

"That a man named Varney might know a way for me to put a little money in my pocket." She reholstered her Colt.

"Could be that I do. Been waitin' here for Cal for over a week." He lit his smoke. "'Bout to give up on him, as a matter of fact, especially now that I need to get word to the boss about Killian."

"Boss?" Torey was careful to keep her reaction indifferent, though her heart hammered wildly. He had to be talking about Pike. "He the one who wants Killian dead?"

Varney nodded. "Dead in his own way and his own time, mind you. The hate the boss has for Noah Killian goes back a long way. He wouldn't want things rushed."

"If he wants Killian alive, I'll bring him in trussed up like a damned turkey. Makes no never mind to me." Torey was shaking. This was almost too good to be true.

"And who's to say I won't take him the coward myself?"

"Killian might've run off from a band of renegade Indians," Torey said, "but he didn't look so easy to take one on one. You and I could work some kind of deal."

"Tell you what, Langley, I'll be seeing the boss tonight. Me and my friend here." He gestured behind her, his mouth twisting in a smirk.

Torey straightened, her hand moving surreptitiously to her gun, even as she cursed herself for a fool. She should have figured Varney wouldn't be alone. Now some bastard could have the drop on her.

Keeping her face expressionless, she dared a glance over her shoulder. She nearly gasped aloud. Behind her was a tall, burly blond whom Torey recognized at once—the young man who had kept himself apart from the others the night of the attack, the one who had watched the horses, who had even seemed sickened by what his friends were doing, but who hadn't had the courage to stop it. She felt a fierce surge of triumph. The circle was complete. Tomorrow she would have them all.

"This here's Bobby," Varney was saying. "Don't expect too much from him. He's dumb as dirt. Ain't ya, Bobby boy?"

"Yes, sir, Mr. Varney." The boy gave her a slack-jawed grin.

"Ol' Bobby got kicked in the head a few years back by a feisty mule. He don't think too good no more." Varney laughed. "Not that he ever did. Right, Bobby boy?"

"Yes, sir, Mr. Varney."

"Fetch the horses, Bobby. We're ridin' to see the boss tonight."

A shadow of fear crossed those boyish features, but Bobby turned quickly and headed for wherever Varney had left their mounts.

"You be back here at first light, Vic," Varney said. "Maybe I'll have good news from the boss."

Torey knew she was being dismissed. For the briefest instant she considered trying to follow Varney and his simpleton friend, but decided against it. If he caught her, he'd kill her. Besides, as furious as she was with Noah, she had to warn him. He was in more danger than he could even have imagined.

"I'll be here at dawn," she said, then stalked away. She could feel the bastard's eyes boring into her back. Did he suspect something? She assured herself, it didn't matter. Tomorrow morning she would be back. She would be back, and she would bring Noah. She would present him to Varney as her prisoner. The outlaw wouldn't be able to resist taking such a prize back to Pike. They would have the murdering bastards right where they wanted them. The promise she'd made so many months ago beside her father's grave would be fulfilled at last.

Then why did she suddenly feel so empty, so lost?

But she knew. The foreboding was back. As angry as she was at Noah, she still loved him. And one way or another tomorrow she was going to lose him forever.

18

Torey paced beside the wide, muddy Platte, her roiling emotions in stark contrast to the placid waters of the river. She had been at the rendezvous point since just after sunset, the time she and Noah had agreed to meet. It was now past midnight, and there was still no sign of him. More than once she'd considered riding off to try and find him. But where would she look? Especially in the dark. And what if he finally rode in only to find her gone?

No, she had no choice but to stay, stay and be alternately terrified that something terrible had happened to him, and furious that there was all too likely a less ominous reason for his tardiness, an exquisitely beautiful reason named Katherine.

Torey stalked over to the nearest cottonwood. Even in the dim light of the half moon she could see the shadowy outline of the two-foot-high X scarred into its trunk, a wound years old, but still clearly visible. She traced her fingers over the lightly fissured bark. Noah had told her the story of the X. Left by an emigrant heading for Oregon, the man had written to his fiancée back in Baltimore, telling her to look for it on her journey west with her family the following year.

Near the X, he wrote, she would find their initials carved in the tree. The young man assured his intended bride that their love would endure as long as the tree lived and beyond. Tragically, the young woman died in a cholera epidemic the next year near this very spot. The last thing she was said to have asked was that her father carve a heart around the initials.

Torey traced that heart, then on impulse tugged her knife from the sheath in her boot and began to pick at a separate section of the tree trunk, chipping out *VL + NK*. "Take that, Katherine," she said, stepping back to admire her handiwork.

"What did you say?" came Noah's disembodied voice.

Torey whirled, startled. "Where the hell have you been?" she demanded, ignoring the flood of relief that coursed through her to see that he was unhurt.

He shrugged. "Something came up."

"Yeah, I'll just bet it did."

His jaw tightened. "Did you find out anything at the fort?"

"I found out you're a son of a bitch."

"You should've already known that."

Torey clamped down on the retort that rose to her lips. They could exchange insults the rest of the night. As appealing as that prospect might be, she needed to talk to him about what they were facing in the morning. "Can we sit somewhere?"

"I wasn't planning on staying."

"A pressing appointment?" she asked, shoving her knife back into its sheath.

He told her about the payroll wagon. "I want to ride out with the men Dodd is sending to intercept it."

"That's all well and good," she allowed, "but you can't be certain Pike is going after the payroll."

"It's worth a chance. And right now it's all we've got."

"What if it isn't?"

He frowned, puzzled. "You've got a better idea?"

"We can get to Pike tomorrow."

His frown deepened. "What are you talking about?"

"Varney was at the fort. He was one of the men who came at you in front of the colonel's office."

"Are you sure? You got a good look at him?"

"I did better than that. I talked to him."

Noah's voice was still as death. "You did what?"

"I talked to him. We meet tomorrow at first light. You act like you're my prisoner and—"

He had her by the arms, shaking her so savagely her teeth rattled. "You swore to me you wouldn't do anything stupid."

She tried to twist away from him, but he held her fast. "Noah, you're hurting me."

"I'll break your fool neck."

His face was inches from her own, his features twisted in a mask of fury. But there was more than fury in his eyes—there was fear, fear for her. The realization helped her keep her own temper under control.

"Look, Noah," she reasoned, "I was careful. You were in more danger in front of Dodd's office than I was from Varney."

He released her so abruptly, she fell back. "That doesn't excuse your facing him alone," he said. "Anything could have happened. He could've recognized you."

"But he didn't! Blast it all, aren't you even hearing what I'm saying? In less than six hours we've got a chance to bring in Pike."

"Not we. Me." He jabbed a finger at her. "You, Miss Lansford, are not going anywhere."

"The hell I'm not," she countered. "Varney expects me."

"I don't give a damn what he expects!" Noah roared. "I'll tie you to that tree if I have to."

Torey began to pace. "I know you're afraid for me, Noah," she said, struggling to keep her voice even. "But this is something you can't do for me. Not this. Not when it involves Pike. You and I are partners, remember? Pike is as much my enemy as he is yours. You're not being fair."

"This isn't about fair. It's about keeping you alive."

She stopped pacing. "I'd like to think it was about keeping you alive too."

"My life doesn't matter."

She stared at him. "You *are* a son of a bitch," she gritted. "How dare you say such a thing. Your life matters, Noah. It matters a helluva lot. To me. You may think that being some kind of damned martyr will redeem you in the eyes of your peers, but I've got news for you. They're worried about their own lives. Not yours. And not mine. When we leave here, guilty or innocent, the only opinion of you that should matter is your own. And," she added quietly, "maybe mine. Just a little. Dammit, I love you."

"Don't say that."

"Why? Because you heard it already today from a woman you were once going to marry?"

He had the good grace to look flustered, embarrassed. "How did you—?"

"I came looking for you. Believe it or not, I wanted to tell you about Varney right away. Before I went to talk to him. But you . . . you were busy."

"I'm sorry. I had no idea you were there."

"Yeah, well, what can I say. The woman has good taste."

He dragged his hat from his head, twisting the brim in front of him, feeling, Torey suspected, supremely awkward all at once.

"She's beautiful, Noah. Petite, a real lady."

"Torey, you mustn't—"

"It's all right. I'm tough, remember? But my pa always told me to pick on someone my own size. I guess that leaves Katherine out. I'm afraid she wouldn't stand much of a chance against me."

"No," he said softly, "she wouldn't. Not a chance in hell."

"I can't say you didn't warn me. Whoever's convenient, right? Belle, me, Katherine. I—" She stopped. "What did you say?"

He shoved his fingers through his hair. "I said Katherine wouldn't stand a chance against you."

She allowed a sad smile. "Right. I could arm wrestle my pa to a draw. Sometimes, anyway."

"That's not exactly what I meant. I wasn't late because of Katherine, Torey. I was with her father. Talking about the payroll wagon, the court-martial, Pike, a lot of things. Katherine wasn't there."

Torey was quiet for a minute, a glimmer of hope sparking to life inside her. She tried to tamp it down, telling herself she was just going to get hurt all over again. "You could've let me go right on thinking you were late because of her. Why didn't you?"

He shifted uncomfortably. "I don't know."

"Maybe you do."

Her gaze locked with his, the sudden hunger in his gray eyes so fierce it was almost frightening. Her heart pounded. "Why didn't you stay with her, Noah?"

He turned away, and she had the sense that he was waging an inner war of some kind, a war he was rapidly losing. "She's married."

"Is that the only reason?"

"Don't do this." His voice was a plea.

"Is that the only reason you didn't spend the night with her, Noah? She wanted you. I know she did. Why didn't you make love with her?"

"You know why." The words were ragged-edged, raw.

"Tell me anyway."

"Dammit, I swore this wouldn't happen. I don't want to hurt you, Torey. Not you. Not ever."

"You only hurt me by shutting me out. Not giving me a chance to show you how special you are, how very much I love you."

"I've got nothing to give you in return."

"You've got yourself."

He touched her cheek and she felt his fingers tremble.

"In the morning," she said, "we're going after a murderer. We both know the price we might pay for that. But tonight we're alive, Noah. We're together. We can't waste that time being angry or afraid or . . ." she added gently, "or even being noble." She caught his hand, brought it to her lips. "Are your women interchangeable, Noah? Are they?"

He closed his eyes. "Maybe they were once, when I used women like I used whiskey—to forget who I was."

"And now?"

He regarded her intently but didn't answer.

"And now?" she repeated softly.

"Now," he said slowly, "I don't want to forget. I want to clear my name. I want . . ." He stopped.

"What do you want, Noah?"

"I want you, Victoria. Only you."

"Say it again."

"Only you."

"Say it again . . . and again . . . and . . ."

With an oath he pulled her to him, brought his mouth down on hers. The kiss was savage, relentless. He gave her no quarter. She asked for none.

His hands were all over her. Wild, desperate, he bore her down onto the riverbank. In a frenzy he tore at her clothes, even as she tore at his.

With a cry part profanity, part prayer he drove himself inside her, gloried in how wet she was, how ready. Raw, primal, he took her, took her hard and fast. Afterward, he collapsed beside her, awestruck, gasping.

Her hands were already moving. "Tell me again, Noah," she pleaded. "Tell me again how much you want me."

He did. Over and over he did.

Varney could wait. Pike could wait. The whole damned world could wait.

Hours later, Torey came awake, heart thundering, misty dream images swirling through her mind, images alternately wondrous and terrifying. Noah had been there, in her dream, much as he had been so many weeks before. His smile, his touch, his words. *I'll teach you. I'll teach you so you never forget . . .* The words had been a threat to her then, a threat to her own buried feelings of being a woman. But this time the words were not a threat, but a promise. She had reveled in them, gloried in them. Noah had held out his hand to her, and she had taken it and gladly.

Then Noah was gone, vanished. And another man was holding her hand. Torey opened her mouth to scream.

Pike.

Pike with his soulless black eyes and malevolent smile. Pike with his own whispered promises. Of brutality and death. She tried to wrench herself free, but he held her fast, twisting her arm savagely behind her back.

"Come with me, my dear," he whispered. "Come with me and watch Noah Killian die. Watch him die a thousand deaths because of what I'm going to do to you. And then . . ."—he laughed—"then I'm going to cut his heart out . . ."

Torey shuddered, clutching her blanket tight around her, assuring herself the dream meant nothing. Today was the day she and Noah were going to bring Pike to justice. It was only natural that she be thinking about him.

Determined, she sat up, careful not to disturb Noah, still slumbering peacefully beside her. In the soft orange glow of their waning campfire she studied his shadowed features and allowed herself a tender smile. Lovemaking obviously agreed with him. He looked years younger, almost boyish, content.

Yet the contentment, she knew, was an illusion. He had been desperate tonight, taking her again and again, gifting her with pleasures beyond imagining, as though somewhere in the deepest part of him he too suspected these brief hours together could well be their last.

Another shudder rippled through her.

Noah stirred, pushing up on one elbow. "Are you all right? What is it?"

She told him about her dream, taking care to leave out Pike's threat to her. "We can't go after him, Noah. Pike's going to kill you. I know it. I feel it."

Something flickered in his eyes, and Torey experienced a stab of fear beyond any nightmare. He looked away, but it was too late. She had seen his own certainty in that gaze. Noah too did not expect to return from his confrontation with Pike alive.

But when she pressed him, he would not discuss it. Instead he pulled her to him, kissed her hard, his mouth hot, hungry, her breasts crushed against the heated wall of his chest.

"Are you trying to distract me, sir?" she murmured shakily, when he let her draw back a little.

"I'm trying to kiss the hell out of you."

"You succeeded admirably, I must say." She traced her fingertips along the sensual curve of his lips. Though she longed to talk about her fears, it was obvious he would only deflect her at every turn. Instead she asked, "Does this mean you're not sorry anymore for making love to me?"

He closed his eyes. "I should be, for your sake, but I'm not."

She smiled. "Good. I don't think I could bear another round of apologies for your making me feel so . . . so alive, so wanted, so cared for." She paused, worrying her lower lip with her teeth. "Can I ask you something?"

"What?"

"You said once that you tell your women lies when you make love with them. To flatter them, to make them feel good."

He looked away, and she was sure he was blushing. "Torey, I—"

"It's all right," she interrupted. "It's not like you and Belle knew each other well enough to worry about sincerity. But what I want to know . . . I mean, those words you whispered to me tonight, when you told me how pretty I was, how much you wanted me, needed me, were those only lies to make me feel good too, Noah?"

His eyes seemed overbright all at once, but Torey decided it could have been a trick of light. He laid his hands on either side of her face. "No lies, Victoria. There were no lies between us tonight. I swear."

"I love you, Noah Killian."

His gray eyes darkened with yearning, want, but he did not say the words back to her. "We'd best get riding. We wouldn't want to keep Varney waiting."

"How are we going to handle him?"

"Whatever way works best to keep you out of danger."

"I'm in this, Noah. Don't even try to keep me out."

"I know. Believe me, I know. Even though it goes against everything in me. I was raised to protect women, take care of them, remember?"

"Because we're weaker?" She said the words without censure.

"Because it's who I am."

"Protecting someone you love cuts two ways, Noah. It's why I had to catch up with you after you left Denver. I couldn't let you ride into Fort Laramie alone."

He pressed a kiss to her forehead. "Knowing you has been one hell of an education, Miss Lansford."

She smiled again. "That cuts two ways too, Mr. Killian." Then she sobered. "So how *are* we going to handle Varney?"

He sat up and reached for his clothes. Torey did the same.

"I want to get to the fort before dawn," Noah said, pulling on his shirt. "I can alert Dodd. We can take Varney prisoner, convince him he doesn't want to hang alone."

"You really think he'd take us to Pike?"

"Men like Varney are rarely brave when they're cornered. He'll take us to Pike if only to keep me from breaking his neck."

They broke camp then and saddled the horses. But before they mounted, Torey caught Noah's arm. "I need to tell you something, in case . . . well, in case . . . " She didn't finish.

He waited.

"That night on the farm," she began, twisting Galahad's reins between her fingers, "I felt helpless against those murderers and their guns. Later on, when I strapped on my own gun, I thought I'd found the great equalizer. But it wasn't long before I realized, it was all an illusion. I felt safe only as long as I was Vic Langley. You changed that, Noah. You made me feel strong and capable as Victoria Lansford. And I want to thank you for that."

He tipped her chin up. "If that's true, then I can honestly say I've done at least one thing I'm proud of these past three years."

She laid her hand against his chest, tears threatening. "Promise me it's going to be all right, Noah. That when tomorrow comes I'll still be able to feel your heart beating beneath my hand."

With his thumbs he brushed away her tears. "Is this any way for a tough bounty hunter to act?"

"I suppose not. But this bounty hunter loves you so damned much."

"I don't know what I ever did to deserve you in my life," he murmured, trying and failing to make his voice light, "but I sure as hell am glad I did it."

She wanted so much for him to say the words, to tell her he loved her. But maybe it was the very uncertainty of what lay ahead of them that kept them unsaid. She fixed a brave smile on her face and mounted. "Let's ride, Killian. We've got killers to bring to justice. And I'd like to get it done before supper."

They rode out, heading for the fort. They were still a mile from its gate, when they spotted two riders heading their way.

"Varney," Torey said.

Noah cursed under his breath. "What the hell is he doing out here?" He looked at her. "I want you to make a run for it."

"I will not."

"Dammit, Torey . . . "

"Give me your gun, Noah. Hurry, before they're close enough to see. If you're armed, they'll know we're together."

With an oath he handed over his rifle but stopped short of giving her his sidearm. Swiftly, he shoved the Colt into the back waistband of his denims. Grabbing up his duster, he shrugged into it, effectively camouflaging the weapon. Then he flipped open his saddlebags and withdrew a double-barreled derringer. He tucked the hideout gun in the top of his right boot. "If I think for one minute we can't get out of this, I'll blow them both out of the saddle."

"But Pike . . . "

"Your life means more to me than catching Pike."

There was no more time for discussion. Varney was fast closing the distance between them.

"Who the hell has he got with him?" Noah whispered.

Torey studied the hulking shape of the man riding beside Varney. "The last of them," she said. "His name's Bobby. The one who watched from the corral the day of the attack."

Varney raised a hand in greeting. "That you, Vic?" he called.

"It is," Torey returned tightly. The outlaw was still at a full gallop. He waited so long to rein in, his dun gelding slammed haunches with Galahad.

"I thought we were supposed to meet at the fort," Torey said, sending him a murderous glare as she soothed her agitated mount.

Varney gave a dismissive shrug. "Change of plans." He shifted in his saddle. "I told you I had a surprise for you, Bobby boy," he told his partner. "See? Your old friend, Captain Killian."

The boy stared at Noah, his jaw dropping.

"My God," Noah murmured.

"What's the matter, Killian?" Torey demanded, assuming her role of Vic Langley. "You look like you've seen a ghost."

"Billy Joe Brown," Noah said. "But it can't be. I saw your body myself. How could you—?"

"I never meant no harm to you, Captain," the boy said. "I swear. The boss . . . he made me."

"Shut up, kid," Varney snarled. "The boss does the talkin', not you." To Torey he said, "I can't believe you got 'im, Vic. The boss is going to be real impressed." His eyes narrowed thoughtfully. "You know, I pondered on it all night, but it still won't come to me. There's something mighty familiar about you. Are you sure we ain't crossed paths somewhere before?"

"I'd remember a man like you, Varney," she said with a cold irony that was lost on the outlaw. "Believe me, I'd remember."

They rode out, Torey keeping her Colt trained on Noah. He sent her a baleful look, one that said if he had his way about this, Varney and Billy would already be dead. But he made no move to go for his guns. He would play the hand they'd been dealt, for now anyway. Torey could only be grateful Varney had not thought to search Noah.

Several miles went by before Varney began to slow his dun. He pointed toward a dilapidated, tree-shrouded shack sitting atop a bluff.

Torey swallowed nervously, wondering how many men were in that shack. As they reined up in front of it and dismounted, a chill skittered up her spine. She had to crush the urge to tell Noah to run. Even with her gun in her hand, she wouldn't be able to react in time if Pike chose to shoot Noah down the instant they stepped through that door.

Damn, this was all her fault. She and Noah should have gone back to the fort last night. But she'd wanted so much to make love with him . . .

"Keep that thing pointed away from me," Torey gritted at Varney, who had drawn his own gun.

"Boss gives the orders, Langley. You'd best keep that in mind."

Inside the shack, her heart all but stopped. She'd thought she'd been prepared to see him again. But nothing could have prepared her for those malignant black eyes. He was seated behind a spur-scarred table, an ivory-handled Colt in his right hand.

"Pike." Noah was stiff with hate, rage.

"Come in, Noah," Pike crooned. "So kind of you to drop by. I couldn't have timed your arrival at Fort Laramie better if I'd sent you an engraved invitation."

"You didn't have anything to do with his being here," Torey put in. "You've got me to thank, mister. And you can do it with cold, hard cash."

"All in good time, Mr. . . . Langley, is it?" Pike said softly, too softly.

Torey felt the hair along the nape of her neck prickle. Instinctively, she started to thumb back the hammer on her Colt, but she was too late. Varney's hand flashed out and grabbed the gun.

"What the hell is this?" she demanded. "I did what you wanted."

"You fooled my men, Langley, but you didn't fool me." Pike stood, leveling his Colt in her direction. "You see, I know exactly who and what you are. Exactly."

Torey saw the undisguised fear in Noah's eyes. She knew what he was thinking. If these animals had discovered she was a woman, they would be on her like a pack of wild dogs on a blood scent. Her mind's eye recalled the battered, bloodied body of her sister. Despite her best efforts not to, Torey trembled.

"Never send a boy to do a man's work, eh, Noah?" Pike said. "I thought you of all people would know better. After all, you once made the supreme mistake of trusting Billy Joe Brown."

"What is this, Pike?" Noah demanded. "This son of a bitch

Langley draws down on me last night and now you're not even grateful."

"Give it up, Noah," Pike said. "Vic Langley is not who he pretends to be, and we both know it." He eyed Torey with a new contempt. "I'm afraid you didn't kill dear Cal Grady over a horse, did you, Vic?"

"What are you talking about?" she asked.

"You killed him for the reward money. But isn't that what bounty hunters do?"

Torey nearly staggered with relief. They didn't know she was a woman. They knew she was a bounty hunter! As fine a distinction as that might be regarding her life expectancy, she found the prospect of dying as a man at Pike's hands far more palatable than suffering what the bastard was capable of doing to a woman.

"A friend of mine in Cuttersville wired me soon after Mr. Langley left town in your company, Noah." Pike signaled for Varney to open the door. "You might recognize him."

A red-bearded man strode into the shack.

"Remember me, Killian?" Farley asked, his mouth twisting in a smirk. "I gave you one black eye in Cuttersville. Mr. Pike promised me a chance at the other one."

"You see," Pike said, "I know you and Langley are partners, Noah. And this little performance was all part of a plot to get to me." He grinned unpleasantly at Torey. "Let me assure you, Mr. Langley, my old friend has made a fool of you. There are no reward dodgers on me. Though I understand Cole has been stupid enough to get his face on one up Dakota way."

"Haven't seen it," Torey said, disgusted with herself for being suckered in to this. She and Noah were both going to die here today, each of them too worried about the other to try anything reckless. What chance they might still have rested with Noah's undetected guns.

"Search Killian!" Pike ordered.

Torey's shoulders slumped. With Pike's gun aimed at her

chest, Noah could only stand helplessly by and submit to Varney's search. The outlaw found the Colt right away, hefting it up with a triumphant smirk.

"Check his boots and his hat," Pike said. "We can't be careless. Not with Noah."

Torey's last hope vanished when Varney snagged the derringer. And then she remembered the knife in her own boot.

"Scared, Vic?" Pike taunted. "I certainly would be, in your position. Especially since I also know about Jensen and Scott. Farley filled me in. Ah, Vic, you shouldn't have gunned down my stalwart associates."

"Hurt Vic and I'll kill you," Noah said. "No matter how many bullets you put in me, Pike—my hand to God, I'll kill you."

He laughed, a cold, lethal sound. "Always the hero. But not this time, Noah." He rubbed the barrel of his gun against his cheek. "What would you think if I skinned your friend alive? Maybe cooked him. Let you hear him scream. That was the disappointment three years ago. That you didn't actually get to hear your men scream. Though I'm certain a man of your intelligence can use his imagination . . ."

"Let Langley go, Pike. Please. He's just a kid. Do what you want to me. Anything. I won't fight you."

"I'm touched by your concern. But I think not. He knows too much. Dead men don't tell tales, do they, Noah?"

Noah's mouth twisted in disgust. "You should know." He turned toward Varney. "I don't suppose he's told you that any man who works for him eventually winds up as fertilizer."

"Cole is loyal to me. Give it up, Noah. Besides, Cole's looking forward to the payroll wagon we're planning to rob. Of course, it will be your body that will be found at the scene. Deserter, coward, thief. A fitting end. But before it happens, believe me, you'll wish for death, pray for it."

Torey shivered, but thought of the extra guards Noah had arranged to be riding with that payroll shipment. At least if

Pike won here today, the bastard wouldn't savor his victory for long.

"How did you do it, Pike?" Noah asked. "The massacre. How?"

Torey held her breath, knowing what the answer meant to Noah, yet knowing too that he'd asked only to buy them more time.

Pike smiled, an oddly indulgent smile. "It helps to hire the killers," he said. "More than a dozen men dressed up like Sioux warriors. When they were finished, I couldn't have told my own body from that of the poor unfortunate soul we killed in my place. Right down to the tattoo. We added another body to account for Billy boy. Monstrously clever, don't you think?"

Noah looked sick. " 'Monstrous' is the right word, all right. But why didn't you kill me too?"

"Killing you would have been too easy. Better to leave you alive with the deaths of your men on your conscience and on your record. A revenge worthy of Shakespeare."

"I never meant it to happen, Captain Killian," Billy Joe said. "Honest. I never knew what Mr. Pike was plannin'. He promised he was just going to escape. And if I helped him he would forget about all the money I owed him from some card games."

"Stop whining, you worthless idiot," Pike snapped.

"Just escape, you said," Billy went on. "That's all. And then maybe rob a bank or two. Those soldiers were my friends, Mr. Pike. And then those ladies, those ladies in Kansas . . . "

"Those bitches wanted it, begged for it."

Torey dug her fingernails into her palms. For an insane moment she wondered how many times Pike could shoot her before she drove her knife blade into his heart.

"They begged, all right," Billy said, tears rolling down his cheeks. "Begged for you to stop."

Pike cocked his gun. "If you don't shut up, I'm going to blow away what's left of your brains. Now"—he turned back to Noah—"where were we? Oh, yes, I had had Billy put something in Eli's whiskey at the fort. Made the old coot sick as a dog. I couldn't risk his being along. He was the one man in your command who could've rallied your troops. When you ordered a rest for the horses at midday, Billy added a little something to the water in your canteen and several others. Dear Sergeant O'Reilly was beside himself when so many men took sick at once. After you passed out, my men butchered the lot of them.

"I dumped half a bottle of whiskey on your uniform and had Billy take you back up the trail a couple of miles. The drug made you seem intoxicated. The smell of whiskey clinched it. Admit it, Noah. I'm the smarter one, the more clever one, the one who by rights should have finished first in our class at West Point. Say it. Say it!"

Pike took a menacing step toward Torey.

"You're right, John," Noah said quickly. "You are the clever one." He had to keep the bastard talking. "You did it. You ruined my career, destroyed everything that mattered to me."

Pike smiled. "Ah, yes, even dear Katherine threw you over, didn't she? Too bad you don't still love her. I could've invited her to our little party. Now, there would have been the proper icing on the cake." He glanced again at Torey. "Maybe you'll do, boy. Noah seems to have an affection for you. We'll make you rue the day you ever met him."

He jerked his head toward Billy, who went immediately to fetch a length of rope.

"Pike, leave Vic out of this. It's me you want."

Torey straightened. "You're some son of a bitch, Pike. It was Killian who was convicted of cowardice. But I can see a yellow streak running all the way down your back."

"Vic," Noah gritted. "Shut your mouth."

"Don't worry, Killian," Torey said, "I don't hold you accountable for this. It's my own fault for wanting this vermin dead so badly." She prayed Noah would get her message, that she didn't want him blaming himself for anything that might happen to her.

"Why should you want me dead?" Pike demanded, actually looking affronted.

"Maybe you're not so clever, after all," Torey said.

"*Vic,*" Noah emphasized. "Stop it."

She wasn't listening. They were going to kill her anyway. Why not prick at Pike's staggering arrogance? Besides, if there was even a chance to distract him . . .

Taking care to make no sudden moves, she tugged off her hat and began to fluff her hair. She spoke to Pike again, this time making her voice more lilting, feminine. "In fact, Pike, maybe you're pretty damned stupid."

Varney stared at her, wide-eyed. "I don't believe it. A woman. Jesus Christ, I don't believe it."

"She's one of those l-ladies," Billy stammered.

"I'll be damned," Varney said. "Long legs. Of course."

Noah was out of his mind. Torey had laid herself open to her greatest terror—rape. And for what? To give Pike a more hideous opportunity for revenge?

Varney gripped her chin, ran his hand down the front of her shirt, squeezed her breasts. "I don't know about skinnin' her alive, boss. I've got a better idea, a lot better."

Pike laughed, an eerie, amused sound that set Torey's flesh crawling. "Icing on the cake, after all," he said. "Strip her naked. Now."

"I'll kill you!" Noah spat out. "I'll kill you an inch at a time." God above, he couldn't fail Torey as he had failed his troops. She trusted him, trusted him with her life.

"Strip her!" Pike repeated. "Billy Joe, tie up the good captain. I want him to have the best seat in the house."

Torey's blood was icy with terror. But she kept a firm grip on her senses. If she and Noah couldn't get out of this, she would at least die bravely. For Noah's sake, if not her own.

Billy Joe approached Noah with a section of rope. Varney

had his mouth on Torey's, his hands groping her, pawing her, tearing at her clothes.

Noah let out a roar of hell-spawned rage and dove at Varney. He would tear the bastard apart with his bare hands.

A gun erupted, a bullet whizzing bare inches past Noah's head.

Billy Joe moved to block Noah's path. Noah slammed a fist into the boy's jaw, then realized belatedly what Billy Joe was attempting to do. He wasn't trying to restrain him; he was shoving the butt of a pistol into his hand. "So sorry, Captain. So sorry."

Noah gripped the gun, even as he shouted a warning to Torey.

But Torey was already grabbing for her knife.

The shack exploded in gunfire.

Bullets gouged out chunks of wood in all four walls, impacted on flesh and bone. Men screamed. Noah kept firing.

When the smoke cleared, Varney lay staring at the ceiling through sightless eyes. Farley was crumpled in a lifeless heap in one corner of the shack. Billy Joe lay on the floor, gripping his stomach and moaning pitifully.

Noah stood over Pike, his chest heaving. The bastard was trying vainly to stanch the flow of blood from a gaping wound in his chest. Blood gurgled from his mouth. He tried to form words, but failed. Hate still sparked in those black eyes. Noah levered back the hammer on his gun.

"Don't." Torey staggered over to him, pushed the gun away. "He's not worth it. Let him go to hell in the devil's own time."

Pike's eyes rolled back in his head.

Noah caught Torey by the arms. "You took a helluva chance, woman."

"Maybe not," she said, though her voice shook. "Varney had respect for Vic Langley. None for Victoria Lansford. Once the son of a bitch knew I was a woman, he had only contempt for my ability to defend myself. It's ironic. My being a woman gave me the edge I needed to beat him."

Noah gave her a swift kiss. "We'll talk about it later." He bent over Billy. The young outlaw was bleeding badly. "I'm so sorry, Captain."

"Will you tell the army the truth about Noah?" Torey asked.

"I will. I swear."

"We need to get him to a doctor," Torey said.

Noah nodded, feeling strangely light-headed all at once.

Torey threw her arms around him in a fearsome hug. "Oh, Noah, I can't believe it. We're both alive. And it's over. It's really over."

He caught her face between his palms, kissed her hard and deep. "You scared bloody hell out of me, woman. Bloody hell—" He gasped, winced, tried to straighten.

Torey's eyes narrowed with sudden alarm. "Noah?"

She seemed so far away. He had to tell her something. Tell her before it was too late. "I love you." The words came out in a croaking whisper. He felt his knees begin to buckle, aware only now of the warmth of his own blood seeping across his middle. "Love . . . "

He heard Torey scream his name as the darkness claimed him.

19

For three weeks Torey didn't know if Noah would live or die. For three weeks, day and night, she hovered beside his bed in Colonel Dodd's private quarters, praying for him, pleading with him, cursing at him to stay alive. But he'd lost so much blood that the post surgeon, Dr. Frederick Sanderson, offered her little hope that even a man of Noah's strength and constitution could rally against such a devastating wound.

"You don't know Noah," Torey had told him. "He can overcome anything. You'll see."

But by the end of the third week even Torey's rock-solid faith in Noah's will to live had begun to falter. She sat beside his bed, holding his hand, staring at the haggard features of the man she loved, his long, dark hair now set in agonizing contrast against the ghostly pallor of his skin.

Tears trailed unheeded down her cheeks. "Don't you die on me, Noah. Damn you, don't you die."

Coma. That was what Dr. Sanderson called it. "The body goes into a deep sleep to try and heal itself, but most times the patient doesn't wake up. They can't take nourishment and weakened as they are . . . "

He didn't finish. He didn't have to. Torey had seen the truth of the medical man's words in Noah's sallow flesh. He was slowly starving to death. Determined, single-minded, she had fought Sanderson's death sentence, spending hours on end spoon-feeding chicken broth into Noah, massaging his throat until he swallowed at least some of it. Even so, he continued to lose weight.

Bone weary, Torey pushed to her feet and crossed to the washstand. If she'd once thought herself unrecognizable as Vic Langley, the pallid creature with bruised circles for eyes that looked back at her from that mirror was no one she could identify by name. "No wonder you don't want to come back to me, Noah," she said, a half-hysterical laugh escaping her lips.

She dipped a clean cloth into the basin and brought it back over to him. His fever had long since broken, but she still liked to smooth the cool cloth over his face and chest, slipping past the bandage that circled his middle.

"Just think how much we could both enjoy this," she teased softly, running the cloth over the flatness of his belly, stopping at the edge of the blankets that covered him to his waist. "All you have to do is wake up."

She set the cloth aside and lifted his hand, kissing the backs of his fingers. "Do you know how much I miss your touching me? Do you have any idea?"

Eyes burning, she pressed his hand against the side of her face and gently squeezed his fingers. For a moment at least she could believe he was caressing her again as he had done on those two magical nights. Then she skated his hand along the front of her shirt and lay it against her breast.

"Noah, please," she whispered, "you can't let Pike win. I know I've told you this a hundred times, but Billy Joe confessed to everything before he died. You have your name back. No one can ever take it from you again."

He winced, gasping slightly, as he did often, but he did

not wake up. Behind her, she heard the door to the bedroom open.

Torey kept her attention on Noah, expecting the visitor to be Dr. Sanderson or Colonel Dodd. Instead a feminine voice inquired softly, "How is he?"

Torey blinked, startled to see Katherine. Dressed in golden silk with ebony accents, she glided across the room like some fairy princess from another world. Did the woman ever have a hair out of place? Sighing inwardly, Torey said, "The same."

"I, uh, don't mean to intrude, but I wanted to say goodbye. My husband's transfer back East has come through."

Torey only nodded. She hadn't had to ask who had requested the transfer. She and Katherine had come to an understanding of sorts these past three weeks. If it had meant the difference in keeping Noah alive, Torey would have stepped aside in an instant in Katherine's favor. But even Katherine had known the futility of such a sacrifice and had said as much when Torey had brought Noah back to the fort, wounded and barely breathing.

"He doesn't love me, Miss Lansford," Katherine had said, following wary introductions. "I saw it in his eyes that afternoon in the barn. Noah needs a woman of courage, a woman to be his equal. A woman like you."

"I love him," Torey had said.

"Then fight for him. Like I wish I had."

Torey had done just that. Now she rose beside Noah's bed and eyed the lovely woman standing pensively on the far side of the room. "When are you and Major Duncan leaving?"

"Tomorrow."

"Your father's going to miss you terribly."

"He knows it's for the best."

"I might even miss you myself."

Katherine smiled. "Now, Victoria, this isn't the time to start telling tales to one another."

Torey blushed.

Katherine stepped over to the bed. "I brought him something." She held out two separate pieces of what had once been a masterfully crafted sword forged of the finest silver. "Noah left it in the dirt out on the parade grounds that awful day. It belonged to his father, and his grandfather before that. I think a good silversmith might be able to repair it somehow." She swallowed a shuddery breath. "I know I had no right to take it, but it was all I had left of him."

"I'm sure he'll appreciate it." Torey waited for Katherine to leave, but the woman remained by Noah's bed, her wistful gaze all too easy to decipher. "You still love him that much?" Torey asked.

"Could you ever stop?"

Torey knew the answer to that one. "I'm sorry, Katherine. Truly."

"Don't mind me, dear. The better woman won, I assure you." She turned to leave. "I wish you well. Both of you. Tell him I . . . just tell him I said good-bye."

"I'll do that," Torey promised.

After Katherine had gone, Torey again took up her vigil at Noah's side, even forcing a false cheeriness into her voice as she leaned forward to fluff his pillow. "Did I tell you I got a letter from Lisbeth? She's getting very impatient. She wants us to come visit. She and Aunt Ruby and Eli are all praying for you, you know. Maybe God will get so tired of hearing about you, he'll make you well just to—"

Her voice caught, her eyes tearing up all over again. "Damn you, Noah Killian, how can you do this to me? How can you leave me now, when we have our whole lives ahead of us?"

Her question brought no response from the still figure on the bed.

Heart aching, she stroked his hair, his face, his body, as if somehow her touching him could infuse him with the very strength he had given her by believing in her. But her only reward was the blessedly even rise and fall of his chest. Finally, exhausted, she spooned herself beside him and fell asleep.

She woke to a gentle nudge on her shoulder. Instantly alert, she looked at Noah, only to feel a bitter surge of disappointment to find him still unconscious.

"It's only me, Torey," a woman's voice said. "I'm sorry."

Torey glanced up to see Millie Yates and her son Tyler standing beside the bed.

"My fault," Torey said. "I was getting my hopes up again."

Millie clucked sympathetically, then pointed toward the linen-covered tray on the bedside table. "I brought your supper over and more soup for Captain Killian."

"Thanks, Millie, but I'm not hungry." Millie had been among the first to stop by and offer her support and apologies for the injustice that had been done to Noah. And when Torey had refused Dr. Sanderson's orders to rest, it had been Millie who had offered to sit with Noah, an offer Torey had eventually, reluctantly, accepted.

"We've been through this before," Millie said. "It won't do you or Captain Killian any good if you get weak as a lamb yourself. Now eat."

"Yes, ma'am." Torey picked up a fork and made a stab at a couple of green beans.

"That's better," Millie pronounced. "Oh, and here." She handed Torey the blue cotton dress that had been draped over her arm. "I took it in quite a bit. It might be an inch or two shorter than you'd like, but it should fit."

Torey studied the simply styled garment. "I don't know. Noah probably wouldn't recognize me."

Millie smiled. "That's the girl. You keep believin' he's going to wake up."

Torey's voice shook. "I wish I did believe it."

Tyler, who had been ogling the broken pieces of Noah's sword, piped up with, "How much longer is Captain Killian going to sleep? He's been hibernatin' longer than a bear.

Doesn't he know I want to talk to him? Tell him I'm glad he's not an outlaw, and that he didn't kill my pa?"

"He's going to wake up real soon," his mother said. "Real soon." She pushed a package wrapped in brown paper at Torey. "Maybe this is the one you should wear."

Torey accepted the package. "Is this . . . ?"

Millie nodded, looking acutely embarrassed all at once. "I sure hope you know what you're doing. That was some piece of sewing I did, girl."

Torey hugged the package. "The day I wear it, Millie, that's the day I know everything really will be all right."

"You go on and rest awhile," Millie said. "Take a bath. I'll sit with him."

Torey knew better than to argue with Millie. Though loath to do so, she went downstairs to Colonel Dodd's private bathing room. The bath felt heavenly, but she didn't linger. She toweled herself off and pulled on the blue dress Millie had brought her. It was astonishing how foreign it felt.

Back upstairs, she discovered that Colonel Dodd had stopped by to look in on Noah. The army commander had kept a surprisingly low profile around her. She suspected he was as riddled with guilt about Noah's conviction as his daughter had been. Torey had to smile a little though, when she noticed him regarding Millie and Tyler with unmistakable affection.

"He's looking a little better," Dodd said, too polite to comment on the obvious astonishment he was experiencing to see her in a dress.

"You look wonderful, Torey!" Millie exclaimed. "I've got a couple of other dresses I could take in for you too."

"You mustn't trouble yourself on my account, Millie."

"Nonsense. Glad to do it. We want our patient to perk right up when he finally opens his eyes, don't we? The sight of his pretty lady bounty hunter should do it just fine."

Torey blushed. "Thanks, Millie." She gave the woman a

swift hug. "Don't tell anyone though, but I prefer the pants."

Millie giggled. "Now come along, Vernon. You too, Tyler. Leave Torey in peace."

Dodd took a minute to clasp Torey's hand. "I really do think he looks better, dear."

Torey bit back tears. "I hope so." When they'd gone, Torey again took up her vigil at Noah's bedside.

It was well past sunset, and she supposed she should just curl up on the cot near the wall and try to sleep. But she was feeling too jittery tonight for some reason. She found herself checking again and again to make certain that Noah was still breathing.

Finally, to relieve her own tension, she crossed to the washstand and mixed up a batch of shaving soap for Noah. She had become quite proficient at her tonsorial efforts on his behalf. A glance at that still-stubborn jawline suggested a fine shading of stubble. She'd already shaved him this morning, but it would give her something to do.

Using a shaving brush, she daubed the white, foamy soap along his chin, his jaw, his neck. Then she picked up a straight razor the colonel had provided her. Only then did she notice her hand was trembling.

Taking a deep breath, she stroked the razor along his cheek, startled when his head moved slightly. Torey cursed at the small nick in his flesh. Grabbing up a towel, she dabbed at the spot of blood.

"Ouch."

She stilled. The word was soft, so soft she wasn't sure she had even heard it. She stared at him, willed the word to come again.

Slowly, so slowly, his gray eyes opened, the words that followed coming only with great effort. "Still . . . hoping . . . to slit . . . my throat?"

Torey's heart thundered in her ears. "Noah?"

"Is Pike . . . ?"

"Dead."

"Others?"

"The same."

"You . . . all right?"

"Of course," she managed in a voice that trembled even more than her hands. "You refused to pass out until you made certain I was, remember?"

He gave her a weak smile. "What kind of knight in shining armor would I be if I let you slay the dragon without me?" He closed his eyes. "How long have I been out?"

"Three weeks."

"My God."

"You scared me to death."

He touched her face. "I'm sorry."

"Just don't ever do it again, all right?"

"Deal." He shifted, trying to sit up, but succeeded only when Torey did most of the work. Briefly, he passed out again, the change in his position after so long a time on his back causing him to faint. When he came to, Torey found him regarding her closely. "What on earth is that you're wearing, Miss Lansford?"

She blushed and stood up. "I understand it's called a dress. Do you like it?"

"I'd like you in anything." He gave her that crooked smile she had fallen in love with all those weeks ago. "I like you best in nothing at all."

"I love you."

His smile faded. "This will probably sound absurd, but I'm exhausted. I think I'd better sleep."

She leaned over and gave him a gentle kiss on the mouth. "I missed you so much."

"I'm really tired, Torey."

She let him rest, assuring herself that his mood was the result of his wound, his exhaustion. Yet over the days and weeks that followed, his mood did not change, even as he gradually regained his strength. Initially, sitting up in bed wore him out, but soon enough he was taking short walks, first around his room, then around the house, then finally around the fort.

His aloofness, however, remained. It was subtle, not at all the kind of stubborn demeanor Torey knew how to meet head-on. But though she didn't understand, neither did she pressure him. She concentrated instead on helping him get stronger.

Eight weeks after he'd been shot, her patience gave out. She'd been sitting up with him, reading letters from Aunt Ruby, Eli, Lisbeth, trying to ignore the increasingly strong demands of her own body—how much she ached to hold him, touch him, have him touch her.

Finally she could take it no longer. She settled herself on the bed and planted her hands on her hips. "Do you have any idea what you're doing to me?"

He gave her a blank look.

"Night after night I conspire with Millie to have Colonel Dodd gone from his own home—they walk, they picnic, they have supper together. And night after night, Mr. Killian, you and I sit up here and discuss the weather, the Sioux, the Cheyenne, and the general lack of mosquitoes this time of year. Dammit, what is the matter with you? I remember your last words to me before you passed out, when Pike had shot you. Do you remember them, Noah?"

He knotted his hands together. "I remember."

"Did you mean them, or were you just making some grand gesture, thinking you were about to die?"

He grimaced. "That isn't fair."

"Fair?" she all but shouted. "I've been more than fair. And I might add, patient. Patience is not a virtue I come by naturally, let me tell you."

"Torey, I do . . . " He hesitated. "I do love you," he said softly. "So much."

"Then why don't you say it?" Tears blurred her vision and she swiped them swiftly away.

"Because I don't intend to . . . to hurt you any more than I already have. When I think of how close you came to being killed . . ." He shuddered.

She bristled. "So we're back to that, are we? How many times, how many ways do I have to tell you that it was my choice to be there? Mine. You couldn't have driven me off with a cudgel. Dammit, Noah, I love you."

He trailed his fingers lightly along her cheek, then curled them regretfully into his palm. "Torey, I haven't thought two days ahead for three years, and now lately I've been thinking about the rest of my life. What the hell do I have to offer you? I've got a horse, a saddle, and the clothes on my back."

"You've got your name."

"That's not enough."

"The army offered you your commission back."

"My army days are over. I'm afraid I've become much too undisciplined for the service."

She smiled impishly. "We could always be bounty hunters. Or Pinkertons perhaps. I can see the shingle now, can't you? Mr. and Mrs. Noah Killian, private detectives."

"What am I going to do with you, woman?"

"I've got a few fairly lascivious suggestions."

He shut his eyes. "You're incorrigible."

"I know, but so are you. We're meant for each other." She spooned herself next to him, felt his body tense.

"Don't, Torey. Please, I . . . The spirit is willing, but the flesh is still weak, I'm afraid."

"Your flesh is quite healthy, thank you." She eyed the telltale bulge beneath the coverlet. "Top of its form, in fact."

"Dammit, woman, I love you too much to offer you a life where tomorrow is nothing more than an educated guess."

"I've got news for you. Growing up on a farm can sound pretty ordinary, but we were never sure what tomorrow would bring. It would rain when we didn't need it, then go for weeks dry as dust when we did. Locusts, wind, hail. I've seen them all, seen them destroy a year's work in a day, in an hour. I never really gave it much thought before, but my whole life has had a measure of uncertainty attached to it. You see, it doesn't matter what tomorrow brings, Noah. As long as I'm with you."

He grew thoughtful. "A man could start a ranch."

"A man and a woman could start a ranch."

"And maybe raise a few horses, a few cows . . . "

"A few kids."

His eyes darkened, his hand coming up to caress the side of her face. "I can just picture you, your belly swollen with our child."

"Anything to keep me from wearing pants, eh?"

"You can wear pants every day of your life, as long as you take them off when you come to bed."

"I've got a better idea." She stood and grabbed up the package Millie had brought her weeks before. Then she hurried over to the dressing screen in the far corner of the room. "I asked Millie to sew me something special," Torey called out. "I would've done it myself, but I'm afraid my sewing is even worse than my cooking."

"Why doesn't that surprise me?"

"Well, I assured her this wasn't anything I would ever wear out in public. Anyway, what do you think?" Shy all at once, uncertain, Torey stepped from behind the screen and did a tiny pirouette in front of the bed. She was wearing a red silk nightdress. "Your lady in red, sir."

Noah's mouth went dry.

He had dreamed it, fantasized it, believed that it could never be possible. Not for him.

Torey climbed into bed beside him. "A woman named Mamie LaRue told me once that if I ever found a man who cared as much about a woman's feelings in bed as he did his own, I should grab him, hold on to him, never let him go."

He caressed the silk where it covered her breasts, teasing the nipples to swift arousal. "You saying you want to keep me?" he asked hoarsely.

"For a while at least. Fifty or sixty years. Then we could talk again."

He chuckled. "Maybe we can reconsider that Pinkerton idea. I like the notion of investigating you, madam—most intimately."

She kissed him then, hard, deep. He tried to draw back, but she wouldn't let him. "You've made me insatiable, sir. It's your own fault, for being so good at what you do."

He groaned, his hands joining the fray. The kiss grew hungrier.

They made love. Gentle, tender, sweet.

Afterward, Torey snuggled close, reveling in the achingly tender endearments he whispered in her ear, words meant only for her, thoughts so intensely personal, private that she knew they came straight from his heart. It humbled her to think that he loved her that much. And filled her with an indescribable joy as well.

She stroked his hair, kissed his cheek, then rested her palm against the hard, flat plane of his chest. For a long time she just lay there and gloried in the strong, measured beating of his heart.

Noah Killian. Friend. Lover. Partner. A man who could by turns be sweet, noble, vulgar, shy, arrogant, funny, ill-tempered, gentle, and the fiercest and most tender of lovers. And who allowed her the freedom to be all those things and more right back at him.

"Eli was right," she murmured. "You indeed have a magic touch, Noah Killian." A magic touch that had healed [illegible] heart, and given her the courage to heal his in return.

He kissed her cheek, her chin, her eyes. "I love you, To-rey. I love you more than my life."

What had begun in a fiery promise of hate and revenge had come full circle.

Torey twined her hand in Noah's and smiled, a supremely contented smile. This was the only promise that mattered. A promise of love to last them a lifetime.